BIRTHRIGHT

BOOK ONE IN THE
SHEPHERD'S MOON SAGA

J. ANNE FULLERTON

This is a work of fiction. The events and characters described herein are imaginary and are not intended to refer to specific places or living persons. The opinions expressed in this manuscript are solely the opinions of the author and do not represent the opinions or thoughts of the publisher. The author has represented and warranted full ownership and/or legal right to publish all the materials in this book.

Birthright
Book One in the Shepherd's Moon Saga
All Rights Reserved.
Copyright © 2012 J. Anne Fullerton
v4.0

Cover Photo © 2012 JupiterImages Corporation. All rights reserved - used with permission.

This book may not be reproduced, transmitted, or stored in whole or in part by any means, including graphic, electronic, or mechanical without the express written consent of the publisher except in the case of brief quotations embodied in critical articles and reviews.

Outskirts Press, Inc.
http://www.outskirtspress.com

ISBN: 978-1-4327-9459-0

Library of Congress Control Number: 2012911063

Outskirts Press and the "OP" logo are trademarks belonging to Outskirts Press, Inc.

PRINTED IN THE UNITED STATES OF AMERICA

*For my husband and my mother,
who unfortunately never met.*

ACKNOWLEDGEMENTS

I have to thank my husband for his unwavering support as I made my way through this book. He's been more than a little understanding about the creative process. Fortunately, he's artistic, too, so he gets me.

I hate this part, because I don't want to forget anyone, so I hope my friends and family know how much I value them and their support. If your name isn't here, and there are many that aren't, it's not because I don't appreciate you. I do, I really do.

In particular, I have to hug and kiss Kirsten Bird, Susannah Rogers and Katie Wilkinson. Kirsten is my best friend and has suffered through my personality quirks for thirty-odd years. She's such a good sport. Susannah is my other best friend and literary nemesis, an amazing writer who needs a little more confidence (hint, hint), who pushed me to improve my writing skills to keep up with hers. Katie is my nit-picky quasi-editor, who was afraid to read the initial manuscript because she can be "too critical", but who found fewer errors than her little red pen expected. Nya, nya.

I have to give a big shout out to Catherine Russell, author of *The Stage*, who paved the way for me to open myself up and self-publish. If I hadn't met her, this would all still be in my head.

I'm hesitant to include this, except that credit is due where it belongs, but this book wouldn't have been written if I hadn't been inspired nearly twenty years ago by the talented Sam Neill to create the character of an Australian sheep farmer who marries a werewolf. I've never actually met the man, but I have the utmost respect for him and his craft. He has unknowingly become my muse over the years, helping that simple idea grow into the Shepherd's Moon Saga. I've built the foundation for an entirely new world history, giving life to characters that are near and dear to my heart, and for that, I am eternally grateful.

    Lastly, I have to give the biggest thanks to my mother, who is no longer with me and regrettably never read anything I wrote. She gave me my love for life and encouraged my wild imagination. I know she would be proud of me and what I've accomplished in my life. Thank you, mom. I miss you and I love you.

CHAPTER ONE

"It is the nature of the beast for a man to want what is beyond his reach."
John Nigel, philosopher

Sydney, Australia, December 1874

"Mr. Buchanan," said Eliza Forth-Wright with a startled smile. "I wasn't expecting you this evening."

She stood in the glossy wood-paneled foyer of her gothic revival townhouse addressing her unannounced guest, Copernicus Buchanan. The imposing stone edifice was situated in the Peddlington suburb, an affluent and park-like district of Sydney. On this night, New Year's Eve, it was crowded with revelers celebrating the turn of the year.

Around them floated strains of Baroque music as a string quintet played from the broad staircase landing. Male and female shadow fae, dressed in fine clothing, mingled and meandered through the rooms and halls on the main floor of the expansive home. Several curious glances took in the sight of an attractive human male in their midst. Two familiar faces passed by in the crowd, stopping when they recognized him.

Dirk van Amersvoot approached Eliza with a predatory grin. His younger brother Lars stood alongside him, looking and feeling quite out of place. Lars was only there because Dirk had agreed to let him tag along.

Dirk was a helf, half-human and half-elf. Lars was full elf, Dirk's half-brother through their mother. They were tall and fair-haired with similar features, only Lars sported the small fangs inherited from his father. They came from the same hometown as their human counterpart, but were almost half his age. They knew the man well considering they had grown up around him. He was their father's best friend and an accepted member of their family.

"Nick," said Dirk, puzzled by the man's presence. "I didn't think I'd see you here."

Nick shook Dirk's offered hand. Lars also extended a hand in goodwill. The young men were other names on Eliza's list of eligible marriage material along with Nick's. They had been formally invited to the New Year's Eve marriage ball to seek wives. Nick was not on the guest list. It was not an event for humans so their surprise was evident.

Dirk was the eldest son of Buren and Bloem van Amersvoot. The Buchanan and van Amersvoot families shared close ties as they had been founding members of the Falmormath Shire community more than fifty years ago. Nick's father had established Gilgai Station and Buren, being of a race that outlived humans, had built Willowbrook. Their sheep stations abutted one another in the rural region north of Sydney. Buren had watched Nick grow from a babe to a man and in turn Nick had been an uncle figure to Dirk, Lars and their sister Beshka.

"I'm a bit surprised myself," Nick laughed. He felt slightly out of place in the company of the much younger men. He was a widower in his fifties, not a pup on the prowl. He paid no attention to the other people in attendance. He had one thing on his mind this night and nothing could distract him. "This was rather a spur of the moment decision."

"If you'll excuse me, Mr. van Amersvoot," said Eliza, touching Nick's arm and gesturing towards a large dark door. "I need to speak with Mr. Buchanan."

Intrigued glances followed them as she led Nick into her office. Dirk glared at their backs, lips pulled away from his teeth. He stalked into the crowd, head cocked menacingly. People stepped out of his way. Lars remained in the foyer looking lost.

"I'm sorry to arrive without corresponding," Nick apologized as Eliza closed the door for privacy. "Although with the number of times you've invited me to one of your marriage markets, I would think you'd be pleased to finally see me."

Eliza moved behind her polished walnut desk as though it were a barricade. She was a large woman, nearly as tall as most men and given to eating well. She wore a harebell blue dress that matched her stern eyes and complimented the towering mound of red hair on her head. She appraised the man before her with a calculating eye.

Nick still wore his driving habit. Wide framed goggles rested on his high brow. Well worn leather gauntlets were tucked under his left arm. His knee length oilskin coat was still buttoned and a brass buckled belt was wrapped around his neat waist. A tooled leather holster with a long barreled .44 Riggins Manhunter hung from the belt. Australia had only recently departed from its duty as a Victorian penal colony and was still a dangerous place. Dark trousers peered out from beneath the hem of his coat and he wore a pair of hard soled work boots that had seen many miles.

As for his physical appearance, he was a strapping buck of a man. He showed few signs of his age other than a sprinkling of grey throughout his dark seal-brown hair and a few crow's feet at the edges of his eyes. Those eyes were alert and expressive, alternating between a soft grey-blue and a sharp clear sapphire depending on his mood. His skin was not afflicted by the dark colouring and heavy lines of most men his age that spent the majority of their lives working in the elements. He looked a dozen years younger and it reflected as well in his easy going nature.

"I'm afraid this isn't the event for you," Eliza said gently. She opened the leather bound book on her desk and flipped past several pages. "I have another arrival date of February 18th. Those will be ladies more suited to your needs."

Eliza Forth-Wright was the premiere marriage broker in Sydney and throughout most of the continent. She provided a much needed supply of women to the male dominated country. Females were in short supply in the new frontier and Eliza's minions found them in every corner of society around the world. There was a niche to be filled at every social level. It was ironic that her personal preference was for her own gender. After her husband had passed away she allowed herself to indulge in familiar female company. She and Beshka van Amersvoot, Dirk and Lars' younger sister, had been involved in a relationship for several years, since Beshka's arrival in Sydney to attend university. Their intimacy was a well guarded secret in the closed minded Victorian society in which they lived.

Tonight's event was for a particular section of the populace. Australia was attracting more than its fair share of werewolves as well as elves, fae and humans. She had arranged this private social occasion to bring together mates of the shadow fae and werewolf races. The shadow fae consisted of a variety of species that included vampires, incubi and their female incarnations, bunyips, harpies and all other manner of creature that tended to prey on humans. For that reason, among others, they had remained in the shadows of human and elf society since the origin of time. Werewolves had suffered their own misfortune and were shunned.

"I've driven a very long way," said Nick, trying to hide his exhaustion and disappointment. "I don't know when I'll be back in Sydney. As you've often pointed out, I'm not getting any younger. I'll need sons to keep the place running after I'm gone. I'm going to need a wife if I'm to have those sons and you, Mrs. Forth-Wright, offer the best choice of female stock in the country. I'm here tonight. I think I'll have a look around if it's all the same to you."

Despite his crude summation, he was correct.

Eliza considered his position. She had been after him for years to take another wife. The men who lived in more isolated areas paid the heftiest premiums for her services. Copernicus Buchanan was worth a small fortune to her. Why on this of all nights had he chosen to accept her offer? In February she would have a shipment of fine young human women from Britain. Tonight, the available ladies were not meant for human husbands. They were not exactly ideal matches for a quiet, gentle man like Nick who lived on a secluded sheep station.

"Regrettably, this event is a private affair," she told him. "You may find it strange that the van Amersvoots were invited, but the women here tonight are more suited to their marital needs. Perhaps you would allow me to select a lady from the collection arriving in February. I could make all the legal arrangements and send her to you. You wouldn't need to return to Sydney at all."

Nick shook his head. He removed the goggles from his forehead and stashed them in his coat pocket. He was intent on his mission. He wanted to see it through before his nerve failed him.

His first marriage had been a disaster and he hoped to avoid that same fate the second time around. He knew that he needed sons to continue his name and run the station, but he didn't want to marry a local Falmormath woman. He knew the families too well, it could create unwanted tension. Many of the men with whom he was friends would push to combine their lands with his and he didn't want that. He liked the privacy and control of running his own station. He supposed the right term would be to call him an alpha male. It was a werewolf expression he had had once heard, but it was certainly applicable.

Eliza was thorough in her screening of the women she offered. She knew their backgrounds, their health histories and their personalities, ruthlessly culling the undesirables. He trusted she would be able to find a woman who was complimentary to his temperament and lifestyle, but he wanted some involvement in the final decision if at all possible.

"As unconventional as all of this is to begin with, I would actually like to meet the woman I marry before any nuptials take place," he said firmly. "I may not be in a position to properly court a woman, but I can at least take a moment to get to know her before entering into marriage. Surely there is one woman here tonight that you would suggest. I've come prepared to pay your fee in gold."

The mention of money made her reassess the situation. Eliza mentally scrolled through the fae creatures in attendance, determining which would be the most acceptable for a union with a human. She couldn't think of any, but she did have access to some human women who had not been selected in the last go round. She would have them brought post haste.

"I do have a few eligible ladies I can bring in this evening," she said with a satisfied smirk. "Why don't you wait in here and make yourself comfortable. Help yourself to a drink while I make those arrangements."

After Eliza slipped out, he hung his coat and gun belt on the rack by the door and set his gloves on the marble surface of the liquor cabinet. He poured himself a whisky. The ice cubes rattled in the glass as his hand trembled with anxiety. He didn't imbibe often, but tonight his nerves were jangling and he felt a little liquid courage would see him through.

He had lost Birgitta to cholera over ten years ago. She had given him no children, which was no surprise with her distaste for sex. He had only himself to blame for marrying Birgitta. He had been in Germany on business and met her at a party. She had been young, attractive and intelligent. It had been a whirlwind romance and they were married in less than two weeks. She had seemed so passionate in the beginning. He hadn't known at the time that she was just acting out in an effort to get her overbearing father's attention. She hadn't realised that marriage was not a game and her father would not come to her rescue. Everything had gone wrong upon arriving at her new home in the bush. Her attitude became bitter and cold. He had thought he had known her well enough to live out a happy life together, but he had been deceived. Birgitta had been distant and frigid. This time he hoped to find a woman that was at least friendly, if not loving.

He had never thought to use a marriage broker to procure a wife, but Eliza was a force to be reckoned with. She had a catalogue of every unmarried man in the entire Victoria/New South Wales region and she never backed down from a challenge. He had been at the top of her list for some time through his connection with the van

Amersvoots. Beshka van Amersvoot attended university in Sydney and lived with Eliza. Eliza's letters and personal visits had eventually worn him down. He knew it was time to make some changes in his life and prepare for the future.

He was on his second whisky when the office door opened. He turned, expecting to see Eliza.

Instead, a tawny haired young woman slipped into the room. She shut the door and leaned against it, eyes closed. She had high cheekbones and a softly pointed chin. Lips, full and pink, were parted slightly as she panted. Her breasts heaved above a silver and black brocade corset as she struggled to catch her breath. A black lace shawl covered alabaster shoulders and satin gloves concealed slim hands. The rhinestones on her black satin skirt flickered like sparks from a fire. When she opened her eyes and saw Nick staring at her with mouth fallen open she sucked in a gasp and held it. Her golden eyes were frozen in fear.

Agatha Whistleton realised that she had gone from the frying pan and into the fire. In her blind panic to seek refuge from Dirk she had gone through the first unlocked door she found. Now she was alone with a strange human who was staring at her with unabashed interest. Her senses were reeling and she was finding it difficult to gather her thoughts. The wolf that shared her skin was aggravated by this turn of events. It did not like being pursued or trapped.

"I'm sorry," Nick said, collecting himself. Eliza must have sent her in. Searching for the right thing to say, he added, "I didn't mean to frighten you. Would you care for a drink?"

"No, thank you."

Nick identified her American accent. He studied her furtive movements as she began to work her way around the room, looking for another exit. She was as nervous as he was. He took a moment to covertly examine her.

She was solidly built with slender, muscular arms. He had heard that women from the central part of America were hard working and sturdy. He could use that sort of woman on his land. He wasn't after a delicate hothouse flower. He would be content with a weed that once planted was impossible to uproot.

"I'm Nick Buchanan," he said, hoping to put her at ease. He wasn't one for small talk so he wasn't certain if he would say the wrong thing. "Are you one of Eliza's….other guests this evening?"

She cocked her head. Her gold eyes raked him from head to toe. The tension in her body eased somewhat. The wolf relaxed. This man was nonthreatening, unlike the man she was running from. All the males she seemed to meet were aggressive, but this man was docile. There was a sense of calm about him that attracted her and allowed to her relax slightly.

"Yes. I'm Agatha Whistleton. You aren't….you're…." she struggled with her choice of words. "I wasn't expecting to meet someone like you here tonight."

Taking that as an invitation, Nick stepped closer. She was standing by the stained glass windows at the front of the room. Moonlight poured though the panes, spilling a complex rainbow of colours on her white skin. She looked like some ethereal creature from a fairy tale. He was no knight in shining armor, but he felt confident approaching her.

"You're American," he said, feeling ridiculous for stating the obvious. "Have you had a chance to see much of Sydney?"

"A little. Do you live in the city?" she asked hesitantly.

"No," he answered, watching the colours shift and collide across her face. "I have my own sheep station north of here. I know this is forward, but I'd like a wife who can work alongside me, who'll give me a few sons to keep the place running after I'm gone. I'm not expecting more than that. I'm a hard working man. Anyone who knows me can tell you I'm a decent mate. I don't smoke or gamble or drink."

He quickly set down his glass. He felt a fool for rambling, but nerves had gotten the better of him and he couldn't seem to switch it off.

The office door swung open and Eliza appeared. Her expression was one of horror when she saw Nick talking to Agatha. Her worst fear was realised. She had hoped to keep Nick safely sequestered away from the shadow fae and werewolf females, but here was Agatha in uncomfortably close proximity to her prized client. The last thing she needed was an incident between a werewolf and a well respected, unsuspecting human.

"Mr. Buchanan, if you please. Agatha, you are needed elsewhere."

Agatha fled the room, shooting Nick a promising glance over her shoulder.

"I like her," Nick said, ignoring Eliza's look of disapproval.

"I'm afraid she isn't one of the ladies I've chosen for you to meet," replied Eliza. Her tone was firm. "They're waiting in the music room."

Nick held his ground. He picked up his glass and took a gulp of whisky to bolster his courage.

"I'll take Miss Whistleton."

"She isn't an option," Eliza replied sternly. "If you'll come with me, there are some lovely young women who are more suited to your particular needs in a wife."

Nick didn't move. He was man who made up his mind once and stayed the course, even if it was the wrong decision. He should have learned his lesson a dozen times over in his life, but he was stubborn that way.

"And why not Miss Whistleton?" he asked.

"She wouldn't be an appropriate match for a man with a sheep station. It would create a difficult situation for both of you and that is all I can say on the subject. Now, if you will please come with me."

Nick set down his whisky glass and walked to the coat rack. He plucked his coat and gun belt from the hook and collected his gloves from the bar.

"I'll be going then," he announced, turning towards the door.

"What?" Eliza echoed, stunned.

Nick came around to face her. His expression was grim.

"You've invited me here on no less than a dozen occasions to meet a wife. I finally made the effort to accept your offer and you refuse to allow me to marry the one woman I've met. I don't like playing games, Mrs. Forth-Wright. I don't need you to trot out a handful of women just so there's a better selection. I've made up my mind what I want. I'll even double your fee."

Eliza was flabbergasted. It was the worst possible scenario she could imagine. He was offering her more money than she could reasonably refuse, yet she would be handing him a potential disaster in return. Still, she was in the business of match making. If she wanted to stay in business, she needed to make money and marriages.

She had come to know Agatha well in the six months that the girl had been in her stable and she felt fairly confident that Agatha would toe the line. There was an innate sense of loyalty in Agatha that stemmed from a pack mentality and the necessity of forming unbreakable bonds for survival. She had grown up in a repressed society so her full potential as an alpha had never been realised. She had been raised with considerable restraint and that would be important if she married Nick.

Agatha was a Birthright. She had been born a werewolf. She was in complete control of her wolf and her ability to keep it inside, unlike a Sauvage. Sauvage were werewolves that had once been human. They had contracted the infection through the Bite of a Birthright, whether of their own accord or not. The Sauvage were at the mercy of the moon's cycle and were under the influence of the personality of the Birthright who had given them the Bite. More than just the wolf gene was passed with the infection.

"Very well," Eliza relented with a measure of apprehension. "If Agatha consents, I'll draw up a marriage contract. You must know that my liability is limited in regards to any unforeseen difficulties."

Nick nodded, satisfied. He was confident that Agatha would agree. He handed Eliza a weighty leather pouch.

"Just draw up the contract," he told her. "I'd like to be heading home before midnight. It's a long slog back to Falmormath."

Within minutes, Agatha found herself back in Eliza's office, standing beside Nick. When Eliza had approached her in the garden with the proposition of marrying a human, she had thought the woman had lost her mind. Eliza knew her history with humans and what her experience had been growing up on the Blackpaw Reservation in Colorado. The firm set of Eliza's jaw had told her that this was no joke. Knowing her only other option was to marry the aggressive Sauvage, Dirk van Amersvoot, Agatha chose what she hoped was the lesser evil.

She looked up at Nick's handsome face, wondering what her life would be like with him. She would never have imagined being married to a human. Her experience with humans was limited to the Regulators who kept the peace on the Rez and the missionaries that had raised her. The Regulators were ruthless, brutal men who would use force at the drop of a hat. The missionaries had been little better in their treatment of the young werewolves. The men of her own kind with whom she had grown up were bitter, simmering with rage. Nick had a neutral quality, not overly assertive but not submissive. The fact that he owned a large spread of demilitarized land would be a dream come true. She would no longer be confined. He also had sheep. Her mouth watered at the thought.

"Sign here," Eliza instructed them. "And here. Well, there you are. Married. Congratulations."

Nick glanced down at Agatha. Her gaze was apprehensive. He cautiously lowered his lips to hers and pressed down in an awkward first kiss. She didn't resist, but didn't respond either. They both accepted that there was time to adjust to the more intimate aspects of their new relationship.

Suddenly remembering he had brought something special for the occasion, he fumbled in his trouser pocket and withdrew a simple gold band. He took her left hand in his and gently slipped it into place on her third finger. It was slightly loose because her fingers were so slim, but it did not fall off. She looked it with curiosity, not entirely comprehending its significance.

Outside, Eliza took Agatha aside as Nick loaded her trunk onto the bed of his steam wagon. The vehicle rattled as its engine rumbled inside its housing. It was a large canvas topped utility truck not designed for comfort.

"I am taking a grave risk by allowing you to marry that man," Eliza hissed. She clutched Agatha's arm with rigid fingers. "If you do anything to jeopardize my reputation I will ship you back to Blackpaw and let you rot. Am I clear?"

Agatha nodded stiffly. It was always about Eliza and her business.

"I'm a Birthright, remember," Agatha replied in a low voice. "You just keep an eye on the Sauvage you have in there. It's a full moon in two nights. He could become a handful. You made a mistake thinking I would ever choose to be his mate."

"Are you ready?" asked Nick, coming up behind Agatha. He rested his gloved hands on her shoulders. His goggles were perched high on his forehead. "We've a long drive ahead of us."

Eliza watched the tension form in Agatha's face.

Benevolent human contact was foreign to her, but Agatha found the gentle squeeze of his fingers on her shoulders was more pleasant than she had expected. Living in an all female household for six months with only two other female werewolves for company had made her appreciate the rough nature of the men she had known back home. Women in general, especially those of several fae races, were manipulative and unkind to one another. At least all men were animals to some degree and were fairly predictable. Their needs in life revolved around food and sex. Eliza had spent the last several months drilling into her brides the attributes men sought in a wife based on those two main principles. Agatha prayed she remembered her lessons, especially when it came to sex. She did not want to disappoint him and make him seek other women for pleasure.

Eliza waved them off as they departed in Nick's sputtering steam wagon. She prayed that she had made the right decision letting him go off into the bush with a werewolf.

Another pair of eyes followed the happy couple's exit. Dirk van Amersvoot glared out through the salon's bay window, his features fused into an angry mask.

CHAPTER TWO

"A woman's joy and love of life begins the day she becomes a wife."
Excerpt from the Victorian pamphlet, "A Woman's Place"

The night passed in amiable silence as they sped through the darkness. Agatha dozed in her seat, head tilting over to rest against Nick's shoulder. He shifted so that his left arm went around her shoulders. She snuggled closer, pushing her cheek into his chest. He found the pressure of her body against him extremely comforting. She naturally fit into the curve of his body.

Agatha woke shortly before they reached what would be her new home. The sun was above the horizon, casting bright rays over the countryside. The canvas top of the steam wagon shielded them from the direct harshness of the sun, but it shone through the glass windscreen into their faces.

She sat up, raising her arm to block out the glare. Nick pulled off his goggles and gave them to her. She put them on and smiled at him gratefully. He felt his heart skip a beat.

The steam wagon bounced over the rough track, jostling them violently. She was thrown into him again and again, which he didn't mind. Her hand rested on his knee for balance. She was warm and soft and her fingers squeezed with a distracting sensation that he had not experienced in years.

Agatha looked through the dark green lenses at the landscape as it flew past. Low forested hills rolled for miles in all directions. The valleys were clear of trees so that flocks of sheep could graze on the summer yellowed meadows. The shorn creatures seemed to be everywhere she looked. She breathed in the heady odors of the terroir. It was a distinct blend of the local ecology: the soil, topography, vegetation and climate all attributed to the individual scent. It would remain in her olfactory cortex indefinitely as the smell of her territory.

"It's beautiful," she said, admiring the undulating waves of sheep that filled the grassland.

Her stomach rumbled. Nick grinned. It had been a long journey for them both. He realised that he hadn't eaten since the morning before. He didn't know when she had last had a meal.

"We're almost there," he assured her.

Agatha settled back in her seat. This was an ideal place to live. She would have room to stretch her legs, plenty of prey to hunt and a home to call her own. She also had a husband to please, once she figured out exactly how to do that. He was so different from the werewolf males in that he was not driven by rage. He was nothing like the other human males she had come in contact with during her life either, the ones from the Rez who feared her and took sadistic pleasure in controlling her.

Almost thirty years ago, several years before she was born, the government of the United American Territories had taken steps to control the werewolf population in the burgeoning young country. They had drafted a measure to protect human settlers as they spread across the fertile continent in search of prosperity. The werewolves were rounded up by Territorial Regulators and sentenced to a life on tracts of inhospitable land. There had been several bloody skirmishes, but eventually the werewolves were captured and forced onto reservations.

Agatha's pack had been restricted to the Blackpaw Reservation in the Colorado Territory with several other competing packs. Tensions had run high on a daily basis. Hunting had been outlawed, changing shape was a crime and spreading their bloodline through birth or the Bite was a federal offense, punishable by death. They were expected to suffer in filthy, run down encampments with no freedoms and not bite the hand that fed them.

The clandestine arrival of Eliza Forth-Wright's agent from Sydney had been a blessing. Of all the young females trapped on Blackpaw only she had been selected to travel to the new world in the southern hemisphere. In addition to Agatha, two other werewolf females from other reservations had been chosen by the agent to make the journey to a new life. Mrs. Forth-Wright supplied demand, so there were limited openings. Agatha had impressed the agent, sent to secretly interview potential mates, with her wit, her understated strength of will and her exceptional looks. She also was an alpha female without her own pack and therefore made the grade.

Nick saw the kangaroos before they reached the road. He braked hard, reaching out to prevent Agatha from crashing into the dashboard. She yelped in surprise. Her gilded eyes widened as she observed the strange creatures that hurtled across their path.

"What are those?" she asked as the large beasts leaped with deer-like grace across the track ahead of them. Her wolf perked up. It was attracted by the prospect of the chase.

"Scrubbers," he answered, shifting into second gear. The wagon lurched forward.

Agatha stared, transfixed, at the great animals bounding across the field. She was reminded of the elk herd she had once pursued with a few other Birthrights. They had snuck off the Rez one time to hunt and had barely avoided getting caught by the Regulators.

"What are they?" she asked again. "Scrubbers?"

"Kangaroos," he said, realizing that there would a bit of a language barrier until she settled in. "Bloody things eat all the grass we need for the sheep. They're a plague on the stations."

She cocked her head, peering at him through the green lenses.

"Weren't they here first? Wouldn't that make it your sheep eating their grass?"

"You'd do well not to say that around here," he advised, reminding himself that this was all new to her. She would come to understand in time. "We keep a manageable number of head on the land to prevent overgrazing. We need to keep it sustainable. Otherwise we graze ourselves out of business. But they aren't the real problem. It's the dingoes. During lambing season they're the worst. They'll pick off every lamb they can get."

She nodded, turning to follow the receding herd of kangaroo. They looked like the ideal answer for her urge to hunt. The sheep were obviously more important to humans and would be off limits. The kangaroos would provide more of a challenge.

"Here we are," he announced proudly. "Home, sweet home."

They passed a low river-stone wall with metal lettering that read *Gilgai Station*.

Agatha's first impression was that he must be wealthier than she had imagined. There was a large, whitewashed single story house and a separate building for the kitchen and laundry with attached living quarters for servants. An outhouse was tucked away behind a stand of bushes and trees. Orchards and gardens spread out away from the buildings. There was a bunkhouse for the station hands as well as a meat house, shearing shed, grain silo and windmill. Barns and horse pens took up a large amount of the immediate property. Several fine grade stock horses loitered in the morning sun. A garage stood a slight distance off, where the steam wagon spent most of its time.

They were met by a heavyset fae woman in her late seventies who came bustling out of the house as soon as the sound of the wagon's engine reached her ears. She wore a simple uniform of a plain blue cotton smock dress under a crisp white apron. Her steel grey hair was braided and wrapped in a bun on top of her head. Her brilliant blue eyes were lit with excitement to greet them.

"Welcome home, Mr. Buchanan!" Mrs. MacLeach called out in a thick Scottish brogue.

She slammed open the gate of the wrought iron fence that formed a barrier around the house and garden. The fence prevented the bush from encroaching on the urban setting. It gave the house an illusion of civilization. She approached Agatha's side of the vehicle, hesitating when she saw the metallic gold gleam in Agatha's eyes as the girl removed her goggles. It couldn't be possible that he'd brought home a werewolf for a wife, but here she was. Mrs. MacLeach glanced at Nick, who was busy undoing the straps that held the girl's trunk on the back of the wagon. Knowing the man's uncomplicated thought processes, he probably had no idea. What disaster had he wrought?

"Oh, she's a lovely bairn, she is. What a sweet sight," she announced, determined to treat her new mistress like the queen of Gilgai that she was. She had endured the first Mrs. Buchanan's haughty, condescending attitude. Surely she could handle a werewolf.

Agatha smiled uncertainly. She had never received a positive welcome anywhere before. It was a foreign concept, but she made up her mind to accept it. Things were not the same as in America. She wanted to make the best of every moment of her new life. She tried to exit the wagon to get her land legs back. She fumbled with the latch on the door. She had not been in a motorized vehicle before in her life and the lever confounded her.

"Allow me," said Nick, who had made his way around to her side while she was pawing at the latch in futility.

He opened the door and offered her his hand. She eyed his upward facing palm for a moment then slipped her hand into it. His skin was warm and dry. His grip was firm as his fingers closed on hers. She felt a sense of security pass into her body from the power of his grasp.

Without the green hue of the goggles she was able to look around her and see the true colours of her new world and the people in it. The landscape was rather drab, much like the Rez, but she didn't mind the comparison. She would be able to explore as far as her eye could see and discover the similarities and differences for herself. The muted palette was actually soothing and familiar.

The small crowd that collected in the yard around them was more colourful. The men were rough cut, like the cowboys back home. A few of the men had dark, dark skin and she identified them as the native people. Other than the Scottish woman, Agatha was the only female in sight. The crowd hung back, eyes wide with curiosity. Sheepdogs growled from a safe distance and the horses began to move about anxiously, but no one seemed to notice.

Nick put his arm around Agatha's shoulders and pulled her close. She wanted to melt into him and become invisible. Humans made her nervous under the best of circumstances. These people were watching her with intense scrutiny. She realised that she was still wearing her black satin skirt and brocade corset. She looked as out of place and unwanted as a fly on a wedding cake.

"I want you all to meet Agatha, my wife," he said. A murmur of surprise went through the group of witnesses. "She's from America, so she isn't familiar with how a station runs. I know you'll all help her and make her feel at home." He looked down at her encouragingly. "Say hello."

She was so overwhelmed by the events of the past twelve hours that she could only muster a shy nod. She wanted to prove herself to him, to show him that she could be a strong mate, but she wasn't sure how to do that yet.

"That's enough," said Mrs. MacLeach, nearly dragging Agatha away from him. "Can't ye see the wee thing is done in? I'll take her from ye now. Come wi' me, dear. Ye'll be needin' a bath and a change o'clothes. Mr. Buchanan can see to yer things."

Agatha was swept away by a tide of Scottish enthusiasm.

She soon found herself soaking in a copper bathtub filled with hot, rose scented water. The tub was in a room just off the master bedroom. The water came up to her chin as she sank down into its inviting depths. The first hot bath in her life had been at Eliza's. On the Rez she either washed in the river or sponged herself down from a communal bucket shared with the other females of her pack. The warm fragrant water was a delight that she hoped would become a routine occurrence.

Mrs. MacLeach was an urisk, a fae race commonly known to humans as brownies. She refused to handle Agatha with kid gloves. She used a washrag to scrub the girl's back, arms and legs, making no remark about the numerous scars she discovered. Judging by the marks of puckered flesh that appeared randomly on her body she had lived a hard life. She could tell that the young woman was not well socialized. She felt pity for the girl. Mr. Buchanan's first wife had been educated, a proper human lady from Berlin. If Birgitta had born him children he would not have resorted to a marriage broker and brought home a stray from America. A werewolf on a sheep station was a recipe for disaster. She would have to keep a close eye on her.

Agatha squirmed under her rough hands, but didn't make a peep of protest. She suffered through the cleansing until Mrs. MacLeach was finished. Once the torture was over she stood in the tub with the cloudy water up to her knees, dripping like a wet dog. Her skin tingled from the abrasive scrubbing, but she felt clean. Mrs. MacLeach wrapped her in a towel and left her there while she went to fetch clothing from Agatha's trunk. It had been hauled into the master bedroom to be unpacked later.

As Agatha waited and shivered, she heard the door open behind her. Water splashed over the sides of the tub as she turned.

Nick paused in the doorway, eyes taking in the vision of her slender, towel clad body. He had come in to get soap and a towel to wash off the road grime under the outdoor shower that the station hands used. He hadn't expected to encounter Agatha still in the bath.

They stared at one another, each too insecure to speak or move.

Agatha desperately searched her mind for what she should do. Eliza had instructed her brides that they should always be ready to accept their husband's sexual demands. A man might want her at any time and she should be ready and willing. Thinking that this was that kind of situation, she allowed the towel to fall to the floor. Water trickled from her hair as it lay in wet strands across her shoulder and chest, forming a bead on the peak of her right nipple.

Nick's brows rose above startled blue eyes as he took in the spectacular vision of her naked flesh. His gaze followed the drip of water as it fell from her breast. He might have assumed it was an attempt to seduce him if not for the trembling of her slender figure. She was clearly unsure of herself, but seemed to think it was what he wanted. He approached her, picking the towel up off the floor. After a brief but appreciative close up view of her nubile body, he brought the towel around her shoulders and covered her.

"Och!" cried Mrs. MacLeach in shock as she stumbled onto the inappropriate scene. "Ye cannot be in here, Mr. Buchanan. Out! Let the girl in peace."

Nick quickly took his leave, forgetting the soap and towel. At the moment, he just needed some cold water to bring down his arousal. She certainly was a delectable morsel that he anticipated savoring.

Agatha stood in the tub, immobilized by fear and something she couldn't identify. The damp on her skin was not from the bathwater. An unfamiliar pulse beat between her legs. She smelled her own body's sexual response to Nick's closeness and was astonished by it. None of the males on the Rez had elicited that kind of response from her. A slight curl lifted her lips as she realised she liked what she was feeling.

Mrs. MacLeach clucked like a hen as she helped Agatha to dress. She rambled on about life on the station while Agatha listened as best she could. She tried to focus on what the housekeeper was saying. Mrs. MacLeach took time to braid her hair into a thick tail and pinned it in a coil behind her head. Once dressed in a high-necked, long-sleeved cream blouse, rust coloured underbust corset and heavy layers of calico skirt, Agatha was led to the dining room to join Nick for a late morning meal.

CHAPTER THREE

"Something to Sink Your Teeth Into"
Advertising slogan for the Australian Sheepmeat Association

Nick had given himself a quick sprucing up, changing into a suitable combination of khaki trousers, white shirt and brown vest. His hair was still wet, combed against his scalp as it dried. He got to his feet as the women came into the room.

Agatha stared at the bounty of food on the table. She had not seen so much food in one place at one time. Even at Eliza's she and her werewolf sisters had eaten separately from the other women, being given a plate of raw meat each. Here, platters of fruits and cheeses shared the table top with plates of sliced meat, kippers, bread and an array of jam jars. Dizzily trying to remember Eliza's lessons in table manners, she accepted the chair Nick had pulled out for her. She eyed the tableware uneasily. Eliza had drilled home rules of etiquette in all her potential brides, but Agatha came from a world without such trappings. Tableware was alien to her.

Mrs. MacLeach served them their meal, which included soft boiled eggs in delicate silver cups.

Nick watched the confusion grow in Agatha's face as her anxiety increased. He had not known what to expect from her, considering he had spent no time actually learning anything about her. Eliza had always provided him with a dossier on each woman she had lined up for him to review. Agatha had not come with an owner's manual, nothing to hint at her personality or past. He didn't know where she was from, how she was raised, what she liked or didn't like. She was a total stranger at his table. Judging by her worried eyes he gathered that she was not from the better half of society. Perhaps that was why Eliza had wanted him to avoid her. He was still trying to figure that out. He just knew that Birgitta had been too refined, too well bred to find the relaxed atmosphere of the station to her taste. He hoped that Agatha would be more suited to the pastoral lifestyle.

Agatha's hand hovered over the silverware laid out beside her plate as she strained her memory for which was the right piece to choose. Nick's fingers closed over hers. Her uncertain eyes came to up meet his.

"Any one will do," he said with a comforting smile. "I don't put much stock in formality."

She visibly relaxed, shoulders dropping.

"I'm sorry," she said, blushing. "I don't have much experience with fine dining. My people are simple. We live off the land."

"I'd like to hear about your people, where you come from," he told her. He released her hand and sat back. "How did Eliza find you?"

Agatha knew that she could not tell him the truth, at least not yet. She might never be able to reveal that she was a werewolf, but she would tell him as much as she could.

"One of Mrs. Forth-Wright's agents came to the mission where I was living in Colorado," she began, studying the egg in its cup. She had no idea how to eat it, but she didn't think that it was meant to be consumed whole. "We didn't have much. It was a struggle to get by, but we managed."

Nick admired her resolution. She knew the value of hard work. It was vital to the maintenance of the station.

"What about your family? Do you have brothers and sisters?"

She gave up on the egg and instead used a knife and fork to cut into a piece of lamb on her plate. Despite being cooked, it tasted divine. Restraining her hunger with an effort, she forced herself to eat slowly and chew.

"I have a large extended family, but no immediate siblings."

"And your parents?" he asked.

BIRTHRIGHT

The silverware clattered onto her plate. An expression of distress was frozen on her face.

Presuming they had not approved of her being a mail order bride he let the subject drop with an apology for bringing up an unwelcome topic. Not many families would be pleased that their daughters had left home to become wives to anonymous men in a foreign country.

"I didn't mean to bring up something painful," he said.

Using Eliza's tactics, she steered the conversation back to friendlier waters. She could not discuss her parents because she had never known them. She adroitly changed the subject back to him.

"Do you have brothers or sisters?" she asked, giving him her complete attention to make him feel important. It had been part of her bridal boot camp training.

He shook his head. He used his knife to crack the shell of his egg, catching her intrigued gaze as she watched his demonstration. He found it amusing and strange that she was confounded by boiled egg.

"No, I'm an only child," he answered. "My parents passed on years ago. I consider everyone here on Gilgai my family. That includes you now."

Her smile could fill a room with its cheerful energy. She was such an innocent, which brought up a particular subject that he had failed to broach with Eliza.

"May I ask how old you are?" he inquired.

Following his example, she worked methodically to crack the egg in front of her.

"Twenty-four," she said. She looked up at him. "How old are you?"

The truth was she didn't know exactly how old she was. She had been told she was somewhere around twenty, but the missionaries at the school where she had been raised had only been guessing. There were no birth records for werewolves. They were not even supposed to be breeding on the reservations. Eliza had estimated her age at twenty-four so that was what she repeated.

"Fifty-four." He smirked at her speculative gaze. "I hope you don't think I'm too old."

The egg gave itself up to her persistent attack and she beamed at her simple success. Her smile flattened for a moment as she contemplated his comment.

"Too old for what?" she asked.

Nick laughed at her naïveté, banging his hand on the table. Silverware jumped and so did Agatha. When he saw her flinch, he caught himself. Displeased by her response, he was quick to reassure her. He couldn't imagine what had happened to her that would make her so frightened. There was real fear lurking in her eyes.

"I'm sorry," he said, lightly touching her arm. "I didn't mean to startle you."

She pulled back, automatically acquainting human contact with pain. She was afraid it would always be her first reaction. It would take time and a concerted effort to change that.

"It's alright," she replied, her smile beginning to return. "I'm just a little excited."

He understood. He was a bit on edge side as well. He wanted everything to go well so that she would feel comfortable in her new home.

"What's it like in America?" he asked, sipping his tea.

"It's not too different from this area, I suppose. Mostly farmland. We were rather isolated where I lived."

Mrs. MacLeach stepped in to pour tea for Agatha. Agatha leaned forward to sniff it.

"Ye'll like it, dear. Earl Grey."

"You've never had tea before?" Nick asked, surprised.

Agatha felt ridiculous that so many things he took for granted were completely new to her. She sampled the tea and found it unappealing. It tasted like boiled grass.

"I like coffee," she said, carefully putting the delicate tea cup back on its matching saucer. "They gave us coffee."

Mrs. MacLeach huffed, offended. She stomped away from the table.

Nick picked up on Agatha's comment, "*They gave us coffee.*" She must be talking about the missionaries. If she had lived in a mission then she came from a controlled environment. As she didn't seem keen on revealing her past all at once, he let it rest.

"Then we'll have to make sure we keep it stocked," he said. He raised his teacup to her in a toast. "Is there anything else you like? Any favourite foods?"

Agatha chewed slowly on a bit of lamb, contemplating the question. Her tastes were simple. She liked raw meat.

Life on the Rez had been a challenge to survive. Once a week the Regulators would come through on flatbed rail cars and fling animal carcasses out for the packs to fight over. The train tracks formed one boundary that the werewolves were not allowed to cross. The meat that they were given was usually rancid, filled with maggots, mold and disease. The packs scrambled to gather what they could from the rotten carrion. Fights were an everyday occurrence. Sometimes people were killed in the battle to survive. It was all part of the government's plan to eradicate them slowly and painfully.

"I'd like to try kangaroo." She paused, considering. "Do you eat them?"

Nick nodded, resisting the temptation to touch her arm. He didn't want to frighten her again. She was definitely a flighty creature that required a gentle, slow approach. He would not rush things.

"I'll eat almost anything, really," she went on. "We didn't have much to choose from on the-on the farm."

"Well then, we have our work cut out for us, don't we, Mrs. MacLeach?"

The housekeeper nodded and disappeared through the hall door to fetch coffee for her new mistress.

Agatha was trying so hard to remain well-mannered, but the texture of the meat was activating her predatory nature to bite and tear. The wolf took over. She didn't realize she had stopped using her utensils and was eating with her fingers until there was a crash of porcelain shattering on the floor. She looked up, hands poised over her plate. Her mouth and fingers were smeared with lamb grease.

Nick merely sat back and watched Agatha sink her teeth into the meat, pulling and ripping like a dingo with a kill. It was a little unsettling to witness, but it was strangely appealing to see a woman eat with a real appetite.

Mrs. MacLeach had dropped the coffee pot in her shock of seeing Agatha hunched over her food, devouring it with the savageness of an animal. The girl was behaving in a manner that would expose her true nature.

Agatha wiped her mouth with the napkin, her stomach quivering. She tucked her elbows tightly against her ribs as she cringed, awaiting discipline. This was when the violence began. She knew better than to resist, though her wolf began to simmer with suppressed rage. It would be no different here, despite Eliza's promises.

Nick studied her posture. She was shaking like a dog about to be beaten.

He was beginning to understand how difficult her life must have been before now. When she had said that life had been a struggle he felt she was not exaggerating. He had heard that America was a land of plenty, filled with prosperity, where people lived like kings. Apparently there was squalor among the gilded lilies.

Thinking about her uncivilized eating habits he recalled stories he'd read about the Regulatory government clamping down on the fae races, keeping some of the more violent species like werewolves confined to prison camps called Reservations. For those people competition for food must be fierce. It could explain her behavior, but he had not heard many reports of them in Australia yet. Surely the Victorian government was keeping track of their whereabouts if they reached Australia's shores. He hoped Eliza took precautions to prevent dangerous creatures from slipping into the country. Although their infamous uprising against humans was three hundred years past, werewolves had yet to live down a reputation as dangerous beasts that were not to be trusted. He couldn't just come out and ask her what race she was. It would be hurtful and rude. He had married her without knowing if she was human, fae or something else and there was no point questioning it now. He was in for a penny and a pound.

"It's alright," he said softly. A reassuring smile played about his lips. "There's been a time or two when I've been hungry enough to eat a wallaby with my bare hands."

She peered up at him from beneath sheltering lashes, disbelieving what she'd heard him say. He had every right to reprimand her for her behavior, but that was her past talking. Eliza vetted every man she selected, assuring that they were not prone to violence, alcoholism or other destructive habits. There was no way Eliza would have allowed her to go with Nick unless he was good man. He was proving it to her right now.

"You're not going to punish me?" she asked skeptically.

"For what?" he asked, finding her apprehension upsetting. "Appreciating good food? As long you remember to use the flatware when we have company, I don't care how you eat when we're alone. It's a breath of fresh air to see a woman with a healthy appetite. Mrs. MacLeach won't say anything to anyone, will you?"

The grey haired housekeeper nodded. She was on her hands and knees picking up the pieces of the coffee pot. She would have to work on the stain in the carpet later. It was definitely best that no one mentioned it ever again.

Agatha was taken aback by his generous absolution. She didn't know how to express her deep gratitude. Werewolves were contact oriented among their own kind and she knew that humans showed affection by embracing. She left her chair and went to him. She slipped her arms around his neck and pressed her face beneath his chin in a very wolf-like gesture of submissiveness, a request for approval.

Nick was stunned speechless. Her hair retained the smell of rose water and it tickled his cheek. He rested his chin on the top of her head and put his arms around her as well. She was so unlike any woman he'd ever known, almost child-like. In such a short time she had completely invaded his world and turned it upside down. No other person had ever done that.

Acting on her basic instincts, she nuzzled under his chin, breathing in his scent. It penetrated the deepest part of her brain, becoming a permanent fixture in the framework of her olfactory synapses. It would allow her to distinguish his individual scent from all others. Even if millions of smells assaulted her nose his would stand out like a beacon.

Her warm breath on his neck caused his tongue to dry out like a cotton pad. She had a specific impact on him that he couldn't deny. It was fortunate the table hid the stiffness in his trousers from view. What was it about her that caused his body to behave like he was reliving puberty?

"We should finish breakfast," he said, gently pushing her away before he carried her to bed. "Mrs. MacLeach worked very hard to put it on for us. And if you're not too tired, I wanted to show you around the property after we're done."

Agatha returned to her chair and made a determined effort to behave like a proper human woman.

Mrs. MacLeach finished gathering the large pieces of porcelain and got to her feet. Her glower warned the werewolf that she was on thin ice. She carried the broken shards cradled in her apron as she went out of the room.

Properly chastened, Agatha decided to eat something other than meat. She dipped her spoon into the now topless egg and scooped out a mound of gooey yolk. After all her effort to get into the egg, she wasn't sure she wanted to eat what was inside it. It was unappetizingly gelatinous. Still, she didn't want to appear ungrateful or rude so she licked the soft yolk off the spoon with quick flicks of her tongue.

Nick's attentive gaze was pinned to the furtive movements of her tongue as she lapped at the spoon. There was nothing deliberately suggestive in her behavior. He was beginning to realise that she was completely unaware of the erotic nature of her simple actions. She was merely eating the way she knew how. He gathered that she had no idea what she could do to a man. The tension in his trousers was almost unbearable. He had thought he was mature enough to have better control over his impulses than he had in his younger days. If he was a man even half his age he would have cleared the table and ravished her on the spot. There was going to be a time when he would need to relieve his desires. He hoped that she would be ready. He reminded himself that he could afford to be patient and take his time to make her feel at ease. Now was not the moment to take action. He forced himself to think of anything that would deflate the pressure in his loins. It only took one thing. The Ice Queen Birgitta. His erection was gone in an instant.

"Shall we take a tour of the station now?" he asked, giving up any pretense of eating breakfast.

"Yes, I'd like that," she answered eagerly, willing to do anything he asked.

Mrs. MacLeach came in to clear the table. She could see that life on the station was going to change drastically. She wasn't sure if it would be for better or worse.

CHAPTER FOUR

"A woman's realm is the home. The rest is a man's domain."
Excerpt from the periodical, "Ladies of a Victorian Age"

Agatha followed Nick through the house as he started the tour indoors. When they reached the master bedroom he cleared his throat uncomfortably and moved on quickly. Agatha got only a brief glimpse of a large bed with mosquito netting curtains before being led away. She supposed that was where they would spend their nights as husband and wife.

On their way out, Nick grabbed a dark brown slouch hat from a peg by the front door to protect his head and face from the brilliant glow of the summer sky. He offered another hat to her. Agatha wasn't bothered by the glare. She had grown up enduring long hot summers. To be polite she took the hat, which was too large and rested above her eyebrows instead of on the crown of her head. She looked like a child wearing an adult's clothes. Nick put it back on the peg.

"We'll have to get one that fits you," he chuckled.

Out in the yard he spoke to an Aboriginal lad who darted off towards the barn.

"It's a nice day," he said, turning to Agatha. "I thought we could take the scenic route."

Agatha shrank back as a pair of riding horses were brought out of the barn. She clung to Nick's arm, her hand tightening on his biceps.

"I can't ride," she said with a tremor in her voice.

"I made sure they saddled the calmest horse we have," he told her, patting her hand. She was surprisingly strong for having such a slight build. "All you have to do is stay on it. It isn't as difficult as you might think."

"This isn't a good idea," she whispered.

Nick gave her a curious look as she took a step behind him. She peered around him as the horses caught scent of her wolf. She knew what was about to happen and she wanted to be out of harm's way.

The horses went in to a frenzy of squealing and rearing. They pawed the ground before absolute panic made them crazed juggernauts, tearing free of their handler's grip. They bolted out of the yard like rockets, leaving a plume of dust in their wake.

Bewildered, Nick turned to face a cowering Agatha. Her eyes hesitantly met his.

"I warned you," she mumbled.

"It's alright," he said, rubbing the back of his neck in consternation. "We can take the wagon. It won't be as smooth as horseback, but there's plenty of track. We can cover more ground anyway."

Her insecurity was endearing, but suspect. As for the horses being spooked by her, he chalked it up to the new smell of her. Horses were notoriously high strung animals and could easily be sent into hysterics. It didn't mean anything more. He did not want to think that everything she did meant she could be a werewolf. It was crazy. She was from America and their culture was different, that was all.

She waited in the passenger seat as Nick climbed into the steam wagon beside her. He had put the canvas top down so they could enjoy the fresh air. He gave her a pair of tinted goggles before putting on his own. The goggles were far more necessary protection from the sun than a hat. He put the wagon in gear and it rumbled forward, throwing Agatha against him. Her fingers clasped his thigh for balance. They both looked down at her hand on his leg, the backs of her fingers brushing his groin, then at each other. She lowered her gaze first, but didn't move her hand. He wasn't about to ask her to. He just made himself mentally repeat Birgitta's name over and over to keep from responding to her touch.

They drove across vast open spaces, past flocks of grazing sheep and large scrub kangaroos lounging in the shade. Their blue-grey bodies were stretched out on the hard ground with their upper halves propped up on bent arms. Satellite ears flicked as flies buzzed around their heads.

Agatha stood up, gripping the top of the windscreen. She focused intently on the scrubbers. The wolf whined within her, longing to run. Pulling down her goggles as she stared at the lazy beasts, she remembered what she had seen of them earlier. They were deceptively sluggish at the moment, but she knew they were capable of impressive agility.

Nick stopped the wagon under a canopy of heavy branches to block the sun.

"Are they fast?" she asked, remembering their lunging strides.

"Oh, yeah," he said, leaning out the window to watch the brutes sunbathe. He removed his goggles and hung them on the side mirror. "Outrun a horse at top speed and they can clear any fence we put up."

"They look stupid," she observed, referring to brain capacity not their appearance.

Nick howled with laughter, taking her comment completely wrong. She tilted her head down to watch him as he wrestled with his amusement. She scowled, thinking he was laughing at her.

"I'm sorry," he muttered at last. "I never thought how they would look to someone who's never seen them before."

Her expression mellowed. She looked back at the kangaroos.

"I meant they don't look like they're very smart," she huffed.

For all her social awkwardness, she was well spoken and intelligent. It was refreshing to have someone to talk to other than the stale company on the station. There were few new topics among the hands and he knew the opinions of those around him ad nauseum. Agatha was a gust of fresh air and he intended to breathe deeply of her essence whether she was human or fae, or something else.

Ready to move on, he sat back in the driver's seat. As he did so, he realised that she had shifted to lean over him. He found his cheek

BIRTHRIGHT

pressed against the fabric of her skirt and his face nearly imbedded between her thighs.

Feeling the contact, Agatha looked down. Their eyes met and she held her breath.

Presented with the opportunity and feeling the sudden need for some kind of gratification, Nick put his arm around her hips and brought her closer. He buried his face in the hollow of her thighs. His fingers tensed on the backs of her legs, pulling her tightly against him.

Startled, but not afraid, Agatha ran her fingers through his hair in an intuitive response. He wasn't hurting her. Maybe she should have protested or pushed him away, but his firm grip was rather pleasant. She wasn't sure why he was digging his face between her legs and making deep noises in his throat, but it induced a liquid warmth within her belly. Her fingers tightened in his hair, encouraging him.

The earthy smell of her was almost most than he could take. His prior decision to bide his time had all but flown out the window. Even a man his age had a difficulty restraining himself under these circumstances. All his inner dialogue about maturity tempering his desires had gone silent when presented with such a rare and delightful chance to enjoy female splendor. Still, this wasn't the time or place to take advantage of her inviting nature.

With supreme strength of will Nick pulled her down into the passenger seat and released her. Their wedding night couldn't come soon enough. He was fooling himself to think that he could be patient. As she watched a kangaroo leap across the road he surreptitiously adjusted his erection into a more comfortable position in his trousers. He slipped on his goggles and put the wagon in gear.

Agatha turned away from him, breathing unsteadily. What had just happened? What was the unfamiliar burning deep inside her body? She assumed it must be related to sex. Her knowledge of sex was limited to the overly aggressive posturing of the males on the Rez and the ridiculous pamphlets provided by Mrs. Forth-Wright. The ink drawings had been prudish and uninformative. This was so much more enticing, more visceral. She trusted that Nick would know what to do when the time came.

They didn't speak for quite some time as they followed the perimeter of the station. He pointed out some landmarks, identified stations that occupied the other side of fences and in general gave banal details of the property. He avoided any discussion of a personal nature.

Agatha had tremendous memory for landscapes. She memorized each hill, stand of trees, meadow, watering hole and even the angle the sun as it spread across the countryside. She could navigate her way through every inch with an internal compass and would always know exactly where she was.

By the time they returned to the homestead, she was feeling the weight of exhaustion on her body like a lead cloth. She had endurance far beyond that of humans, but her emotions were raw, her sleep cycle had been interrupted over the past twenty-four hours and she had eaten little in that time. The day was hot and she was encased in fabric from neck to wrist and ankle. Her energy was sapped. She slumped in her seat, eyelids resting heavily over her golden irises.

Pulling off his goggles Nick glanced at her. She looked like drowsy kitten. He tried to erase the memory of what had happened between them earlier. There was still a good deal of daylight left and he was at a bit of a loss about what to do with it. Typically he would be out in the field or otherwise involved in the daily work on the station. He wanted to stay with Agatha and get to know her more, but he could tell she was drained. He couldn't take advantage of her in that state.

He came around to her side of the wagon and she nearly poured out into his arms. He slid the goggles from her face, leaving them on the seat beside his. He gathered her up, surprised that she weighed so little. With her forehead resting against his shoulder, he carried her to their bedroom.

Mrs. MacLeach bustled along behind him.

"Leave her to me," she instructed, shooing him out the door.

Nick stood in the hall for a moment, marveling at the fact that he was once again a married man. He had a beautiful young wife with a mysterious history. He needed to contact Eliza for a clearer picture of Agatha's past.

Mrs. MacLeach unlaced Agatha's corset and set it aside. Agatha inhaled deeply, expanding her ribcage to fill her lungs. The urisk's gnarled fingers worked on the row of small buttons that went up the front of Agatha's blouse. She folded it neatly and put it in one of the drawers assigned for her clothes. That left Agatha wearing only her camisole and skirts.

Agatha was unaccustomed to such treatment. She could undress herself and she preferred her own company when she was tired. She slipped the layers of fabric down her legs, revealing long pale limbs. Mrs. MacLeach collected the skirts she flung carelessly away. Agatha hated the confinement of clothing. If she never had to wear human garb again she would be happy.

"Please, just leave," she said, brushing away the housekeeper's hands as Mrs. MacLeach tried to remove her camisole.

"You seem to hae made some impression on the master," Mrs. MacLeach replied, stepping back. "I've never seen him so taken wi' a woman, not even his first wife."

Agatha cocked her head, pale amber eyes fixed on the housekeeper. "He had another wife?"

Mrs. MacLeach chuckled. She disobeyed her mistress's order and continued to aide in her undressing. She unlaced the mid-calf boots and slipped them off. Agatha wiggled her toes, willing the blood to return. She undid the plait of her hair by herself and allowed the mass of tawny waves to unfurl down her back.

"Ye dinna think you're the first Mrs. Buchanan, did ye? The master's of an age when a man has known many a woman. He's a widower. Dear Birgitta passed on near ten years ago. Left him no children, I fear. That's why he went to Sydney, tae that marriage broker. He needs a wife tae give him sons. A human wife."

Agatha wore only a camisole and short bloomers as she perched on the edge of the bed. This was closest to her natural state, her most comfortable existence. She bridled at the housekeeper's remark. Where she was submissive to Nick, her alpha side began to surface around Mrs. MacLeach. Urisk were lower fae, historically rating even below werewolves. She did not need to be chastised by one.

"I can give him all the sons he wants," she said defensively. "That's not your concern."

The older woman wasn't fazed by her tone.

"I've been here since Mr. Buchanan was a bairn," she said. "I've watched him grow from a wee 'un into a braw bloke who's buried one wife already. If ye aren't careful, he'll be buryin' a second, mark my words."

"I understand your concern and I appreciate that you have Nick's best interests at heart," Agatha replied tersely. "So do I. This is where I belong now. I won't do anything to jeopardize that. I'm not going to lose what I have."

Mrs. MacLeach nodded stiffly. She pulled the curtains closed to darken the room.

"I'll wake ye for supper."

Agatha sprawled out on top of the quilt and lay still, listening to the unfamiliar sounds of the world outside. Horses whinnied. Sheep bleated. Men shouted. Dogs barked. Sheets flapped in the breeze as they dried on the line. Strange birds cried out. The blade of a saw grated through a board. Hammers pounded. This was the symphony of her life now. It was music to lull her to sleep.

CHAPTER FIVE

"Remember this on your wedding night; a husband's pleasure is a woman's delight."
Excerpt from the Victorian pamphlet, "A Woman's Place."

Nick was seated at the dining table alone, waiting for Agatha. It was seven o'clock in the evening and the sun was still up. Gas lamps gave an extra luminescent glow to the room.

He had been distracted all afternoon by thoughts of Agatha's soft thighs pressing against his face. He could still felt the texture of her skirt on his skin. He was looking forward to a quiet meal with her then retiring to the marriage bed for dessert.

Mrs. MacLeach appeared in the doorway, her expression dour.

"I'm afraid the bairn's all in," she said. "I tried waking her, but she won't stir."

Nick understood Agatha's need to rest. Her entire world had changed overnight. He had eaten in solitude so many times over the years that one more night was no problem. She would be at his side for the rest of his life.

"That's alright. Let her sleep."

Mrs. MacLeach nodded and set about serving him his meal.

Agatha woke, sensing the presence of someone else close by in the darkness. She turned over to find Nick lying on the quilt beside her, fully clothed except for his boots and socks.

His pale blue eyes searched her face, devoting every nuance to memory. He brought his hand up to touch her cheek. When she didn't pull away, he slid his fingers along the angle of her jaw. His thumb traced the rise of her lower lip, pulling it down gently.

Agatha smiled trustingly, parting her lips. She bit down on his thumb, tasting the saltiness with the tip of her tongue. She was careful not to break the skin. She allowed him to smooth his hands up and down her body, creating warm waves on her skin. Following instinct, she curled into the shape of his body, pressing her face beneath his left ear. Her tongue slipped out and followed the curve of his earlobe. Her fingers tentatively spread across his chest, gripping the cotton of his shirt. She found his mouth with hers and was driven to explore the recesses within. He tasted of rosemary and lamb with a hint of wine and garlic. It was a delicious meal in a kiss.

Nick rolled to the side of the bed, pulling his shirt over his head. He unbuckled his belt and shoved his trousers down, kicking them away. He turned to her and she fell back submissively, arms above her head and legs slightly parted. His gaze roamed over her with a hunger that she recognized on a primitive level. His fingers passed beneath the hem of her camisole, lightly brushing the flat surface of her stomach. His hands were callused but gentle as they slid along her ribs to reach her breasts. Her nipples were like pebbles under his palms. He kissed her neck, sliding one leg over hers.

Agatha gasped as he applied a gentle pressure to her breasts, massaging them. A small whimper escaped her lips. She felt a churning between her legs in a deep part of her that had never been touched. It was a tingling, aching sensation that grew stronger with each caress of his hands on her skin.

He pushed the camisole over her head, flinging it onto the floor. Her breasts were firm and full. Her nipples blushed pale rose pink in the low light. He lowered his mouth to one taught peak, sucking it into his mouth and grazing it softly with his teeth.

Agatha caught her breath when his hand moved under the waistband of her bloomers. His palm put delightful pressure on the mound of her groin. His middle finger entered the wet crease he found there to discover the pulse pounding in her clitoris. She gave a gasp as the rough tip of his finger circled it with expert ministrations. Her breathing turned to ragged gasps while he toyed with her, bringing forth a rapturous sensation unlike any she had ever known. She bucked against his hand, pushing up into his palm as a wave of delight cascaded over her. She fell back into the mattress, trembling.

Her unbridled enthusiasm was a welcome difference from Birgitta's frigid reaction to his touch. He hadn't known how Agatha would respond to him. With no vision into Agatha's past, he had not known what to expect from her. He had anticipated some hesitation on her behalf stemming from the unfortunate history she had hinted at. He had assumed that her prior experience with men had been unpleasant or even hostile. From her reaction over breakfast to implied violence he suspected she had been physically abused at some point in her life and would be resistant to his touch. For all he knew she may have been raped. If that was the case she would certainly have been on the sale rack at Eliza's, intended for a life among the lower class. She would not have been at a formal marriage ball. Perhaps she was a widow that had endured an abusive husband. He had not been prepared for her pleasure to be authentic. He found her uninhibited passion refreshing and exciting.

He drew the bloomers down her legs, letting them fall where they may. His fingers trailed up the inside of her thighs to find her warm feminine core. He stopped when he encountered the flimsy veil of tissue guarding the entrance.

She was a virgin.

It was a shocking revelation and it briefly stalled his momentum. He had not expected her to be unclaimed territory. What was her history then? Who was she?

He peered into her dilated eyes. She looked up at him with willing anticipation.

He stroked her arm, settling himself between her pale thighs. She shivered as his weight came down over her. He kissed her throat, working up to her mouth. There was no awkwardness in their kisses now. He covered her lips with bruising force which she gave back with equal intensity.

With his face resting against hers and the head of his penis touching the frail barricade of her hymen, he whispered, "I'm sorry this is going to hurt."

She could feel the hard round tip of him pushing inside her followed by the intense pressure of his forcible invasion of her body. It was a searing pain that seemed to go on forever, making her cry out. He smothered the sound with his mouth, swallowing it with his own moan of pain as he felt the sharp raking of her nails down his back.

They began to move together, feeding off each other's energy. He found her moist and accommodating, the pliant tissues inside her gripping him like a velvet fist. She ignored the distant burning as he thrust deeply, meeting her rising hips each time. The pain had faded to a tolerable level, becoming a sensation of endurable pleasure. The friction created between them accelerated until Nick could not hold back. He buried himself completely, touching the deepest part of her as he felt the explosion of his need spill forth. Agatha released a long wail of satisfaction, clutching him to her.

Spent, he relaxed on top of her. She snuggled in beneath him, using the weight of his body as a welcome blanket of warmth and protection. Werewolves slept in piles for the same reasons. This was the most intimate exchange of physical contact she had ever had with a human. It was like being with one of her kind. She promptly fell asleep under him.

Nick slowly regained his breath as he looked down on her tranquil face. She seemed so fragile, but the burning scratches on his back told him otherwise. There had been no hesitation in her energetic lovemaking. She had been a strong partner, keeping up with him and matching his pace. Birgitta had been cold, a completely unwilling participant. Agatha's sense of enthusiasm was invigorating and he hoped was a taste of things to come.

He gathered the quilt around them, keeping her tucked against him. She fit perfectly into his shape like the piece of a puzzle he hadn't realised was missing from his life.

CHAPTER SIX

"A woman does not make excuses. She decides what truth she chooses."
Excerpt from the banned publication, "The Voice of a Woman"

In the feeble morning light that peered into room, Nick lay awake, memorizing every detail of her body.

He was amazed by how much he hadn't realised he missed real intimacy. He had settled for sexual tidbits thrown his way by Birgitta in the years of their marriage. After her death he had devoted his time to the station, giving little thought to his own needs and desires. A few lovers had crossed his path before he had resigned himself to the chore of finding a new wife to give him sons. He accepted that love was not required to produce children, thus his decision to use a marriage broker to procure the second Mrs. Buchanan. Birgitta had demonstrated that love was overrated.

Making love to Agatha was anything but a hardship. Everything about her was desirable and she was eager to please him. It was shame so much of his life had been spent without her in it. He felt like a young man again.

He lightly drew his hand along the rise of her hip and down into the curve of her waist. Her skin was soft under his work worn palm. He touched the scars on her shoulder, counting five small round marks like a bite. She had odd scars in various places all over her body. What the hell had happened to her in America? As his gaze continued to take in the sleeping beauty of her he noticed significant scarring on the inside of her right forearm. How had he not seen it before now? He traced the thick lines with light fingertips. They looked like deep scratches.

He was so engrossed in studying them that it took him a moment to realize she was watching him intently.

She made no attempt to withdraw from his touch, but her muscles were tense as if she might spring away without warning. Her wolf was leery of being revealed. She calmed it by telling it that every inch of her belonged to him now and that meant it did, too. That was the decision she had made. She had nothing to hide, besides the obvious.

"What happened to you?" he asked, staring at the scars with a sickening twist in his stomach.

"This is my previous experience with men," she said. She meant humans in general, but as they had mostly been male she felt it unnecessary to clarify.

The scar covered her Regulatory Identification Brand so she wore it with pride. She would never forget the day she had been branded. She had been ten, the same age as all werewolves when they were marked with the government's RIB. It had taken four human adults to hold her down so that the Regulator could place the red hot metal to her forearm. Each letter and numeral had been applied separately, dragging out the torture for over twenty minutes. She had clawed it out the day she had been smuggled off the Rez by Eliza's agent, relishing the pain she inflicted upon herself. She took it as a personal victory over the government's tyranny. The physical discomfort had been nothing compared to the mental torment of seeing the burn mark every day and knowing it branded her a monster. The RIB marks helped the government keep records on all werewolves, listing their whereabouts, behavior and threat level.

Nick was appalled by the confession of the suffering she had endured. He was amazed that after such abuse she would have been willing to sell herself to a complete stranger in a foreign country. Whatever she had lived through must have been so bad that she figured nothing could be worse. He knew Eliza's business well enough to know that she would not have accepted Agatha without having the full story. If Agatha wasn't willing to discuss it then he would make Eliza provide him with her file. He should have asked for it before leaving Sydney, but he had been so carried away with emotion and alcohol that it had slipped his mind.

"I don't understand why you would sign a contract with a marriage broker," he said, at a loss to understand her motives.

"I know a woman's choices in life are few. A woman is meant to be a wife." Her smile was a sad shadow of the one he had seen the day before. "In America my options were limited. There was no future for me there. I jumped at the chance to start over. And I wasn't expecting to marry a hu-you. I can tell a great deal about someone when I meet them and I always trust my instincts."

His gaze searched her face for clues to her nature. He trusted his instincts as well, but he could not read her expression. There was a wall she kept up. He wasn't sure what lurked behind it. If she was fae, it could be good or bad. He just didn't feel she was a threat. Nothing about her hinted at danger.

"What do your instincts tell you about me?" he asked, rubbing her hip in a soothing manner.

"You don't have a cruel bone in your body," she replied, reaching down to squeeze his flaccid penis out of curiosity. She felt it harden in her grasp, stretching across her palm. This was what he had put inside her that created such wonderful sensations.

His fingers splayed across her waist. He saw the dried blood on her thighs and on the quilt beneath her. He would give her time to recover before plundering her feminine depths again, but there was no denying his response to her touch. He needed a bit of time to heal, as well. His back was on fire from her scratches. It was the first time a woman had done that to him.

He placed his hand over hers and began to draw her palm up and down the length of his shaft, encouraging her to continue. He felt the pressure building as he guided her through the rapid motions. It took almost no time before he spilled a flood of white fluid over their entwined fingers.

She looked down at the pearlescent semen on her hand.

"If you want sons, you shouldn't waste it like that," she commented.

He laughed and slipped his fingers between her legs, probing into the hollow he encountered.

"Is that better?" he whispered in her ear before playfully kissing her neck.

She giggled, but pulled away slightly. She was tender in the spot his fingers were invading. She tried to cover her discomfort by claiming to need to relieve herself.

"I hope someday you'll tell me more about what happened to you," he said as she clambered to the edge of the bed. He wiped his fingers on the quilt. "I want you to know that I will never raise a hand to you."

Recalling a quote from one of Eliza's pamphlets entitled A Woman's Place, she lowered her head submissively and said, "It's a husband's right to show his wife his might."

Hooking a finger under her chin, he raised her face up to look into her eyes. The meekness of her words did not extend to her golden gaze. He suspected that somewhere within her lurked a dominant personality waiting to come out.

"Who told you that?"

"Mrs. Forth-Wright."

He should have known. Leave it to Eliza to brainwash her brides into supplicating slaves for their new husbands. He did not want Agatha to believe that was expected of her in any way.

"Eliza means well, but she leaves much to be desired when it comes to her instructions on being a good wife," he explained. He lightly ran his fingers up and down her arm, watching her nipples turn into tight buds in response to his touch. "I'm not your master, I'm your husband. That makes us equal partners in all things. I'll need to run Gilgai when I'm not here."

She straightened up, alarmed. She couldn't imagine losing him now.

"Where are you going?" she blurted.

He saw the panic in her eyes and he pulled her back to the bed to embrace her reassuringly. His arms encircled her waist and he held her tightly. She pressed against him, shivering. He kissed her hair.

"Nowhere, at the moment. I didn't mean to frighten you like that," he said. "I only meant there will be times when I have to leave the station on business. I'll more than likely take you with me, but there may be times when I go alone. I'll need you to keep the station running smoothly while I'm away. I'll be counting on you. This place can't run itself. Now, let's going."

Nick rolled out of bed and her eyes followed the red striations that paralleled his spine. She had not meant to hurt him. She would need to be much more careful and restrain her wilder impulses. She could kill him or accidentally infect him with her Bite if she became too carried away. She was opposed to giving the Bite to anyone for any reason. She remembered her kind's history all too well.

She relaxed on the bed with a content smile. The people on Gilgai were her pack. Nick was her alpha mate. She was quite comfortable with how her choice turned out.

———

The day went on at a smooth pace.

Nick went out with the men into the south paddock after a brief morning meal brought to their room by Mrs. MacLeach. The housekeeper said nothing about the crimson smears on the top quilt, though she was secretly relieved to know Agatha had at least been a virgin. She changed the bed sheets while Agatha soaked in the tub.

The men relentlessly teased Nick about leaving his lovely young wife's side so soon to return to work. They hadn't expected to see him on his feet for at least a week. He took the jibes in stride, accepting their brotherly teasing with a knowing smile.

Once dressed in another uncomfortably stiff and heavy outfit,

Agatha began to take instruction from Mrs. MacLeach about the regimental pace of the household. She struggled to pay close attention, but her thoughts wandered from time to time to the great spread of land beyond the windows. It called to her wolf with a distracting whisper.

CHAPTER SEVEN

"The process of changing from human to wolf shall be forbidden under any circumstance."
UAT Werewolf Statute

She didn't see Nick again until the evening meal.

Eating in the dining room had always been at Birgitta's insistence. It had seen little use in the last ten years. He was so informal that he typically took meals with the station hands. Unaccustomed to feminine company at the table, he had gotten into the habit of coming in straight from the fields and tucking into his food without regard for his appearance or smell. He was oblivious to a layer of dust in his hair from the paddocks and his clothes were streaked with animal waste and blood. His boots were caked with clay and manure from the horse pens. There was a smear of Dextril's Drenching Formula blended into the creases of his forehead.

Agatha's nostrils twitched, picking up on the scent of viscera clinging to his clothes. The cooked meat on her plate paled in comparison. The wolf wanted to rub itself against him, absorbing the stink of his clothes.

It took Nick a moment to realize that he was inappropriately dressed for dinner with his wife. He glanced down at himself with a grimace.

"I'm so sorry," he said as he stood. "I should clean up before coming to the table."

"You've had a long day," she said. She placed her hand on his arm and he returned to his seat. "This is your house. You're entitled to eat whenever you like and not have to put on airs just to sit at the table. As long as you wash up when we have guests, it's alright with me."

Mrs. MacLeach uttered a noise of dissent. Agatha's narrowed eyes silenced her.

"I must smell like I've rolled in dingo shit," he said, suddenly embarrassed that he had sworn in front of her. "I'm sorry. I need to watch my language. It's just been so long since I've been in the company of a woman. Mrs. MacLeach excluded."

"I don't mind." Agatha smiled shyly. "The men I grew up with were pretty coarse. You can't say anything I haven't heard before."

"Aye, he can," muttered Mrs. MacLeach.

He found Agatha's sentiment sweet. He would remember to wash up prior to dinner and to mind his language, but he appreciated her forgiveness.

"Oh, I nearly forgot to mention that we've been invited to a party to celebrate our marriage," he said, cutting into a thick quarter steak. "It's at the van Amersvoot's, Buren and his wife, Bloem. They're very good friends, more like family."

Agatha was curious to meet the people he knew. It would give her a chance to learn more about him and to get to know the people in the area. It was an excellent opportunity to gather knowledge. Then she recognized the name and a chill went through her. There could not be too many families named van Amersvoot in the area. That mean Dirk van Amersvoot had to be related in some way. He had been most aggressive in his pursuit of her at Eliza's. She did not like the idea of meeting him again, but she could keep him in his place between the moons.

"When?" she asked, keeping her unease to herself.

"Next Saturday. I know it's rather sudden." He chewed slowly, measuring his words. "I was thinking about going into town tomorrow to pick up a few things. There's a dress shop. I thought you might like a new frock for the party."

Agatha's smile swelled. His generosity and kindness meant more than he would ever know. It would be something she could rub in

Dirk's face, demonstrating her position as Nick's mate.

"I don't need much," she said humbly. She saw rejection seep into his face and hastened to add, "But I'd like that. The dresses I have are too confining. I'm not used to wearing anything so restrictive."

He beamed. He had to remember that Agatha was nothing like Birgitta, but he had only his experience with his first wife by which to judge marriage and women in general. Mrs. MacLeach didn't count. She was too matronly and her company was mostly peripheral. He hoped that Agatha wouldn't become bored with life on the station. Birgitta had suffered through it, making both their lives miserable in the process. His first day with Agatha was already better than all his years with Birgitta.

"Then it's settled," he said, satisfied.

After a round of energetic intercourse that night, Nick fell fast asleep. His days were filled with strenuous activity and apparently his nights were going to be just as physically demanding. He was grateful to be in good health at his age, but was still risking a strained back or heart attack with all his exertion. Agatha was already becoming bolder. He needed all the sleep he could get if he was going to keep up with all his responsibilities.

Once she sensed his sleep rhythm was consistent, she slipped from the bed. Pale light from the full moon embraced her naked body as she padded outside. She stood in the formal garden behind the house, the earth warm beneath her bare feet. Her loose amber hair was aglow with moonlight, shifting in the breeze with a life of its own.

She could hear the horses whickering nervously, detecting her scent. A dog barked in the front yard.

Although she was capable of changing her shape at will, it was always more exhilarating under the gaze of a full moon. The full moon had just passed, but there would be plenty more. She had been forbidden from transforming on the Rez, though it was not something she could completely banish. Her few transformations had been done in secret, fearing for her life. Now it was time to release the wolf. She couldn't keep the ring on her finger in wolf-shape. She should have left it inside. She removed the gold band and let it fall.

The full power of her blood surged like raging floodwaters. She felt the animal rising within her, shaking off its hibernation. It began to push outward, stretching her skin. Bristles of fur pierced her flesh from the inside like the quills of a porcupine. Claws ripped through the tips of her fingers as paws forced her hands to swell and split open. Her back arched, flesh peeling away as the reshaped spinal column broke through. She dropped to the ground, head down. She was giving birth to the wolf through every inch of her body. The animal inside was tearing its way out.

The complete change took only minutes. Bloody shreds of her skin lay in the dirt, remnants of her humanity. Once she was more in the habit of changing it would only take seconds to pop her skin off and let the wolf out.

She shook out her marbled grey fur, relishing the slap of ears against her head. The weight of her tail was a welcome counterbalance as she regained her bearings. She walked in a circle, stretching and shaking out her limbs.

Another dog began barking. Horses banged against the rails of their pens.

Agatha loped away from the house, leaving the stress of the human world behind her for the night. The moon guided her path along the hard dirt track she and Nick had driven the day before. She wanted to map out the property on her own, to see how well she recalled their tour. She made a clear point to avoid any contact with the flocks of sheep that dozed in the fields. A few of the dogs growled, but kept their distance.

She knew that the sheep were the reason Nick survived. They were his livelihood, what kept him going. He was born of the land, raised with the responsibility of maintaining it and providing for its future. All he was and all he knew was the bounty that nature laid out before him. She would not do anything to jeopardize that.

BIRTHRIGHT

She returned to the homestead a few hours before dawn. The horses whinnied at her arrival, bumping into each other in their pens. The racket woke the dogs, who sounded off with energetic baying.

Nick stirred, attuned to the natural sounds of the station. The animals were uneasy and their agitated noises broke through the barrier of his sleep. He lay on his back, listening to the familiar heartbeat of the night. Glancing sideways he found the bed beside him was empty. He sat up, the quilt pooling in his lap. Putting his hand on the mattress he felt the coolness of the fabric, picking up none of Agatha's body heat.

"Agatha?" he said, peering into the dim corners of the room.

Thinking she had gone to relieve herself, he reclined on the bed, arms behind his head. He waited for several minutes, listening to the animals grow more anxious. Something wasn't right. There was only thing that caused such a disturbance.

Dingoes.

He shot out of bed, grabbing his trousers and tugging them on as he stumbled across the room. He fell against the doorframe in his unsteady rush, bruising his shoulder. The injury was forgotten as quickly as it happened. He snatched the gun from its resting place on the dresser, checking it for ammunition as he raced out the front door. Mrs. MacLeach did not like loaded guns in the house so he usually emptied the bullets when he came in. This time he had left it loaded for which he was thankful.

The yard was empty, but the animals were still making a racket.

He didn't see any of the slinking canine shapes in the area, but that didn't mean they weren't there. They were sly devils. If Agatha had gone out to the dunny she was at risk. Dingoes typically didn't bother people, but he had heard of them being brazen enough to go after children and women. Heart pounding, he charged around the side of the house.

In the back garden, Agatha heard him coming. She had been

trying to locate her ring, but couldn't find it. She ran in the opposite direction, keeping the house between them. She ducked back inside through the open front door, still in her wolf shape. She was out of practice shifting back and forth. She had just gotten the hang of letting the animal out, now she had to put it back and it did not want to be stifled. It still wanted to run. She was caught between states, torn by her conflicting natures. They struggled to dominate each other.

Nick searched the garden and orchard for signs of Agatha. He called out her name over and over.

Mrs. MacLeach had been awakened by his voice. She came out of her bedroom adjoining the kitchen wearing a heavy night robe. She knotted the belt about her thick waist. She saw Agatha in the doorway of the main house, shaking badly in her naked human form. A pile of fur covered her bare feet from her cast off wolf shape. She could barely stand on her own.

The housekeeper bustled towards her as the station hands began to make noise in the bunkhouse. They had woken to the sounds of the agitated horses, angry dogs and Nick's cries as well. They were preparing to come out and check on the yard.

"Agatha?!"

Nick's voice carried on the night air. He stood by the back door. She must have gone outside, so why wasn't she answering? He glanced down and saw the large pugmarks in the soil as well as bits of bloody skin. They were bigger tracks than anything he'd ever seen. They couldn't have been made by a dingo. A shimmer of gold caught his attention and his blood froze as horror overwhelmed him. Her wedding ring lay on the ground between the tracks. He picked it up and stared at it, his breath caught in his throat. She must have been attacked by something large and he had no idea how badly she could be hurt. Where the hell was she? His stomach clenched with fear that she could be dead.

"Agatha?!" he screamed, turning in a circle. He put the ring in his pocket.

She heard the pitch of his voice and realised he was engulfed in panic.

"Come wi' me," chided Mrs. MacLeach. She put her arm around Agatha's trembling shoulders and guided her into the salon. "I'll fix you up. I'll let Mr. Buchanan know yer alright."

Agatha slumped onto the high backed velvet sofa, dragging a knitted blanket around her cold body. Tears slipped quietly down her cheeks. She had only grasped freedom for an instant and now it was gone.

"Mrs. MacLeach," gasped Nick as he came down the hall. His eyes were wild with terror. "I can't find Agatha. I found her ring. I think she's been hurt."

The housekeeper met him with a reassuring expression.

"She's safe in the salon, have a look," she said. "I found her walkin' in her sleep and I brought her in straight away. Not a mark on her."

Nick's panic melted into the deepest relief when he saw Agatha curled up on the sofa with the knitted blanket of armor around her shoulders. He put the gun down on the side table and knelt in front of her, frantically checking her for wounds.

"Bloody hell, are you alright?" he demanded. He turned over her arms to scan for cuts or abrasions. He lifted her chin to check the alabaster skin of her throat, brushing back her matted hair. "You scared the hell out of me."

"I didn't mean to," she said in a pathetically small voice. She noticed the darkening bruise on his shoulder. "What happened to you?"

His own injury was easily forgotten. His eyes scanned her smooth cheeks, chin and brow, finding no marks. Where were the bites and scratches? How was it she was unharmed?

"It's nothing. Are you hurt? I saw blood and I found your ring on the ground."

She froze. She should have thought about the evidence she'd left behind but everything had happened so fast. She had to derail that train of his thoughts before it reached the station and he put things together.

"I'm fine." She spread her arms to show him her flawless skin then closed up again. She looked at her bare left hand. "It must have slipped off. I went to use the outhouse, but I don't remember what happened after that. I'm sorry."

"I'm not angry at you," he reassured her, holding her face in his palms. "I just didn't know where you were. You shouldn't use the dunny at night. There's a chamber pot under the bed. I should have told you that."

Mrs. MacLeach shooed away the station hands that gathered in the doorway. They filed out, shuffling back to the bunkhouse with much grumbling. She followed them outside, closing the door to give the master and his wife some measure of privacy. She looked for the pile of fur Agatha had shed, but it seemed to have scattered in the breeze. That was a bit of good fortune.

Mrs. MacLeach sighed. The girl was going to expose herself as a werewolf. It was just a matter of time. Should she tell Mr. Buchanan the truth, sooner rather than later and let the chips fall where they may? Was it even her place to tell him? It was rightfully Agatha's duty to be honest with her husband. If the girl chose to hide her blood from him then she would need to be far more careful in her nightly endeavors. Unable to decide the proper course of action, Mrs. MacLeach retired to her quarters to sleep on it.

"There are wild animals around here," Nick told Agatha, pulling the blanket tightly around her. He joined her on the sofa, his arms pinning her to him as though he could shield her with his body. "One or two dingoes aren't much worry, but when there's a mob of them they think they can take down an elephant."

She nodded, burying her face in the groove of his neck.

"I'm not afraid of them," she said. There was no humor in her voice. "You haven't seen a grizzly, have you?"

He shook his head, laying his cheek on top of her amber hair. He chuckled at her bravado.

"No, and I'm not sure I want to if that's the only thing that frightens you," he said, kissing the crown of her head.

"I'm sorry that I caused such a problem," she said, pulling back to meet his eyes. "I didn't mean to make you worry."

"You didn't worry me, you scared me to death," he corrected. His gaze softened. "I've only just found you. I don't want to lose you."

"Then you may have to get used to my sleepwalking," she said, giving him the best excuse she could muster thanks to Mrs. MacLeach. "I can't help it. I've even found myself miles from home before. At least it doesn't happen every night."

He thought he finally understood part of Eliza's hesitation to let him marry her. Eliza would have known about the sleepwalking. With thousands of acres of wilderness surrounding them it was a frighteningly real possibility that she could wander off in her sleep and never be found. Or be found dead.

"Then I might have to tie you to the bed at night," he said teasingly, only to receive an incensed glower in response. Realising that she was not only offended, but infuriated, he quickly sought to defuse the situation. "I'm only trying to make light of what's happened. I would never do anything of the sort. I'm sorry. I didn't mean to make you angry."

Her anger was short lived. The wolf backed down. She smiled, hoping for his forgiveness.

"It won't happen again tonight, I can promise that," she said. "It doesn't happen if I wake up in the middle of the night and go back to sleep. I don't know why."

"Then I'll have to watch over you when we go to bed," he mused, thinking of what he could do to stop her from becoming lost in the country around them.

There had to be a way to protect her. There was no lock on the bedroom door, but he decided it might be a good idea to have one installed.

She sighed. He was serious.

"Maybe once I'm more settled it won't happen at all," she told him, preparing to give up her wild nature if it would give him peace. It wouldn't be any different than being back on the Rez and she had spent a lifetime living like that. "It could just be a reaction to all the upset in my life recently. Give it time. It'll get better."

He was still shell shocked by the night's events, but he accepted that she was not responsible for her actions. It was going to be a difficult adjustment. He would have to learn to adapt and find the best way to keep her safe.

His thoughts drifted to the torn skin and huge tracks outside the back door. If she wasn't hurt then what was the explanation for that? There was no dingo or dog that size that he was aware of. What could have made those tracks? A werewolf? He had seen tracks like them before, years ago when there had been a werewolf scare. Nothing had been proven at the time, so no one spoke of it anymore. If there was one anywhere near the station he would have lost sheep. He didn't want to imagine that there was a werewolf on the loose near Gilgai, especially with Agatha's uncontrollable sleepwalking. She had been lucky tonight.

Then he had an even more unpleasant thought. What if she was a werewolf? He disregarded that idea as quickly as it came to him. It was common knowledge that they were savage, barely human. He had no reason to think she was anything more than an unfortunate victim of sleepwalking and a painful past.

"Let's go back to bed," he said, helping her to her feet.

He guided her to the bedroom, one arm around her waist. She was limp against him, as if her will to live had deserted her. She slumped listlessly onto the bed and curled into a ball with her back to him. He assumed that she was embarrassed by what had happened, afraid that she had disappointed him and was completely exhausted by it all. He lay down on the bed, arms wrapped around her. He used the volume of her hair as a pillow, pressing his nose in behind her ear. There was a wild, musky smell to her skin that he didn't remember. It was both disturbing and alluring. He couldn't place it, but if things were different at the moment, he would have been aroused by it. He knew that she was not in a state for romance.

When he heard the soft sound of her sleeping breath, he pulled her tighter, whispering, "I'm never going to let anything happen to you."

CHAPTER EIGHT

"A proper wife is never distressed as long she remains well dressed"
Excerpt from the Victorian pamphlet, "A Woman's Place."

Falmormath was like the small towns Agatha was familiar with. The streets were dirt, the buildings had raised boardwalks. Painted wooden signs designated the shops, hotel and saloon. There was a post office that also provided telegraph communication. In the street, horses outnumbered steam wagons. Modern progress was definitely on the rise. Gas lamps waited for dark to illuminate the town. At the far end of High Street was a small airfield for moderately sized dirigibles and other airships. Work was progressing on laying track for the train.

Nick parked their wagon outside the post office, intending to send a note to Eliza once Agatha was handed over to the dress maker. He took great pride in having Agatha on his arm as heads turned and questioning glances followed when they passed. The wedding ring had been reinstated on her hand. He escorted her down the boardwalk to Lovelace's Ladies' Emporium, the only dress shop in town.

Fashionable dress forms assumed elegant poses in the front window. Music played softly from a battery operated record machine with a large conical speaker. Framed oil paintings hung on the walls, displaying scenes of domestic bliss with ladies dressed in the most current fashion. Ready-made dresses hung on racks on all sides of the room for ease of selection. Shelves along the back wall held stacks of imported bolts of fabric and trimmings.

Nick removed his hat as they stepped into the shadowy depths of the shop. Agatha bristled as a tall thin woman approached with a pack of homely women in her wake. They were studying her with judgmental eyes. She felt their suspicion and jealousy pour over her like acid. They were the resident pack and she was the intruder. She had been through this scenario before, but from the other side. She recognised the tall dark haired woman as the alpha. She was Agatha's biggest threat and the one that needed to be dealt with first.

Nick was immune to the barely concealed hostility emanating from the women in the store. He didn't realize that he had been the crown jewel of marriage material in the area. With a bevy of local daughters to choose from he had gone to a marriage broker and come back with an American wife. He was oblivious to the sentiment that ran rampant among the locals. They were disappointed in him and they resented Agatha's intrusion into their realm. She was not exactly welcomed with open arms.

"Mr. Buchanan," greeted Luisa Lovelace, proprietor and renowned local seamstress. The saccharine in her voice was enough to rot teeth. She pecked Nick on the cheek. "How lovely to see you and your new wife. We've heard rumors that you returned from Sydney a married man. Congratulations to both of you."

Nick gently urged Agatha forward. She was clearly resistant.

"Thank you, Luisa," Nick said, grinning from ear to ear. His hands rested possessively on her shoulders. "This is Agatha. I'm sure you know the van Amersvoot's are hosting a party next Saturday and I'd like Agatha to have a new frock. Actually, she'll need a new wardrobe now that she's here."

"Of course," Luisa oozed, eyeing Agatha like she was something scraped off the sole of her shoe.

Agatha tensed. Nick picked up on her hesitation, but chose not to call attention to it. She had to find her own confidence. He kissed her cheek.

"I'll leave you in Luisa's capable hands," he told her, squeezing her shoulders.

After he abandoned her to the unpleasant women, Agatha's

resolve stiffened. She stood her ground against the wall of resentment. She was not going to be intimidated by these or any other humans. She had fought other starving werewolves for food. These females were of no consequence. She just had to remember not to resort to physical violence, because her wolf was ready and waiting.

"So, you're from America," said Olivetta Hansen disapprovingly. Her husband ran Dunedin Station, producing high quality Merino sheep. "I've heard that only women of low character sell themselves to these so-called marriage brokers. Is that true?"

Agatha looked at her with hard eyes.

"I wouldn't know," she replied coldly. "This is the first time I've met any."

There were hisses and gasps from her audience. The women suddenly felt the tide change.

"How dare you," snapped Hope Cantwell, her puffy cheeks suffused with purple indignation.

Luisa smirked, gaining some respect for the girl. At least she wasn't meek.

"That's enough, ladies," she announced. "I'll be closing the shop for a bit to attend to my newest client. If you could please show yourselves out."

Agatha had definitely ruffled feathers and alienated some of the most influential women in the area. She would have to make amends to keep Nick from receiving the brunt of their antagonism, but she was not going to be pushed around by a weaker pack. She was an alpha and they were going to learn to give her a wide berth.

"Don't mind them," Luisa said, leading Agatha towards the back of the shop where the fabric bolts were stacked. "We're all a little out of sorts with your arrival, that's all."

"Why?"

Luisa began measuring, turning her and posing her as needed. She made notes in a small leather bound book then gathered particular fabric bolts and laid them out on a wide table. She collected trims and buttons from drawers and shelves, arranging them with the coordinating fabrics.

"Mr. Buchanan is quite the catch," she explained as she worked. "Everyone in the Shire wanted him to marry their daughter. Now he comes back from the city with a wife from America of all places, flaunting you in front of the women he snubbed. I'm sure he doesn't see it that way. He's a very modest man. But I can assure you that the women of Falmormath are none too pleased right now. Buren and his wife are making a gracious gesture by throwing a party for the two of you. Mr. Buchanan could use good friends right now. As could you."

Agatha considered this revelation. She had not had many friends in her life and she didn't feel the need to start now, at least not with any of the women she had encountered so far. She had Nick. She also had Mrs. MacLeach for female company. In time she would get to know the men on the station. Most of all she had her wolf. It would always be a part of her. The people at Gilgai would be the backbone of her pack and she was pleased with that, but it angered her that these people that Nick thought of as friends would turn on him so quickly.

Luisa let her stew in silence for several minutes.

"I'm not offering to become your bosom companion," she said at length. "I don't know you well enough yet. I am willing to get to know you. You won't find many other women who will at the moment. I hope you won't be stupid."

Agatha's alpha ego flared. The wolf rose against her skin but she held it back. She put her hand on the notebook as Luisa was writing, blocking her from continuing. Luisa looked up to meet a metallic gold glare.

"Don't pretend to show me kindness," Agatha growled, head cocked in a dominant posture. "I don't know why Nick chose me over the mutts in this town, but he did. I don't care what any of you think of me, but he's a good man who doesn't deserve this treatment."

She quickly pawed through the fabric choices, separating out those that Luisa had picked and shoving them off the table onto the dusty floor. She pushed her own selections forward as Luisa gaped at her with the puckered lips of a fish out of water.

"I'll expect a party dress ready for Saturday. The rest can be sent out to Gilgai when you have them done."

※

Down the street, Nick composed a message to Eliza. Once sent, he stepped out into the warm sunshine. Just down the block Buren van Amersvoot was standing outside the general store with a handful of other men, all deep in conversation. Buren's son, Dirk, was also among the crowd. Nick remembered seeing Dirk at Eliza's and smiled at him. Dirk nodded brusquely, an ugly look in his eye.

Buren was one of a species of elf called hugtandalf. They were Dutch fanged elves. The mildly pointed tips of his ears and slightly extended canine teeth were a physical trait of that heritage. He was nearly as tall as Nick, with a stylish goatee and neatly trimmed mustache that matched his short, pale grey hair. His eyes were a fierce ice blue. He was well muscled from years of physical labour. He dressed the same as the other men in the region, khaki trousers and a short sleeve button down shirt.

The van Amersvoot family had lived in Falmormath Shire for so long that their appearance was unremarkable to those who knew them. The humans were comfortable with the presence of the few elves and fae in their midst. Australia was a cauldron bubbling with human, elf and fae ingredients. Werewolves were still a minority and their presence was mostly rumored.

Buren waved to Nick who sidled over to see what the discussion was about. After a brief round of congratulations at being remarried, the topic switched back to its initial flavor.

"They found three dead sheep at Corriedale," said Buren. He cast a sidelong glance at his son, who shifted uncomfortably. "All torn to pieces."

Nick was stunned. He pushed his hat back on his brow.

"When was this?"

"Last night," answered Arlen Cantwell. "I heard that Longren lost some, too."

"There's been talk over in Bukkalla that it could be a werewolf," offered Tom Havering.

Nick immediately recalled the size of the tracks he'd seen. That would be about right. A purely uninvited thought arose. Agatha had been sleepwalking last night. She would have left footprints, but he didn't remember seeing any. Just the animal tracks. He had been so distraught that he probably had overlooked them. He tried to shake off the feeling of misgiving, but a small voice remained in the back of his mind, whispering doubt.

"You don't really believe that, do you?" he asked, gauging their reactions against whether or not he should tell them about the pugmarks. He sure as hell wasn't going to mention his thoughts about Agatha.

Buren shook his head. He was a man of confidence, to whom others looked for direction and answers. His attitude dictated how the men around him responded. His words inspired action. He was one of the most respected men in the Shire.

"No, I don't think we have a problem with werewolves," he said definitively. "Maybe some wild dogs have formed a pack in the area."

Arlen held up the yellowed pages of the Victoria Daily Herald. It was dated over a week ago, but it was the most up to date news they had regarding the outside world.

"This tells a different story," he said, waving the paper at Buren. "The werewolf problem in America is getting worse. Their government is talking about deporting them to other countries just to get rid of them. Australia was on that list."

"Can I see that?" Nick asked, taking the paper from Arlen.

Before he could finish reading the offending article, Nick caught a glimpse of Agatha storming up the boardwalk towards him, her jaw set at a determined angle. There was a fire in her eyes that he had not seen before. He tucked the newspaper under his arm and took a step to intercept her.

BIRTHRIGHT

A low rumble sounded in Dirk's chest, only to be silenced by a glare from his father. Dirk's lips compressed in a tight line and he stalked across the street, glowering over his shoulder.

"Whoa, whoa, are you alright?" Nick asked, grabbing Agatha's arms.

"I'm fine," she said, head lowered to hide the lingering sheen of anger in her eyes.

He cupped her chin in his palm and lifted her face up to peer into her conflicted gaze. It took a moment to shake off her dark mood and make the wolf settle down. She did not want to give in to the negativity those women had incited within her. She frowned, accepting that this was his world and she had to fit into it as best she could. She could not lose her temper and allow the wolf to surface. Her life depended on it and his probably did, too.

"I didn't expect to see you so soon. Is everything alright?"

The other men stood back, uncomfortable around emotional women. They avoided female confrontations whenever possible. They had wives, but chose to ignore anything that involved a conflict with the fairer sex.

"Yes. It didn't take as long as I thought," she said, forcing a laugh. She lowered her voice to a whisper. "I don't think they like strangers."

He slipped his arms around her and pulled her into his chest in a shocking public display of affection. Her arms slid around his waist and she pressed her face into his chest. He kissed the top of her head, which earned a tsk-tsk from passersby. The other men shifted uneasily, embarrassed.

"They'll come around," he said as confidently as possible. "After all, we've only known each other for a few days. You'll become friends with so many people you won't remember ever being nervous."

She laughed into his chest, breathing deeply of his comforting scent. She looked up and met his warm blue gaze. It was like falling into the summer sky and being engulfed in its infinite grandeur.

"You're right," she said, relaxing against him. "I'm sorry. This is all so new to me."

"I suppose it's to be expected." He realised that the other men were still standing idly by, averting their gazes. "Sorry, mates. Forgot you were still here. Agatha, let me introduce you to a few people."

She agreed begrudgingly, peering out from the protection of his shirt. The women had been trouble enough, but the males of Falmormath were part of Nick's extended pack. He was in his element among them. She needed to tread lightly and measure their level of aggressiveness towards her. To her relief, she detected none. They seemed far more welcoming than the females, but that was fairly typical. The women felt threatened by her, the men were intrigued by her.

The only one who posed a danger was Dirk, but he had already removed himself from the area. For that she was grateful. Dirk was a Sauvage, stronger and wilder than herself. She could handle him on most days. She did not want to face him during a full moon, when he would be capable of killing her.

Nick passed names around, not knowing if she would remember. She would see them all again on Saturday at the van Amersvoot's where she would have the opportunity to cement their faces and names in her memory.

Buren's features stood out to her trained eye. She identified the pinched tips of his ears as those of an elf. His eyes regarded her warily, but she said nothing. She was curious about his place among the humans. He was clearly accepted. Eliza had said that humans were more accepting of elves and she guessed that it was true.

Returning to their earlier subject, Arlen pointed at the newspaper in Nick's hand.

"The werewolf problem in the American Territories is getting worse," he declared. "There was just an uprising on a reservation in the Colorado Territory. If the Regulators hadn't stepped in, those bloody animals would have gotten loose. They wiped them all out, thank God, but lost a good number of men in the process."

"Aren't you from Colorado?" asked Nick, concern etched his in features. He tried not to imagine the worst. "Did you know about this?"

"There's more than one Rez in the Colorado Territory," she said, hoping desperately that it had been either the White Mountain or Elkhorn Reservations. "And I've been in Australia for some time. I'm from Colorado, but this is the first I've heard of it."

"How many reservations are there?" asked Tom.

"A hundred and eighty seven in total," she said. She did not know all the names, but she knew their number.

Arlen whistled.

"Why so many?" he asked.

"Werewolves live in packs," she answered as if it should be common knowledge. "They can't all be shoved together. They'll fight. It's a big problem."

Arlen grunted, "Then maybe they should put them all together and let them kill each other off."

Buren saw a spark in Agatha's eyes as her wolf reacted to the cruel comment and quickly spoke up to quell it before it became an inferno. They did not need her to make a scene and let her wolf loose.

"Mind how you talk in front of a lady," he said harshly.

Castigated, Arlen apologized to Agatha. Women weren't usually given to being part of these kinds of conversations. Agatha shrugged it off. The wolf skulked deeper within her. She knew human sentiment towards her kind. It wasn't anything she hadn't heard before, even from other fae. How far the mighty had fallen.

Nick opened the newspaper and scanned the article.

"Says here it was on the Blackpaw Reservation," he read aloud. "In the southwestern part of the Territory. What part of the Territory do you come from?"

Agatha turned her head away to keep them from seeing that the blood had washed out of her face. She felt sick to her stomach. Her knees turned weak.

"Agatha?"

She couldn't answer because her world had gone dark. She was trembling uncontrollably and there was no way to hide it. She didn't even feel Nick's hand on her shoulder. Bile rose up in her throat and she choked it back. It burned her esophagus as she fought to keep it under control.

Nick was astonished by her reaction. It was completely unexpected for someone to become this upset by the killing of werewolves. Perhaps she had a personal reason for this level of hysteria. He didn't know how close she might have lived to the reservation. It was possible that she had known people who had been killed, perhaps some of the Regulators. He didn't want to think that it was just as likely she had known the dead werewolves. It would stand to reason that if she had grown up near the reservation she would have been in contact with them at some point. She may have even befriended some of them.

"What's wrong?" he asked.

Agatha regained her composure with a supreme effort. She faked a smile, but could see that he was not convinced. She was too emotional to care.

"I lived near that Rez, in Durango," she said. She swallowed the searing pain. "I had no idea it had gotten that bad."

She wasn't lying. She had not realised that the situation between the Regulators and her people had come to a violent climax since she'd left. She had been in Australia for six months under Eliza's strict tutelage. Eliza had cut her ties to America, so this was the first she was learning of anything happening in her homeland. She was under no delusion that the "uprising" had actually been a massacre coordinated by the government. It had happened before on other reservations. It would seem that the government was becoming more proactive about wiping them out. Starvation and infighting weren't doing the job fast enough.

Buren knew the true cause of her distress. He knew that she was from the Blackpaw Reservation because Dirk had reported back to him from Eliza's that she was an alpha Birthright from that particular reservation. She had just learned that nearly everyone she knew had been butchered by humans. Eliza must have kept her in the dark all this time. That was a cruel thing to do, but she must have had her reasons.

Dirk was furious that Agatha had chosen a human. Buren was torn. As much as he wanted his son to have the best female for a wife, he couldn't begrudge Nick's apparent happiness. Nick was his best friend. Agatha had seemed an ideal choice for Dirk, but Buren could see why she had married Nick. Nick was calm and dependable, the complete opposite of Dirk. He did harbor concern about their union, with her inborn tendency toward animal behavior. He didn't want Nick to get hurt or become infected by the Bite. He had seen firsthand what the Bite did to a man by watching it overcome Dirk. Part of the reason for hosting a wedding celebration had been an excuse for him to speak to her and get a feel for who she was and her intentions towards Nick. If she planned to give him the Bite, Buren would be forced to intercede. He would not allow Nick to suffer his son's fate.

"This must come as quite a shock," he said to her with compassion.

She nodded, still reeling. She looked up at Nick, her gaze hollow.

"I'd like to go home."

"Of course," he agreed immediately.

He excused himself and Agatha, leading her towards the steam wagon. He would pick up Eliza's response another day.

CHAPTER NINE

"Sometimes the past is a thing of the past."
Edward V. Schuster, poet and philosopher

They were well out of town before either spoke.

"I'm sorry you had to find out like that," he said, shifting down to round a sharp bend in the road.

Agatha sighed, staring blankly out at the countryside. She hadn't bothered to put on her goggles. At least the sting of the wind in her face was something she could feel because she was otherwise completely numb. Her heart had crumbled to powder in her chest. She expected the wind to blow it away. Now there was nothing left for her but her future with Nick. She had to hold onto him with everything she had.

"I'm not surprised," she confessed. There was a sharp edge to her voice. "The Regulators are always trying to get the werewolves to start something so they can legally come in and kill them. It happens all the time."

"You're sympathetic to the werewolves?" he asked, startled.

"They didn't cause the problem," she snapped defensively. She turned in her seat to face him. "The government uses them as an excuse, blaming them for everything from killing settlers to spreading disease just to turn humans against them and force them off their lands. They shouldn't be locked up like animals in cages, but humans want every inch of land in America for themselves. They won't even consider living with the werewolves in peace."

"In peace?" he echoed. "Is that even possible?"

"Yes. I believe it is. It used to be. I lived alongside them all my life," she said truthfully. He assumed she meant as a human she had lived alongside the werewolves, but it was the exact opposite. "I know how they live, how they think. Only the Sauvage are truly dangerous. The Birthrights are peaceful."

Nick stopped the wagon, pulling into the shade of a gum tree grove.

"I haven't really given much thought as to how difficult all of this must be for you," he said, turning towards her. "I can't imagine what you've given up. You left everything behind to come to Australia and start a new life. That takes courage."

Agatha scowled, but she wasn't upset with him.

"It takes desperation. I had no life in America, no future. I'm twenty-four. I should have children already, a husband and a home. I shouldn't just now be starting to build a family. That should tell you something about the conditions I came from."

"Weren't there any men there you could have married and had a family with?"

She thought about the few werewolf males she would have considered. Adam Steelcuff, Charles Pedersen and Lance Highmoon would have each made a good match. Adam had been her childhood sweetheart and knew her better than anyone. Charles had been a strong alpha who challenged her. Lance had a rebellious streak that made him a target for the Regulators, but also made him a popular cult hero among the young werewolves. Because procreation had been forbidden by the government, she had opted not to take a mate until the opportunity to escape the Rez presented itself. Cubs were taken away by the government and the parents were executed if caught. If the news from the Territories was accurate, it meant everyone she knew was dead; men, women and children. She would have been killed, too, if not for Eliza. She owed Eliza her life.

"There were a few young men I liked," she said with heaviness in her chest, revealing a hint of her history. "But I could never have married them. Things are too different back there."

Nick watched as a single tear breached her defenses, slipping down her cheek. He wished there was something, anything, he could do to erase those painful memories. He was forced to accept that they were a part of her and they would never completely go away. He hoped he could help lessen their hold on her by giving her a home and family to call her own.

She sniffed back her emotions, wiping away the traitorous tear with the ball of her hand.

"Do you want to talk about it?" he asked, trying not to sound too desperate to learn about her.

"I'm not sure it's something you should hear." She touched his cheek with hesitant fingers. "Please, don't ask me again. You'll just have to take me as I am."

His hand closed over hers and he kissed her palm. He pressed her hand against his face, closing his eyes as he relished the soft warmth. He felt the gentle pressure of her mouth on his and responded with terrific restraint. Every time she touched him he wanted to make love to her. It was an astounding change from his life with Birgitta. Once again, he used memories of Birgitta's cold blue glare to squelch the stirring in his loins.

When he opened his eyes, he saw a reflective tint to Agatha's golden eyes that he didn't remember seeing before. It faded while he watched.

The suspicion of her being a werewolf resurfaced, but he suppressed it. He had no idea what life was like where she had been raised. Maybe the people there were less civilized. America was a wild frontier, much like Australia. From what he'd heard about it, it was rife with lawlessness and violence was rampant. In Australia they still had the refined influence of the Victorian Empire, although the collapse of the penal colonies was taking its toll. America had broken ties with the crown and behaved like a child without parental guidance.

He could only think that Eliza had to know more about Agatha. Miles Loughton, the telegrapher, would send him the message once it came through to Falmormath. If she hadn't responded by Saturday, he would make a trip to Sydney the following week and speak to her face to face.

"I won't pressure you," he promised. "I want you to feel comfortable enough to tell me in your own time. I don't think there's anything you could tell me that would change how I feel about you. I know it's only been two days, but it seems like you've always been in my life. I really can't explain it."

Agatha could, but she didn't, not yet. It meant they were soul mates. Their lives were merged on all levels, from the corporeal to the ethereal. Her kind understood it. His did not.

"You don't have to," she said softly, leaning her head on his shoulder.

He put the wagon into gear and they headed home, neither saying a word.

❖

She said little to Nick all evening and she knew it was bothering him. She couldn't stop thinking of her family and friends slaughtered by the Regulators. Their faces passed through her mind no matter what she did to stop it. She was angry and depressed, confused and in pain. Nick couldn't understand, but he was allowing her time to mourn.

When they retired to bed, Agatha curled up with her back to him and lay awake, listening to him as he undressed. She always thrilled at his touch, but it wasn't welcome tonight. He slipped under the sheets, keeping his distance. He knew better than to make romantic advances. Birgitta had trained him well. Actually she had put the fear of God into him. He was a bit gun shy when faced with the cold wall of a woman's back.

He fell asleep just inches from Agatha while hoping for a sign that she might allow him to comfort her. He tried to remain awake in case she began to sleepwalk, but it was his habit to fall into deep sleep as soon as his head hit the pillow. His days were typically long and strenuous, a good night's rest was crucial to maintain keen physical and mental condition. His snoring alerted her to his slumber.

Agatha slipped outside, but only for a few moments of respite. She didn't transform. She stood in the light of a waning moon, grieving for her friends and family. She allowed tears to cascade down her face. This would be the last time she gave in to the aching emotions within her. Her past was gone and she would face her future with a brighter outlook.

CHAPTER TEN

"When presented with hostility, a lady responds with civility."
Excerpt from the Victorian pamphlet, "A Woman's Place"

It was late afternoon the following Saturday that a package and telegram arrived by local post delivery. Miles Loughton had received the cable the day before, but thought it best to wait as long as he was already delivering the package from Lovelace's.

The package contained Agatha's new party dress. Nick was probably more excited to see it than she was. He was already dressed for the evening in a long gunmetal grey coat, dark blue brocade vest, white shirt and black trousers. He had been pacing the salon floor and checking his pocket watch every ten minutes when Loughton's jalopy finally rumbled into the yard.

"You'd best get into it," he told Agatha, glancing at the grandfather clock in the corner. It had been a gift from Birgitta's parents for their wedding. "As the guests of honour, we should be there ahead of the crowd."

She slipped into the bedroom with Mrs. MacLeach to help her dress. She opened the brown paper packaging to expose a shimmering red fabric. The dressmaker had done a beautiful job with the cut and stitching details. It far exceeded her expectations.

Alone in the salon, Nick read the cable from Eliza.

Dear Mr. Buchanan stop I appreciate your inquiry into Agatha Whistleton's life in America stop I hope you will understand that some of my ladies have less than respectable histories stop I give them a clean slate and chance to start over stop If you have any further questions you will need to address them with your wife stop *Sincerely Eliza Forth-Wright*

The rustle of fabric caught his attention and he crumpled the note in his fist, shoving it into his pocket. Why had he expected Eliza to cooperate? The woman had his money. He had a wife. Her side of the contract was fulfilled. She didn't owe him anything else and she was right. If he had questions about Agatha he should be asking Agatha.

He whistled in approval as Agatha appeared in the doorway. His heart stuttered in his chest at the sight of her. Now he understood what it meant to have his breath taken away. She was the most beautiful woman he had ever seen.

The crimson dress fell in flounces off her shoulders with strands of matching red crystals tucked amid the layers to add sparkle. It was cut low in front, giving a grand view of her décolletage. Her waist was cinched in by an overbust corset in the same bold red. The floor length skirt had a multi-layered bustle and was trimmed with a beaded fringe that just brushed the tops of her fancy high heeled shoes. Mrs. MacLeach had styled her hair and stacked it on top of her head with the red feathers provided by Luisa. One long winding curl dangled behind her right ear to rest on her collarbone.

Agatha took his silent stare as a negative response. She felt like was covered in blood with all the red fabric dripping down her body. No wonder he didn't like it. She sighed, lowering her head.

"I'll change into something else," she muttered, turning away.

He gently grasped her hand to stop her. She looked up at him, hope burning in her eyes. She wanted so badly to please him.

"Why? You look…" he searched for an appropriate word, but all adjectives seemed inadequate. "You look like you've come down from the Heavens."

She turned a shade of red that matched her dress. The blush went down her throat and across her cleavage, which he found adorable and attractive.

"Really?" she asked, peering out from beneath thickly protective lashes.

BIRTHRIGHT

"Oh, yes," he assured her. He suddenly remembered something that would be the icing on the cake. "Wait here."

Agatha looked to the housekeeper curiously, who shrugged. Who knew what men thought when confronted by a vision of divinity? Their brains turned to mush.

Nick ducked into the bedroom and began frantically rummaging for an old jewelry box that he had shoved at the back of a drawer. He tossed shirts onto the floor in his haste, not caring that Mrs. MacLeach would scold him for the mess he was making. He pulled out the ancient wooden box inlaid with malachite and mother of pearl.

"Where is it?" he muttered, digging through bits of jewelry that he had bought for Birgitta as bribes for her affection.

His fingers finally found what they sought. He retrieved a faded satin bag and undid the drawstring with trembling fingers. He withdrew a strand of large, perfectly matched white pearls. At the end of the pearls was a swirl of rubies set in white gold. There were also matching pearl and ruby clip-on earrings. Vindicated, he hurried back to the two women waiting patiently for him to return.

"I want you to have these."

He stepped behind Agatha and draped the pearls around her slender throat. The rubies nestled against the pale cream of her breasts. He carefully attached the earrings to her barren earlobes then walked her to the mirror above the fireplace mantle so she could see herself through his eyes. He wanted her to know that she was the most stunning creature to set foot on earth, which was exactly how he saw her.

Agatha stared at her reflection. She had never seen herself like this. Her gaze shifted to Nick's proud face beside hers. She couldn't believe that she had allowed a human into her life, much less found one so kind, compassionate and handsome.

Mrs. MacLeach recognized the jewelry. The rubies had been mined on another parcel of land owned by the Buchanan family. The set had been a wedding present from his father, Barker Buchanan, to his mother, Sarah. Nick hadn't even given it to Birgitta. It represented his family, his respect for his mother's memory and his desire to show his devotion to Agatha. He was more than smitten with the girl. He was already in love with her. It was going to make their relationship either unbreakable, or that more easily shattered when the truth came out.

"Ye two should git goin,'" Mrs. MacLeach said. It warmed her heart to see him so happy, but she feared it wouldn't last. "They'll be expectin' ye."

Agatha was walking on clouds when they arrived at Willowbrook. She clung to Nick's arm for security, but only because she thought her feet might leave the ground if she didn't have an anchor. She tried to keep thoughts of Dirk from ruining her bliss.

Willowbrook Station was designed similarly to Gilgai, but the house was larger and more formal. Where Gilgai was all business, Willowbrook was also a family home. Buren and his wife had raised three children there and held out hope for grandchildren. Agatha might have been part of that scenario if not for Nick, but the elder van Amersvoot's were forgiving. Nick had been part of their family his whole life, so any children of his would be theirs in spirit regardless.

Nick and Agatha were met at the front gate of the main house by Buren, dressed in elfin finery. His ankle length cloak was woven through with leaves and vines. Beneath it he wore a lightweight burgundy tunic over tan trousers and soft kidskin boots. A heavy silver chain hung around his neck with chunks of amber, bone, feathers and other talismans. On his brow sat a simple crown of fragrant eucalyptus leaves denoting his status as a Custodian of Nature. He was responsible for monitoring the balance of nature in the shire and reporting any issues to the regional council.

"Welcome!" he announced, embracing Nick with enthusiasm.

Buren also wrapped his arms around Agatha, who stiffly accepted the gesture of goodwill. He knew that elves and werewolves were typically at odds. Throughout history, werewolves had allied with humans for protection and power. Elves looked down on them as primitives, whether Birthright or Sauvage. He was not as elitist as most of his brethren because he harbored the secret of Dirk's werewolf infection. It was not his place to decide who was superior.

"Welcome to our home," he whispered in her ear, hoping to put her at ease.

Nick slipped his arm around Agatha's waist and followed Buren up the front walk towards the house.

Bloem van Amersvoot stood in the doorway, her long slender shape backlit by gaslight from within. She was a remarkably ageless woman with waist length white blond hair that remained unfettered by any modern style. It hung loose, creating a cape of curls over her sleeveless emerald green Grecian gown.

"Bloem, you look stunning as always," Nick told her, giving her a brief embrace.

Bloem kissed them both on the cheek.

"You're charming as always," she teased. She turned her attention to the startled young woman beside him. "You must be Agatha. Buren told me you were quite pretty, but I don't think he likes to make me jealous by telling me the truth. You are a beautiful young woman. Very beautiful, indeed. Copernicus is a lucky man."

Agatha immediately liked the woman. She was a woodland spirit. They were less prejudiced against werewolves. There had been a time when werewolves had lived in peace in the forest elves, but those days were long past.

"Thank you," she mumbled, leaning into Nick with a relieved sigh.

He kissed her ear playfully and she squirmed, giggling.

Bloem met her husband's expectant gaze. She smiled and nodded approvingly. They were a good match, typical newlyweds. She had not seen Nick acting so young in far too long. She could tell that Agatha would never have been happy with Dirk, nor would she have made him happy. Despite the potential problems associated with any mixed marriage, Bloem felt confident that Nick and Agatha were mates in the truest sense of the word.

"Come inside," she said, stepping back to allow them past her. "Our home is yours."

"It's been my second home all my life," said Nick as he crossed the threshold with Agatha in tow. "I practically grew up here."

She was sure that Bloem was a High Elf, an elf of the oldest and purest bloodlines, yet her husband was a hugtandalf. They were considered commonplace elves. She was curious about how they had come to be married because Dirk was half human. That was a discussion for another time.

Buren brought up the rear as they entered the house. He left the front door open as a welcome sign to later arriving guests to come inside. Doors were always open in the shire.

"Bloem is the local midwife," he told Agatha with a wink at Nick, who promptly went eight shades of red. "You'll be in need of her services at some point, I presume."

Bloem's smile never faded. She looked at Agatha, who seemed less embarrassed by the nature of the comment than her husband. To placate all present, she put her long fingered hand on Agatha's flat belly. To her surprise, she felt the essence of a new life as it nestled itself in Agatha's womb. It was faint, barely detectable, but to a nature spirit, there was no mistaking it.

"I hope to be of assistance to you soon," she stated, eyes shining with gladness. "Nine months should be about right."

"What? It's been less than a week," Nick blurted, stunned. Thinking he was the brunt of Bloem's unpredictable humor, he muttered, "You're having me on."

Buren nudged him with an elbow in a male gesture of approval.

"She's never wrong. Congratulations, my friend," he said. He threw his head back and laughed. "I've never known you to waste time when you set your mind to something, but this is a new record, even for you."

Bloem touched Agatha's flushed face in a maternal manner. She gave Nick a reassuring smile. He looked shell-shocked.

"I don't think it's something we need to announce just yet. Give the locals time to adjust to the idea that you're married then perhaps we'll have another party to announce the little one's impending arrival. That will keep down any inappropriate murmurings," she said softly.

She knew that there were going to be those in Falmormath who would not be above gossiping if it was known that Agatha was already pregnant. The new couple did not need to hear rumors to the effect that the baby might not be Nick's if she was with child so quickly. Wagging tongues could cut deeper than a knife.

She remembered all too well from her own experience. When she had come to live with Buren as his new wife there had been no hurrah, no fanfare or celebration. She had already been showing the evidence of her pregnant state and the good people of Falmormath had made it plain they knew what it meant. Buren had taken the rudeness with his typical staid composure, refusing to allow it to affect his good nature. He had, however, stood up for Bloem with the ferocity of a tiger when the comments had reduced her to tears. It had taken years to overcome the judgmental nature of the local people, but Bloem's considerate personality and outstanding care as a midwife had eventually turned the tables. Bearing Buren two other children had also been to her benefit. It proved that she was faithful. She still did not associate often with the local families and they were content to keep their distance for the most part. It was a truce, nothing more. She suspected it would be the same with Agatha.

Nick knew immediately what Bloem alluded to. It anyone found out Agatha was pregnant now there would be talk that she had been with child when he married her and that the baby might not be his. He didn't care what anyone thought, he knew the truth, but he wanted to spare Agatha the cruelty of evil rumors. There was no call for those kinds of hurtful accusations. He also clearly recalled what had happened when Buren brought Bloem home already well pregnant from her human lover. There was no way in hell Nick was going to allow that scenario to replay itself with Agatha in the title role.

Agatha also understood the insinuation. Her eyes shimmered with anger. The wolf snarled below the surface. Before she could respond, there came the clattering sound of a horse drawn wagon from outside. It kept her wolf at bay.

Nick put his arm around her shoulders. She looked up into his bewildered, but supportive gaze.

"Don't let it get to you," he told her, giving her shoulders a loving squeeze. "Small towns breed small minds. You'll learn to ignore it."

He suddenly pulled her against him with strong arms, holding her there for what seemed an eternity. He buried his face in her mass of tawny curls. She melted into him, inhaling his warm scent as if they were the only two people on the planet.

Buren went out to greet the new arrivals, relieved to be away from the overly romantic scene. Bloem quietly cleared her throat to get their attention. It was an honor to be in the presence of two people so clearly meant for each other. Their union was exceptionally rare, made even more unique by their two different species. If they could keep their partnership together it would mean great things to future relations between humans and werewolves.

Within an hour, the house was overflowing with local residents and some people from towns quite a distance away. Nick was well known in the shire and beyond. He was instantly liked by everyone he met. His friends and acquaintances were legion. There was no shortage of well wishers filling the house and yard, even if many would have preferred he had married a local girl.

Buren had arranged a dance floor in the back. It was a square of hard packed dirt, really, but it served its purpose admirably. A band from Sydney played a wide selection of music to keep people up and active. Gas lit lanterns hung from the trees, strung in rows from the house to the top of the gazebo that sat in the middle of the formal garden. That was where the table of honor had been placed for Nick and Agatha. Brightly coloured paper streamers fluttered in the breeze. Other tables and benches were arranged around the dance floor and gardens for people to rest and enjoy a tremendous banquet of food and drink. As was tradition, guests had brought their best dishes to share. A table had been set up inside the house to receive gifts and it groaned under the weight of cheerfully wrapped packages.

CHAPTER ELEVEN

"Let not fear rule your soul. Let love be thy heart's embrace."
Halyconius, Roman poet

Set away from the heart of the celebration was a fire pit over which slowly turned one of Willowbrook's choicest lambs. Buren tended the spit, keeping out of the limelight, despite being the host. He let Bloem drift through the crowd, charming their guests. She was born to it. It was one of the greater differences between them.

Agatha managed to escape the clutches of some of the younger women, new wives themselves, as they complained about their marital duties. They seemed to find sex an unpleasant chore. Agatha deduced that their husbands must fall short of expectations in the bedroom. She kept her pity for them to herself, fleeing the conversation as soon as she could. Perhaps Nick should speak to their husbands and offer them advice. He had no difficulties in that area of expertise.

She used the outer garden paths to keep herself from the public eye as she made her way to the rotating spit with its tantalizing aroma. Too many people were vying for her attention. It caused her thoughts to jumble and her tongue to tangle. She was certain they must think her a half-wit. Nick was being mobbed by other sheep farmers so he was unable to come to her rescue. Her wolf had withdrawn deep within, leaving her feeling isolated.

Buren met her with a kind smile as he turned the spit with a foot pedal. The device controlled the speed at which the meat rotated. Coals simmered red hot beneath the slowly revolving carcass.

Flames jumped up from time to time as grease dripped from the meat.

"Overwhelmed?" he inquired.

She nodded, keeping to the shadows as best she could. Too many people wanted her attention. She felt like she was drowning. On the far side of the dance floor, Nick was involved in a discussion with Tom Havering and some other graziers. He caught her gaze and smiled. There was a dazed glint in his eyes that was due to the giddiness of finding out he was going to be a father sooner than expected. The men gathered around him had no idea. They presumed he was silly in love with his beautiful, desirable young wife.

"No one will bother you if you stay by me," Buren promised. "They fear my bark as well as my bite. How do you like your lamb?"

"On the hoof," she replied absently.

He arched a brow at her response. A true werewolf answer. She quickly realised her gaffe, but had no idea how to recover.

"You don't have to worry about me," Buren said, brushing a homemade glaze on the lamb's crackling skin to keep it moist. "I know what you are and I have no intentions of telling anyone. I just want to know that Nick is safe around you."

"Why wouldn't he be?" she snapped, wounded by his suggestion.

"You tell me."

Fat dripped into the fire and hissed loudly.

"I don't answer to you," she said, teeth slightly bared. She was confused by his change in attitude, suddenly questioning her when he had been so accepting of her before.

"Typical response," he grunted. He could see that she was at a loss so he continued. "Let me be blunt. You do answer to me. Nick is my closest friend and it's my job to look out for him and protect him. I like you, and Bloem certainly has a positive feeling towards you, but I don't know if I can trust you."

She exhaled, frustrated. The rubies at her ears and on her chest sparkled in the fire's light as she thought of a response. She was deeply hurt, which aroused her animal defenses. She knew she had to keep her wolf under a tight leash, but it was difficult to think rationally when she was angry. Her eyes glowed with a brassy light. Blood stained her lips as her wolf threatened to emerge. She held back with a tremendous force of self-control.

Buren was measuring her reaction to determine her ability to remain calm and focused under emotional duress. She didn't disappoint him. He watched the emotions chase each other across her face until she settled on one and it was not one he wanted to see.

She looked defeated.

"I won't cause any problems," she said softly, lower lip quivering. Her gaze dropped to the band of gold on her finger. It might as well have been another brand because it prevented her from letting the wolf out. "I've made up my mind to live with him as a human."

"But you aren't," Buren wisely pointed out.

"I've lived twenty-some years like this, what's another fifty or sixty?" Tears stung her eyes. "It won't even be that long. Nick won't be around for more than what, twenty, thirty years? When he's gone I can do what I damn well please."

The conversation had gone horribly wrong and Buren tried to bring it back on course. He ignored the cooking meat to focus on her.

"No one is asking you to change who you or what you are," he told her in as kind a tone as he could manage under the circumstances. "I only needed to know that Nick isn't in danger of receiving the Bite and I have my answer."

Her eyes widened in astonishment.

"Why would I give Nick the Bite?" she asked, rattled to her core. "I would never do that. I've never given the Bite to anyone and I don't intend to. Birthrights don't just give the Bite without due cause. We remember the Paradeus Uprising better than anyone. Sauvage are dangerous without guidance and training. Nick is the kindest human I've ever met, the Bite would-"

"The lamb is on fire!"

Buren turned to see flames working their way up the blackened carcass. He grabbed the bucket of water set aside to put the fire pit out at the end of the night and splashed it over the burning animal.

Laughter filled the air from the bemused guests.

Seeing Agatha standing near Buren, Nick came over to check on things. He clapped Buren on the back, commiserating.

"It's not a complete loss," he observed. "Cut off the top layer and there should be plenty of good meat left."

Buren chuckled at his own foolishness for letting the meat catch fire. He shook his head, grinning crookedly.

"Can I interest you in a slice of lamb?" he asked Nick.

While the two men enjoyed the moment with a crowd of hungry and amused party goers, Agatha slipped away into the darkness.

She didn't get far before she felt the oppressive presence of a Sauvage. It was like a heavy net had been cast over her. This was what she had been dreading. Her wolf reacted to it, wanting to come out to protect her. She kept it back, knowing she could release it if she was forced to.

"Come out where I can see you," she ordered.

Dirk emerged from the black depths of the trees. He circled her slowly, making her turn to stay face to face. He knew she didn't want to have her back to him even though he was weakened by the waning moon. She was the powerful one tonight and he had to watch his step, but that didn't make her lower her guard.

Agatha breathed in his madness. His Birthright had created a monster. It was bad enough that any Birthright would even give the Bite, but whoever had infected Dirk had transmitted all their negative energy into him. He was dangerous at any time.

"You chose a human over me?" he snarled. His eyes flashed with unrelenting rage. "And Copernicus Buchanan of all people. Do you know how pathetic he is? His first wife kept his balls in a jar next to their bed and only let him use them when she said he could. Where are they now?"

She had to be under constant restraint around Nick and the others, but here alone with Dirk she had no compunction about showing her teeth. Baring a set of long fangs she took a threatening step in his direction. He backed up, offering no challenge.

It was pack etiquette that if another werewolf displayed submission in any way the dominant werewolf accepted the gesture as a bloodless victory. The subservient werewolf was allowed to slink away in defeat, usually escaping unscathed.

Agatha had been through an emotional ringer of late. She now had her unborn child to protect and Dirk was a definite threat. She didn't care that he supplicated himself. This was her moment to be the alpha she knew she was. She lunged at him, catching his hand in her mouth as he raised it to shield his throat. He squealed in pain, feeling flesh tear and bones crack under the pressure of her jaws.

He dropped to the ground, showing his belly in the ultimate posture of submission. Unless she was prepared to kill him, she had to take it seriously. His hand was bleeding profusely and he grasped the hem of her dress. There should have been fear in his eyes, but what reflected back at her was even more frightening. Her attack aroused his dominant side.

Agatha stood over him, wiping his blood from her chin.

"Stay away from me, from Nick and from Gilgai, or I'll rip you apart," she warned, her words falling on closed ears.

"I have the full moon on my side," he growled, slinking into the shadows. "You will be mine one way or another."

She stalked away, back towards the house. She licked the blood from her lips as she stewed over the incident. It was fortunate that her dress was the same colour as his blood to mask the evidence of the attack.

She had seen the power-hungry excitement in his gaze and realised she had made a mistake. Rather than putting him in his place, she had thrown down a challenge. She knew that he was mad. Now he was more determined than before to have her.

Nick met her as she erupted from beneath the branches of a eucalyptus tree and into the bright light of the dance floor. He dismissed the high colour in her cheeks as excitement. Around them people began to applaud. She stopped, startled.

"There you are," he said, taking her hand. "Everyone is expecting our first dance as husband and wife. We can't disappoint them."

She allowed his awkward enthusiasm to envelop her. It was an antidote to her dark mood, but she could not fully shake off the disquiet that had taken up residence within her.

As they took center stage on the dance floor Buren introduced them to the congregation as Mr. and Mrs. Copernicus Buchanan. Loud cheers and applause echoed through the yard. The band struck up a heartfelt and romantic tune. The siren vocalist captured the mood with her lilting voice. All eyes were focused on them.

Nick peered into her golden eyes. He was nervous. A light sheen of perspiration lined his brow and upper lip. He thought back to when he'd been fourteen and his mother had forced him to learn to waltz. He'd been humiliated as she paraded him in front of his father, demonstrating proper technique to his father's loud amusement. He had angrily sworn to them both that he would never need to know how to dance. On the dance floor tonight with Agatha's light body in his arms, he was fourteen all over again with two left feet and a much larger audience.

"Eliza did teach you how to dance?" he inquired hopefully.

The smile that overcame Agatha's features made his heart race. She nodded, eyelids lowering seductively.

"She did teach us a few things we might need to know," she replied, assuming the correct pose for their inaugural dance. Her shoulders were square and her head was turned up toward his. Her eyes monitored the colour that crept into his face. "Do you know how to dance?"

"It's been a very, very long time. I'll try not to step on you, but I can't make any promises."

She laughed, head tipped back. She caught sight of the moon in the black sky. The thin rind was missing from one side as it shrank away from its full size. It was the only thing that had kept her safe on this night. Determined not to give Dirk any satisfaction, she gave herself over to Nick's embrace as he started to move to the flowing strains of music.

In the shadows, Buren slipped his arm around his wife's narrow waist and pulled her to him. They swayed slowly to the music, lost in a world of their own. She rested her head on his shoulder.

Nick felt like a three legged dingo as he led Agatha in a clumsy rhythm at first, but she followed his fumbling steps with graceful ease. His uneven strides smoothed out after a few turns and he began to feel the natural sway of the music. They moved in unison, gliding across the floor. Their eyes never let the other's face.

Everyone around them took notice of their obvious bond. Blissfully unaware, Nick and Agatha shattered any remaining doubts among their audience, but animosity and resistance lingered. No one could deny their affection for one another. It did not excuse his decision to use a marriage broker rather than marry a local daughter or widow. There would be a mountain to climb to overcome petty small town jealousies.

CHAPTER TWELVE

"Being human is not necessarily a human trait."
Edward V. Schuster, poet and philosopher

It was long past midnight when the last visitors departed, leaving the guests of honor and their hosts exhausted, but satisfied by the turn out and the mostly positive reception of Agatha as Nick's wife.

Hired servants cleaned up outside while Bloem personally prepared Beshka's room for Nick and Agatha to spend the night. Agatha sat in a padded velvet chair in the corner of the room, half asleep already. Nick and Buren stood outside talking, leaving the women to it.

"How is it Dirk is a helf?" Agatha asked drowsily. If she was in complete control of her senses she would probably never have had the courage to ask such a rude question.

Bloem's movements slowed as she digested the question. She continued to make up the bed where the newlyweds would sleep.

"I allowed myself to be deceived," she said softly. "His blood father was quite convincing in avowing his love for me. I wanted to believe it was true."

"But he was human," Agatha surmised, based on Dirk's genetics.

Bloem straightened up and turned to face Agatha. She was not put off by the questions coming from one who would find it difficult to understand.

"I have never judged humans as a whole," she said. "Nor any other race. When I met him I found him charming. I did not intend to have a relationship with him. It evolved somehow. I kept it from my family until I became pregnant."

Agatha was bewildered that such a thing could have occurred. Bloem was far too intelligent and wise to not take precautions. It didn't make sense.

"You must be thinking I should have been more careful. You ought to know that not every method of birth control is effective," she said to Agatha's dubious gaze. "It is something all women should understand."

"What happened to your human when he found out?"

Bloem sat on the edge of the bed, hands folded in her lap. She had not reminisced over such painful memories in years. She had thought the key to that door had been lost long ago.

"He left me, as my family said he would," she sighed.

"When did Buren come into the picture? Did you already know him?"

The questions were cruel in their words, but not in their spirit. Agatha had only just realised that humans were capable of kindness. She was curious to hear someone else's view and experience with them.

A radiant glow came to Bloem's face when Bloem thought about her husband. Her love for Buren could not be dimmed.

"I knew him through a cousin's marriage. We didn't have much contact, being in different social circles, but I found him handsome and polite. I didn't realize that he had been making inquiries about my marital status even before my affair. My parents had refused him. He was a hugtandalf and he owned a sheep station in the middle of the bush. He wasn't their idea of acceptable marriage material for their daughter. My family is of noble blood. I was expected to take my place among the High Elf court. When they learned of my condition, they urged me to abort the baby. Because I refused they had to find another way to keep our reputation from being sullied. My father approached Buren with an offer. If he married me and took on my bastard, my family would give him a title and position. Buren didn't care about that. He agreed because he loved me."

BIRTHRIGHT

Agatha unlaced her shoes and tucked them under the chair. She was tired, but she wanted to hear the rest of Bloem's story. It gave her promise that she and Nick could make their differences work.

"Did your family force you to marry him?"

Bloem shook her head, but her expression was conflicted.

"Not exactly. Family relationships are complicated among elves. I married Buren because I liked him and he was willing to accept my mistake without question or judgment. The decision was mine, but my family took the credit." She paused to soothe the sting of her family's resentment towards Buren. It had never completely gone away. "Because of their position in elf society they treat him like he's no better than a stable hand. No matter what he accomplishes he'll never be up to their standards, but it doesn't matter. I never planned to become a socialite. I was never as happy as the day I married him. All I ever wanted was to have a home and family. Perhaps that was the reason for my affair. I wanted something my family couldn't understand."

Agatha's heart went out to the elf. She could understand the emotions Bloem felt. She didn't feel it necessary to bring up Dirk's current condition. Bloem was wrung out from reliving her memories.

"You need sleep, young lady," said Bloem, resuming her duty as hostess and midwife. "I will send Copernicus in, but I want you to get sleep."

Agatha's shy smile was sweet. She nodded. She was too tired to engage in sex tonight.

CHAPTER THIRTEEN

"Corruption often begins as good intent."
John Nigel, scholar

1872 Perth, Australia

A garden of delights beckoned within high stone walls. Roses filled the air with their heady scent. Jasmine vines wrapped their spindly arms around wrought iron shapes. Fingers of ivy crept down the water stained walls. Stone figures watched over the meticulously tended flower beds from pedestals stationed around the perimeter. Low boxwood hedges created a Celtic knot work maze in the middle of the garden with a large fountain at its center featuring a naked marble maiden pouring water over a reclining and fully aroused satyr.

Dirk breathed deeply of the perfume that surrounded him. He found peace in the beauty of nature. Perth offered many such escapes from reality. This one happened to be the private gardens on the grounds of the Russian ambassador's home.

Perth was often called the poor man's Sydney with its street grid pattern and architecture mimicking Sydney's example. It had its own unique style and ambience, but it definitely aspired to be more like its sister city to the east.

"I thought I'd find you here," said a soft female voice.

He turned to see the graceful figure of Natassia Goreyevskaya sweeping towards him. His heart danced each time he beheld the vision of her sensual features, but he recognized the palpitations were signs of a simple boyish crush. She was well out of his league. He didn't know why she was attracted to him.

The daughter of aristocratic Russian family, seventeen year old Natassia was the epitome of what a woman should be. She was tall with robust cleavage, a narrow waist and womanly hips. Tar black curls were arranged in a crown on her head. Stars sparkled in her midnight blue eyes. Her smile could stop traffic. She was educated, wealthy and currently in circulation, looking for a husband.

"I love the gardens here," he replied. He took her gloved hand and laid his lips on the back of it. "But it doesn't compare to the loveliness of you."

"I heard a rumor that you're returning to your station," she said, lower lip distended in a pout. "That cannot be true."

He sighed and began to lead her along the path that wound through the garden.

"It's true. My father and I are leaving at the end of the week. We only came to purchase rams for this season's breeding. Now that our business is done, we'll be going home," he explained. "I shall miss you."

Natassia found rejection a foreign concept. She was the daughter of the Russian ambassador to Australia stationed in Perth. As an only child, she had been denied nothing her entire life. Her parents had gone further overboard to provide her with her heart's desire since arriving in the relative desolation of Australia. She had not wanted to leave the familiar climate and gilded domes of Moscow so they lavished her with attention and gifts to make up for it.

She wanted Dirk van Amersvoot. He was the choicest bachelor she had met so far in Perth.

Dirk was half-elf, half- human and she found the combination intriguing. He had the elf's fine features and regal stature combined with the human's broad shoulders and ruddy complexion. He was also possessed of a human's unassuming demeanor, not the arrogance of an elf. He was incredibly easy to get on with. What mattered most was that he was related to the Threadwells, one of the families in the upper echelon of High Elf society. She had designs on improving her place in the world by any means necessary.

"Surely you'll stay if I ask you to," she suggested, running her finger down his cheek.

Dirk found her beauty like that of a spider. There was something delicate and deadly about her.

"I can't," he said gently. "I have to help on the station. My father needs me there."

Natassia frowned. Her eyes crackled with pewter lightning.

"You'd put your sheep above me?" she asked with distaste.

He shrugged self-depreciatingly. He failed to identify the increasing danger.

"You're very sweet and beautiful, Natassia, but I have a responsibility to my family. I can't stay in Perth without a good reason." He didn't realize until after he'd said the words how they sounded. "I'm sorry. I didn't mean it like that. You're a very good reason to stay, if we were serious about pursuing a relationship. We've only just met a few days ago and haven't spent much time together. I'm not sure I'd be the right bloke for a brilliant girl like you."

She calmed down slightly. A coquettish smile played about her ruby lips.

"If you stayed we could learn all about each other," she said, leaning close.

Dirk was tempted by her wiles. It was a nice thought, but that's all it was.

"If I had a career in the city I could see staying on," he said, trying to be as polite as possible under the circumstances. "I'd have something to offer you. It would impress your family more than my potential as a dirt farmer."

Natassia wasn't going to let him get away. He was the man she wanted. His family connections could get her out of this Gods forsaken country.

"But you have potential you don't even realize," she told him, stroking his arm. She took a step closer. "You could be so much more than a grazier. I could help you reach heights you never dreamed of."

She had no idea that his human blood was a deterrent to achieving any of the goals she had in mind. His very existence was a blight on the Threadwell family tree. She didn't realize that his being a bastard prevented him from having any future among the elite of elf society.

"I don't dream like that," he replied with a shake of his head. "I have my place and it's a good one. I'm sorry."

Natassia curled her fingers in his hair, keeping him in place. She pulled his head to the side.

"I do dream like that," she hissed.

Dirk pushed Natassia back, heart pounding. She moved in a circle around him, head lowered. Her black hair came loose from its pins and tumbled over her bare white shoulders. She began to untie the ribbon holding her burgundy corset tightly bound.

"What are you doing, Natassia?" he demanded, confused by her unexpected aggression.

"I'm taking what I want."

The corset fell to the gravel path at her feet, exposing small high breasts with dark nipples. She stepped out of her matching skirt and bustle. She wore no undergarments. Her long slim body was an alabaster column.

Dirk thought she was attempting to seduce him. He wasn't averse to the idea, but he didn't trust her motives. She was behaving so strangely.

"Please stop," he urged, glancing around the secluded garden. "You shouldn't be doing this."

It didn't stop there. Her clothes were not the only thing she took off. As he watched, her skin split into seams and fell to the ground. As the flesh fluttered down it landed at the feet of a black wolf that stood where Natassia had been a moment before.

He knew immediately that she was a Birthright werewolf. He'd heard stories that they were fairly common in Russia and were even socially accepted. He suspected that the Australian government was not aware of their ambassador's true nature. There was a definite bias against them and he would probably be run out of the country.

"Natassia, this is madness," he attempted to reason with her. "I'm sorry I don't feel the same way about you. Please, we can discuss this over tea. Not like this."

She snapped angry white teeth at his extended hand. He jerked back.

A primitive voice spoke in his head, telling him he was in mortal danger. It was purely instinctual, an understanding that he was in the presence of an apex predator. Dirk turned and broke into a fleet stride that rivaled any deer or horse. He darted between towering topiaries, sending small pebbles flying in his haste.

Natassia predicted his direction and came around a giant yew swan to cut him off. She jumped towards him, but he was able to push the topiary swan over to block her attack. She got only a mouthful of leaves and twigs.

He raced in the opposite direction, aiming for one of the two exits out of the walled garden. He could hear her crashing through the foliage close behind him. She was gaining. His foot struck a rock and he crashed into the stone wall. He put out his hands to catch himself. The ivy vines slipped through his fingers. He went tumbling to the ground among a field of snowy white lilies.

The wolf advanced with measured steps, dark eyes reflecting his fear.

"Natassia, no, please," he begged, hands up to ward her off.

She stood over him, muzzle pointed towards his throat like the barrel of a gun. Her teeth were long, sharp and too close for comfort. He grasped at her snout, trying to wrestle it aside. His futile gesture infuriated her. No one pushed her away. She made her move.

He felt a spark on his skin as her teeth grazed his throat. It became a white hot sensation when they entered his flesh. A tremendous surge of heat went through him. He waited for her to rip and tear, violently ending his life. It did not happen.

Natassia had no desire to kill him. She had given him the Bite to make him need her. She hoped it would work with his fallible human blood. As a Sauvage he would be at the mercy of his new power. He would require her mentoring to survive. She would keep him like a pet, grooming him for greatness and taking advantage of his status in High Elf society to propel herself into a world of royalty and wealth. She owned him.

Dirk scrambled backwards, out from under her four legged stance. Blood was smeared across his neck and it stained the collar of his shirt. Small holes were visible on the surface of his throat just below the ear, each set with a sanguine jewel.

Voices reached his ears as a crowd of visitors neared the garden. He turned over and crawled away from her. Natassia recognized her father's deep tone. She gave Dirk a warning growl before bolting into the bushes, abandoning him to his fate.

He managed to regain his feet, one hand clamped to the wound on his neck. He stumbled towards the gate that led out to the street. Using a handkerchief to conceal his injury and staunch the bleeding, he staggered onto the footpath and stumbled the two blocks to his hotel.

He was feeling light headed and nauseous, confused and terrified. She had tried to kill him. If her father hadn't inadvertently interrupted her Dirk was sure he would be dead. He only wanted to get back to the hotel where he and his father were staying. He needed to have his wound tended and he had to tell his father what had happened. It was his word against hers, a grazier's son from the east and a foreign aristocrat's spoiled daughter. He knew who the authorities would believe if he reported the incident.

He was barely able to make it up the stairs to reach his room. His body was beginning to burn inside. He fell against the door, his hand weakly grasping at the brass handle.

Buren heard the sound of something heavy hitting the door. He put down his pen and stepped away from the desk where he had been logging notes about the rams he had purchased.

"Did you forget your key?" he asked, opening the door.

His son collapsed in his arms.

Buren dragged him to the bed and laid him out on top of the coverlet. He saw the marks on Dirk's neck. There were too many for it to have been from a vampire. They left two, maybe four puncture wounds. This was two rows of holes. It had come from an animal and only one came to mind. A werewolf.

He was livid that his son had been attacked. There were few documented accounts of werewolves in Australia, but at least one had gotten in. He would be expected to file a report with the Guardianship. If it had been a Sauvage they would seek to destroy it. If it had been a Birthright, which was his greater fear, they would have to approach the situation with caution. Sauvage were animals and could be put down. Birthrights were considered a separate race and therefore had rights and were afforded legal sanctions.

Only humans were vulnerable to the infection from a Birthright and Dirk was half human. Buren had no way to know how the Bite would affect him. It was possible that there was no reason to be alarmed. It was just as likely that Dirk could become Sauvage because of the influence of his human blood. Dirk's current reaction to the Bite caused Buren grave concern. If his suspicion was correct, there was no way he could make a report to the Guardianship. He had to get Dirk home to his mother before anything worse could happen. She would know what to do.

Dirk was burning up with fever. Buren sat with him through the night, sponging down his sweating body. As cramps gripped Dirk's muscles he would groan and contort into painfully awkward positions. He spent the night drifting in and out of consciousness, which was a blessing. At least he wasn't aware of what was happening.

By dawn the worst was seemingly over. Dirk lay calmly under the sheets, his skin dry and cool. He slept deeply.

Buren gathered their things, packing for their return to Falmormath. They could not remain in Perth another day. He made arrangements for a private airship to take them back to Falmormath before he woke Dirk. He helped his son to dress because Dirk was weak as a mouse from the muscle torture he had endured during the night. It was all he could do to stay on his feet. His entire body ached as though he'd been battered by an iron bar. They caught a cab outside the hotel and headed for the Perth Airyard.

Natassia slowly climbed the narrow steps that led up to the roof of the three story embassy house. She held up her full skirt as she made her way. The stairwell was narrow, confining as a casket. She took deliberate steps, counting them in her head.

Seventeen. Eighteen. Nineteen.

She opened the door to the roof and stepped into a wave of golden sunshine. It poured over her like cold water. She no longer felt its warmth. She felt nothing.

The sun followed her with its great yellow eye as she walked to the front of the house. The roof was flat. A small seating area with a covered arbor was used occasionally for afternoon tea. She stood at the ledge and gazed down on the street and footpath.

Only that morning she had stood on the front balcony, hands gripping the wrought iron railing, and watched Dirk leave his hotel with his father. Her rage knew no bounds. He was hers. He could not leave.

She stormed down the wide mahogany staircase, skirts swirling loudly around her legs. She wore a deep blue dress that matched her eyes. Her hair was a riot of black curls bouncing down her back.

Her father met her as she crossed the foyer. He was a large man, built more like a bear than a wolf.

"I will speak with you now," he said, his tone brooking no opposition. He pulled her into the salon and closed the double doors. "I saw the state of the garden yesterday. I have asked the staff and they informed me that you were there with Dirk van Amersvoot. What happened?"

"He wouldn't have me," she replied, wavering between anger and petulance.

"He is the son of a sheep farmer," said her father disdainfully.

Anatoly Goreyesvkiy was stern, but she had always been able to manipulate him. He had to take a hard stance this time. "I would never allow you to be with a man like that. You will forget him."

She threw herself onto the sofa, pouting.

Anatoly realised she was still naïve and filled with unrealistic ideas about the world. He studied the conflicting emotions that crossed her face. He knew what she had done.

"You gave him the Bite?"

She nodded shamefully.

"Where is he now?"

"His father is taking him back to the east," she answered sullenly. "He's a Threadwell, papa. He could bring us great favour with the High Elves."

"I don't think they've filed a report, or we would have Guardians at our door," Anatoly sighed. He stood over his daughter. "He's a bastard. The Threadwells banished his mother for her dalliance with a human. They married her off to a hugtandalf, by the sake of the Gods. If you paid more attention to your lessons you would have known all that, but you chose to listen to gossip and rumor. I don't know what we're going to do now. It's a good thing he's half elf. If the Gods are with us, the Bite will have no impact on his system. But if it does, you are responsible for what you've created and my guess is he will want nothing to do with you. If word gets back to his family we could all be condemned because of your impulsiveness. We do not give the Bite for selfish reasons. It is a powerful gift. Few humans can control the infection. Paradeus was an exception and it still got him killed. Your vanity, possessiveness and ego are now part of this young man. Natassia, my daughter, you may have cost us our lives."

Those words replayed in her head as she stood on the precipice, gazing out over the rooftops of Perth. It was called the poor man's Sydney for a reason. It was a bustling port city like its east coast sister, but it lacked the culture and refinement of Sydney.

How could she have been so stupid? She had dreamed of becoming a member of High Elf society, holding Dirk's arm as they moved through royal circles. Her desire to escape the drudgery of Perth's social scene had cost her more than she could afford. Immaturity ruled over her emotions, blinding her to reality. She had made a fool of herself and ruined her future with one unfortunate decision that she couldn't take back. The damage was done. She could never have a life of her own without always being haunted by what she had done. She had made an unforgivable mistake, causing Dirk to spurn her.

Below her people meandered past; ladies with parasols and men with tall hats. They were quite surprised when her body struck the cobblestones at their feet.

A week later Dirk read that the daughter of the Russian ambassador in Perth had fallen to her death. He felt overwhelming pity and anger. She had gotten off easy.

CHAPTER FOURTEEN

"A bored dog will chase its tail A contented dog will wag its tail."
Excerpt from the parable, "The Lost Shepherd"

Weeks passed and Agatha began to chafe under the yoke of normal life on the station. There had been no sign of Dirk and it made her uneasy because she heard the reports of mutilated sheep after the next full moon. He was making his presence known, but she didn't know what he was waiting for.

Luisa had made several sleeveless cotton dresses for summer which made the heat bearable. The waist cinchers were double layered fabric without boning which made them pliable and less confining. They would become obsolete when her waist began to expand in the coming months. For now, she wore them out of habit and fashion. She would soon require another, completely new wardrobe of maternity clothing.

True to her word she maintained her human shape at all times which meant her sleepwalking ended as unexpectedly as it began, much to Nick's relief. She kept herself sequestered inside the house while Nick was working in the paddocks. She knew that the animals would start acting up if she went outside and she didn't want their behavior to raise questions. He had decided to wait until after the baby was born to begin her education on running the station from a hands-on perspective.

Mrs. MacLeach attempted to alleviate her ennui by teaching her to cook, but certain smells made her queasy which led to the discovery that cooked meat made her violently ill. Mrs. MacLeach prepared her meals in secret. Because Nick was out the door by sun up she was able to eat raw meat for breakfast and lunch. When he returned home for dinner she ate almost nothing which concerned him. She wasn't losing weight and her colour was good, but he worried that she wasn't feeling well. He would have been even more troubled to know she never set foot outside the house. She spent most of her days sitting at the front window, staring out at the world like a dog pining for its master.

She was further devastated that since learning about the baby he had withdrawn all sexual contact and slept alongside her without touching. He was terrified of hurting her or the baby, so he kept his desires to himself. He relieved the urges manually when necessary, which was usually daily. Being so close to her made him want her like mad and he woke fully aroused each morning. It was almost impossible to keep his hands to himself, but he forced himself to treat her like she was made of glass.

Another month passed with no sign of Dirk, but more sheep were killed on the night of the full moon. Agatha couldn't understand Dirk's motives and it kept her on edge.

Bloem stopped by for her first formal prenatal visit, pronouncing Agatha and the baby off to a healthy start, quelling Nick's concerns over her nutrition. She did her best to reassure him that all was as it should be and that he could still make love to Agatha, but he wasn't taking any chances.

Bloem took him aside, leading him out to the yard to speak privately. Agatha remained inside, helping Mrs. MacLeach wash the china for the second time that week.

"Have you been intimate since we last spoke?" Bloem asked as he walked her back to her carriage. She was old fashioned, preferring horse and buggy to steam wagon. Elves as a rule despised technology.

He coughed and looked at the ground. It wasn't his custom to speak openly about sex.

"No," he said, distinctly uncomfortable with the topic. "I don't want to do anything that would put the baby at risk."

Bloem laughed lightly, touching his shoulder. Buren had been the same way when she had been pregnant with Dirk. Men were convinced women were fragile vessels that could be damaged by a gust of wind. They also highly overestimated their own strength.

"You won't, as long as you aren't overly energetic," she told him with a knowing grin. "Agatha isn't going to break. She is much stronger than you realise. There isn't any risk to the baby by having sex and your wife would appreciate the attention."

When they retired to bed that night, Nick decided to heed Bloem's advice. He removed his shirt, keeping a watchful eye on Agatha. She stood by the window still fully dressed, gazing longingly out into the moon drenched night. He slipped out of his trousers and shorts, already half erect at the sight of her.

Nick approached her on bare feet. He hooked his fingers in the laces of her cincher and gently loosened the stays. Once undone, he let it fall to the floor and nudged it aside with his foot. His strong hands encircled her waist and worked their way up to her breasts. They were fuller than he recalled and she winced at the lightest pressure. He felt her tense. Discouraged, he pulled away.

She turned to face him, keeping a small gap between them rather than pushing into him as she normally would. Her breasts were too tender for that at the moment.

Her fingers wound up through his hair and she brought his head down. She kissed him deeply, her tongue filling the warm well of his mouth. His hands gathered the material of her dress, pulling it up and over her head. Once she was naked, save for a layer of silver moonlight dappling her skin, his hands greedily roamed over the swell of her backside and up her spine. He stepped backwards to the bed and fell onto the mattress, pulling her on top of him. She gasped, rolling away.

"I'm sorry, I'm sorry," he said, mentally kicking himself. He should never have attempted to seduce her. "I knew this was a bad idea."

"You haven't hurt me," she said with a low laugh. She lay on her

BIRTHRIGHT

back next to him, head turned so she could see his profile. "My breasts are sore, that's all. Bloem said it's normal."

He rolled onto his side to study her lean naked shape, imagining how it would change over time. He put his hand on her belly, in the hollow just below her navel. There was no sign yet that a baby was growing inside her. Her abdomen was still flat and smooth. He looked forward to watching it grow as their child developed.

They proceeded to a delicious embrace that evolved into a slow session of lovemaking. He drew her on top of him so that she sat upright, straddling his hips. He was buried inside her, her tight muscles gripping him like a fist while she maneuvered up and down the rigid length of him. They took their time, relishing their first intimate contact in nearly two months. Fingers splayed across his stomach for balance, she rode him in a slow, deliberate rhythm until he cried out and erupted inside her.

She fell onto her side with a satisfied sigh. Her skin shone with perspiration. Strands of amber hair clung to her cheeks and neck. Nick lay on his back, eyes closed, letting his breath settle. His eyes opened when he felt her hand on his chest. Ignoring the discomfort of her breasts, she leaned against him and rested her head on the rise of his ribs. He kissed her forehead and held her until they fell asleep.

✦

Her sleepwalking affliction started again.

With the return of an active sex life, Agatha also felt the return of the urge to hunt. Her hormones were on the rise and she needed another outlet. The sex just seemed to light a match under her wolf. It was agitated, trapped, resenting its containment. She asked Nick to invite the van Amersvoot's for dinner so she could speak to Bloem without alerting him to a problem.

It was a relaxed affair, the men dressed in casual working clothes and the women in simple country dresses without frills. Conversation was chipper with a cascade of wine for everyone but Agatha. After the meal, of which Agatha ate nearly nothing, she and Bloem took a stroll in the back garden while the men went to play cards with the station hands.

Round glass bulbs strung on cables were hung from poles to provide soft illumination. Flying insects danced in the halos of light. The two women walked side by side in the shallow dark. They listened to the concert of the night as it played around them.

"I'm having cravings," Agatha confessed. "I don't know what to do."

Bloem suspected that this would happen. She had tremendous sympathy for the young woman. It was one thing to pretend to be human; it was another to make it work. Agatha had good intentions, but there was a flaw in her design.

"Then you must give in," advised the elf.

"I can't," said Agatha, aghast.

They walked in an awkward silence for a few minutes until they reached one of the wrought iron benches. Once seated, Bloem took Agatha's hands in hers and stared fixedly into her eyes.

"You are a werewolf. It will only get worse if you do not let it out," she explained. "Your body is changing in a different way right now. It needs to know both halves are fulfilled."

Agatha was beside herself with guilt. She so desperately intended to keep her promise and never change again. It was an enforced punishment, not unlike life on Rez, but she was doing to this to herself. At least her treatment here was better. She had Nick's affection. Still, she lacked freedom, the one thing that had brought her to Australia in the first place.

"What about the baby?" she inquired, struggling with her dilemma. "It won't be affected?"

Bloem laughed like a bubbling stream. She patted Agatha's hand.

"Goodness, no, your body is designed to protect it," she said. "It will be perfectly safe. You forget how strong you are."

The metallic shimmer returned to Agatha's eyes as she contemplated Bloem's words. Her blood began to rush. The wolf strained at its tether. She wanted to transform there and then, but held back. With the training of a lifetime, she kept the beast inside.

BIRTHRIGHT

"Thank you," she said sincerely. The relief in her face was obvious. "I needed to know that. I'll be careful."

Bloem caressed her cheek.

"See that you are. Enjoy yourself."

<hr>

Nick was too tired and subdued by alcohol to wake when Agatha left the bed later than night. She tucked her wedding ring beneath the mattress then exited through the rear of the house, shedding her human shape as she slipped through the garden. The earth felt exhilarating beneath her paws. She took a moment to roll in it, enjoying the pure carefree sensation. It was a guilty pleasure.

She left the yard on long loping legs, moving with graceful strides. The moon painted her with a pale brush, making her grey fur appear even lighter. She moved like a ghost through the shadows.

A flock of sheep woke as she neared them and they broke into a frantic gallop, scattering in all directions. The dogs keeping watch were too busy trying to maintain order to give chase. They snarled in her direction, but she was already in the distance.

This was her first real hunt. She had tagged along with Lance Highmoon on another venture years ago, sneaking off the Rez to hunt elk. She hadn't been very good at it, almost getting herself killed by the elk's knife sharp antlers. She was older now with a more mature sense of her animal self and an overconfident measure of her capabilities. Her reflexes were rusty, but that would improve in time. She was just out of practice.

She was after one particular animal. She could smell its musty odor more than a mile away and she closed in on it. The mob of kangaroo heard and smelled her approach. They began an unhurried retreat to higher ground into denser trees, not recognizing her scent. They still identified her as a predator. They used the trunks of the trees for shelter, hoping to confuse her. When they realised their plan was not working, they turned back towards the flat open ground in the valley. They surged forward, leaping with powerful thrusts of their hind legs, gaining valuable ground.

She picked her victim out of the dozen fleeing animals, a young female that seemed more panicked than the rest. Agatha maneuvered with speed and agility even she had not been aware of possessing. Her feet flew over the ground as if borne on wings. The rudder of her tail made ninety degree turns possible even at full speed. She predicted the frightened animal's moves and closed in like a bullet, ramming into the kangaroo with jaws agape. She closed her mouth on its throat. Her teeth connected with fur and flesh, driving deeper into muscle. The animal squealed and lunged sideways to dislodge her. She held on fiercely, digging her front claws into the kangaroo's hide. Her back feet dragged on the ground while the creature struggled to jump. Keeping her claws securely anchored in the kangaroo's shoulders, she readjusted her grip on its neck. Her jaws clamped down, cracking the spine with one savage bite. The kangaroo dropped to the dirt with her muzzle still clenched around its throat.

The rest of the mob was long gone, not one kangaroo was visible in the valley below.

Agatha loomed over her first kill. Blood dribbled from her lips and off the end of her tongue as it flopped out the side of her long mouth. Dynamic energy flooded every fiber of her body. She trembled with its power.

The howl that burst forth from her was the sound of her tortured soul being set free.

Morning light poured into the bedroom as Nick drowsily came to life. His head throbbed from the residual effects of all the wine he had consumed during dinner and the whisky afterwards. He did not ever drink like that and now he remembered why.

Agatha lay sprawled in a tangle of sheets, her skin seemingly infused with a new glow that he credited to her pregnancy. He'd heard that women glowed when they were expecting, but he hadn't believed it was meant literally.

Still partly under the influence of the wine in his system, Nick leaned over and peeled the coverlet back to expose the pale moons of her bare buttocks. She shifted slightly, but didn't rouse. His fingers smoothed a pattern on her leg before finding their way up between her thighs.

She sighed in her sleep, legs parting instinctively at his touch. She squirmed against his hand while his fingers flickered and massaged her furthest recesses. Pressure from his thumb activated a sudden blood flow to her clitoris, making it bulge with desire like a flower about to bloom. Her tissues continued to absorb the blood of passion, becoming swollen and sensitive to the lightest touch.

He was incredibly swollen, too. He needed to get inside her or release the pressure himself. He rolled over and positioned himself between her legs. He braced his arms on either side of her smooth back.

He had never mounted a woman from behind. There had been no experimentation with Birgitta. The few times she relented to his requests for sex he had been required to enter her in a missionary position, usually with her head turned aside, and be as quick as possible with his orgasm.

Agatha awoke to the pressure of his penis sliding into her. She reared up, startled.

"Ssh," he whispered, cupping her throat in one hand. He pressed his cheek against hers. "Ssh."

His deep, powerful thrusts made her whimper with pleasure. She grasped at the sheets, uttering quick, sharp cries. He moved his hips with the natural rhythm of a horseman. She bucked back into him with wild abandon. She arched back with a shriek as he dove into her with a final thrust. His guttural moan echoed in her ears as he sank down on top of her.

He had never imagined being able to truly enjoy himself like this with a woman. He did not have to worry about boring his partner. It was always amazing with Agatha and she wanted more.

Bloem's words echoed in his mind, "As long as you aren't overly energetic."

A stab of concern made him slide off and check to see if she was alright. He had surprised himself with this sudden, more aggressive advance on her. He was even more shocked by her excited response. He prayed they hadn't been too energetic and done anything that would injure the baby.

"I didn't hurt you, did I?" he whispered urgently. "I don't know what came over me. I've never done that before."

Agatha stretched out, arms and legs taking up the length of the bed. Her sated smile told him volumes. The ring glinted on her finger.

"You're experiencing dominance," she said, knowing that it was being triggered by the release of pheromones caused by her hunting success. There was a renewed sense of vigor and lust for life that he was subconsciously feeding on. "It's good."

His brow furrowed briefly at what she said. He wasn't sure what she meant exactly, but he did feel a kind of power that he hadn't felt in years. He couldn't explain it, but he welcomed it.

CHAPTER FIFTEEN

"Confidence is essential to success, but arrogance is a fool's undress."
Excerpt from the Victorian pamphlet, "A Woman's Place"

When another full moon came and went with no challenge from Dirk, Agatha began to relax about his threat. More sheep were found slaughtered at other stations, but there was no indication that he had been anywhere near Gilgai. She felt that he might have been lashing out because he was a sore loser who was jealous of Nick. She hadn't said anything to Bloem about it, but she suspected that Buren may have stepped in to keep Dirk in line.

The high she had felt from her first hunt began to fade as the weeks wore on. Her body was telling her to go out again and taste blood. The wolf demanded it. Four days past the moon's peak, she went out for another hunt. This time, she bit off more than she could chew.

She charged after the kangaroo mob, driving the scrubbers down towards a broad, open field. She was filled with confidence from her prior triumph of having taken a young kangaroo with ease. Her legs propelled her with lightning swiftness and she found herself pursuing a big male that had separated itself from the mob.

It took more stamina than she expected to run the beast down. It could throw itself forward in a leap greater than twenty feet, clearing scrub and rocks with ease. She didn't have the endurance of a Sauvage. She was ready to give up when it suddenly collided with a section of wire fence hidden in the darkness and became entangled. It thrashed in terror, making loud noises of pain.

With it mostly immobilized, Agatha thought she had an easy kill. She just needed to keep out of the reach of its deadly rear feet. There was a long claw on each one that could eviscerate her in a single thrust. Thinking it was completely wrapped in the wire, she went for a direct charge, aiming for the throat. She wanted to get a hold on its windpipe to kill it quickly. In the darkness she couldn't see that it was caught with only its upper body snared in the wire mesh, but its massive hind legs were loose. As she leaped both rear feet came up to stop her.

It scored a direct hit.

She went sailing through the air, spinning like a kite in a storm. Her body bounced like a stone skipping over the surface of a lake before coming to a rest. The wind went out of her from the impact and she briefly lost consciousness.

She lay still for some time, half awake, regaining her breath and taking stock of the injuries to her body. Her left hip was bruised to the bone from striking a rock. Her left shoulder felt shattered, but she knew it was just dislocated. She looked down at her right side and saw the fur was parted by a deep gouge that ran across her ribs. Blood ran through her pelt like rainwater.

The scrubber struggled against the wire, flailing and screaming. She wished she had the strength to kill it, just to shut it up.

Agatha staggered to her feet, unable to put weight on her left foreleg. It dangled like a broken tree branch. She thought only of getting to Willowbrook to nurse her wounds. She needed Bloem to check on the baby. If she miscarried because of her stupidity she would never forgive herself and she wouldn't expect Nick to forgive her either. Even if the baby was unharmed, her other concern was how she would explain her wounds to Nick. She had gone too far to hide her true nature now. In shame, she hobbled on three legs towards Willowbrook, leaving a trail of blood in the dirt.

◆

Bloem sat up in bed, the thick braid of her platinum hair coiling in her lap. She leaned over and lit the gas lamp on the bedside table as Buren responded to the plaintive scratching at the bedroom window. He peered out at Agatha's bruised face as she leaned against the outside wall for support, her cheek pressed against the window pane.

"By Gods, it's Agatha," he said in alarm.

Dressed only in his sleeping trousers, he rushed outside. He caught her as she slid to the ground. He carried her inside, depositing her on the empty bed in their daughter's vacant room.

Bloem donned a beautifully embroidered white robe, tied around her waist with a silver rope. She sat on the edge of the bed, making an immediate visual diagnosis.

The bleeding had mostly stopped, but the jagged wound that ran along her right side gaped open to reveal torn muscle and the white arches of her ribs. It was a blessing that werewolves were endowed with supernatural physical power. Although they healed with incredible speed, Agatha would be out of action for weeks. A human would have been killed.

"Bring me my kit," Bloem instructed.

Buren obeyed without question. He had assisted her many times and knew when to be a silent participant. Bloem would tell him what she required.

Agatha's eyes opened and she gazed up at Bloem. Tears crept down her temples and into her hair. She whimpered, eyes pleading.

"I wasn't careful enough," she said meekly.

Bloem ran her fingers over the girl's brow in a calming gesture. Her other hand moved to the flat expanse of Agatha's belly, seeking proof that the life inside still held on. A strong spirit emanated from her core, allaying Bloem's fears. The baby was alive and safe.

Buren returned with the large wooden box containing his wife's medicinal arsenal. He set the cabinet on the nightstand within Bloem's reach then stepped back. He waited to be given orders.

"Send Lars to fetch Copernicus," she instructed.

"No!" Agatha cried in a panic. She grabbed Bloem's wrist. "No, he can't know about this."

Buren leaned against the doorframe, muscled arms crossed over his bare chest. His cold blue gaze was pointed at her like a knife.

"You should have thought about that before you got torn up," he chastised her. He wasn't entirely unsympathetic, but it was difficult to be kind when she had made such a mess of things.

"Buren, please," Bloem said sharply with a stern look over her slim shoulder. She turned back to Agatha. "Now is the time to tell Copernicus the truth. This is not something you can hide from him. He needs to know."

Agatha went limp on the mattress. She had sabotaged her own future. It felt like the depth of winter awaited her.

"How do I tell him?" she implored Bloem.

The elf gave her an encouraging smile, opening the medicine cabinet. She had her work cut out for her with the numerous injuries Agatha had suffered. Agatha gasped when Bloem's fingers probed her left shoulder. The bones were badly out of alignment and needed to be put right as soon as possible.

"We'll come to that soon enough," she answered. She motioned to Buren. "I'll need you to help me set her shoulder."

Buren held Agatha with hardened arms around her torso, taking care with the severe gash down her side. Bloem used one quick motion to put the scapula back in place. Agatha shrieked into Buren's shoulder, leaving tear stains on his skin. He half expected her to sink her teeth into him as would a wounded animal. He laid her back on the sheets as gently as possible, but there was no doubt she was in agony. He was impressed that she had not bitten him in her pain.

Bloem began the arduous task of putting Agatha back together before her husband got a look at her.

Lars didn't knock when he arrived at Gilgai. There were no locked doors in Falmormath Shire and he had spent much of his life at Gilgai. He marched down the hall to the master bedroom and turned on the light.

"Get up," he ordered.

"Wha-?" Nick sat up, eyes rolling. He was completely disoriented. "What's going on?"

Lars opened a drawer and threw clothes at him. He regarded Nick as an uncle, someone he respected and admired, but tonight elfin arrogance got the better of him. He was on a mission from his parents and their expectations took precedence.

"Get dressed."

Nick was so flustered that for a moment he couldn't think straight. He sat up in bed and pulled on a shirt, fumbling with the buttons in his half asleep state. It suddenly occurred to him that Agatha was not in bed with him and Lars van Amersvoot was glaring at him from across the room. The last vestiges of sleep were wiped from his brain as he realised something was very wrong.

"What's going on? What the hell are you doing here? Where's Agatha?"

Lars gave nothing away. He had been ordered to bring Nick back to Willowbrook and that was all. He secretly wished to he could get the Bite from Agatha so he could join his brother, but as an elf he was immune to the infection. He looked up to Dirk and had tried to be like him all his life. The change in his brother was frightening, but at the same time appealing. Dirk was stronger than he ever had been. He stood up to authority. He wasn't afraid of anything. Lars wanted to be like that.

"Just hurry up. Father will tell you when we get back."

Nick's heart sank. Agatha must have been sleepwalking again. If Buren had sent Lars to Gilgai she must have made it some distance. Hadn't she told him before that she had found herself miles from home? Lars didn't seem too concerned so perhaps everything was alright, but why hadn't Buren come himself? That got Nick's nerves twitching.

He quickly pulled up his trousers and stomped on a pair of boots. The mattress shifted as he stood and he heard a small metallic clink. He noticed Agatha's ring spiraling in a circle on the floor. He snatched it up before following Lars outside.

The sun was cresting as they arrived at Willowbrook. Virgin rays of sunlight pierced the navy blue of the night sky overhead. Hazy shapes became distinguishable as the light grew bolder.

Nick stepped out of the steam wagon before it came to a stop. He saw Buren coming out of the house to meet him.

"Where is she?" he demanded.

Buren put his hand out to slow Nick's bullish advance. His eyes were sharp and they gave Nick pause.

"Settle down," he said. "Come inside so we can talk."

"Talk? I want to see Agatha. Isn't she here?"

Buren nodded, guiding Nick into his office. The gaslights would soon be extinguished as the morning brightened, but for now they provided brilliant ambient light.

"Yes, Agatha is here. She's been hurt," Buren said to get it out first thing. He noticed the pale expression on Nick's face and hastened to reassure him. "Bloem is seeing to her. She'll be alright."

Nick's legs failed him and he sank onto a high backed leather chair. His chest felt like he'd taken a kick from a horse. He looked at Buren beseechingly.

"I knew I should have put a lock on the door. I should have done something to keep her safe," he moaned, head falling into his hands. "This is my fault."

Buren uttered a sound of disgust that brought Nick's head up.

"This isn't your fault," he commented with a curled lip. He didn't want Nick to blame himself for Agatha's condition. "She brought this on herself."

Nick quickly came to her defense.

"She can't control her sleepwalking," he said. "I thought it had stopped, but maybe being pregnant has something to do with it happening again."

"That is part of it," said Bloem as she came silently into the room. Her robe was stained with blood and dirt, which brought a gasp of horror from Nick. "But there is much more you need to know about your wife."

"How badly is she hurt?" he asked, getting to his feet. His legs almost failed to support him. "Did she lose the baby?"

Bloem bestowed a tender smile upon him.

"Your child is strong and safe in her womb," she replied to his obvious relief. He almost lost his balance, but gripped the back of the chair to stay on his feet. "Agatha will heal in time. Her wounds are severe, but she is already recovering. Don't be afraid of her, Copernicus. She loves you more than life itself."

Her statement confused him. He had a sinking suspicion of what she meant by being afraid *of* Agatha, but right now he was afraid *for* her.

Nick entered the bedroom with trepidation, not knowing what to expect. Agatha was lying on her back beneath a quilt, eyes closed peacefully. There was no colour to her flesh except for areas of dark bruising and ugly red abrasions. If not for the low rise and fall of her chest he would have thought she was dead. He fell to his knees beside the bed, tears of helplessness careening down his face.

Bloem stood behind him like a sheltering tree. She placed a hand on his shoulder.

"I've given her a sedative," she explained. "She needs to rest."

"What happened?" he asked, eyes never leaving Agatha's tranquil features.

"I'll let her explain that when she wakes."

Nick struggled to wrap his head around what was happening. He just couldn't grasp the entirety of the situation. Why were they being so evasive?

"I'd like to stay with her."

Bloem nodded. She squeezed his shoulder reassuringly.

"Of course. I'll bring you something to eat in a bit."

She softly closed the door on her way out.

Nick stared at Agatha's serene, waxen features. She looked like she was at death's door. He could almost hear her knocking. He couldn't lose her. He would give anything, do anything to keep her.

Out of morbid curiosity, and to assuage his concerns over her injuries, he gently pulled back the quilt to reveal her battered and damaged body. She did not respond in any way. He could see the deep blue bruising that marred her pale skin over her entire left side. There were cuts and scrapes amid the angry dark splotches. Her left arm was bound tightly to her side. It was when he looked at her right side that he felt his stomach constrict. He knew a wound from a scrubber claw when he saw one.

He sat back on his knees and studied the script of scars written on the parchment of her skin. They told a story that didn't have a happy ending. He had been right all this time. She was a werewolf.

Agatha woke to a burning fire on her right side. She gasped, tears dripping down her face. The sheets were soaked with sweat, blood and the residue of the unguent Bloem had used over the sutures that sealed the ragged claw inflicted wound.

Her sudden cry brought Nick awake. He had been dozing in a chair in the corner and was jolted to his feet by the sound she made. He crossed the room in two long strides and perched on the edge of the bed. His frantic eyes searched her tense face.

"I'll get Bloem," he said, starting to rise.

Agatha's right hand clamped down on his wrist, keeping him there. He looked down at her, a wary expression in his eyes.

"No," she said in a soft breath. "I deserved this. I haven't been honest with you."

He waited, his bowels churning. He didn't want to hear this, but he knew there was no avoiding it.

"Have they told you what I am?" she asked, eyes searching his tense face. She released his wrist. When he shook his head she said, "But you know, don't you?"

"I've suspected it for awhile, but I didn't want to believe it," he admitted. At this point, there was no reason to hold back. They needed

BIRTHRIGHT

to get it all out in the open. "Why didn't you tell me?"

She was surprised, blurting out, "I heard how the men in town talked about werewolves. How was I supposed to tell you?"

"I'm not like them. You should know that." He sighed, running his fingers through his hair in frustration. "Don't you know you can trust me?"

"I've never trusted humans," she said in a quiet, angry voice. Her eyes were downcast. "You're the first human I've ever allowed to get close to me. You don't know how hard it's been to lower my guard for you. I do trust you, but I didn't know how to tell you."

"So you haven't been sleepwalking," he deduced, finally seeing the whole picture.

"No." She raised her gaze briefly then looked down again. "I've gone out a few times to stretch my legs. That's all. It's not something I could do back home on the Rez, but I can here. I tried not to, but the wolf inside me needed to get out."

"Have you been killing sheep?" he asked.

Her eyes came up to meet his. She was deeply insulted that he would think such a thing of her.

"Why would I do that? The stations rely on sheep to stay in business. Why would I go after their livelihood?" she inquired as though he should have known the answer. Her voice took on an urgent quality. She needed him to understand. "Australia is the answer to my prayers."

Numbed by everything that had transpired in the past few hours, he asked, "Then what am I?"

"Everything."

In her vulnerable state he couldn't deny that she seemed nothing like the stories he'd heard about werewolves. She wasn't some mindless beast. There wasn't anything about her that gave credence to those old wives' tales. He was too old to believe in monsters anyway. Putting a name to it didn't change who she was and what she meant to him. She was the same woman he had married and who shared his bed every night. The revelation of her true nature made no difference in his feelings towards her.

Agatha waited, holding her breath. If he denied her now, Eliza would send her back to America. She would rather die than be placed on another reservation. With the massacre at Blackpaw, she would be assigned to a different Rez where she would have to fight for her place in a pack. With a baby on the way it would make her struggle that much greater. Because it was Nick's it would be Kindred. He had only one part to contribute to the baby's development, so the extra werewolf piece from her would be dormant. Kindred were unable to transform, though they shared werewolf blood. No pack welcomed a female with another male's cub, especially if it was Kindred. They wanted to keep their own bloodlines and perpetuate purity. They would probably kill it, if the Regulators didn't take it away first. The accidental children born on the Rez were removed by the government and placed in institutions run by missionaries. She knew that from experience. She also knew that the Regulators would execute her for unlawful breeding.

Nick was thinking of the baby, too. Having a werewolf wife was one thing, but was he prepared to raise a werewolf as his child? He had no notion of their culture. Would they have to teach it to control itself during the full moon? Would they have to lock it up? Would Agatha become more of an animal with another werewolf around? Questions assailed him until his head pounded. The only way to find out was to move forward.

He sat on the edge of the bed and took her hand. She was so cold and weak. He gently rubbed her hand in his to give her his warmth and strength.

"I love you," he told her, feeling the heaviest weight rise from his shoulders. "There's just so much I don't know."

She offered him a wilted smile.

"Then let me tell you our history."

CHAPTER SIXTEEN

"There is no greater mystery than a woman's history."
Anonymous

"Did you know that we were once the companions of kings?" Agatha asked, slipping into a dream-like state as she spoke.

"From the beginning, in the Time of Mist, Birthright werewolves lived in peace with humans, elves and fae, sharing the First Forest. Then humans began to extend their reach. They cut down the trees and built cities. The elves retreated to the sanctity of the mountains, but the werewolves were curious about the human domain. They left the forest to dwell among the humans, taking on more and more human traits. They were seduced by what humans had to offer. They learned to crave power, personal comforts and to be desired. To achieve that which they sought, they sold themselves to the highest bidders. Only the wealthiest and most influential people kept werewolves as status symbols. They guarded merchants on their travels. They engaged in royal hunts. They were seen in every court and castle across Europe. Werewolves were fashionable, collectable, like jewelry or fine art."

Agatha took a moment to catch her breath. She was exhausted. Nick helped her drink some water before she continued.

"Until the first Bite. It was an accident. A young noblewoman was waylaid by a highwayman on her way to meet her lover. Her Birthright guardian defended her, but the robber escaped with a deep bite wound. That is how the infection is passed. If a weak person receives the Bite, the wolf will take over. It senses fear and seizes control. It will twist the body into a thing born of nightmares as it tries to become the dominant shape. It will never completely win, but it becomes a permanent state of being. A stronger soul can withstand the wolf's advance, but will still fall prey to its strength under the force of the full moon, day or night. That is when the infection burns hottest. Even the strongest man cannot keep the wolf inside during the full moon. If a person can join the wolf with their human nature they can achieve a state closest to the Birthrights. I've only heard of one Sauvage who could do that, but his story is coming."

"No one realised at first what it meant to give or receive the Bite. When the noblewoman's father learned about what had happened, he organized a posse to track down the highwayman, not knowing about the nature of the Bite." She stopped, brow furrowed as she sought to translate her choice of words. "I'm sorry, posse is an American expression. You'd say mob."

Nick grinned, offering her another drink of water. She sank back against the pillow with a sigh.

"In any case, they captured the man just before the next full moon. Imprisoned, he succumbed to the infection as the moon glowed bright. When the nobleman saw this, he understood. He ordered his own Birthright to give the Bite to another prisoner. Sure enough, the following full moon gave him two of the brutal new creatures. In his infinite wisdom, the nobleman saw this as an opportunity to generate revenue. Because of their natural tendency towards violence, he named them Sauvage. The next month, he took them before the king and demonstrated their power as combatants. That began a downward spiral for my kind. Our esteemed position as consorts and personal guards began to change. Not all Birthrights were willing to give the Bite. Many returned to the forest in protest. Those that were willing to pass on the infection received rewards beyond imagining. They used us to make bloodthirsty gladiators for their sport. We created vast armies of Sauvage to fight their wars. There were even humans who volunteered to receive the Bite in the name of king and country. The elves were furious. They warned your ancestors that their bloodlust and greed would lead to ruin. They attempted to reason with them, but humans aren't capable of changing their ways. You are a savage race at heart."

Nick couldn't disagree.

"This abuse lasted for hundreds of years until one Sauvage came to realize that we were more than aristocratic pets, slaves or soldiers. His name was Paradeus. It means 'of two gods'. He had been a Centurion in the Roman army before being captured by the Normans. He had served the human army faithfully for most of his life and he didn't care who he fought for. He was a natural born soldier. He fell in love with a Birthright courtesan. He took the Bite from his lover so that he would be strong enough to return to her when the war was over. It was the pureness and unselfishness of her love that kept him from becoming one of the mindless warriors around him. He is the only one who ever fully mastered his new power. He merged with his wolf. And then he rose up. He organized a rebellion. Thousands of Sauvage turned on their human masters and spilled their blood in rivers across the fields of Europe. Of course the humans ran to the elves for help like children afraid of the dark. The High Council agreed to give them aide, but only for their own egocentric reasons. They wanted to destroy the Sauvage. The Birthright had broken one of the first laws of nature and created a beast with no natural place in the order of things. With their armies combined, the humans and elves went to war against Paradeus and his Sauvage. It was the single bloodiest battle in history, lasting for thirteen weeks. In the end, most of the Sauvage were dead. Even Birthrights were slaughtered for their involvement in creating the monsters who had dared bite the hand that fed them. Those that survived fled, but they had few places to go. The forests were no longer their home. The elves and other fae made sure they did not find refuge among their kind. The Birthrights were able to hide in the cities of the humans that once enslaved them. The few Sauvage that escaped scattered to the four winds."

She paused, breathing heavily in pain. There was a rattle in her chest.

"You should rest," Nick told her.

"I'm almost finished," she said. Her eyes were barely open as her energy waned.

He sat back and waited her to go on.

"Where once we lay at the feet of kings, now we live in the shadows. In Europe we're hunted for sport. In the Eastlands our organs are sold for their medicinal properties. Humans fear us. Elves don't trust us and they will kill any Sauvage they find. We thought the new country of America would provide us a safe haven with its great open lands, but now humans have taken that away from us, too. The government controls everything we do. They've rounded us up like cattle and put us on reservations where we can't hunt, can't let our wolves out, can't breed. They're forcing our extinction."

She lowered her head, tears spilling down. Her wounded eyes met his.

"Do you understand now why I came here? I had to live. When I met you, you gave me that chance. You gave me hope. Please believe me when I tell you I'm no threat to you or anyone. I just want to live my life like anyone else."

Nick wiped away his own tears. He could not imagine the depth of her suffering. How could anyone begin to understand? He wanted so badly to hold her and give her comfort, but with her injuries it was not possible without causing her more pain.

"I know 'I'm sorry' doesn't come close to making up for what you've lived through," he said in a soft voice. He let his fingers caress the curve of her cheek. It was probably the only part of her that wasn't black and blue. "I wish there was something I could do to take all that away. I can only offer you the life you deserve. I'm not afraid of what you are, because what you are is my wife. I told you that you are my partner in all things and I meant that. I married you because I fell in love with you the moment I saw you. Nothing you've told me makes any difference."

The weight of the world seemed to lift off Agatha's mind. How had she doubted him?

Nick retrieved her wedding ring from his pocket, meaning to place it where it belonged on her left hand. She curled her fingers into a fist, much to his surprise. His questioning eyes met hers.

"I can't wear that anymore," she told him.

"I don't understand," he said. "I told you I don't care what you are. You're my wife. This is a symbol of our marriage."

"If I wore it when I changed shape it would constrict and cut off my toe." That brought a look of shock and dismay to his face. "To wear that would bind me to my human shape as much as my brand did."

His expression of horror deepened.

"Brand?" he echoed. He could taste bile at the back of his throat at the mention of it.

She raised her right arm as much as she could to show him the scar that covered the RIB.

"They brand us as children," she explained, sinking into the comfort of the mattress. It was too difficult to stay awake.

Nick almost vomited to think of her skin burning as red hot metal was applied to it. It was inhuman to brand anyone, much less a child.

Bloem appeared in the doorway. She had been listening from the hall. Her heart was filled with mixed blessings for them, but their road was a long, steep one.

"Copernicus, she should sleep."

Nick nodded. Agatha wouldn't release his hand. Her eyes opened a fraction.

"Stay with me," she begged.

Bloem slipped away down the hall.

Nick removed his boots before joining Agatha on top of the quilt. He found a way to put his arm over her that didn't cause discomfort and settled in.

His brain was spinning like a child's top. He lifted her right arm and scrutinized the scar he found there. Any hint of a brand had been scratched out. He knew she had done it to herself. She had broken the chain that held her prisoner and he had merely put another on her with a wedding ring. He turned the band over in his fingers. Guilt consumed him. How was he to have known it had entirely different significance to each of them? How did he explain to her what it meant to him as a sign of his love and fidelity? Was it a concept too foreign for her to understand?

At the moment all that was important was the health of her and the baby. Any culture clashes could be resolved later.

CHAPTER SEVENTEEN

"Creation is to one man as destruction is to another."
Chao Ming, warlord, Cheun Xiang Dynasty

Agatha remained at Willowbrook for a month during her recovery. After hearing from Bloem and Buren the importance of the wedding band, for Nick's sake she agreed to wear it on a chain around her neck that was long enough so as to not strangle her when she changed shape.

Fearing she would go stir crazy on bed rest, Buren and Bloem did all they could to alleviate her increasing boredom. Buren taught her to play chess which she took to like a flea on a dingo. He was astounded by her tactical mindset and how she maneuvered her pieces with critical precision across the board to win almost every time. Bloem attempted to get her interested in herbalism, but Agatha was less inclined to the ancient arts of healing. Alphas were typically warriors. The more arcane lessons of medicine held little appeal.

When Nick learned from Bloem that Agatha had been living as a virtual prisoner in her own home at Gilgai he was devastated. She was afraid of what her presence did to the animals on the station and feared what would happen if the station hands learned of her nature. To make her life more bearable once she returned home, he took the opportunity to make some improvements and drastic changes.

While she recuperated with the van Amersvoots, Dirk made an appearance at Willowbrook. The loud argument between father and son woke her from a sound sleep.

"I know she's here," Dirk snarled, chest to chest with Buren as the elder van Amersvoot blocked the hall leading to Agatha's room. Bloem remained in their bedroom, sobbing into her pillow during the heated exchange. "I've come to take her."

"She's not yours," Buren replied, his voice laced with heavy emotions. "She never was. I don't know why you're obsessed with Agatha, but it's going to stop. You leave her alone or so help me-"

"What?" Dirk sneered, leaning his face close to his father's. "You'll do your elfin duty and kill me like you should have when you first found out I was Sauvage? You can't kill your own son. I know you better than that."

Buren's eyes, so sharp and powerful, were filled with torment. The situation was tearing him apart. He was being put in a position to choose between his oldest son and the rest of his family and close friends. Dirk wasn't his by blood, but that had never stopped him from thinking of Dirk as his son.

"The only reason I haven't done the right thing is because your mother begged me to spare your life. That's the only thing keeping you alive right now. She thought you would be strong enough to control it, but even she can see we're losing you to this infection. If I ever find out who gave you the Bite, I'll kill them."

Dirk's eyes shone with a wicked gleam. He laughed and it was a frightening sound of madness.

"She's already dead," he said chillingly. "And you can't keep me locked up anymore. I'm too strong for you now. You can't force me into that prison cell you built to hold me on the full moon."

"I promised your mother that I wouldn't kill you," Buren replied, a muscle throbbing in his clenched jaw. "But I want you out of the Shire. If I catch you anywhere near here, I'll turn you in to the Guardianship."

That brought a spark of fear to Dirk's eyes though he tried to mask it.

"You would be killing me with your own hands if you did that."

"No. I'd just be pulling the strings. If your mother hates me for it, I'll learn to live with it. I won't let you get your hands on Agatha. I'll do whatever it takes to keep her safe," Buren promised. There was no mistaking the warning in his voice. "Now get out."

Once Dirk was gone, Buren returned to his wife. Bloem clung to him, trembling as she wept into his chest.

Agatha lay awake for hours, replaying the conversation in her head. No matter how she tried to interpret it, there was no changing the fact that Dirk was more dangerous than she thought and Buren had lost control of him.

⚜

A few days later, Agatha returned home to discover that life at Gilgai had taken a new direction. She immediately noticed that there were no sheep, horses or dogs in the yard when they drove up. The barns and buildings were devoid of life. Not a single animal remained except the wandering chickens that were forever underfoot. Oak barrels were stacked outside what had been the shearing shed. Large wooden crates with importation stamps from France waited to be unpacked. The nearest hillsides and fields were furrowed by rows of freshly tilled soil.

Nick helped her out of the steam wagon, goggles down around his neck. He handled her gingerly because her injuries were not thoroughly healed. She was at ninety-five percent, but not back to full health.

A loose cotton dress allowed ease of movement without pulling against her still tender skin and her feet were bare. She walked towards the house with a hardly noticeable limp, eyes and ears taking in the absence of normal activity. It put her on edge.

Mrs. MacLeach greeted them before they reached the gate. Now that Nick knew about Agatha there was no need to ignore her mistress's special needs or keep them hidden. Preparing meals would be a much simpler matter.

"I'm so pleased tae see ye back home where ye belong," she cried, gingerly embracing Agatha. "Ye look gaunt. Weren't they feedin' ye?"

She brought Agatha into the salon and set her on the sofa like a doll on a shelf.

"I'll get ye something to eat."

Nick hung his goggles, gun belt and coat on the rack just inside the door. He surreptitiously checked the Riggins, making sure it was loaded, before putting back in the holster. He walked over to where Agatha sat staring at several stacks of books on the long, low table in front of her. She picked one up and read the title aloud.

"*The Life Cycle of the Grapevine.*" She picked up another. "*Black Rot: A Vineyard's Guide to Fighting Fungal Disease.* What is this?"

"Our new venture," he answered proudly. "I've sold off most of the livestock. We're going to make wine. I know it's a bit of a flutter, but I'm going to make it work."

Making the change from sheep station to winery had not, in fact, been as impulsive a decision as he let on. He had never felt the same desire to be a grazier as his father had. After his father's death, he had broached the subject with his mother about moving away from keeping sheep and planting grapes instead. The land was ideal for it. He had done his research and mined every possible nugget of information from books and correspondence with vintners in other parts of the country. He knew what it would take to be successful, years of hard work and potential heartbreak, but he was game for the challenge. Unfortunately, such a concept had been too outrageous for his mother to take seriously. He was from farming bloodlines, generations of men who kept livestock. All she had known was farming and she had been too emotionally brittle from the loss of her husband to deviate from what was familiar. Nick had put aside his dream and went about his life as it had been planned for him in order to provide his mother with peace of mind and stability. He had certainly never shared his ideas with Birgitta. Now, however, with Agatha's support, he was at last going in the direction he wanted to be traveling. He was on his way to having the vineyard he had been dreaming of for most of his adult life.

BIRTHRIGHT

Agatha had made him realise that it was never too late to pursue his heart's desire.

"Why would you do that?" she asked, confused. It made no sense to her. "You're a grazier. You've raised sheep your whole life. I don't understand why you would want to change."

He sat beside her, his expression earnest. He clasped her hands in his.

"Bloem told me you haven't left the house since you came here," he said in a mild, chastising tone.

Agatha looked down, embarrassed. She had hoped he wouldn't find out.

"I didn't want you to know. I didn't want to worry you."

He cupped her chin in the palm of his hand and tilted her face up to peer into her eyes.

"I do worry. It's part of my nature. Just like being able to run free is part of your nature," he explained. His lips brushed her forehead. "You aren't human and I'm not going to let you give up being who and what you are for my sake. I want you to be able to go about as you like any time of day or night. Although I'd rather you didn't go out at night. And you don't have to hunt scrubbers anymore."

His kindness was overwhelming. Admittedly, she had reservations about his true motives.

"But this?" she asked, holding up a book titled *Biodynamic Viticulture*. "I don't understand why you would do something like this. You raise sheep. You always have. Do you think I might start attacking the sheep if I stop going after kangaroo?"

Her accusation was unexpected. He sat back, studying her hurt expression.

"No, that's not it at all," he said, feeling equally stung by her suspicion of his intentions. "That never crossed my mind. I knew it bothered you that the animals were afraid of you so I moved the horses out to the north paddock with a small flock of sheep to keep for meat. Without so many sheep, we don't need the dogs, although I will miss having them around."

Agatha grinned mischievously, regretting that she had questioned him.

"You have me," she giggled. He had rarely seen her laugh of late. "If you like dogs, you'll love my other shape."

He realised he had not yet seen her as a wolf. He had a difficult time picturing her as anything other than what she was right now. He'd never even seen a real wolf, only illustrations in books. Dingoes were the only living canine predators he'd clapped eyes on in his life. He was intrigued.

"Will you show me?"

"Right now?"

He shook his head and rested his hand on her knee. It felt natural to keep some sort of physical contact with each other.

"Someday, when you're ready," he answered. "You don't have to do anything right this minute."

"Except eat," announced Mrs. MacLeach, carrying a silver tray loaded with slabs of raw lamb. She placed in on the table on top of the books. "I'm goin' tae feed ye up like a proper wife should be. I want tae see meat on yer bones."

"I'll be very round soon enough without your help," she sighed.

Nick put his hand on the slight rise of her abdomen. She giggled, feeling a new sensation in her belly. It was a tiny quiver beneath the warm weight of his palm. It had happened a few times before in the previous days and every time it made her laugh with delight and wonder.

He searched her bright expression with curious eyes.

"I can feel it," she told him, smiling broadly.

He pressed down softly, but could not detect any movement.

"What does it feel like?" he asked, wanting desperately to share in her experience.

"Like tiny fluttering wings." She searched for better way to describe it. She found it would be best to demonstrate. Slipping her fingers under his, she softly wriggled them against his palm to recreate the flurry of movement that was happening inside her.

"Something like that."

The simple action brought home that his child was alive inside her. He so was overwhelmed by emotion that he wasn't able to speak for several moments. He couldn't help the tears that formed in his eyes and clung to his lashes. His fingers tightened on hers and he leaned over to give her a tender kiss.

"That makes me hungry," she whispered against his lips. "But I right now I need real food."

Nick had never been put off by the sight of raw meat, but he was surprised that watching her devour the bloody flesh aroused him. He couldn't explain the connection. It might have been her pure, unadulterated joy at tasting her natural food, the relief of being home or the fact he hadn't been able to make love to her in a month that caused it. In any case, he appreciated her enthusiastic feeding and was hoping for some of the same energy in bed later. He wasn't disappointed.

CHAPTER EIGHTEEN

"The true measure of a woman's worth is in her ability to conceive and give birth."
Excerpt from the Victorian pamphlet, "A Woman's Place"

As she had predicted, Agatha's belly swelled steadily in the following months until, by the end of winter, Nick was both impressed and concerned by the size of it. Bloem reassured him that her body was designed to stretch to remarkable proportions to allow for the baby's continuing growth. The baby was constantly active, the source of many sleepless nights for Agatha with its antics. Nick was fascinated by the rolling, turning, kicking motions that caused ripples and bumps on the surface of her abdomen. He would lie sideways on the bed with his head resting on her stomach, feeling the baby move inside her. He often fell asleep like that until a sharp movement would wake them both.

By August, Bloem was visiting weekly to monitor Agatha's progress. She explained to them the process of giving birth. Nick paled visibly when he heard the more graphic details of what was going to happen to Agatha's body when the blessed moment arrived. Agatha was even less enthused to learn what she would have to endure to provide Nick with an heir. Regardless of her reservations, it was what she had signed up for when she married him so she would have to see it through. Nick knew nothing of her apprehension. She was a master at hiding her thoughts and emotions. It was a survival technique honed by life on the Rez.

BIRTHRIGHT

It was mid September when new life entered their world.

Agatha was helping Mrs. MacLeach in the kitchen, gutting chickens for dinner, when she felt a warm trickle of fluid run down the insides of her legs. She looked down at the stain spreading on the hem of her skirt.

"Mrs. MacLeach?" she asked with a tremble in her voice. Being told about what to expect and actually experiencing it were two frighteningly different things. "What's happening?"

The housekeeper turned away from chopping carrots to see the puddle forming on the floor at Agatha's feet. She dropped the knife with a clatter and quickly wiped her hands on her apron.

"Och!" she cried excitedly. "Yer water's broke. The bairn's a'comin'."

Mrs. MacLeach poked her head out the kitchen door and shouted at Jim Parsons as he crossed the yard on his way to the bunkhouse.

"Fetch the midwife!" she called out. "And send someone out tae the north paddock! Tell Mr. Buchanan that the baby's comin'!"

Jim broke into a full out sprint towards the barn.

Agatha wasn't sure if she was ready, but she was overruled by her body's desire to be rid of its extra cargo. She braced herself on the chopping block as the first of many contractions gripped her.

It was going to be a long night.

Nick was digging holes for a new row of vines when he heard the pounding of hooves coming over the hill to the south. He was drenched in sweat and his bare torso gleamed in the late afternoon sun. The hard work kept him warm in the cool late winter weather. It took more out of him at his age, but he was determined to work the land until the day he died as his father had before him. He shielded his eyes with his arm to see Jim Parsons thundering across the paddock like the Devil was on his heels.

A movement closer to the tree line briefly caught Nick's attention.

He turned to see a small group of dingoes further up the hill. There was a pure white one among them, which was rare. It was as if they were studying him. As the rider drew closer they faded into the shadows.

There had been numerous reports in the region of increased dingo sightings. He found it odd that with the bulk of the sheep removed from Gilgai the dingoes would still come around. The manner in which they had been eyeing him was disturbing, as if they were aware of something that he wasn't.

Jim's horse skidded to a stop, spewing dirt and rocks onto Nick's trousers and boots.

"Where's the fire?" Nick asked, gripping the horse's bridle.

Then he realised there was only one reason anyone would be riding out to the north paddock like a man possessed.

"It's the Missus," panted Jim, leaning forward in the saddle. "You've got to come."

He didn't have to say it twice. Nick hurled himself onto his horse and the two men tore off towards the homestead, leaving Nick's discarded work shirt fluttering on the fence rail.

There was no sleep to be had by anyone that night. Buren kept Nick company while they waited hour after hour in the dark. Nick had been given a clean shirt by Jim, having been barred from entering the main house. The men played cards in the bunkhouse to pass the time that felt as though it was marching in place. The night seemed to linger, never wanting to end. Nick's nerves were fraying with each passing minute. He felt it prudent to stick close to the house so he excused himself from the poker game. Buren joined him.

The elf leaned against a support post on the front porch, arms crossed over his chest. He gazed up at the half moon, grateful that it wasn't full. His thoughts drifted back to a time in his life when he had been in Nick's shoes, waiting for Dirk to arrive. What was he going to do about his son?

"It took Bloem almost two days with Dirk," he said wistfully.

Nick groaned, rolling his eyes in dismay.

"I don't remember it taking that long," he said. "All I remember is getting pissed as a newt when we got the news. I don't know how you could stand it. I can't take much more of this."

Buren laughed low in his throat, "You think this is hard on you? What do you think Agatha's going through?"

Uttering a despairing groan, Nick shook his head. Too many images filled his mind, each more horrific than the last.

"I don't want to think about it. I just keep thinking if things go badly and something was to happen to her. I don't know what I'd do." He looked towards the bedroom window with its drawn shades. "I just want to be with her."

Buren sympathized with him. He had felt the same way. He hadn't anticipated that it would all go wrong nearly thirty years later.

"She'll be fine. She's young, strong. Bloem will take good care of her."

"Two days?" Nick asked with a sour taste at the back of his throat.

Buren grinned and looked up at the moon again.

"She said the hardest part was pushing out his big fat head," he laughed. His eyes reflected the moon's hazy glow. "Dirk weighed almost eleven pounds and most of that was his head."

Nick felt some calm remembering that all had gone well for Bloem and Buren with all three of their children. He hoped it boded well for Agatha.

An hour before dawn they could hear Agatha's pained screams coming from the bedroom. All had been fairly quiet until then. There was a stabbing pain in Nick's heart with every shriek. He clenched his jaws and closed his eyes. Nothing could drown it out.

"She must be close," said Buren. He still leaned against the post, watching the moon as it rested on the trees in the distance like a balloon caught in their branches. "It's hardest towards the end."

Nick just wanted to crawl into a hole and bury himself to block out her screaming. It tore him open as effectively as a knife blade. He could feel every nerve and fiber bleeding onto the ground.

Just as the sun's rays pierced the dark grey of the sky, there was a moment of silence from the house.

Fearing the worst, Nick sank into one of the wooden chairs. It felt like his stomach had been pulled out and his heart dropped into the empty space it left. There was a searing pain in chest that he realised was because he had stopped breathing.

The shrill cry of an infant suddenly rang out. It echoed across the yard, bringing a rousing cheer from the men in the bunkhouse as they saluted their Boss and the Missus with another round of whisky. Their raucous celebration kicked into high gear. They would be doing no work that day as they slept off their binge.

Nick's breath returned in a painful gasp and he leaned back in the chair. Buren stomped over and clapped him heartily on the shoulder.

"That's the worst part over," he said with a beaming grin.

It was still some time before Bloem came out to speak to them. She had removed her birthing robes, which were stained with blood and other bodily fluids, so as not to alarm Nick with the evidence of Agatha's ordeal. Mrs. MacLeach was changing the bed sheets to make the scene more presentable for when he saw his wife.

Bloem was tired, her face worn from the long night. She sent a distressed glance at Buren, who immediately stiffened in alarm. He knew his wife's demeanor and she was deeply troubled.

"How is she?" Nick demanded, getting to his feet as the midwife came out into the morning air.

"Agatha is doing very well," she assured him with an encouraging smile.

He was almost afraid to ask, "The baby?"

"It's not often I'm surprised," she admitted. She wore an expression of duality. She was pleased, but concerned. "Agatha delivered twins."

Buren was almost more startled than Nick. He knew that Bloem did not make mistakes like that. If Agatha had been carrying twins, Bloem should have known. Something wasn't right.

"You have a strong, healthy son," Bloem told Nick, resting her hand on his arm. His elation evaporated when she said, "But the other baby is very small and weak."

Nick took a step back to keep his balance. The news was a complete shock. He didn't completely grasp the rest of what she said.

"What are you saying?" he asked with a shake of his head.

Buren came closer to keep Nick steady. Nick needed the support.

"Your daughter may not survive," Bloem said gently. "She did not receive as much nourishment in the womb as her brother, which kept her from growing as well she should have. Her life spirit was too weak for me to sense, that's why I didn't know there were twins."

Feeling like the world was crumbling under his feet, Nick asked, "Does Agatha know?"

Bloem nodded. She was being kind, but she was not going to lie to him.

"Yes. She needs you now."

Buren folded Bloem in his arms as Nick went inside. This was too close to home. They were losing a child, too, in Dirk.

Agatha was sitting up in bed holding a large healthy infant wrapped in a thick cotton blanket. It looked as though she had gone ten rounds with a scrubber. Her pallid face was splotched red from the strain of pushing. Tendrils of tawny hair stuck to her brow and cheeks, but most of her hair was tied back in a heavy braid. She was physically drained yet filled with the strangest energy. Her eyelids were lowered as she looked down on the baby in her arms. It squirmed and fussed against her hold. She heard Nick in the doorway and raised her head. She gave him a frail, inviting smile.

His tears started as he joined her on the bed. He brushed her cheek with trembling fingers.

"Meet your son," she whispered.

He almost couldn't bring himself to touch the fragile scalp with its thin layer of dark hair. It was so soft. He smoothed his palm over the round shape of the baby's head, his thumb stroking the fine dark strands across the wrinkled brow. He stared, amazed, at the tiny person who had, until an hour ago, been curled up inside Agatha, snug and warm and content to remain there. He had to admit that there was no way he could have done what she had to bring this perfect creature into the world and this was only one of two babies she had brought forth. This was their healthy child. They had a daughter who was not as well off as this infant fidgeting in his mother's embrace.

There was a faint squeak from the crib in the corner of the room.

Cautiously, Nick rose and walked over to peer down on the tiniest baby he could have imagined. Swaddled in a kitchen towel, she was barely the length of his hand with his fingers fully extended. Her skin was nearly translucent. He could see the blue veins in her scalp through the wisps of pale hair. Fists the size of his thumbnails were tucked under her chin. Her eyes were closed, but her lips moved silently as though speaking her own language. One of his tears fell onto her cheek and she stirred, making another soft squeal. Her tiny hand came up to her face, resting where his tear had landed. She wriggled against her tight wrapping.

Nick felt the strongest emotion he'd ever experienced fill every ounce of his being. He was overcome with the deepest love and sense of pride a man could feel. He wasn't going to allow his daughter to die if there was anything he could do about it. It was his job to protect his family and he was damn well going to do it.

Mrs. MacLeach knocked quietly, peering around the door.

"I've brought Agatha a compress," she said, slipping into the room with a wooden tray.

While Nick continued to study the fragile baby, the housekeeper pulled down the sheets to apply the herbal compress to Agatha's tender perineum. She glanced at her master standing over the crib.

"Ye shouldna worry yourself," she said comfortingly. "There's a fire in that bairn that won't soon be extinguished. Mark my words."

Nick wanted to believe her, but he couldn't see how something so impossibly fragile could survive despite his best intentions.

CHAPTER NINETEEN

"There is no force in Heaven or on Earth that supersedes a mother's devotion."
Evelyn Wild-Winter, author, "Family Foundations"

That afternoon, Bloem sat with Agatha as she attempted to nurse for the first time. Agatha's frustration grew each time her son refused to take the nipple he was offered. He would clamp his lips together and turn his head away. Her breasts were painfully swollen, in need of relief. Each time the baby brushed her breast with his cheek she felt pressure that made her wince.

"Why won't he eat?" she asked despairingly. "Isn't he hungry?"

"He is hungry," Bloem replied, equally consternated by the baby's refusal to nurse.

She tried every trick she knew, but he would not part his lips to accept the nipple. He remained steadfast in his stubbornness. Then she had an idea. She returned him to the crib that he shared with his smaller sister. Bloem picked up the girl child and carried her to Agatha.

"I think I know what's happening," she said. She placed the baby in Agatha's arms. "Try with her."

It didn't take more than a second before the miniature lips opened and grasped at the nipple presented to her. It was almost more than she could fit in her tiny mouth. She worked her jaws furiously to get all the milk she could. She had much growing to do and she needed as much nutrition as she could get. Agatha was surprised by the ferocity of her daughter's determination. It was a good sign.

Bloem couldn't resist a satisfied smile.

"Their connection is stronger than I expected," she said. "He was protecting her, letting her nurse first. He knew she needed it more."

"How could he-" Agatha shook her head. She knew. It was ingrained in her blood, as well. Her kind protected its own in many ways. Maybe there was more of her blood in her children than she realised.

Once her daughter was fed and asleep she was able to nurse her son, who quickly latched on with an intense grip. While he was concentrating on eating, Nick came in to check on them. Bloem gave him the promising news that his daughter had fed well. She closed the door on her way out.

Nick sat on the bed and watched in fascination as his son pulled greedily at Agatha's breast.

"He's really strong," she laughed, grimacing. She met Nick's wondering gaze. "What should we name them?"

Nick couldn't take his eyes off his son. Everything about the baby's pudgy face was beautiful, even the puckered mouth. The fact that it was currently attached to Agatha's dark pink nipple made it that much more irresistible.

"What's your father's name?" he asked, having forgotten that one of their earliest conversations about her parents had been a mistake.

"I don't know," she answered with slight shake of her head. It wasn't as difficult to speak of it now. The initial shock of his asking had been what sent her into a panic, especially on their first day together when he hadn't known she was a werewolf. It was no secret now. "I didn't know my parents."

His gaze came up to meet hers. He read the deep pain in her face and that first conversation over breakfast on their first day together came back to haunt him. He immediately regretted bringing it up again. She had told him little about her life on the Rez in their time together and he had sworn to himself that he would wait for her to be ready to tell him. He would not press her for information.

"I was taken away from them when I was born," she explained. Her tone was flat, nearly emotionless. She had deadened herself to

BIRTHRIGHT

the pain. "I was raised by the missionaries. They named me Agatha Smith. Mrs. Forth-Wright changed it to Whistleton to make it sound less common."

It was no wonder she felt lost in the world. She didn't even know who she was. She had never spoken to him about it before now. It was obviously something she was reticent to discuss.

"Why were you were taken away from your parents?" he asked, stunned.

"We aren't allowed to breed," she reminded him.

"Not allowed..." he echoed dumbly. How could he have forgotten?

She shook her head, holding her son closer as he suckled fiercely. Nick couldn't resist touching the baby's face. He had to reassure himself that nothing came between him and his son. His thumb brushed her breast and the baby angrily brought a fist up to clench at her skin as if guarding his claim on it. How could anyone be forbidden from obeying the most basic drive of human and animal nature? It was unconscionable.

"What happened to your parents?" he inquired softly.

"They were killed by the Regulators," she said, gripping her son tighter.

"They were killed because you were born?" he said, dumbfounded.

He couldn't fathom a world existing where children were ripped from their parents arms and parents paid the ultimate price because they shouldn't have had those children in the first place. It turned his stomach and made his jaws tighten.

"That's how it works on the Rez," she said in a cold, savage tone. The baby squawked in response to her anger and she made herself relax her hold. She shifted him to her right breast and he immediately clamped onto it. "I was raised by missionaries like all the children on the Rez. We went to school, like we were ever going to need to learn to read and write. We were never leaving the Rez. We were taught to be human. We were told that what we were was somehow wrong, evil, something to be afraid of. I never knew it could be like this. I'm one of the lucky ones. I never understood happiness until I

– 143 –

met you. You will never know what you've given me."

He hated the people who had treated her so mercilessly in a way he could never have thought possible. To think that Agatha had been taken from her family, that they had been murdered just because she had been born, made his blood boil. He could not imagine allowing anyone to take his children. He would kill anyone who tried. That realization hit him at a primal level that he hadn't known existed. He had never considered himself a violent man, but he felt a surge of protectiveness that possessed every cell within his body. He knew he was capable of killing to protect his family.

"All I ever want is to give you happiness." He gazed intently into her eyes. "I want you to forget everything that happened to you before we met."

"I wish I could."

"So you don't know what your parents named you, or even if they named you?"

Agatha shook her head, smiling at the face of her son. All the pain he had caused was forgiven because he was hers. Had her mother felt the same way when she was born, just before she was taken by the Regulators? Agatha hoped her mother died before the unbearable grief had set in. She knew that if she lost either of her babies she would slip into a dark sea of despair from which not even Nick would be able to rescue her. Her daughter had shown bright promise by feeding so she no longer feared the worst. She was going to survive.

"All I know about them is they were both Birthrights and my mother was related to Paradeus by the Birthright that gave him the Bite. I learned about that from the other werewolves on the Rez. They treated me like I was something special because of it. The missionaries treated me like shit. Sorry."

Nick yearned to wipe those memories from her mind. He had never imagined such singular hatred could be possible. Surely after three hundred years humans could forgive werewolves and learn to coexist, especially if she was an example of what werewolves were

BIRTHRIGHT

truly like.

"We should give our children names meant for them," she said. "Not someone else's name."

He agreed. He searched for names that weren't attached to anyone he knew. One seemed to echo in his mind and he couldn't recall where he would have heard it before. It was a good strong name.

"Logan," he said with conviction. "What do you think of Logan Buchanan?"

Agatha's face brightened. It was a name that evoked power and compassion. It suited the small hungry face at her breast. He had a lifetime to grow into it and she knew he would. She pulled him loose and handed him to Nick.

The last time he had held a baby was over twenty years ago, when Beshka was born. Back then it had been awkward to balance the wriggling mass of arms and legs. Now it seemed the most natural thing in the world. He held his son in both hands, gazing at the angry expression on his son's face. Logan was not pleased to have been removed from his food source and he wanted the world to know it.

"Hold him tightly," she instructed. "He needs to feel secure."

Nick settled Logan against his shoulder, feeling the small warm body press into his chest as Agatha would do. He closed his eyes, savoring the moment. The peace ended with a wet splatter on his shirt as his son christened him with a belly full of breast milk.

Agatha grinned at his appalled expression. She buttoned her blouse, feeling much relieved.

Without explanation, she suddenly knew their daughter's name. It broke into her head like a thunderclap.

"Luna," she said, looking up at Nick as he stared the mess on his shirt with a grimace. "Our daughter's name is Luna Buchanan."

Nick's blue gaze traveled to meet hers. He saw confidence there. By giving their daughter a name it meant she had a permanent place in their lives. They let go of their fear, accepting that she would be with them for a lifetime.

"Tell me about your parents," Agatha said, longing to know more about him.

She wanted to understand what it was like to have been raised by the mother and father who had created him. She was desperate to know what a normal childhood was like so that she could recreate it for her own children. More importantly, she wanted to know how he had come to be the man he was. How was it he was so sensitive and gentle yet so strong and masculine? What had his family been like?

"What do you want to know?" he asked, feeling a fist clutch his heart.

He wasn't sure it was wise to tell her how good his early life had been when hers had been so atrocious. It also raised painful memories for him to think back on his parents. He had lost his father at nineteen in a mining accident and he had forced himself to bury those memories. He decided to keep his answers as innocuous as possible to keep their mutual pain to a minimum.

"Who were they? What were their names?"

"Their names were Barker and Sarah. They came here from Scotland when they were a bit younger than you."

"Where were you born?"

He put Logan down next to his sister in their crib. The babies fell asleep with their faces inches apart. He drew a blanket over them.

"I was born right here in this room," he said, removing his soiled shirt. He placed it in the laundry hamper. "In a different bed, but in this room."

Agatha looked around at the wood slat walls, the large windows and the white washed ceiling. This room had been his first view of the world. She tried to picture him as a newborn, but the image ingrained in her mind was as he was now. She couldn't even think of him as a boy.

"Were your parents kind?"

It was gut-wrenching to hear her plaintive questions as she sought to comprehend the manner in which he had been raised. He felt guilty telling her about his upbringing in a home filled with love and laughter. It was so overwhelmingly unfair that he had been blessed with a nurturing childhood and she had been left to the brutality of the missionaries and Regulators. She had been denied so much. She had never known her mother's embrace or her father's pride. He had lost his father early, but at least he had been able to share the milestones of growing up; first steps, first words, the loss of his first tooth. Those were events in every child's life that parents' cherished. All the simple things that most people took for granted as part of their youth were dark memories for her.

"They were very kind people."

He joined her on the bed. She snuggled into the crook of his arm, savoring the warmth of his bare skin. She settled in against him, tired and unsure of her future. She had given him the children he craved, the reason why had he had married her in the first place. What would happen to her now? Her insecurity knew no bounds. She desperately sought his approval. She wanted to be the kind of mother he had known so he would continue to accept her.

"Did they love you?"

His heart cracked like the summer plains under the baking sun. He pulled her tightly to him. What could he do to put her at ease and alleviate her pain? The only antidote was to give her the care and love she deserved. It was too late to change the past, but he would not let her spend one moment of her life cultivating further remorse.

"They loved me very much. They would have loved you, too, as much as I love you."

She peered up at his earnest gaze as he looked down at her.

"Do you really think so?" she asked tentatively. "If they knew what I was?"

His smile was open and honest. It penetrated the wall of her anxiety and gave her the promise of mending her damaged soul. Her fear began to recede.

"They would have seen how beautiful you are and what a good soul you have. They would have welcomed you into their hearts without question. They accepted everyone in their lives without judgment. I'm so sorry you never had that. I'll do everything I can to make up for it."

He gave her a light kiss then shifted her into a comfortable position to sleep. She rubbed her cheek on his shoulder in a werewolf gesture of affection. They drifted off in each other's arms, content to let each day bring what it would. They would face it together.

<hr />

Agatha recovered swiftly and was on her feet in no time. She felt like a dairy cow with one of the babies always at her breast, yet she embraced the connection she felt with Logan and Luna as they fed. It was difficult for her to allow anyone to take them out of her sight. She experienced a moment of panic any time they were away from her. She couldn't help it given what she knew about her own past.

Having babies in the house brought unending joy to Mrs. MacLeach, who took pleasure in aiding Agatha with their care. She missed mothering. Her own children were long grown and moved away. She had no grandchildren yet to visit. She took Logan and Luna into her charge.

Bloem stayed on for a time to make sure Luna was eating well and gaining weight. She also felt a sense of unease that she could not put her finger on. It was a mother's intuition.

Nick remained at the homestead, not wanting to leave Agatha or the babies for even a moment. Though he was losing sleep with their incessant two hour feeding schedule, he couldn't imagine a better life. He didn't even mind the more onerous duties associated with the babies' care, despite Logan's surprisingly accurate aim when his diaper came off. He relished each moment with his children. He sometimes had to fight Mrs. MacLeach to hold them as she was in possession of one baby or the other at nearly all times. He couldn't be angry with her. The babies were such a blessing to the household that even the station hands made excuses to come into the house and see them.

Nick was so attached to Logan and Luna that he would fall asleep on the sofa in the salon with them both snuggled together on his

BIRTHRIGHT

chest. Agatha would have to wake him up to put everyone to bed for the night, but there were times when she would sit across from him and drink in the serenity before disturbing the scene of peace and quiet.

One night, while she watched silently, his eyes opened a fraction to see her there. He smiled, glancing down at the babies curled quietly together on his chest. He didn't want to wake them, but he wanted to ask her a question that had been on his mind for some time.

Speaking as softly as he could, he asked, "When will they...How old do they have to be before they..."

She cocked her head inquiringly.

"When they what?"

His eyes met hers and he whispered, "When they can change shape."

She laughed louder than she intended and the twins stirred. Nick gently rubbed their backs to settle them and they went back to sleep.

"What makes you think they can change shape?" she inquired in a low voice.

"They are half werewolf," he whispered, hoping to keep them quiet.

"Not really," she said with a firm shake of her head. His look of doubt made her add, "Logan and Luna are Kindred."

There was still a blank look on his face, so she reached into her memory for the best way to explain werewolf bloodlines. She remembered how it had been taught to her by an elderly werewolf woman on the Rez.

"When werewolves breed, the wolf parts and the human parts connect and the offspring have both parts. Even Sauvage have both parts and can reproduce a Birthright by giving both parts to their offspring. Because you're human you only have the human part. You don't have a wolf part for mine to connect with. That isolated wolf part will remain dormant in our children. They will never be able to change shape, making them Kindred werewolves."

Somewhat relieved, Nick also felt rather sad that their children would never know the wild pleasures enjoyed by their mother.

"What does that dormant wolf part do then? Will they have any wolf attributes?"

"They may have some tendencies towards their wilder nature. You've seen them eat. Like little animals," she said with a happy smile. Her breasts ached at the mention of feeding them. She would need to do that before going to sleep. "They won't know any different. Not like me. I knew there was another part of me that desperately needed to come out, but I was taught to keep it caged. They won't have to deal with that struggle. Kindred are as human as you, which is probably for the best."

He hated to see her relive her past and to know the pain it caused her.

"I think it's time for bed," she yawned. Her nights were constantly interrupted by the twins' demands so she wanted to get an early start on sleep deprivation. "Or do you want stay there?"

He followed her to the bedroom carrying Logan. The baby was a heavy lump in his arms. Logan slept deeply when he did sleep. After a prolonged round of breast feeding, Agatha put them in their shared crib. They had tried to separate them, but both babies refused to be apart. Their desperate cries had been heartbreaking so they were kept together. They slept in a pile like cubs would do. Agatha was familiar with the need for warmth and contact.

Nick was already under the covers when she joined him in the bed. He was surprised when she pressed herself along the length of his body. She slid a leg over his waist, slowly moving her hips down until she met with his rigid arousal. It took no time for him to be ready. He groaned as he pushed inside her.

"It's been too long," she murmured, her hair forming a curtain around their faces as she peered down on him.

He couldn't answer. All he could do was gasp in delight as she grasped him with her firm inner muscles. Apparently childbirth hadn't altered her dimensions. She was still taught and pliable just as she had been on their wedding night. He threw his head back against the pillow as he felt the burst of pressure releasing itself from his core.

Agatha relaxed on top him. Her breasts rested on his chest, nipples pointing up at his face. An overwhelming curiosity took hold of him. He lowered his lips to one inviting bud and was rewarded with a flow of sweet fluid that filled his mouth. He could understand why the babies were always hungry. She clutched the back of his head, keeping him there. It was a completely different sensation to feel his mouth on her breast. His teeth lightly grazed her sensitive areola. She shuddered in pleasure.

He eventually released his hold on her nipple, not wanting to take nutrition away from the babies. He lay beside her, taking his time to caress her curves. She fell asleep while he stroked her with a light touch.

He couldn't believe that his life was this good. His history with Birgitta was all but forgotten.

CHAPTER TWENTY

"All Sauvage must be confined two days prior to the crest of the full moon."
Proclamation from the court of King Reginald IV, 1396

Word of the twins spread throughout the Shire like a bushfire. Thanks to the dingoes, it took only a few days to reach Dirk in his lair at Dumfries Castle in the Blue Mountains to the south.

The castle had been built forty years earlier by a homesick Scotsman named Carl Dumfries as a wedding present to his bride, Mary, before she relocated to Australia. The ship she was traveling on sank in a violent storm coming around the Cape of Good Hope before she ever laid eyes on the sprawling medieval structure. He had not remarried. Instead he remained alone inside the barren stone walls until his death in 1870. The castle had subsequently fallen into disrepair as it was too costly to maintain and too remote to be of interest to anyone as a functional place of residence.

Dirk had stumbled across it shortly after receiving the Bite. He had sought refuge there from the emotional albatross placed around his neck by his parents' denial of his new life as a Sauvage. He had been refurbishing it on his own for years and it was nearly ready to be his military headquarters.

He had done what his father asked and temporarily left Falmormath, but he was far from finished with his goal of having Agatha. He was dedicated to the purpose of building an empire of werewolves that would take control of Australia. There was much work to be done. To be the leader of such a government he needed a powerful female alpha at his side. There was only one female who could take that place.

Agatha.

When he learned from the dingoes that she had born Nick not one just child, but two, he was enraged beyond reason. It burned in his belly that she was with a human. Now she had bred with him. She had lowered herself to bear Kindred, children that would never know the thrill of the hunt. They would be trapped inside human skins their entire lives and Nick was to blame. If he hadn't shown up at Eliza's that night none of this would have happened. He had stolen what was rightfully Dirk's.

Dirk decided it was time to make things right. He needed Agatha to bring his plans to fruition.

After weeks at the homestead, Nick could no longer shirk his obligations to the station. Not wanting to disturb Agatha, who was getting little enough sleep, he left the house during the dark hour before dawn. He drove the steam wagon out to the barn in the north paddock before switching to horseback. He had moved the animals out of respect for Agatha, but he preferred to ride when the opportunity presented itself.

He joined a few of the station hands as they scoured the hills for some sheep that had gotten out of their pen the night before. The fence rails had been torn down, allowing the sheep to escape, or more likely be driven out of the pen. Livestock theft was common as freed convicts prowled the bush. It was the primary reason he and his men were constantly armed. It was legal to kill thieves. If the sheep were still in the area he didn't want them to attract dingoes. He also didn't want them to eat the grape vines that were coming along so well.

He was still in a state of euphoria after the birth of the twins. Luna was not the wilting flower Bloem had feared. His little girl had a fighting spirit like her mother. It would take her longer to achieve her full potential, but no one doubted she would succeed. As for

Logan, he had his father's calm disposition, but there was a hint of Agatha's fire in him as well. He did not like to be bothered while eating and when he wanted to be put down he meant immediately. Nick was looking forward to seeing their personalities develop as they became distinct individuals. He was eager for Logan to become old enough to begin learning the ins and outs of running a vineyard.

His horse picked its way through a rock outcropping, carefully maneuvering over the uneven ground. Nick kept his balance in the saddle, hips rocking with the horse's movements. He leaned forward over the horse's neck as the animal continued its uphill climb. The mare chuffed as she worked her way upwards, ears swiveling nervously.

Through the branches overhead he could make out the scythe-like curve of the moon hovering in the gradually lightening sky. He was grateful that it wasn't full, but he was not aware that it actually was. There was a partial penumbral eclipse in effect, which darkened a large portion of the moon's full face. It appeared as a quarter of its complete self.

He briefly thought about what Agatha had told him months ago after the scrubber incident, that the Sauvage were influenced by the full moon. She had said the only the strongest people could control the infection. He didn't want to imagine what it must be like to feel that kind of rage and fear as it ate through layers of his humanity. How could anyone exist like that?

With his head up, staring at the moon and his thoughts occupied, he didn't see the black shape launch itself at him from the top of a boulder until it slammed into him. He was shot out of the saddle with the force of a train derailing. The rocky ground met him with granite fists.

Squealing in terror, his horse disappeared into the bush.

Nick rolled onto his knees in an effort to get his feet under him. He heard a growl that sent fragments of ice through his veins. Lifting his head, he found himself staring down the muzzle of a huge snarling beast. Its teeth were as long as his fingers. Globs of saliva glistened on those ivory blades. The mouth opened and its rotted breath blew over him in a loud growl. Nick felt his bowels clench in fear. His tongue turned to stone, lying heavily in his mouth. His breath came in shallow puffs, if he was actually breathing at all. He couldn't tell.

The thing glaring back at him could only be a Sauvage.

Dirk straightened up, rising to his full height. His body was elongated and out of proportion for its size and shape. He was covered in a thick layer of muscle like ropes beneath his skin. Coarse black hair coated his body, concealing his nudity. His legs were like those of a dog, bent the wrong way for a human being. His sternum was a sharp ridge pushing out his chest. He had a heavy canine head with ears pressed back flat. He was a nightmarish creature towering against the trees.

Nick felt like an insect about to be crushed underfoot.

Dirk reached out with one long arm and gripped Nick by the throat, dragging him to his feet. He wanted to toy with him, to drag out the torture. It would be more entertaining. He liked to play with his food.

The vertebrae in Nick's spine cracked with his full weight pulling against the fist that held him. The toes of his boots traced a pattern in the dirt as his body swung like a pendulum. His jaw was being pulled forward by the Sauvage's grip. His teeth ground together until he thought they might splinter.

He understood belatedly why the Sauvage were considered dangerous.

Dirk effortlessly flung him away. Nick struck the side of a boulder and slid to the ground, half conscious.

Dropping to all fours, Dirk slowly circled his victim. He pawed at Nick's legs, cutting through his trousers with hooked claws. Blood seeped into the canvas fabric, creating abstract patterns. Nick gasped with each slash, kicking at the long hands that repeatedly snagged his flesh. His boot connected with Dirk's snout.

With a roar, Dirk grabbed his shirt and hurled him down the hill.

Nick tumbled violently with the force of gravity, striking rocks and brambles during his short journey. He came to a rest amid a tangle of fallen branches. Broken ribs burned in his chest. It was like inhaling fire with every breath. Blood ran down the side of his face from a deep laceration in his forehead. He turned onto his left side, reaching for the Riggins at his right hip. The last three fingers on his right hand were fractured and he couldn't grip the butt of the gun. With a wail of pain, he struggled to close his hand on the ebony wood hilt.

Dirk leaped down the slope, reaching him before he could get the gun free of its holster.

Nick felt white hot daggers sink into his right shoulder as the Sauvage clamped its jaws down. His entire arm went limp. Blood poured down his sleeve. A scream tore its way out of his lungs.

Further down the hillside, Jim Parsons and Edison Finnerty had caught Nick's horse as it careened towards them. The animal was driven insane with terror. It was washed out with white sweat on its neck, chest and flanks. It was all they could do to hold onto the reins as it plunged, screaming and kicking, in an effort to get free.

The bellow of the beast echoed down the valley.

"What the hell was that?" asked Ed, eyes wide.

Jim shook his head. They stared up into the scrub and trees, hearts crawling up into their throats. Their horses joined the dance of terror until all three animals were rearing and charging in their desperation to run.

Two other horsemen came riding towards them. Craig Williams and John O'Reilly had also heard the animal's roar.

"What the hell was that?!" shouted Craig as his horse shot upwards in a wild pirouette.

"Where's Nick?" asked John, also struggling to control his mount.

"His horse came from up there." Ed pointed uphill. "We haven't seen him."

They all heard Nick's piercing scream split the air.

John's horse spun in a tight circle before obeying his urging to go forward. The men rode up into the trees, not knowing what they would come across.

Dirk raked his claws lightly down Nick's chest, creating shallow furrows that bled in slow trickles. He lowered his muzzle and licked away the blood. His eyes were blazing with hatred as he met Nick's fearful gaze.

Nick couldn't imagine Agatha being anything like this monster, unless she had been lying to protect herself. He refused to accept that. This was what she had warned him about. This was what Paradeus had been. It was no longer human. The infection was altering its mind and body. It did not know right from wrong. This was what people thought werewolves were.

It was going to kill him.

John reached Nick first. He was dumped out of the saddle as his horse unexpectedly shied and stepped out from under him. He hit the ground hard.

Dirk turned to see other men on horseback riding towards him. He had wasted valuable time taunting Nick. Now he had to either fight with several armed men, which he was not opposed to, or turn tail and live to extract his revenge on Nick another day. He bared his teeth in Nick's face and snarled. Rancid saliva mixed with his own blood dripped onto Nick's cheek, running down his neck.

Ed, Jim and Craig arrived within seconds to see the massive creature leaping from boulder to boulder as it escaped up into the thicker trees. Jim got off two shots, both hitting tree trunks. His target shooting was known to be the worst in the Shire.

"Oh, shit, Nick," said Craig, flinging himself off his horse.

Ed grabbed the discarded reins before the mare could bolt. He caught John's horse, too.

"Is he dead?" Ed asked, fearing the answer.

Craig knelt beside Nick's bloodied body. He checked for signs of life. He found a thready pulse in Nick's throat.

"Not yet. We've got to get him back to the homestead."

They did what they could on the spot to tend to Nick's injuries, but they recognized that he was badly wounded. While Craig, Ed and John struggled to get Nick onto a horse, Jim rode off to get the doctor.

※❖※

Agatha paced hysterically, bouncing Luna on her shoulder, as she waited for the surgeon to finish with Nick. Her worst fears had come true. Dirk had finally acted on his threat. Nick wasn't safe. No one was safe when the next full moon rose.

"Let me take the bairn," said Mrs. MacLeach, wanting to lighten her mistress' burden.

"No," Agatha said with a shake of her head. "I need to hold her."

The housekeeper nodded in understanding. Logan was sleeping in a portable crib in the corner of the salon. All the hands were in attendance, all fully armed, waiting for news. They occupied the salon and front porch as they milled about like the chickens in the yard. Mrs. MacLeach returned to the kitchen where she was busy preparing enough food for so many mouths at once. She would be busy keeping them all fed. It was much simpler keeping them all in drink. She had opened the liquor cabinet and let them have at it. It would make it easier to take what the doctor had to tell them when he came out.

Several hours passed without a peep from the master bedroom. Nick's hoarse cries had faded some time ago. Now there was only a depressing silence in the house as evening descended.

Buren and Bloem arrived at the same time Dr. Bastyr Urquhart emerged from the bedroom. He was drying his hands on a towel as he came down the hall. He nodded at Buren, who returned the stiff male greeting. Bloem went to Agatha, wrapping her arms around her shoulders. Agatha was filled with too many conflicting thoughts and emotions to respond. She still held Luna. Her gaze was focused on Dr. Urquhart.

"How is he?" she asked, hating the plaintiveness in her voice.

"He's lost a good deal of blood, but he'll pull through. He's a lot to live for," replied the doctor. "He keeps asking for you."

Bloem took Luna from her. The baby fussed briefly then relaxed in the elf's arms.

Agatha met Buren's guilt ridden gaze as she passed him. Her lip curled. He averted his eyes.

It was Agatha's turn to be mortified by the condition of her spouse. She stood in the doorway, taking a moment to adjust to his appearance. She realised how Nick must have felt when he saw her after the scrubber incident, fearing for her life. She had a more legitimate concern about his ability to recover from the attack. He was human. He didn't have her superior healing power.

He was propped up on a double layer of pillows, head slumped to the side. The blanket was down around his waist, exposing long red scratches on his chest that disappeared beneath the tight binding around his fractured ribs. Black whiskers stood out on his brow and shoulder from the sutures used to close the wounds. His entire right shoulder was one dark purple bruise. The broken fingers on his hand had been set and wrapped in an immobilization device. Thick red scabs had formed on his arms among the bruises. His breathing was so faint that it made her think it could stop at any moment.

His eyes opened a sliver and he looked over at her.

"I must look like something that came out of the back end of a dingo," he commented drily.

She laughed without humor.

"You look good to me," she said, crossing the room to sit on the bed next to him. She wrung out the rag in the washing bowl on the nightstand and gently wiped dried blood and dirt from his chin. "At least you're alive."

His grin was pained. He lifted his head with an effort.

"I wouldn't be if not for Craig and the boys," he said with gratitude. His words came between shallow breaths. "They saved my life. I thought you were the only werewolf in the Shire. That was a Sauvage, wasn't it?"

She nodded. She took a deep breath, dipping the rag into the copper basin. The water had a pinkish hue from the blood. She dabbed at his cheek.

"So I don't have the infection?" he asked, concerned stamped on his features. He gripped her wrist with his good hand. "You said that only Birthright can transmit it. Right?"

She nodded again. With a heavy sigh, she put down the rag and locked eyes with him.

"I know who attacked you," she said.

He waited.

She licked her lips nervously before saying, "It was Dirk."

Nick stared at her in silence for a long, agonizing moment. He didn't believe her at first, but the slant of her eyes and tension in her mouth told him all he needed to know.

"Dirk van Amersvoot?" he said at last. He struggled to make sense of it. "Buren's oldest son? How am I supposed to tell Buren something like that?"

"He knows."

Nick saw a muscle jump in her cheek from how hard she was clenching her jaw. She was angry beyond words.

"Am I the only one who didn't know?" he asked, feeling like a fool.

"No," she answered. She resumed washing his face. "No one knows outside the van Amersvoot family. Buren's been keeping Dirk confined during the full moon until recently. Because of that, he was able to keep it a secret."

Nick dredged up something else she had told him.

"You said that elves kill Sauvage when they find them."

"That's his son. Could you kill Logan?" she said, brows low over her golden eyes.

"Of course not," he snapped, instantly regretting the harsh tone he used. His chest seized up and he gasped in pain. He closed his eyes against the darkness that threatened to swallow him whole, struggling to draw breath. "I could never hurt my children."

Agatha smoothed her hand over his brow.

"And neither can Buren."

He opened his eyes to see her sorrowful gaze. The sheen of tears made her eyes glitter with specks of gold. It took a few minutes for him to gather himself enough to speak again.

"Dirk was at Eliza's the night we met."

"Yes, he was," she replied. A black shadow crossed her face. "I was running away from him when I went into Mrs. Forth-Wright's office and happened to meet you. I suppose we would never have met if not for Dirk."

Nick tilted his head, wincing.

"Running away from him?" he repeated. "Did he attack you?"

Agatha let out a resounding laugh, more like a bark.

"Not without a full moon to back him up," she said self-righteously. "That's the only time he's stronger than I am. He was annoying me with his pathetic attempt to be an alpha male. He aspires to be an alpha, but he isn't one. He didn't seem to grasp the fact that I wasn't interested in him in any way. I have never been attracted to a Sauvage. They're coarse and vulgar, even when they're human."

Nick should have known. Birthrights were apparently the upper crust of her society. Sauvage were from the gutter, at least historically speaking. The lines were more blurred these days.

"I'll let you get some sleep," she said. "You need more rest than I did. Do you want me to stay? I don't want to keep you up."

He gave a low chuckle, "I couldn't keep it up right now, anyway."

She leaned in to kiss him then rested her forehead against his.

"I'm afraid this isn't over. Dirk wants me. I don't know what he'll do now and I can't protect you during the full moon."

"I should be protecting you," he said, clutching the back of her neck with his good hand. He kissed her softly, eyes closing as sleep drew him in. "How am I going to do that?"

CHAPTER TWENTY-ONE

"A modern woman is not governed by her emotions in times of duress."
Excerpt from the periodical, "Ladies of a Victorian Age"

Once she was convinced that Nick would pull through, Agatha made a trip to Willowbrook. She was furious at Buren and her rage overflowed.

"He tried to kill my husband!" she screamed, sweeping the photo frames and porcelain vases off the mantel in the van Amersvoot's salon with a powerful swipe of her arm. Sharp fragments flew wildly. "And you knew it would happen!"

Buren stood his ground. He had to reason with her. He was afraid that she would do something she would regret, not that he would blame her.

"I never expected Dirk to go after Nick," he said rationally. "Please, you need to calm down so we can talk about this."

She grabbed the grandfather clock and sent it crashing to the floor. It made a sound like mechanical thunder.

"There isn't anything to talk about, elf," she snarled. "You knew what your son was and you ignored your responsibility. I almost lost Nick."

All the suffering she had endured on the Rez broke over her in an avalanche. The fear of losing Nick came crushing down with the weight of it. Her emotional adrenaline overflowed and its outlet was Buren.

She lunged at him, her skin breaking away as she leaped. It fell in a shower over the furniture and floor beneath her. Her clothes slipped from her changing body. She landed on top of him in wolfshape, jaws wide. A bone jangling growl hit him like a fist. Agatha lowered her mouth around his throat until her teeth met with the surface of his skin. Saliva rolled onto his face in hot trails. She squeezed softly. She was deciding between tearing out his throat or merely scarring him for life. Either option was equally appealing at the moment.

"Go ahead," he told her, jaw set. His guilt was as powerful as her rage. "I deserve it."

Bloem's voice rang out, "Agatha. You are a Birthright. This is beneath you. Release him."

Immediately ashamed of her actions, Agatha stepped back. She changed back with a snowfall of grey fur and curled into a naked ball on the floor. She began to rock back and forth, sobbing.

Buren got to his feet. There were bright red marks on his skin from the pressure of her teeth, but she had not punctured it. He rubbed the marks to make sure there was no blood.

Bloem stepped past him to kneel by Agatha. She put her hand on the young woman's shaking shoulder.

"Fetch a blanket," she told her husband, who promptly did as he was told.

Agatha huddled on the sofa, wrapped securely in a quilt. Tears continue to seep from her eyes. She held a cup of steaming coffee in her unsteady hands because Bloem knew she did not like tea. The dark liquid sloshed in the cup, almost spilling.

"I'm sorry," she said, her eyes meekly rising to meet Buren's. "I was so afraid of losing Nick and all my frustration just peaked. I took it out on you."

"I meant what I said when you had your teeth at my throat," he replied, going to the front windows. He kept his back to her. "If you had killed me I would have welcomed it. I am responsible for what Dirk has done. I can't deny it."

Bloem sat next to Agatha, arms around her. Her heart went out to the werewolf, but she could not completely forgive her behavior.

"You allowed your wolf to get the better of you and you're

stronger than that. You lost control and that's not like you," she chastised Agatha. "You need to keep yourself together, especially now."

Agatha nodded miserably. She had attacked the best friends she had ever known and she felt like the monster werewolves were portrayed to be.

"I'll be making a report to the Guardianship," said Buren. He stared blankly out at the yard, not seeing the world past his pain. "I can't ignore what he's done."

Bloem nodded as she felt the jagged pieces of her heart digging into the flesh within her chest. She had no choice but to support Buren's decision. It was far overdue because she hadn't been able to accept the truth that her son was no longer the kind, considerate young man she had raised. He was a threat to everyone, especially Agatha and Nick.

Agatha rested her hand on Bloem's arm.

"I'm sorry." She looked up at Buren's rigid back. "Do you know who gave him the Bite? The Guardianship will want to track that Birthright down. Whoever it was is accountable for his actions. Giving the Bite is a tremendous responsibility. It comes with a price on both sides."

"He told me she's dead. I don't know if I believe that," he replied with an aching sigh.

"It would make sense," Agatha said, nodding. "He can't feel that influence anymore and without that he's gone rogue. Her personality traits have affected him and it would help to know who she was."

Buren turned to face her. His face was an angry mask.

"What difference does it make now?" he ground out. "Once I turn him over to the Guardianship they'll issue an execution order. How is knowing who started this going to change that?"

Bloem stifled a sob.

Agatha lowered her gaze out of respect. She spoke softly.

"You're right. I just thought it would explain his temperament after the Bite. Give us some answers."

"I don't need those kind of answers," Buren snapped. His eyes were bright and hot as the midday sun. "The only answers I need are the ones that will keep my son from being executed."

"Those are the answers I was thinking of," Agatha replied sharply, head rearing up. She let out a heavy breath. "But you're right. They won't save Dirk now. If he hadn't attacked Nick he might have been able to go before the Guardian's Court and get an exemption certificate. We would have stood for him. There's no chance of that now."

"We should get you home," said Buren. He was tired of discussing it. "You need to be there for Nick."

In the days following her confrontation with Buren, Agatha made routine perimeter checks in her wolf shape. She kept out of sight of the station hands and men from the other stations who were also out in force to protect their investments. As a warning to the dingoes she encountered she made sure to mark her territory frequently. The small orange canines stayed well away from her, but they were ever present like ants.

Nick despised being laid up. He was missing time in the paddocks. There was much to be done with the vines and his hands yearned for the feel of the earth. He couldn't help with the babies and Agatha was distracted by what she thought of as her duty to protect him from Dirk. He felt as useless as tits on a bull.

Mrs. MacLeach doted on him, treating him like he was a child again. She clucked and fussed, making sure he was comfortable, well fed and his wounds were cleaned. It was the happiest she had been in years. She had Nick to tend to and babies to coddle. She was in heaven.

The station hands kept the place running. Although they were new at tending a vineyard, they put themselves into it with zeal. If that meant learning the ropes from the ground up, they were willing. Nick had been their Boss for long enough to have earned their respect. He was a good man, honest and fair. They would go to hell and back for him.

Jim provided Nick with much needed company one morning nearly a week after the attack. Mrs. MacLeach allowed him out of bed for the first time, so Nick was sprawled on the sofa in just his sleeping trousers and a cotton robe, languishing in boredom. He kept himself occupied by reading about the fine art of wine making, but it was losing its appeal. He was over the moon to see Jim. It was a break in his monotonous routine.

"Have a seat," he said eagerly. "I'm dying here. Tell me what's going on out there."

"There's word in town about hunting down the werewolf," Jim replied, lowering himself to a chair opposite the sofa. "Some of the men are thinking of joining up."

That took Nick aback. He grabbed the arm of the sofa and pulled himself up with a tremendous effort, grimacing the whole time. He slowly swung his legs over and put his bare feet on the floor.

"Careful, mate," said Jim, watching the painful movement with concern.

"When?"

"What?"

Nick leaned forward, eyes fierce.

"When are they planning this hunt?"

"They haven't really decided yet. They're still talking about it. No one's made up their mind. They sound like a bunch of frightened galahs."

Nick had to stop his men from going out on a fool's errand. It would put too many lives needlessly in danger. He had to explain to the men about what was happening around them, but he had to speak to Agatha first. He wanted to talk to Buren also, who had been conspicuously absent in the past week. Agatha had told him about her confrontation with the van Amersvoots, deliberately editing the part about nearly ripping out Buren's throat. He suspected that Buren was in Sydney, speaking to the Guardianship.

"Where is Agatha?" he asked.

Jim frowned, shrugging. He didn't understand Nick's sudden agitation.

"I'll track her down if you want. She must be near the house."

"Yes, do that, please," said Nick with a sense of urgency.

Jim went out on his mission, leaving Nick in a state of near panic. If the men went out in pursuit of Dirk they were putting themselves at risk. They would think the worst of Agatha if her true nature was revealed at a later date. He had to explain the truth to them. They had to know that Agatha was not the same as the werewolf that attacked him. She was going to be living there for the rest of her life and they had to come to terms with what that meant. She might not agree, but he had to do what he felt was right.

Agatha came in through the back, her bare feet padding noiselessly on the wood floor. She came up behind him.

"Is everything alright?" she asked. She slipped her arms gingerly around his neck and put her lips on his ear. "Jim seemed worried."

"I want to tell the men about you," he said abruptly, without forewarning. "Let them know what you are."

Agatha released him and stepped back. It was for the best that he couldn't see her face. Her lips trembled and her eyes went round, filling with hurt tears. She felt betrayed.

"Why would you do that?"

He struggled to turn to towards her. His ribs resisted movement, but he forced his body to obey. By the time he was able to shift enough to look at her she had adopted a less horrified expression. She was watching him warily.

"Because, they should know the truth. You're not going to hide here at Gilgai. This is the one place I want you feel safe to be who you are. At some point they need to find out from us that you aren't any threat. With a Sauvage on the loose, they'll think the worst. I don't want you getting hurt."

She knew he was right, but her fear of being exposed to other humans was deeply rooted. She knew that reactions would vary, but she doubted any would be positive. Her heart began to pound and her hands shook.

"And if they turn against me? Are you prepared for that?" she inquired.

"They won't," he told her with confidence he only half felt. He had the same reservations about his plan. "They know you as well as I do. Why would they turn against you?"

"Either you're naïve or far too trusting," she said, joining him on the sofa. "If this is what you want to do, I can't stop you. I just hope you're right."

The next morning the station hands waited in the bunkhouse for an announcement from Nick. They milled about, muttering amongst themselves. They had no idea what to expect.

It was the first time Nick had been on his feet for an extended period in over a week. He held onto a cane and used the fireplace mantel for support. He had managed to dress with Agatha's help so he was fairly presentable. She remained anxiously in the house while he addressed the men.

"I'm glad you're all here," he announced, looking around the room at the faces he knew so well. "I've something to tell you all that will come as a bit of a shock, but I don't want any of you to worry."

The men exchanged glances. They were gathered around the main room of the bunkhouse, sitting or standing as they waited to hear his news.

"Don't tell us you're selling the place," said Ed. "We're willing to stay on until we get things right. Don't give up on the vineyard yet, Boss."

Nick shook his head, smiling in appreciation.

"That's not it," he replied. His gaze was earnest as he looked at each man in turn. "You've come to know Agatha well since she's been here. I've something important to tell you and there's no easy way to say it. You know that I was attacked by a werewolf and I know some of you are planning to join the hunt to track it down."

"Oh, shit, don't tell us you're one now, too," gasped Craig.

"No, no," Nick rushed to assure him. "That's what I'm trying to explain. What do any of you know about werewolves?"

"I know there are some born that way, Birthstones or something," John responded. He startled Nick by speaking up. "They're supposed to be mostly harmless. They used to live with royalty as pets, or so my mum told me. They're the ones can infect people by biting them. Those that are infected are called Savages, I think. They're the nasty ones."

Nick was silent for a moment, completely stunned that any of the men knew so much.

"That's mostly true," he said slowly. "They're called Birthrights and Sauvage. I was attacked by a Sauvage. That means I'm not infected."

A wind of relief blew through the room. The men visibly relaxed.

"The Birthrights are mostly harmless as you said," Nick continued, doggedly pushing on. "They are a very ancient race, proud and honorable. They've been portrayed as monsters and demons throughout history, but that wasn't always the way it was. They stood alongside humans and elves for thousands of years before humans learned about the Bite. It's the Bite that gives the infection. That infection makes someone into a Sauvage. They are dangerous. The Birthright aren't the ones to be afraid of."

His men were watching him expectantly.

"What's this to do with the Missus?" asked Jim. "Was that a werewolf that attacked her a few months back?"

"No, she wasn't attacked by one. She is one. A Birthright," he quickly clarified.

"That's two dollars you owe me," Craig muttered to John.

Nick caught the comment. He turned to Craig.

"What was that?" he asked.

"You didn't think we were stupid, did you?" Craig replied. "We've seen the signs. We've found her skins."

"What?" Nick echoed dumbly.

"They shed their skin like a snake when they change," Craig explained. "I've heard it's used in Far East medicine to increase fertility."

Nick was too stunned to speak. He just stared at Craig with a dazed expression.

"When we heard the Missus had been hurt, we knew it couldn't have been dingoes," Jim said. "I know that's what you told us, but we found that scrubber caught in the fence out in the west paddock. We saw the blood and those big tracks. It didn't happen on the full moon, either, so we got the idea that she might be one of them Birthright."

"Why didn't you say something to me?" Nick asked, half relieved and half angry that he had been left in the dark.

"We thought you didn't want us to know," said Ed. He leaned his elbows on the table. His brows went up. "You didn't know?"

"That's another two dollars," said Craig to John.

Nick scuffed his toe on the wood boards like a petulant child.

"It's all right, Boss," said John. "It doesn't matter. She's your wife, you've got little ones. She hasn't done anything to hurt anyone. She's been good to you. If you trust her then so do we."

Nick almost collapsed in relief. If Craig hadn't caught him he would have hit the floor.

"I don't want any of you going on this hunt until I can get more information," he told them, easing into a chair. "It's too dangerous. I won't let you risk your lives like that. The elf Guardianship is being notified of the attack and they should be on top it soon enough. We may not need to do anything."

"If the elves haven't solved the problem by the time the hunt is organized, we're going. We've got to look after our own," declared Craig to the agreement of the others.

Nick couldn't very well prevent them from going just because he didn't want them to. He just prayed that the elves got their act together by the next full moon.

CHAPTER TWENTY-TWO

"The bonds of family can be as loose as a ribbon or as tight as a noose."
Anonymous

Seagulls canted overhead as Buren rode down Commonwealth Avenue with Holt Threadwell, senior member of the Guardianship and Bloem's younger brother. They were seated in a carriage pulled by a smartly matched pair of dark skinned centaurs.

The day was aglow with brilliant sunshine reflecting off the water. There was a salty tang in the air that Buren found refreshing. The sights and sounds of commerce surrounded them as downtown Sydney bustled with life. The street was crowded with coaches, dray wagons, pedestrians, bicyclists and the occasional steam wagon. One such newfangled contraption passed the carriage much too close for the centaurs' comfort. One of them shouted obscenities in their native tongue at the reckless driver.

After a few moments of polite small talk, Buren broached the subject that was the reason for his unannounced visit. Elves did not delve directly into the heart of the matter. It was uncouth.

"You're no doubt wondering why I've come to Sydney," Buren said, staring out the buildings they passed. He knew Holt wouldn't ask. "I've come to report a Sauvage that's attacked a human."

Holt's wide set hazel eyes gave away nothing. He sat still as stone. Only his tall, narrowly pointed ears twitched occasionally. He bore a family resemblance to his elder sister, but they were extremely different people.

"I'm glad you brought this to my attention," said Holt. He studied

Buren's stoic profile. "Do you know the identity of the Sauvage?"

"My oldest son, Dirk."

Holt's brows arched then relaxed over his eyes as if nothing was amiss.

"It pains me to hear that."

"It pains me to admit it," replied Buren.

"You've done the right thing by coming to me. Perhaps I can make this easier on Bloem by taking care of it myself. I won't have to make an official report. It's just so sad that one mere indiscretion has led to this tragedy."

Buren's features were suffused with anger.

"You will not put this at her feet," he snapped furiously.

Holt's face was inscrutable.

"You were very kind to have married my sister after her lapse in judgment. Not many men would have accepted her helf bastard as their own. But let's not forget, she is still a High Elf and you're…not."

Buren leaned forward. There was a savage look in his cold blue eyes.

"I married Bloem because I loved her. It didn't matter that Dirk wasn't of my seed or even half human. I raised him as my son because he is my son and he will always be my son."

"That may be, but it was her affair with a human that made him vulnerable to the Bite. He is half-human and only humans can be infected. It is a shame that his elf blood couldn't have prevented it from taking hold."

"I think it was his elf blood that's kept him mostly sane until now."

Holt cocked his head.

"How long has he been infected?" he queried.

Buren's eyes shifted back to the small round window and the view beyond.

"Three years."

"Three…" Holt threw himself back in his seat, making the cab rock sharply.

One of the centaurs glanced back and asked if things were alright.

Buren answered yes.

"You've kept this from the Guardianship for three years? You could have petitioned for an exemption. Why didn't you?" Holt demanded.

"Would you or anyone in your family have supported it?" Buren countered.

Holt's silence was louder than words.

"That's what I thought. Bloem knew it, too. I suppose it would have worked out for all of you if we had reported him when it happened," Buren said in disgust. "You could have ordered his execution and then she would have been cleansed of her sin. Your family would have welcomed her back with open arms. My only question is where would that have left me?"

Their eyes met.

"Back to the stables, no doubt," Buren grunted, turning back to the window. He used a common derogatory elf colloquialism that described someone of lower breeding. "Never good enough. I'm only the Custodian of Falmormath Shire because I married Bloem and your family wanted to make sure I had some kind of title so they didn't lose face. They threw me a bone, hoping I'd choke on it. Well, I've worked myself half to death to make Willowbrook one of the top sheep stations in the Shire. Bloem is part of that and part of my life. I don't want her hurt by this."

Holt pursed his lips. Buren had always been blunt and correct with his observations of the world.

"I will handle this myself," Holt said. He pounded on the roof of the carriage. It rocked to a gentle stop. As he exited, he turned to give Buren a reassuring smile. "I've always taken care of my sister."

Buren clenched and unclenched his jaws during the ride back to his hotel. He wasn't sure which way things would go from here.

⊱✦⊰

A week prior to the next full moon the men of Falmormath gathered in town to decide the best way to go about hunting for a werewolf. There was a large contingent from all across the area. Most had lost sheep to the beast and its recent attack on one of their own made them angry and afraid.

Nick attended without Agatha. It was an all male meeting, rife with ignorant masculine attitudes. She wouldn't have been welcome and he didn't want her to hear what they would have to say. It would be too damaging to her current emotional state. He hoped to talk some sense into the mob, but as soon as he stepped into the meeting hall he realised that there was no way he could reverse the anti-werewolf sentiment. His only chance to maintain any semblance of order and safety was to provide the most information pertaining to what they were up against.

The men were pleased to see him up and around. They greeted him with hearty masculine sentiment, but they didn't listen to anything he had to say. He could have gone into the bush and shouted at rocks for all the good his words did.

He had the opportunity to speak privately with Buren after the meeting about Buren's conversation with Agatha. Buren repeated the story Agatha had told him with the same specific exclusion of his near death experience. Nick hoped the elves got to Dirk before the men of the Shire.

He returned home to find Agatha in the garden with the twins. She had spread out a quilt on a bit of lawn and the babies were lying side by side on it. She wore a white button up blouse, a dark brown vest corset and a canvas skirt with cotton petticoats. Her feet were bare, the soles darkened by dirt.

Luna remained incredibly tiny compared to her brother, although she ate like a champion. Logan had been born with a size advantage and he was growing in leaps and bounds because of it. Agatha still felt like a milking heifer with how often she fed them. Her breasts were always on standby, full and ready at their beck and call. During their intimate moments, Nick enjoyed their richness as well.

Nick sat with her on the blanket, his frustration evident. He picked up Logan, who had been nearly asleep. The baby started to cry then recognized who it was that held him. His eyes homed in on Nick's face and he gurgled happily. Nick wiped froth from the puckered lips and kissed the soft round cheek Logan presented to him. His stress slipped away as he put his son on his shoulder and patted the small warm back until Logan fell into a deep slumber, whimpering in his sleep.

"You couldn't stop them," Agatha guessed. She stretched out on the quilt with Luna curled against her belly. Her fingers smoothed the pale cap of hair that had begun to sprout on the frail scalp. "I didn't think you'd be able to talk sense into them. What are you going to do now?"

"I don't have a choice. I'll have to ride with them."

"You'll do no such thing," she replied sharply. "If they want to die they can. Dirk will be almost unstoppable under the full moon. I am not losing you."

"There will be over a hundred heavily armed men out at the same time, in groups of ten or more," he explained. "There will be men in the air keeping an eye on our backs. Besides, I can't imagine he's even still around. He'd be thick as a brick to still be in the Shire. Our quarry will have gone to ground if he knows what's good for him. Until this is done, I want you and the twins to stay at Willowbrook. Dirk will come here looking for you and that may give us a chance to surprise him."

Agatha fervently wished that was true, but Dirk had already proven himself unpredictable.

CHAPTER TWENTY-THREE

"Fear the man, not the moon."
fae proverb

The hunt began at dawn on the day of a rare second full moon in the same month. Nick had been attacked on October 2nd. It was now October 31st, All Hallow's Eve. Men on horseback rode out with dogs, scouring the bush while airships patrolled from the skies. Rifles and shotguns at the ready, men sat in the back of steam wagons as they bounced down rutted tracks throughout the valleys. The search was concentrated near the site of Nicks' attack, but the radius grew as the day wore on. The first signs were spotted well past Queen's Empire Station far to the west. Large pugmarks in the mud near a watering hole alerted the men to the werewolf's presence. They sent up flares and the airships moved in. In the sky, spotters with telescopic and binocular goggles combed the thick tree line. Their job was to prevent an ambush if possible.

Nick was finding it difficult to stay in the saddle. His injuries were still painful, especially his shoulder and right hand. He had opted for a mount that would work with minimal commands. Bob was a gelding that was mellow and obedient. Nothing seemed to faze the bomb proof horse.

Once the signal went up, all hands followed the direction of the leaders, including Nick. He tried to keep up with the mob, but every jolt from the horse sent electric shocks through his right hand and arm until his shoulder felt like it would explode. He just needed to stay on the horse's back. Bob would take care of him.

Buren rode alongside him with his younger son, Lars. Their big black Friesian stallions made Bob look like a prospect for the knackers. They were keeping a vigilant eye on Nick to make certain he didn't hit the ground. It was a legitimate possibility in his current condition.

<hr />

Agatha, Mrs. MacLeach and the twins waited with Bloem at Willowbrook. It was an ounce of prevention should Dirk actually put in an appearance. If he showed up at all, Jim, John and Craig were waiting at Gilgai, armed to the teeth. Agatha refused to abandon her home, despite a heated argument with Bloem. The elf had no grasp of what it meant as an alpha to defend what was hers. Agatha also wanted to draw Dirk away from her children on the odd chance he did come for her at Willowbrook. She left the van Amersvoot's in wolfshape to Bloem's ardent protests and travelled back to Gilgai on foot. She felt confident with her decision. She did not expect to see Dirk at all that night.

<hr />

The hunt continued for a few miles before the trail went cold.

Buren pulled up his horse, looking down at a different set of tracks faintly impressed into the ground. He immediately knew the four toed marks weren't Dirk's. They were chasing something that left perfect canine prints. Dirk's tracks were more like hand and foot prints with thicker toes. These were leading back to Gilgai.

Agatha.

Lars turned his horse away from the mob to stay with his father. He studied the tension in his father's face with mounting concern. Nick brought his horse around as well.

"What is it?" he asked.

"We're following a rabbit, not a fox," Buren replied. "These are Birthright tracks, not Sauvage."

"Oh, shit," Nick gasped. "Agatha."

Buren flagged down the nearest riders, shouting out that they were heading for Gilgai.

They wheeled their horses about and put in the spurs. They were almost an hour's ride away from the station, even at full tilt. That was more than enough time for Dirk to do anything he liked.

Other men saw them riding in the opposite direction and they waved to the airship spotters to alert them that they would be changing direction. Nearly twenty men joined Buren, Nick and Lars as they headed back to Gilgai.

Dirk slunk through the orchard that spread out beyond the back garden at Gilgai, his angular ears constantly flickering back and forth. He walked on four feet, his long hands leaving telltale imprints in the soft earth. He wanted them to be found.

Agatha was in the bedroom when she felt Dirk's presence. Craig had insisted she remain inside. She sat up on the bed, nerves dancing throughout her body. She simmered with anxiety like a cauldron about to boil over.

She let her skin fall away, revealing the sleek body of her wolf. It was her best defense against Dirk. She stood no chance in her human form, lacking the claws and teeth of an animal. Without hands she couldn't open the bedroom door, but that suited her plans. She would make Dirk come to her.

He could smell Agatha everywhere. It was the only scent he was after. He let it lead him to the back door of the house. He paused, ears twitching. There were light scratching sounds from inside, boots on wood planks. He lowered his massive head and nosed at the screen door. It opened easily. He tuned in to the other smells.

Tobacco. Leather. Nervous sweat. Gunpowder. The tang of metal.

He backed away, allowing the door to bang shut.

Two men appeared in the hall inside. One held a Merriman rotating tri-barrel shotgun and the other aimed a Riggins' Manhunter at him. The shotgun's first blast ripped a gaping hole in the screen, but missed its intended target. The pistol flared four times, also firing wide of its objective.

Dirk sought the quickest escape route at hand. He leaped, catching the edge of the roof and pulling himself up. He moved quickly to the front of the house, looking down into the yard. There was only one man standing out in the open.

Jim felt vulnerable on his own, but he figured Craig and John had the Sauvage cornered out back. His gun was in his hand and his heart in his mouth. He heard a growl and whirled in time to see the werewolf an instant before it struck him. He went down with its jaws clamped around his throat. The gun bounced out of his limp hand, skittering in the dirt. The gleaming blue sky overhead was the last thing he saw.

John bolted around the side of the house, reaching the yard to find Jim lying on his back with his throat gaping open. Blood was still seeping from the wound. He skidded to a stop, staring in horror.

Dirk hit him from behind, sending him sprawling in the dusty yard. The shotgun discharged its second shell as it hit the ground, uselessly shattering a fence post with buckshot. With one set of long claws, Dirk drew deep furrows down John's back. The fabric of his shirt split open as did his flesh. His shriek lasted only a second as Dirk sank his teeth into the back of his head and brought his jaws together. The skull gave way like the rind of a melon. He tasted the sweet nectar of the man's brain as it squeezed into his mouth through the fracturing bone.

Agatha paced. Her claws ticked on the hard floor with each pass as she crossed the bedroom from door to window repeatedly. She knew that she was going to have to fight Dirk. He wasn't there for a social call. It was all or nothing. There was no way the station hands could stop him. John's shrill cry cut deeply, but she couldn't let it break her focus. She had to be ready to face Dirk. She needed every fraction of concentration to enable her to find the means to defeat him. On a full moon she knew it was impossible, but she wasn't going to sabotage her courage by allowing that to enter her thoughts.

Only Craig remained to give any protection. He worked his way through the hall, past the bedrooms and into the salon. He reloaded the empty chambers of his Riggins as he stepped quietly through the house. It was ominously silent.

Dirk waited just outside the front door, hunkered under the window. His ears swiveled as he tracked the human's footsteps. He could tell the man was approaching with caution.

Craig peered out the window at the yard, seeing the two dead men on the ground. His lips tightened in anger. Raising the pistol, he nudged the front door open with his boot. He leaned out, catching sight of the crouching Sauvage as Dirk came at him. There wasn't time to get off a shot. Craig was slammed backwards into the salon by the force of Dirk's lunge. Dirk slapped the gun from his hand. Craig struck the writing desk in the small of his back. The blow to his spine briefly paralyzed his legs. As he collapsed to the floor, he grabbed the first thing his hand touched. He used the base of an inkwell to whack ineffectually at the werewolf's head.

Dirk appreciated the man's attempt to fight back. He liked it when they put up a struggle. It made his effort that much more satisfying when they died.

He pinned Craig beneath him, looking into the man's defiant glare. He pushed a claw into the soft flesh of the man's belly, enjoying the scream it elicited. He pulled his claw downward, opening the abdominal cavity like a tin can. He grasped a handful of entrails and withdrew them from their casing. With a growling laugh he raised the bloody prize up for Craig to see. The life faded from Craig's eyes as he stared at his own intestines clutched in the werewolf's fist.

Dirk flung the viscera away, turning his attention to locating Agatha.

Agatha smelled Dirk's approach over the scent of blood. His claws scraped outside the bedroom door. She trembled.

He leaned his upper body on the door, pressing his wolf face against the wood. He scratched a claw down the surface of the door with an ear grating screech.

Agatha backed into the far corner, giving herself the most defensible position.

Dirk shoved the door open in splinters, filling the frame with his hulking shape. His eyes locked onto Agatha's figure tucked into in the corner. He inhaled her fear and defiance. It was as sweet as any blossom.

She lowered herself onto her belly, baring her teeth as a warning. Her hackles stood up in a long streak down her back. He came towards her, ignoring her threat. He was without fear or rationale. He had one thing on his mind and it controlled his actions.

She knew she had one chance and she took it. Springing upwards, she went for his throat. He met her move with both hands, gripping the fur of her neck in his fingers to stop her momentum. She was caught, her body hanging from his fists. She struck out with her claws, unable to get a purchase on the floor or against his body. Teeth clashing, she swung her head side to side in an effort to connect with any part of him.

Dirk looked down into her panicked eyes. He didn't want her to be afraid of him. He wanted her as a mate, an alpha partner. She was his perfect match, but in his current state he was past being gentle. He would make her realize that she was made to be his.

Dirk tossed Agatha effortlessly onto the bed. Before she could get her legs under her, he was on top of her. He clamped his jaws on the back of her neck, pinning her to the mattress. He brought his arms around her waist, holding her tightly. He arched his back and brought his erect penis forward, stabbing into her.

Agatha squealed, lowering her head. She writhed against his strangle hold. He continued to thrust inside her, deepening his hold on her neck. Blood began to trickle through her fur. She clawed the quilt and sheets, shredding them beneath her. He was driving into her with a violent force that tore her flesh and there was nothing she could do to stop him. She screeched agonizingly. Dirk felt the flood of his release and he reared his head back, bellowing his dominance. When the pleasure passed he withdrew, leaving her bleeding and shaken.

Agatha wasn't out of the running yet. She was now at a point beyond anything she had known. Her animal side took over. A thousand years of predatory nature consumed her in a swarm of strength and raw energy. In his moment of vulnerability she attacked.

She struck him in the chest, knocking him into the window. The glass shattered and they tumbled out into the yard among the glittering fragments. Dirk rolled away from her, astonished by the force of her charge. She didn't hesitate to go after him. Her teeth scored a hit on his forearm. He swept her away with his other hand, sending her flying into the dirt several feet away.

She dragged herself up, ears pressed flat back on her head. Her black lips were parted to expose the savage tusks inside her mouth. They were coated with his blood.

Dirk hadn't expected Agatha to return his aggression. He had hoped she would see that they were meant to be together and would submit to him. He didn't understand why she was fighting back.

Agatha didn't wait for him to get up. She lunged at him with jaws spread wide. He rolled away as she closed her teeth on his lower leg. He kicked her in the face, but she wouldn't release her hold. He reached down with a fist of claws, raking her scalp and tearing her right ear in half. She tried to hold on, but he struck her again and she was blinded by her own blood. She let go and backed away, hoping to get another chance to strike at him.

Dirk brought himself up to a squatting position and stared at her. She wasn't backing down. He could kill her if he wanted to. She wasn't strong enough to win against him, so why was she trying?

CHAPTER TWENTY-FOUR

"Secrets hide like wolves in fleece."
John Nigel, philosopher

They both heard the thunder of hooves at the same time, but made no effort to acknowledge it. They did not take their eyes off one another. The hoof beats drew closer until the snorting of the horses could be heard over them.

Dirk rose up to his full height. Agatha tensed, preparing to launch.

The horses were blown out when they reached Gilgai. They ran white with sweat and several were limping from thrown shoes. The riders were almost as exhausted from the journey.

The first thing they saw when they crested the western hill were two dead men lying in the yard and two animals fighting above them. One was a large wolf and the other was a distorted bipedal creature with wolf-like features that towered above its opponent. The pair was engaged in a bloody skirmish. Their snarls and growls reverberated across the hills. They scrabbled and slashed at one another, each struggling to gain the upper hand.

Nick's stomach turned inside out at the sight of what could only be Agatha as she was kicked in the ribs by the other creature. She skidded backwards several feet, but didn't go down. The massive beast was what had attacked him. He could hardly believe that it was Dirk, the same person he had known for thirty years. That was what the infection did to a human.

Nick dug his spurs into Bob's flanks and the brave horse lunged forward despite its weariness. Buren and Lars were ahead of him, driving their mounts to their utmost. They thundered into the yard to stop the battle between Birthright and Sauvage if at all possible.

Agatha paid no mind to the men on horseback. She dove at Dirk's already torn calf muscle, intending to sever it completely and bring him to his knees.

Lars kicked his feet free of the stirrups, preparing to jump from his horse onto his brother's shoulders. His plan was to knock Dirk to the ground and break off the fight. Dirk turned as Lars leapt out of the saddle. He caught his brother in a brutal embrace, crushing Lars' ribcage with his unrestrained strength. Lars gasped once then went limp in his brother's arms. Blood dribbled from the corner of his mouth and his eyes turned to glass.

Dirk stood for moment in utter disbelief of what he had just done. Lars flopped against him with the softness of a ragdoll. Dirk dropped him and stepped back in horror. His brother crumpled to the ground like a broken toy.

Taking matters into his own hands, Nick urged his horse forward, slamming into Dirk. The Sauvage turned to see the blackest hatred burning in Nick's eyes as their glares met. Dirk roared his anger, sending the normally unflappable horse into a panic. Nick barely stayed in the saddle as Bob spun rapidly in a tight circle like a child's top before lurching across the yard in terror. Nick could only hold on for dear life.

Behind them the hunting party continued down the hill, guns drawn. They galloped towards the beasts in the yard with the intent to kill them both. There was no distinction between the types of werewolves as far as they were concerned. The only good werewolf was a dead one.

Dirk realized he was in trouble. There were horsemen closing in on the yard. Bullets whizzed past him. He dropped to all fours and loped towards the northern tree line above the newly planted grapevines. Several men gave chase.

Buren watched helplessly as the events unfolded in front of

him. Tears fell down his face as he stared in numb shock at the discarded body of his son Lars. His pain and grief knew no depth. He had raised Dirk as his own, never showing favoritism after Lars and Beshka were born. They had all been his children, equally loved and treated with fairness. He had done so much more for Dirk to include him, risked everything to protect him. If he had thought for one split second that his efforts would have led to this, he would have killed Dirk with his own hands after the infection took hold.

Agatha found herself surrounded by a gun toting mob. She tried to get past the horses' legs but the men shifted their mounts to prevent her escape. She was cornered. One of the horses swung around and lashed out with an iron shod hoof, catching her in her side of the head. While Dirk had failed to take her down, the well placed blow from the flat of a hoof knocked her unconscious. She dropped like a stone, lying motionless in the dirt.

"No!!" Nick screamed. He dismounted in one fluid motion and ran toward the men who had her trapped. He shoved horses out of his way to reach her, reinjuring his broken fingers. "Don't shoot her! That's my wife!"

He dropped to his knees, gathering up the wolf's limp body in his arms. As he pulled her to his chest it occurred to him what a beautiful animal she was. From the colours and pattern in her fur to the sleek muscular design of her body she was an astonishing creature. She was built for speed, to hunt. She was a spirit of wilderness like her ancestors. She was also terribly injured. Her blood soaked into his clothes as he cradled her tenderly.

"What do you mean?" demanded Tom Havering. "That thing is Agatha?"

"She's not a thing!" Nick railed, pressing her long muzzle against his cheek. His tears fell onto her fur and clung to her whiskers. "She's my wife."

Before anyone could respond, Agatha's coarse fur began to slough off to expose the human body the men recognized. She was naked and bloody, but familiar. It took them aback and gave them pause.

They would have eagerly butchered the wolf, but seeing the woman they had to reevaluate their course of action. Whatever she was, she was indeed Nick's wife. It would be murder if they struck now.

Randall Lundquist leaned forward and handed Nick his coat to cover Agatha.

"It's the other one you want," Nick snapped hoarsely, pulling the long coat over her. "That's the one that attacked me and attacked Agatha tonight. He killed my men. She was just defending herself."

"He's right," said Buren. All eyes turned towards him. "The one you want is my son, Dirk. He did this. He's the Sauvage you want."

Tom rode forward. He kept his rifle cocked, the butt resting on his thigh.

"You knew? Both of you knew about this?"

"I've kept him locked up during the full moon for three years," Buren angrily replied. "No one knew but my family. There wasn't a problem until she got here. That's when Dirk's obsession started. I tried to stop him, but he won't listen to me anymore. He won't listen to anyone. He's gone crazy. I didn't want any of this to happen. I am so sorry, Nick."

Nick huddled over Agatha, blocking out Buren's voice. He understood Buren's motives, but there was an anger inside him that would not soon dissipate.

It was a difficult pill to swallow for the local men. They knew Dirk, or thought they had known him. He had been involved in their lives for thirty years. That wasn't something easy to ignore.

"With all due respect, Buren," said Terrence Mannerly, one of the town Elders. "This isn't something we can overlook. You may have had good intentions trying to protect your son, but he's killed people now. He's dangerous. You understand if we find him, we have to kill him. We don't expect you to be part of it. He is your son. I'm sorry."

Buren's eyes squeezed shut, tears trembling on his lashes.

"What about Agatha?" asked Tom with a glance at Nick and the pale figure he held in his arms.

Terrence sighed, holstering his pistol. He rode through the circle of men and horses to reach Nick. They crowded around him, waiting for his decision.

"You have my sympathy for what's happened tonight," he said as kindly as possible. "Agatha didn't deserve to get hurt. But she is a werewolf. We can't have her running loose in the Shire. She has to be under strict limitations. She isn't allowed off your property. She is not to step foot in town or on any other station. Is that clear?"

Nick's outrage simmered just below the surface. It would be condemning her to another Rez, but at the moment he had no choice. The other option was unspoken and unthinkable.

"Yes, I understand," he agreed with undisguised hatred.

"We'll arrange a meeting to discuss this situation further. We'll expect to see you, Nick, and you, Buren."

The men rode out as the sky began to turn violet for the evening. They would leave the clean up to Nick and Buren and the remaining station hands.

Nick carried Agatha into the house while Buren stabled the horses. That was where Nick discovered the mutilated body of Craig. He almost dropped Agatha as bile surged up his throat. He stepped over the station hand's torn corpse, careful not to slip in the blood, and took Agatha to their bedroom. He found the bed a shambles with red smears on the sheets. His heart shrank. He turned, adjusting his hold on Agatha, and took her into the spare bedroom. As he settled her on the quilt her legs parted slightly and he saw the rusty smear of blood on the insides of her thighs. He choked on a mouthful of acid, forcing it back down his throat. Leaving her on the bed, Nick went back to deal with the carnage.

CHAPTER TWENTY-FIVE

"A man goes to his grave but once; he goes to his maker often."
Reverend Aloysius Froid

Buren loaded Lars' body into the back of the steam wagon, refusing assistance from anyone. There were no words spoken. The men stood in the yard and watched the red rear lights disappear down the road as Buren took his son home to Willowbrook.

The other station hands returned under the glow of the moon's wide open eye to find Nick digging fresh graves in the family cemetery past the orchard. They silently joined him at his task. Ed was familiar with the routine. It took the rest of the night to properly bury Jim, John and Craig. Nick stood over the graves and gave a simple eulogy. Then it was back to the house to clean up the wreckage.

Agatha regained consciousness shortly after sunrise. Her skull felt like the inside of a church bell as it tolled the hour. The entire right side of her head was a numb lump from the horse's hoof. The left side burned from the scratches left by Dirk's claws. The back of her neck was raw from his teeth. Her right ear was a mangled pulp. She didn't want to admit to the sharp sting between her legs.

She was alone in the spare bedroom. She could hear Nick and some of the other hands talking in muted tones down the hall. There was a strong odor of bleach in the air, but it couldn't completely mask the taint of blood.

Dirk had been more violent than she could have imagined. He had killed four men, including his brother, and raped her. She would heal. She would need to get a particular herbal mixture from Bloem to prevent conception, but that could wait. Even if she did conceive, there were ways to purge it from her body.

Her thoughts turned back to Lars. He had worshipped his older brother. He must have felt that Dirk would recognize him and he could somehow get through to his brother. Lars had not realised that Dirk was past reasoning and he had died for it. She was more upset about that than what Dirk had done to her.

She slowly crawled from the bed and limped to the door. At least Nick had dressed her in a sleeping gown. She made her way down the hall, moving at a snail's pace. Her skull felt lopsided.

Nick was on his hands and knees, scrubbing the floorboards with a harsh brush. He glanced up when she shuffled closer.

She looked around the salon with an aggrieved expression. The writing desk was on its side on the floor. The front door was off its hinges. A bloody inkwell rested under the sofa, its contents spewed across the hardwood. The station hands were sweeping up glass in the master bedroom and boarding up the shattered window.

"I can't believe I've brought this on you," she whispered. "None of this would have happened if I hadn't married you."

Nick clambered to his feet, dropping the brush into a bucket of soapy water. He wiped his damp hands on his shirt as he approached her.

"You didn't cause this," he said, taking her in his arms. She was stiff, resistant. He wove his fingers through her tangled hair, pulling her sore head against his chest. "This is not your fault."

"It is," she said, letting out her torment in a river of tears. They drenched his shirt as she suddenly grasped him as though he could keep her from being washed away by a tide of despair. "I should have known I would bring you nothing but trouble."

He rocked her gently, murmuring words of endearment. It tore him apart to see her blaming herself for the disaster that Dirk had brought into their lives. He wanted Dirk to pay for what he had unleashed. Death would be too good for him.

"How could you have known any of this would happen? You

can't blame yourself."

She pulled back and stared at the dark stain on the floor where Craig had died. Most of the blood had been washed clean, but the blemish would never completely go away. The shadow of death would remain.

"Have they caught him?" she asked.

"I don't know."

He gently guided her across the room and into his office. He closed the door to speak privately. She gave him a curious look as she carefully lowered herself into a chair. He remained standing.

"I have to ask you something," he said haltingly, unsure how to go proceed. It was a delicate subject.

Agatha had an idea of the cause of his unease. Her eyes met his.

"Yes," she said, relieving him of the burden of asking the terrible question. "Dirk raped me."

He took a long, deep breath to steady his nerve. He hadn't thought the night's events could get worse, but this was the most disturbing news he could have imagined. He wasn't sure how to feel. He was furious, hurt, jealous, sickened, terrified. His emotions momentarily spiraled out of control. In a rare moment of rage, Nick grabbed a framed picture from the wall and threw it across the room, making Agatha jump.

"What the hell were you even doing here?" he thundered. "I left you with Bloem so you'd be safe. Why did you leave Willowbrook?"

"What if Dirk had gone there?" she countered. "What if he had hurt Logan and Luna?"

She realised he was struggling to come to terms with everything that had happened during the night. His outburst was understandable, but startling. He always kept his emotions close to the vest. To witness a glimpse of his temper was unsettling. It was like seeing fire through the smoke.

Seeing fear briefly cloud her eyes, he quickly collected himself. He remembered her natural reaction to human violence was to withdraw. Now was not the time to let his emotions take over. He needed to be focused and rational to get through this. They needed each other's support. They had much to discuss and he had yet to inform her of the Elder's declaration.

"I knew he'd follow my scent if he showed up and I couldn't put our children, or Bloem, or Mrs. MacLeach, at risk," she said defensively. "If I had stayed there he would have attacked them. I wasn't going to let that happen. You've seen what he can do. Would you rather have found your babies slaughtered?"

He turned his head, nostrils flared. The mention of Logan and Luna being victims of Dirk's rampage sent ice through his veins. Images of their small bodies ripped open came unbidden to his mind and he shook his head to dislodge them. His gorge rose once more.

"I did the only thing I could to protect our children," she said. Her tone had a pleading quality yet her teeth flashed. "If I'd had to give my life to keep them safe then I would have done it."

Nick took two long steps to kneel in front of her. He enveloped her in his arms, burying his face in her hair.

"You almost did," he said, holding her so tightly that she couldn't breathe. "I could have lost you. They could have lost you. I don't know what I'd do if that happened."

Agatha melted against him. His strength was so comforting that she could remain in his arms for the rest of her life. Sadly, they had much to do so it wasn't a practical option.

He reluctantly released her. His hands rested lightly on her knees and he gazed intently into her eyes. He couldn't bring himself to tell her about the Elder's decision. It was too soon. He needed to attend the meeting and state his case. He wanted to shield her from the ugly truth as long as possible.

"Speaking of our children, we should go to Willowbrook and check on them," she told him. "I know they're fine with Bloem, but I need to see it for myself. I have to hold them."

His plan was shot out of the water by her statement. She was right, they needed to check on the babies, but she couldn't leave Gilgai. He rose and walked to the desk. He trailed his fingers over the edge of the wood.

"Perhaps they should stay there for now," he suggested, trying to delay the inevitable. "I'm not sure it's completely safe here."

"Bloem can't look after two babies right now," she replied sensibly. "She'll be grieving for Lars. She'll be in seclusion for weeks. When the mourning period is over we can visit. I'm sure she'll want to see the babies then. But we should bring them home. I need them here."

"Then I'll get them."

She peered up at his elusive gaze. He couldn't meet her eyes. She felt a pang of fear.

"What aren't you telling me?" she demanded.

"I don't know if you remember Terrence Mannerly. He was at the van Amersvoot's the night of the wedding celebration. He's one of the town Elders. Because of what happened, he's ordered you to be confined to Gilgai until there can be a meeting to decide what's to be done."

"To be done?" she repeated sharply. Her brows wrinkled with suspicion. "To be done about what? Me?"

Nick nodded with a difficult sigh.

"They don't have all the facts about what happened yesterday so they're taking precautions," he explained, hoping it didn't sound as bad as it was. "It won't be permanent. I'll talk to them. They'll see you aren't the problem."

She leaned back, her face a mask of shock. She stared at him with resentment flaming in her eyes. The wolf reared up.

"The problem? Is that what you think I am? A problem?" she growled.

"Absolutely not," he fired back. "The problem is Dirk and his family. Buren should have stopped him a long time ago."

She shook her head harshly.

"I've already told you, Buren sees Dirk as the boy he raised. He doesn't see the Sauvage, he sees his son. You watched Dirk grow up. You know what he was like before the Bite changed him. How can you just forget that? Does it make it easier for you to hate him? He can't help what he's become."

"He raped you. How can you defend him?"

"Because I'm the only one who knows what the Bite does and how it affects someone. It's an infection, not a choice. You have no idea what it's like to have a wild animal suddenly thrust inside you, sharing your skin. Either you make it submit or it consumes you. If you aren't strong enough to tame the wolf then it will take over. It's different for each person. The infection brings with it the essence of the Birthright's personality. It doesn't have to be detrimental, but it almost always is."

Nick considered her words.

"What about this Paradeus?"

A golden light appeared in her eyes like a halo around her irises at the mention of his name.

"Paradeus was the only one of his kind. I'm honored to share his blood. He was fortunate that his Birthright was sound minded."

"I don't know who gave Dirk the Bite, but they must have been some kind of insane bastard," Nick grunted. He rubbed his stubble lined jaw with the back of his fingers. "It doesn't really matter now, though. Dirk isn't the same person I knew, that any of us knew. I can't begin to imagine how difficult this must be for Buren and Bloem, losing Lars like this and knowing Dirk has a death card over his head now."

The death card was an old expression. It referred to the Fate's deck of cards, also called the Fatal Deck. In centuries past it was a common provincial practice to use the cards to determine a criminal's punishment. Feudal lords would shuffle the deck and stand behind the convicted prisoner. Drawing a card, the lord would hold it above the condemned's head for the waiting public to witness. The card's denomination would reveal the fate that awaited the poor soul standing beneath it. There was usually more than one death card in a deck.

"You have to let go of your anger towards Dirk. I know what he's done, better than you. I can't forgive him, but I can't hate him because I know it wasn't entirely his fault. The wolf has gotten the better of him and he can't stop it. He'll never be able to stop it. It will only get worse. He does need to be killed. It's his only chance for peace."

Nick didn't know why the thought came into his head, but he asked, "Do werewolves believe in Heaven?"

"We believe in an afterlife. If you lived a good life, you're rewarded by going to the Summer Fields where game is plentiful and the days are warm and long," she said with a wistful smile that turned hard as she continued. "If not, the Winter Fields await you. There is only rock, snow, ice and suffering. I'll tell you more about it sometime, but right now I want my children home."

CHAPTER TWENTY-SIX

"A tree will bend against the wind; a man will break before he gives in."
Edward V. Schuster, poet and philosopher

Arriving at Willowbrook on horseback, Nick was met by a shuttered house. All the windows were dark, the curtains pulled tight. There was a profound quiet in the yard.

He was greeted by Bruce Ramsey, Willowbrook's overseer, who came out of the barn when he heard the horse approaching.

"How's Agatha?" Bruce asked, taking hold of the horse's bridle.

Nick swung down, his boots creating a dust cloud as he landed. He winced as he followed Bruce to the barn.

"She'll recover. How are things here?"

"The Missus is beside herself. She's locked herself away in mourning. The master and the lads are digging the grave right now. It's a dark time for everyone."

Nick agreed. He left Bruce and made his way to the house where he found Mrs. MacLeach. The rotund woman's boundless energy was dimmed by the mood of the house. She embraced him briefly.

"Och, this is a terrible day."

She held the twins as they drove back to Gilgai in the steam wagon that Buren had borrowed to bring his son home. Neither she nor Nick spoke during the trip. Even the babies seemed unusually subdued.

Agatha was waiting anxiously in the yard as they pulled up. She moved as quickly as her bruised body would allow when they came to a stop. She gathered up Logan first, snuggling and kissing him with frantic vigor. The baby giggled, blowing bubbles in his joy.

Nick took Luna, helping Mrs. MacLeach down from the wagon. The baby fit in the crook of his arm with room to spare. She looked up at him, making soft sounds of delight. It was obvious even at such a young age that she was daddy's little angel. He was wrapped around her finger.

The housekeeper bustled inside, determined to set the place right.

⁂

The days passed in somber retrospection. Everyone at Gilgai had grief to work through. Nick stayed close to the house, keeping tabs on Agatha. She was withdrawn, giving all her attention to Logan and Luna.

Their nights were spent with a wedge between them. Nick didn't know how to cross the chasm created by Dirk's assault. He didn't want her to think he was put off by the fact that she had been brutally violated, although it did give him pause. She hadn't spoken about it and he wanted her to be the one to break the ice. He couldn't just blurt out what he was feeling. His needs came after hers. What she needed most was time.

In truth she was afraid to say anything, not knowing how he would react. He kept his distance when she desperately needed him to be close. She couldn't tell if he was disgusted by her now that she had been intimate with another man, even though it had been against her will. He made no attempt to open lines of communication. She felt cut off.

Several nights after the incident they lay in bed, awake and silent.

Agatha could think of nothing else but the lack of contact between them. She wanted to erase the memory of Dirk, to overpower it with something stronger. What Dirk had done was not going to keep her from loving her husband, unless Nick no longer felt the same.

She rolled onto her side, facing him. He turned his head on the pillow to look at her.

"I miss your touch," she said, seeking his approval. "If you don't want to have sex with me, I understand."

He turned towards her, bringing his hand up to caress her cheek.

"Not until you're ready," he said softly. "I know he hurt you. I thought you might not want to, that it might make you think…"

She smiled, leaning in to kiss him lightly. She reached up and stroked his hair.

"It may seem odd to you that I can let it go so easily," she said. "But it's part of my culture for males to take females by force sometimes. We accept it. It's a means of showing dominance. That's all he was doing."

Nick sat up. He stared down at her like she had lost her mind.

"You think what he did was normal?" he asked, sickened by her admission.

She shrank back. She pulled the sheets close around her as a shield.

"If it was only about sexual gratification then no," she replied defensively. "That had nothing to do with it. He was doing what our nature dictates." When Nick continued to stare with unblinking shock, she felt a knife cut through her belly. "You know so little about me and my kind. You're judging our behavior on what you know about human nature. I'm not human. Don't ever forget that."

She rolled away from him, but remained awake for most of the night, listening to rain fall on the roof. So did Nick.

Word finally came that the town Elders were ready to meet.

The Town Hall was overcrowded. People stood against the wall and spilled out in the hall or stood beneath the open windows under darkening skies. Attitudes were mixed. Nick had a large supportive contingent. He had been born and raised in the Shire and his reputation as an honest, decent, hard working man was in his favour. There were those who didn't feel that was enough to overlook the introduction of predators to the area.

The Elders were seated behind the long rectangular table at the front of the meeting hall. There were twelve members including Terrence Mannerly. They were all dressed in formal attire for the occasion. They ranged in age from fifty to eighty. All had lived in the Shire all or most of their lives. They knew Nick and had known his parents.

Nick sat in the front row with Buren, Edison Finnerty and a large collection of friends and allies. Agatha had opted to remain home with the twins. She felt she might be a detriment to her own defense if she became angered by what was said. He was relieved to have Buren at his side. Their friendship was still strong despite the events of the past few months. He knew that things might go against him with Buren's presence, considering it was Dirk that had caused all the damage, but he would never have considered excluding Buren from the proceedings.

Terrence called the meeting to order with a loud bang of his gavel.

"This session has been called to deliberate the course of action to be taken in regards to the werewolf, Agatha Buchanan," he announced in a deep stentorian tone.

"Now hold on," said Nick, immediately on his feet in protest. "She's not on trial."

"Of course not," Terrence agreed placatingly. He gestured for Nick to be seated.

Nick grudgingly returned to his chair.

"We are here to discuss this matter in a diplomatic manner," Terrence continued. "Now, it has come to our attention that Mrs. Buchanan, who is not present, is a Birthright werewolf. May I inquire as to why she is not here?"

"You know we have newborn twins," said Nick. "We felt it was best she stayed with them."

Terrence and the other Elders nodded. That showed her instincts as a good mother.

"Very well. We shall move on. It is our understanding that the werewolf that attacked you, Mr. Buchanan, and your wife, is a Sauvage. Is that correct?"

Nick nodded.

Terrence consulted notes resting on the table in front of him. He looked up, his gaze finding Buren.

"That Sauvage is Dirk van Amersvoot. Is that correct?"

Buren nodded, jaw clenched. His arms were folded over his chest.

"He has already been reported to the Guardianship," he replied. "The elves are handling it."

"Not well enough!" shouted someone at the back of the crowded room.

Speaking over the dissenting voice, rapping his gavel for order, Terrence plowed on, "According to our research, it has been determined that only a Birthright werewolf is capable of transmitting the infection that causes the condition known as Sauvage. Therefore, Mr. Buchanan, your wife is capable of passing her infection to others."

"She's never given the Bite to anyone," Nick said loudly. "She was raised believing it's a crime to give the Bite. Believe me, it was beaten into her and there is no way in Heaven or Hell that she would go against that."

"We cannot guarantee that," said Wallace Dougherty. He sat to the far left of Terrence. "I'm sure you want to think the best of her, she is your wife after all, but we must take no chances. She's been here barely a year and we don't know her background. We know that in the United American Territories they keep werewolves on reservations for their own protection-"

"The Regulators forced them onto reservations in an effort to kill them off," Nick shouted, fed up with the direction the discussion was going. It was obvious the Elders did not want Agatha around and they were attempting to justify their decision. "The government treats them like vermin. They aren't even allowed to have children. If they do, they're killed and their children are raised to be human. They're forced to be something they aren't."

There was a ripple of voices around the room. Some were astounded by what was previously unknown information. Most applauded in agreement.

Nick turned to the crowd. These were people who supported their own native people being "enlightened". To a lesser degree the Aborigines were being treated much like the werewolves. Why had he thought they would be sympathetic? Before he could make a comment that would turn the tide completely against him, Ed put his hand on his arm and shook his head as a warning.

"I understand your desire to protect your wife, Mr. Buchanan," said Terrence condescendingly. "But we have a larger population to consider. If she were to even accidentally give the Bite to someone there could be serious consequences. We must think of the greater good. It is our decision then to enforce the current order that she remain on your property and have no contact with the citizens of the Shire."

"I hope you don't intend to stop people from going to Gilgai," interrupted Buren. "Are you going to post guards on the road leading out there?"

That sentiment was echoed by several people across the room.

"Of course not," Terrence answered sternly. The gavel rapped on the table to regain order. "We cannot prevent individuals from visiting the station, but we must caution anyone that would that they do so at their own risk. Any injuries incurred will be handled in a legal manner. It is further our decision that she not use her other shape at any time for any purpose. She is to remain human for as long as she resides in the Shire."

Nick was just about ready to explode with fury. They had effectively turned Gilgai into another reservation with the same arcane rules and collar around her neck.

"She's isn't going to attack people like a fucking rabid dog," he bellowed. "Why don't you just chain her up and throw her scraps while you're at it. That's what they do in America. She came here to have freedom and a life of her own. She doesn't deserve this kind of treatment from assholes like you."

Ed and Buren tried to restrain him in his seat. Nick managed to shove them back and lunged to his feet.

"Mr. Buchanan, please!" said Terrence, banging the gavel loudly.

"No, I won't sit here and listen to you talk about my wife like she's a dangerous animal," Nick replied with a hoarse shout. "Do what you want, but I won't listen to any more of this bullshit."

He stormed out, too enraged to hear the arguing that continued in his wake. He climbed into the steam wagon and drove out of Falmormath without caution.

He was so incensed by what he had heard that his concentration was not on the road. He knew the route by heart, so he was not careful in his navigation. The wagon bounced and jolted over the pitted track that qualified as a road.

He was well out of town, climbing over one of the higher ridges, when a white dingo shot out into his path. It stopped in the road and stared at him with malevolent yellow eyes. Overcompensating in his agitated mind frame, he swerved sharply. The wagon's narrow front wheels struck the road's hard edge, sending it off the track. It slipped in the rain soaked soil, unable to gain traction, plunging downhill, crashing through brush and branches. The windscreen shattered, spraying glass in Nick's face. He instinctively threw his arms up, releasing the steering bar. The wagon turned violently, flipping onto its side.

It slammed into trees, ricocheting from one to another as it slid down the grassy slope. The wagon eventually barreled over a steep embankment, plummeting ten feet onto a rocky dry river bed to land on its roof. Nick was pinned by the full weight of the vehicle, the doorframe crushing his abdomen.

Rain stung his eyes as the clouds began to unload their moisture. He lay on a bed of nails with the rocks digging into his back and the wagon resting on top of him. He could barely draw breath. Every time he tried to get air into his lungs they filled with fire. The pressure of the wagon on his body was excruciating.

He couldn't die like this. He couldn't leave Agatha to the mercy of the Elders. If he wasn't there to protect her from the men of Falmormath he would have failed her. He didn't know what they would do to her. She wasn't safe on her own with the twins. He needed to be there for them.

Staring up at the falling rain, thinking it was the last thing might see before he died, he blacked out.

⁂

"He's not here?" Buren asked, stepping inside the house at Gilgai.

Agatha's pacing never slowed. She walked back and forth in the salon with Luna on her shoulder. Her strides were frantic with tides of nervous energy flowing through her. Mrs. MacLeach sat on the sofa holding Logan.

"No. We haven't seen him since he left this morning," answered the housekeeper.

"He should have been here a long time ago," said Ed. He hesitated in the doorway, glancing back out at the dark storm. "Or we should have passed him on the road if the wagon stopped."

"Where's my husband?" Agatha insisted.

A hard knot twisted in Buren's gut. He didn't want to worry her unduly.

"We'll go back out and look for him. If he came over the southeast ridge, the road's been washed out. He may have had to take the long way like we did. That would have put him close to Willowbrook. Maybe he pulled in there to wait out the storm. We'll find him."

"I can track him faster than you can," she stated, passing Luna to Mrs. MacLeach.

Buren put his hand on her arm, his expression unyielding.

"Under no circumstances are you to leave this house," he said to her. "The Elders ruled that you cannot leave the station. If we have to get more men to search then I can't have you out there on the loose. Let us find Nick. You stay here."

Agatha watched them leave in Buren's wagon. Her heart was pounding. Her hands twitched uncontrollably. The wolf chafed against its human bonds. It wanted to do what it did best. It was a fight to keep it inside.

By nightfall there had been no word.

Mrs. MacLeach put the twins to bed. She came into the salon to find Agatha in a state of severe anxiety. Her clothes were damp with sweat and her hair was slick like she had been out in the rain. She was shaking with a need to unleash the wolf. It was tearing her up from within.

Knowing what it could cost, the housekeeper helped her undress. "Go find him."

CHAPTER TWENTY-SEVEN

"The difference between life and death is a flip of the coin."
vagabond adage

The rain had let up, but it made tracking virtually impossible. It flushed away scents and blurred prints in the dirt. She stuck to the road until she came across a section that had been flooded out. She spent a few minutes scouring the immediate area but didn't pick up a trail. He had not made it past that section of road before the slide struck. That meant he had to be further down the ridge. She picked her way over the rocks and mud to follow the track east.

She hadn't gotten more than a hundred meters before she hit on Nick's scent. She backed up, turning in a circle to get her bearings. She located its strongest point.

He had gone over the side of the ridge.

Skittering on four stiff legs, she made her way down the slope. It was like riding an eel. She slipped and slithered in the thick mud, pinging off trees in her haste. Once she reached the bottom of the hill, she perched on the edge of the embankment overlooking the now rushing creek.

The steam wagon lay in a crushed heap on its roof among the rocks and splashing water.

She leaped down, landing on sharp stones. She ignored the pain as she picked her way towards the wreck. Her golden eyes searched quickly and frantically for Nick. She came around the front of the wagon to the reach driver's side where she discovered him lying beneath the wagon's full weight.

His face was red with blood from a gash in his forehead. He was half immersed in the flowing water which contributed to the pale blue of his cold skin. His eyelids were parted slightly open. His breathing was shallow, almost nonexistent. His chest didn't move as a weak gasp passed through his lips.

Agatha shed her wolfshape in the blink of an eye and dropped to her bare knees at his head. She didn't feel the rocks cut into her flesh nor the frigid water that flowed over her feet.

"No, no, no, no, no," was all that came out with each breath. With animal rage she flung the wagon off of him. She put her trembling hands on either side of his face. Her voice rose to a shriek. "Nick?"

He blinked, eyes rolling unfocused towards her. He could only see darkness, but he heard her voice. She was there with him. He tried to speak, but there was almost no strength left in him. He used every remaining ounce of life to make a last request.

"Please, give me the Bite," he begged.

Agatha rocked back on her heels. He was asking for her to go against everything she believed. It was taboo, absolutely forbidden. She knew the risks and what it could cost both of them. To become Sauvage was to give up part of what made him human. It was also the only way to save him. She could either lose the man she loved, or lose what she loved about the man.

With her heart breaking and tears cascading down her face, she lowered her mouth to his. She kissed him with fervent passion then took his lower lip in her teeth and bit down. She ran her tongue across the wound, mingling her saliva with his blood. She sucked his blood into her mouth, savoring the purest part him. It was one last taste of his humanity.

One moment Nick felt himself drifting, floating towards a beautiful white light, the next he was engulfed in flames. Fire flooded through him as if a blast furnace had been opened inside his chest. He screamed, arching his body in response to the life that blazed back into him. It was unbearable, but it faded as quickly as it came on.

Then he felt it. Another presence within his body. It was timid at first, weak and fragile as a newborn. It was everywhere inside him; in his head, his muscles, his viscera and bones. Its spirit was a part of him, yet it had a unique personality. It was a physical presence, a separate intelligence. The foreign entity lurked like a shadow below his skin, content for the moment to rest and wait. It required the influence of the full moon to bring out its full potential.

Agatha watched with frightened eyes, crouching near the riverbank. She had never witnessed what happened during the birth of Sauvage.

Nick swallowed a great breath, feeling the fire recede to comforting warmth. He opened his eyes to see the vast black sky with its sprinkling of diamond dust sprawling above him. He had never seen it with such vivid intensity. As he slowly gathered his reclaimed strength and pulled himself to a kneeling position, he realised the ground beneath him felt more like the skin of a living creature. Under the layer of rocks and water beat an ageless heart. He looked to Agatha to validate what his senses were telling him.

"Is this what it's like for you?" he asked, awed by this new awareness.

She knew what he meant. She nodded warily.

He unsteadily rose up, holding his arm around his waist. There was still major damage done by the hours pinned under the steam wagon. The fact that he could even stand was miraculous and thanks entirely to the new life that filled his veins. He could already feel the tissues knitting together inside his body. He wiped the blood from his eyes and stared up at the swaddling sky. It held the Earth in its secure embrace like a mother with a babe at her breast. How had he lived his life until now without this intrinsic connection?

She watched him with wide eyes, not knowing what to expect.

Other than the influx of improved healing power, and a feeling of invincibility, he didn't think he was any different. Whatever was part of him now was quietly curled up inside his skin. It wasn't what he had been expecting, but he was grateful to be alive. He would pay any price, accept any consequence, as long as he could remain with his family.

Agatha slowly stood, cautiously taking a step towards him. She could sense his wolf. It was nothing like the wolf in Dirk or any other Sauvage she had known. It had a Birthright type of aura, a natural sense of belonging. It was strangely subdued, as if it did not need to challenge him. That would change when the moon became full and the infection reached its peak. That was weeks away. She just knew that at this moment he was alive and he was with her.

She took a step toward him.

"Down there! I can see the wagon!"

She and Nick turned to see lights flashing among the trees above them.

"You have to go," he said urgently. "They can't find you here."

"I can't leave you," she objected, stumbling into his arms.

He shoved her away, unaware of his new strength. She staggered backwards, nearly falling.

"Go now," he commanded.

Agatha knew he was right. She picked her way over the rocks on the edge of the river, keeping close to the high embankment to remain hidden should any of the men get close enough to peer down into the riverbed. Once she was past the overturned wreckage of the wagon, she allowed herself to slip free of her skin. It drifted downstream and away from any potential discovery. She paused, looking back at Nick, and then loped into the darkness using the river to mask her tracks.

The first person to each Nick was Edison Finnerty. He immediately picked up on something different about Nick, but he couldn't put his finger on it. He chalked it up to Nick being in shock from the accident.

"I've got him!" Ed shouted up to the search party that gathered on the ledge above them.

Buren scrambled down after him. He, too, noticed a change in his best friend, only he was able to identify it. Nick was a Sauvage. It would not be obvious to everyone, but he was a Custodian of Nature and when things were out of alignment he felt it. He also recognized the sickness from his experience with Dirk.

Buren had a moment of terrible indecision. He had an obligation to kill any Sauvage he came across. It was one of the corporal laws in elf society. He had failed to kill Dirk and that had led to the death of Lars and three other men, as well as Agatha's rape. Now he was standing before the man he knew better than any other and it was up to him to decide Nick's fate. If he made a move now to kill Nick the other men would know that Agatha must have given him the Bite. They would go after her next. There were two babies to think of. Buren didn't believe for a second that Logan and Luna would be spared. Fear would take over otherwise rational minds and normally decent men would become murderers.

Nick faced Buren, reading the thoughts that crossed the hugtandalf's features. He knew exactly what Buren was wrestling with in his heart and mind.

"I asked her for it," he said, hoping to convince his friend not to act on his duty. He doubled over in pain. He wasn't invulnerable now, just stronger.

Buren's jaw tightened. It changed things to know that it had been a voluntary acceptance of the Bite. He knew that it could make the difference between a successful transition or a downward spiral into lunacy and violence. Praying he wasn't making the same mistake twice, Buren shook his head.

"You're a fool," he replied. "But I'll help get you through this if you'll let me."

Ed was helping Maxwell Singer-Hall down the greasy slope and didn't hear the exchange. The rest of the search party soon joined them on the riverbank, each man relieved to see Nick up and around. They acted like nothing was different between them, that they hadn't just been part of the proverbial lynching of his wife. They treated him with the same bonhomie reserved for all native sons. It was fortunate that they were blind to the subtle alteration in Nick's personality. They were too human and unfamiliar with the symptoms.

Their concern was for his injuries.

"Let's get you home," said Buren, leading Nick downriver where there was a stack of rocks that could be used to climb up to the overhanging ledge. "I think there's someone waiting to see you."

"Thank you," Nick said with the sincerest gratitude.

"You may not thank me when the full moon comes," Buren replied, aiding Nick as they scaled the rubble. "But you're the one who has to live with your choice."

CHAPTER TWENTY-EIGHT

"The sun brightens the heart, the moon exposes the soul"
fae Proverb

By the time Buren delivered Nick to Gilgai, Agatha had taken a quick bath and put on a loosely flowing dress. She bolted out the door to meet Buren's steam wagon as it rattled into the yard. Mrs. MacLeach followed at a more sedate pace.

Nick stepped down and as was instantly struck by the richness of the air. It was a thick mixture of all the earthly ingredients combining within his nostrils. It amazed him. It was a shame that humans weren't able to experience it.

Agatha gave no care for his injuries as she launched herself into his chest, wrapping her arms around him. She nearly took him off his feet. If he had still been human she would have bowled him over. He was able to keep his balance and meet her enthusiasm without falling down, but he felt an intense pain in his belly from the accident. He needed to lie down and rest.

Buren came around to their side of the wagon. He watched their reunion with bittersweet satisfaction. He had never seen two people so in love or so well balanced in their relationship. Maybe he had made the right decision. Nick had slept during the drive back, still fairly weak from his wounds and worn out from the early onset of the effects of the Bite.

Ed hurried off to the bunkhouse to relay the news of Nick's safe return.

"Inside, all of you," ordered Mrs. MacLeach. She clucked at Nick.

"You're soaked through. I'll run you a hot bath while you get out of those wet things."

"I'll be by later in the day to discuss a few things," Buren said to Nick, standing close and using a low voice. He looked at Agatha clinging to Nick like a starfish on a rock. "With both of you."

She nodded, understanding his concerns. As Buren drove away, Agatha pulled Nick into the house. She took him into their bedroom and closed the door.

He didn't object as she stripped the muddy wet clothes from his body. Her touch was so much more intoxicating than before. Every time her fingers met his skin it was like tiny electrical shocks passing between them. There was a fresh surge of energy through his system. He no longer felt the aching pain in his abdomen. It was as if her touch absolved him of all ills.

He gazed down on her soft, round breasts and gave in to the sudden impulse to grasp them. His palms supported their weight as his thumbs gently grazed the stiff nipples. The fabric of her dress turned dark with the discharge of milk. He pulled the dress down to release her breasts from their confines. His mouth sought one hard bud, pulling at it with more force than necessary. She whimpered but made no effort to stop him. He was rewarded with a flood of sweet milky nectar that would aid in his healing.

She was surprised by his boldness, but she welcomed it. She gripped his hair, pressing him harder against her breast. His teeth brushed her nipple, biting teasingly. She uttered a deep groan, feeling a warm pool of pleasure fill her lower belly.

Something gripped Nick from within, an unfamiliar wild sensation. The wolf was aroused by the taste of her. It began to infiltrate his thoughts and actions, sharing his wants and needs, bringing an awareness of primitive power. It gave him a stronger drive to satisfy his hunger for her.

Nick ripped her dress away, leaving it in tatters on the floor. He pushed her onto the mattress, coming down fully on top of her. He clutched her head in his hands, forcing her mouth open with his. His tongue swirled up the inside of her cheeks and across her palate. She moaned into his mouth, driving her tongue forward in response. He positioned himself between her thighs, sliding his hardened penis along the ridge of her clitoris in a scintillating dance of desire. He stroked her repeatedly until she was crying out and her hips were undulating desperately beneath him. Bringing his lips down along her neck, he nibbled lightly on her sweat beaded skin, relishing the increased sensations that assailed his brain and body. He rose up, staring down into her pleading eyes. He shoved himself into her as deep as he could until their hips collided. Her inner flesh was hotter than he remembered. It felt like he had entered a volcano only he was the one who would be erupting. Her muscles strained to accommodate the size of him. They worked with a rippling motion, squeezing from the base of his shaft to the head each time he thrust into her. He caught his breath as he plunged again and again with strength and endurance he had lacked before. He wasn't even sure when he would reach his peak. There seemed to be no end to his ability to remain hard and pierce her with indescribable pleasure. After what had to be an eternity of Agatha screaming his name and raking her claws up and down his back and buttocks he felt the rise of his climax. It exploded from the depths of his groin and tore through the rigid tissue of his penis to shoot into her like a lightning bolt. He let out a sound of primal ecstasy that was matched by Agatha's animal scream.

They fell away from each other, drained, but their hunger sated.

"Did you know it could be like that?" he gasped. His lungs burned, but he felt incredibly energized. He could take her again right away. The wolf certainly wanted to.

She wagged her head, panting from the exertion. Her body still reverberated with the release of her pleasure. She wanted it to keep going as long as possible, but it was slowly fading. There would be more opportunities in their future.

Mrs. MacLeach knocked tentatively on the door.

"Your bath is ready."

Nick and Agatha laughed, rolling together on the quilt. He kissed her again. His fingers sought the swollen tissues at the crux of her thighs. He pinched the nub he found there between the sides of his first and second fingers and rubbed them together, squeezing it until she thrust her pelvis in his palm with a squeal of ecstasy. An internal wave of molten delight crashed through her.

"Let it get cold," he said, rolling on top of her again.

Morning brought more than the light of a new day. It brought a sense of renewed commitment between Nick and Agatha. They were worn out from a night of endless lovemaking and he was feeling the effects of the extra stress he had put his body through in the wake of the accident. Werewolves did have their limits. Mrs. MacLeach brought them breakfast in bed.

After they ate, Nick dressed for a day in the paddocks. He was hurting in places he hadn't realised had been injured the night before, but he persevered with the typical stubbornness that defined him as a man. He had responsibilities to the station. Being Sauvage hadn't changed that. He knew Buren would be showing up at some point, but he had to get out into the vines and make a progress check. They were his cash crop, what would keep Gilgai going without the sheep.

Buren arrived a little past noon. He chose to drive the steam wagon rather than ride a horse that would be terrified by the werewolves. Thinking in plural terms was going to take some getting used to.

There was no one in the yard when he stepped down from the wagon. Chickens wound their way between his feet as he walked to the house. He managed to avoid tripping over them. His knock on the replaced front door was answered by Agatha.

It was the first time they had been alone together since Dirk's attack.

Buren removed his hat respectfully. His eyes were hesitant to meet hers.

Agatha was glad to see him. She did not hold a grudge. He had done what any father would have. He had tried to protect his child. If anything, he had gone above and beyond in an effort to keep not only Dirk safe, but the entire Shire. Dirk had proven to be more than he could handle. He had never done anything to intentionally hurt her or Nick. If anything, he had been overly supportive, knowing what she was from the beginning.

She embraced him tightly, which stunned him at first. Her open forgiveness was more than unexpected, it was almost unwelcome. He didn't know if he deserved it because he hadn't forgiven himself.

"You're a good friend, Buren," she said, holding him close. "We've missed you."

He shared her sentiment, allowing himself to give in to the comfort she offered. He let his arms go around her and he accepted her gesture of friendship.

When they parted, she smiled broadly.

"How is Bloem? Is she up to coming for a visit, since I'm under restriction?" she asked hopefully.

"I think so," he answered. "She needs to get out of the house. I'll talk to her. I know she'd like to see the twins again."

"Why don't you go inside? I'll send someone out to get Nick."

Buren and Agatha were engaged in a light conversation when Nick came in. His trousers and boots were caked with dirt which he tried to stomp off outside, but managed to track in regardless.

Mrs. MacLeach was not pleased when she saw it. She brought a tray of coffee in from the kitchen, muttering under her breath about Nick being born in a barn.

He took the tray and placed it on the low table between the sofa and his chair. He poured the steaming coffee into tall cups and offered the first to Agatha. She quickly added several lumps of sugar and a splash of cream. Buren took his black. Nick liked sugar, no cream.

"How are you doing?" Buren asked, looking pointedly at Nick.

BIRTHRIGHT

"It's not what I thought it would be like," he admitted. "I can feel something inside me, like Agatha talked about, but it isn't what I thought. It's there, but it's like it's asleep."

He didn't mention the extra sexual potency he experienced with Agatha. He didn't feel it was necessary to divulge all aspects of his new gift.

"It won't be for long. The full moon is in twelve days," Buren reminded him. "What are you going to do then?"

Agatha spoke up, "I'm going to teach him how to control it."

Buren wasn't convinced so easily. He had heard Dirk's promises.

"Do you have any idea what it's going to be like?" he questioned. He leaned forward, elbows on knees. He looked from Agatha to Nick. "Do either of you know what's coming?"

"I haven't been able to fully explain it to him yet," she said somberly. "He only took the Bite last night. I don't even know where to begin."

Buren centered her in his sights. He was not going to let her squirm her way out of her obligation to Nick.

"You'd better find a starting place soon. I'm not losing Nick to this infection like I lost Dirk."

Nick's cup clattered on its saucer as he set it down with more force than necessary. He didn't want to think that he could end up like that. It shook him to the core.

"I'm sorry about Dirk," he said, recovering his composure. "Have you heard anything from the Guardianship?"

"No," Buren replied, gaze downcast. His voice was laced with bitterness. "But then I don't expect they'll send a bouquet to let me know he's dead. I'm sure Bloem's family will hear about it first. They're well connected."

For many minutes no one spoke.

"I built a concrete room," said Buren, "to hold Dirk during the full moon. It worked, as long as I could get him into it. He went in on his own most times. After he met Agatha that all changed. I had to force him in, but I could only do it once or twice. He was just too strong. I thought it would be a good idea for him to find a wife. He was so lonely, so depressed. I wanted him to be happy for a change. Eliza told me there were a few Birthright females available so I sent Dirk to Sydney, hoping he would find one that he could make a life with. He wanted you and he couldn't let it go."

"I remember seeing him at Eliza's that night," Nick said, recalling the evening with remarkable clarity. "It never occurred to me that everyone there was a werewolf."

"Why would you have thought that?" Agatha asked. She tilted her head slightly. "Dirk was only one of a handful of us there that night. He was the only Sauvage. He was so aggressive. He wouldn't leave me alone. I had to hide just to get away from him." She glanced at Nick. "That's how we met. If I had realised then what he was capable of, I would have done something about him that night. I'm sorry, Buren."

"I wish you would have."

"This concrete room you built," said Nick, changing the subject. "You think I should use it on the night of the full moon?"

"I think it's a good idea," Buren replied. "Remember, the full moon doesn't always happen at night. I learned that with Dirk. The moon can reach its peak during the day, too. You have to be aware of it. I know you mean well, Agatha, but you haven't seen what I have. Becoming Sauvage isn't a picnic. It might be best the first time if Nick was confined."

"You may be right," Agatha said. "If I don't think Nick can control the wolf then he'll need to be locked up. But I want him to learn to work with it."

"Maybe he can, but at first it's better to take precautions," argued Buren.

"I'm right here," snapped Nick.

"I'm sorry, Nick," said Buren. "We want this to go well for you and you won't be able to make that kind of decision when the full moon hits. We have to make some choices for you, whether you like it or not."

Agatha was determined.

"I will teach him to master the wolf. It can be done. Paradeus was able to do it and I'm his descendant. His blood flows through me and with the Bite I passed it to Nick. That has to account for something."

"Maybe it will and maybe it won't," Buren sighed, leaning back on the sofa. "We can't take that chance. I would feel better if on the first full moon if Nick was securely put away."

"And I think the confinement could be detrimental. If the wolf feels trapped it could be worse. He could hurt himself."

Nick was feeling like a toy being pulled between arguing children.

"That's enough," he said sharply. "I can make that decision before the time comes. Agatha will teach me what she can and if I'm not confident about my ability to control the wolf then I will let you lock me up. I don't want to hurt anyone. If I can't control it, you'll have to kill me."

"No!" cried Agatha. That was not an option. "There's no reason why you can't overcome the infection. I won't let it destroy you. I won't let that happen."

Buren laid his hand on her knee in a reassuring manner.

"We'll do our best, but Nick understands the risks of taking the Bite."

Agatha felt the burn of tears. She didn't know yet if she had truly saved Nick's life or merely delayed the inevitable.

CHAPTER TWENTY-NINE

"However enticing its scent or lovely its bloom, a rose still has thorns"
Olivia Morgan-Townes, author "Women United"

It had been three years since Dirk's last visit to Perth. The journey had been delightful, traveling along the southern coast of the continent by airship with stops at Melbourne, Adelaide and Esperance before arriving at his intended destination. He had taken passage on board a second class workman's ship to avoid attracting attention. He was sure that by now his father had reported him for his attack on Nick. The Guardianship was not swift to react when it came to situations like that, but he was taking no chances. He had injured a human, not an elf or a fae. Had his victim been an elf or a fae they would have issued a bulletin across the country and he would be hunted down. Elves didn't really put much effort into human affairs, even if it involved a Sauvage. They talked a good game, but their inaction was legendary.

Dirk hung his head out the window of the airship's passenger compartment to look down on the sprawling city. It curved around a deep harbor filled with ships. The multitude of masts created a forest of commerce. His eyes searched the rooftops and streets until he found what he was after. From three hundred feet up he could make out the familiar building and gardens of the Russian Ambassador's property on Murray Avenue. He had already done his research to learn that Anatoly Goreyevskiy was still in residence. The old Birthright was going to be surprised to see him.

"A visitor, Mr. Ambassador," announced the butler.

Anatoly peered up from his book. He had chosen to take tea in the rose garden that afternoon and wasn't expecting company.

"Who is it?"

Before the tailored butler could answer, Dirk stepped out of the shadows behind him. He stepped forward with measured strides. He studied the Birthright with calculating eyes. The thick black beard was mostly grey now. His wide shoulders seemed to have collapsed inwards. There was little left of the powerful man Dirk remembered. Apparently grief had devoured him.

The book fell to the ground at Anatoly's feet. He stared, mouth agape, at the ghost who had invaded his sanctuary.

The butler obediently retreated.

"What the hell are you doing here?" Anatoly demanded, remaining seated. He couldn't trust that his legs would support him in his state of shock. "Why didn't your father kill you?"

Dirk chuckled, slowly making his way around the rose garden. He sampled the various blossoms to choose the richest fragrance.

"Because he's weak," he answered with a smirk. "My mother begged him to spare my life and the old fool couldn't bring himself to break her heart. So he built me a concrete coffin where I spent two years worth of full moons. I buried my wolf in that coffin every time the full moon rose."

He plucked a heady dark red bloom and held it to his nostrils. It had a sharp spicy scent.

"That was your daughter's gift to me," he went on, circling around his prey. He leaned close to Anatoly's ear. "She blessed me with her Bite. Now I know so much more about her. She was a self-centered, arrogant, greedy little bitch. She wanted the world on a platter and so do I."

Anatoly turned to stare into maddened eyes. Now he understood how Dirk had come to be like this. He had been confined during the full moon in much the same way as his ancestors. It was a technique to create berserkers. Immediately after receiving the Bite, a human would be sealed in a stone room until the first full moon. They would have no contact with the outside world. The wolf would eat away at their sanity as they endured endless days of misery, pain and fear with no way to channel their newfound power in a healthy manner. They went insane. It was how monsters were made.

His health was too poor to take this pup by the throat and put him on his back, where he belonged. After Natassia's suicide he had all but given up on living. Looking at Dirk he realised that in a strange way it was like having her back. Birthrights looked upon their Sauvage as a sort of offspring. The Sauvage assumed many of their Birthright's habits and personality traits through the infection. He could hear the pompous tone in Dirk's voice so much like Natassia's. Dirk had even picked a red rose called Superior, Natassia's favourite. Her influence was alive in Dirk.

"What do you want from me?" he asked, eyes narrowed.

"I want you to help me raise an army."

"For what?"

Dirk picked up the empty chair beside Anatoly and set it down across from him so they were face to face. He reclined negligently, legs crossed at the ankles. He continued to breathe in the rose's spicy floral scent.

"I want werewolves to rule this continent. Those high and mighty elves will answer to us for once and humans will know we aren't their pets or their pariahs. Werewolves aren't going to bow down to anyone anymore. I want a place where we are royalty. I want werewolves to take back what we lost when our ancestors were slaughtered and scattered across the globe. This will be our nation."

It was a grand scheme, so reminiscent of Natassia's desire to become a member of bigger and better social circles. It sounded so much like what she would have wanted.

"It could take years to assemble an army of Birthrights large enough to attempt such a coup," said Anatoly. He wasn't turning the idea down, he was merely pointing out the difficulties inherent to such a plan.

"I don't need an army of Birthrights," Dirk sneered. "I only need enough Birthrights to make an army of Sauvage. We can create all the soldiers we need."

Anatoly shook his head. He knew better than Dirk the dangers of forming a Sauvage army.

"You seem to have forgotten our history," he said. "Paradeus attempted to unite werewolves three hundred years ago and he was defeated. Now we are persecuted. Do you know what will happen if you fail at this?"

Dirk leaned forward. His expression was chilling.

"What makes you think I'll fail?"

"No offense, but you're not Paradeus," Anatoly remarked.

"I don't have to be Paradeus when I have his descendant as my mate," Dirk replied smugly. He leaned back. "And I will."

"I wasn't aware anyone had traced his bloodline to find a living descendant," said Anatoly with an amount of suspicion. "It's believed he never took a mate. How did you locate this relative?"

"I've done very tedious research to trace that lineage to the modern day. It's taken me almost three years to put it together, but I've found the documentation to prove it. He bred with his Birthright. She was a companion in the court of Beranger, Comte de Manville, in Normandia. She took Paradeus as a lover while he was a human soldier. Before he was sent to the front lines in the battle of La Fleche he asked for the Bite to improve his chances of returning to her. Unbeknownst to Paradeus, she bore him a son while he was at war. We know Paradeus and his lover were executed after the rebellion was brought to its knees, but their son survived. His descendant was born on a reservation in the UAT. Only those closest to the bloodline know. She's here in Australia now. Her name is Agatha Buchanan."

"By Gods," Anatoly breathed. He took in the hardened glint of Dirk's eyes. "You're serious."

"Did you think I wasn't?"

"I thought you had plans, I didn't think you had already begun to take action. You mean to do this."

"I mean to become the Alpha King. Are you with me?"

To refuse was to deny his heritage and to risk being on the wrong side of an ugly war. Yet Anatoly was a diplomat above all else. He could see another way to accomplish Dirk's goal with less bloodshed.

"I will support you if you allow me to pursue another alternative to an all out war," he said. "This is a young country with a fairly small population as yet-"

"Which will it make that much easier to dominate."

The older werewolf shook his head disapprovingly. Such reckless behavior was a recipe for ruin.

"I have tremendous influence with both the Victorian government and the High Council. If we bring in large numbers of Birthrights here they will not be able to ignore our presence. We can petition both courts to recognize our rights as an equal race. There does not need to be any blood spilled."

"I'm not going to give them the opportunity to reject us. They're going to feel our teeth as we rip our way through them. We aren't their equals, we're their masters. Are you with me?"

Anatoly saw no way to avoid a brutal confrontation. He, too, dreamed of werewolves being the apex predators they were born to be. He never expected a new rebellion would rise in his lifetime. This was his chance to make amends to his daughter's memory and was she had left behind in Dirk. He still had reservations about how the events would unfold.

"What if the Birthrights are resistant to your plans?" he asked. "Giving the Bite is forbidden."

"I have access to gold and sapphire mines. They'll be well compensated for their efforts."

"What do you plan to do about the massive rural areas? How will you control such a large territory?"

"I'm in negotiations with the dingoes," Dirk answered. He grinned crookedly. "Wollaweroo is a tough nut to crack, but I can convince them to work for me. They make excellent spies and their communication skills are second to none. There isn't anything that happens on this continent that they don't know about."

Impressed with Dirk's well laid plans, Anatoly could not refuse.

"Very well," he relented. "I will make contact with my people in Russia. It will take some time to convince them, but I think I can get you your army."

Dirk nodded with satisfaction.

"Good. I have several American Birthrights to meet with back in Sydney. Between our forces, we will squeeze this country into submission."

He breathed deeply of the rose before crushing it in his fist.

CHAPTER THIRTY

"A man's relationship with his father prepares him for the day he must raise his own son."
Barker Buchanan

The twins responded to Nick's change with different reactions. Luna was as calm and unruffled as ever, but Logan was unsettled around his father. He did not welcome Nick's touch and was vocal about his rejection. Logan would stiffen and scream if Nick picked him up. The slightest contact sent the infant into paroxysms of wailing and kicking. It was a blade in Nick's heart each time his son refused his embrace. He sought Bloem's advice because he didn't want to burden Agatha with another problem. She was already under the pressure of his upcoming full moon.

Bloem sat on the sofa in the salon at Gilgai, cradling Logan in her slender arms. She had lost considerable weight in the months since Lars' death, making her slim elf physique even more gaunt and hollow. The bones in her elegant face pressed against wan skin and her eyes had lost their brilliant glow.

Buren had confessed to Nick that he was afraid she was allowing herself to waste away and there was nothing he could do. She existed in a twilight state of grief, unable to rejoin the living. It was decided to move Bloem to Gilgai, although it was the site of Lars' killing, in an attempt to remove her from the darkness she had created for herself at Willowbrook. It would offer Bloem the opportunity to experience the joys of new life with Logan and Luna. Buren hoped it would give her a reason to rise from the well of her despair and learn to enjoy life again. It was also a blessing for Agatha to have more female company. There was concern that Bloem would have a negative reaction to Nick being a Sauvage but she accepted him with cordial familiarity. Through her knowledge of how the infection worked, she had no fear of him. Agatha's influence was a positive one.

"I don't know why Logan reacts like that," Nick said, exasperated. He paced by the window, his frustration clear in his tense posture. "It's been like this since I took the Bite. Luna doesn't cry when I hold her, but Logan won't let me touch him without screaming."

"Have you asked Agatha about it?" Bloem inquired, gazing at the chubby face asleep in her arms.

"I think she's avoiding it," he answered. "I've tried to bring it up, but she shrugs it off and says he'll come around in time. I don't want to put any more stress on her right now either, but I just don't understand it."

Bloem was upset with Agatha for skirting an important issue. It was her responsibility to explain these situations to Nick.

"Go get Agatha," she said.

Nick located his wife in the kitchen with Mrs. MacLeach. Luna was in the portable cradle in the corner. At least his daughter wasn't afraid of him. He reassured himself of that by picking her up and holding her close to his chest. She gurgled and snuggled against him.

"What brings you out here? I thought you were checking the south paddock," observed Agatha with a content smile. It never failed to warm her heart to see Nick with their children, with the current exception of Logan's attitude shift. "Is everything alright?"

"Can I talk to you in the house?" he asked brusquely, putting Luna back in her cradle.

Brows lowered questioningly, she followed him. He was behaving in a peculiarly irritated fashion. She wasn't expecting to find Bloem waiting with Logan in her arms. There was disapproval in Bloem's expression. She felt ambushed. Her defenses went up.

"What's going on?"

"We need to speak about Logan's behavior towards Nick. You

should have addressed it already, but we will discuss it now," said the elf.

"Oh," said Agatha, redness creeping into her face. "That."

"Yes, that," replied Bloem.

Agatha scuffed her toes on the floor in her discomfort at being caught out. She licked her lips nervously.

"I know I should have said something before," she mumbled, eyes downcast. "We can't really do anything about it for now so I let it go."

Nick stood in front of her, trying to read her face. She was plainly distressed, but he was feeling a heightened sense of aggravation.

"About what?" he demanded. "Why won't Logan let me touch him without crying?"

She sighed, expelling pent up energy in a long breath. She met his gaze.

"His wolf is reacting to your wolf."

"I thought you said his wolf part was dormant."

"It is, but it's still there. He'll never be able to change and the wolf is angry. When he's older he'll know how to master it, but he doesn't have that mental or emotional capacity as an infant."

"He doesn't react to you like that," Nick said with mounting frustration.

She put her hand on his arm, squeezing gently to calm him. He was becoming angry, which was out of character for him. The wolf was exerting its influence and he was too distraught to bring it in line.

"Because it's all he's ever known about me," she explained. "You've changed. The wolves have to work it out."

"How? How long will it take?"

"Your wolf is dominant, the alpha male. His wolf is giving in to you by being submissive. He's a baby. He doesn't understand what to do or why it's happening. He can't do anything but cry. Give him time to adjust. You can't force it."

Nick let out a loud groan of exasperation, raking his fingers through his hair.

"Then why doesn't Luna cry?"

"She's female. It's her nature to be submissive to an alpha male." To his baffled expression she said, "A male child will naturally want to challenge its father, but Logan can't, really. His wolf knows that. He'll learn to accept it, but right now it's something beyond his grasp. He doesn't have any other outlet."

Nick was forced to accept that there would be better days ahead with his son. In the meantime, he would have to deal with the fussing and screaming. He wasn't going to stop showing affection to his son. His wolf would have to learn to back off.

Bloem nodded, satisfied that Agatha had finally explained it. Logan whimpered in his sleep and she readjusted her hold on him. It was a blessing to be in a house filled with life and love. She knew she needed to let go of her grief over Lars and start to regain her health. Buren was worried to death about her and so were Nick and Agatha. She had more to live for.

Nick's ubiquitous placid nature became even more antagonistic as the full moon approached. He had not told his men that he was Sauvage and they had no reason to suspect. They merely assumed that he was carrying residual anger and resentment from the Elders' decision and all the violence that had played out in recent months. He lost his temper without warning and at one point raised a fist to a new station hand that accidentally uprooted an established vine. The men tried to ignore it, but his actions were so out of character that they went to Agatha with their grievances on a day when Nick was away from the station.

Ed spoke on behalf of the hands. He stood in the salon with Danny Rivers. The brothers Spencer and Rake Jones flanked him. All held their hats in wringing hands. Though they knew Agatha to be a somewhat shy person, she was still the Boss's wife and a distracting piece of female flesh.

Agatha was seated on the sofa with Luna in her lap. Logan was lying on a blanket on the floor at her feet.

"I know things have been rough lately," Ed said, trying not to mumble in his nervousness. "And we understand what the Boss has been through. Both of you. But he's been acting so strange. We don't know what to do. He almost hit Danny the other day."

Agatha realised it was time to have *the talk* with Nick. She had been trying to find the right way to explain the transition during the full moon, but in truth she wasn't familiar with Sauvage. There were four days until it happened to him for the first time and she was obligated to make it as non-terrifying as possible. She just wasn't sure how to accomplish that.

"I'll speak with him when he gets back," she assured them. "I'm sorry if he's done anything to alarm you. He has been under terrible stress. I'll let him know you're concerned."

Agatha was in a difficult position. These men would follow Nick through hell and back. A few of them already had. They did not deserve to be kept in the dark about his condition, yet she knew that they were still reeling from Dirk's attack and what it had cost. Three of their friends were dead because of a Sauvage. Was their respect and devotion to Nick strong enough to get beyond their hatred?

"Ed, could I speak with you a moment in private?" she asked.

The other men filed out, leaving Edison alone with the Boss's wife.

He stood near the door as if he might need to escape. He couldn't imagine what Agatha would have to say to him. She rarely spoke to the station hands and when she did it was with Nick by her side. The men all knew and accepted that she was a werewolf, but she still seemed to feel the need to use Nick as a shield. For her to want to address him without the Boss present was unsettling.

"You've worked for Nick a long time, haven't you?" she inquired, shifting Luna to her other arm.

"Yes, ma'am," he answered. He watched her face for clues. She was a blank slate. "About twenty years, I'd say. I wouldn't be here today if not for him."

She cocked her head, an invitation for him to explain. Ed's smile was somewhat timid. He continued to mangle the hat in his hands as he spoke.

"I came to Australia through the penal system," he confessed. "I was convicted of stealing back in Britain and I was sent here on a convict ship."

Agatha's brows went up significantly. She would not have suspected he had a criminal past. He was as honest and upstanding a man as she had ever met.

"I know what you're thinking," he hurried to say. "But I've been on the right side of the law since I came to Gilgai. Nick set me straight and I've never let him down."

"How did you get to Gilgai?" she asked.

"I escaped from Newtown during the revolt and went into the bush like most of the men who got away. I stole what I needed as I went. I'm not proud of it. I just kept going further inland from the coast until I reached Falmormath. I stumbled onto Gilgai, really. I planned to just take a few things from the house, but when I came through the orchards I found the Boss in the graveyard, digging a hole for his mum. She'd just passed the night before. He was a right mess, couldn't see anything through his tears. He wasn't making a dent in the dirt, so I took over. I helped him bury his mum and he was so grateful he offered me a job. He didn't ask any questions, so I just started working here and that was that." He paused. "I have to say you're a much better wife than the first Mrs. Buchanan. You've made him a very happy man."

Agatha smiled appreciatively. It had taken courage to share his history. He had also provided another piece to the puzzle that was Nick's past. She had not asked him again about his parents after Logan and Luna were born. Neither of them spoke about what was dead and buried. She now had Nick's future in her hands. She was about to jump in with both feet by sharing Nick's secret with him.

"I need to tell you something, Ed," she began, keeping her eyes on his wary face. "I have to trust you right now and from what you've just told me, I think I can."

He nodded, not knowing what to expect.

"The night Nick was in the accident with the steam wagon, I had to do something I've never done before," she said. She hesitated, heart pounding. "I gave him the Bite and made him a Sauvage. It was the only way I could save his life."

Ed digested the information in silence. It answered many questions about Nick's change in behavior. It was somewhat frightening to hear, but it made no difference in how Ed was going to treat his Boss. Nick obviously needed more support and understanding now than ever before. Ed would be there for him. He owed Nick his very life. He would give it to him without a second thought if it came to it.

"Thank you for telling me," he said. "I'll do what I can to keep the boys from finding out, or if they do I'll make sure it stays here on the station. No one's going to take the Boss away from us. Don't worry, Missus." Ed turned to leave, but paused to look back at her. "I don't know what it took to make you do it, but thank you for saving his life."

<hr>

That night in bed, relaxing after a strenuous sexual work out, she brought up the subject of the full moon.

Nick lay on his side, tracing trails of perspiration on her skin with his fingertips. He felt more alive than at any point in his life. There was more energy and passion in him now that when he had been a young man. It was all due to the wolf that resided within him and he had her to thank for that.

"I need to talk to you about what's happening to you," she said, looking into his distracted eyes. He was staring at her damp naked beauty with hungry appreciation. "About the full moon that's coming up. The men have noticed the change in your behavior and they came to me."

His gaze focused quickly, connecting with hers.

"I haven't been myself, that's true," he admitted with chagrin. He recognized the change in himself and was at a loss to correct it. "I can't seem to keep my temper in check. I almost hit Danny when he ripped out a one of the vines. It was an accident. I got so angry so quickly that I almost couldn't stop myself. I was so embarrassed that I didn't even apologise. I just walked away. I should apologise."

"I told Ed the truth."

"What?" He sat up quickly.

"You need him on your side in this," she said. He relaxed, acknowledging that she was right. "The wolf is testing you. It's pushing its boundaries to see what you'll let it get away with. You have to keep it from dominating your personality. You aren't a violent man, so you need to show it that you won't allow it to become aggressive."

"How? It just happens. I don't even realize it until after I've done it."

"You have to think of it more like the physical embodiment of an emotion, not like the actual animal. It's more like a knee-jerk reaction right now. You have to learn to control it like any other emotion. You don't allow sadness or jealousy or even happiness to just take over. It has to learn that you are in charge of when it gets to come out. It may be tempting to give in because it feels good. That's when you have to consciously work harder to maintain control. I'm not saying this will be easy or painless. I can't honestly tell you what to expect when you actually change."

Nick flopped onto his back, hands resting on his stomach. He stared at the ceiling, wishing it would open to reveal the mysteries of life.

"Will I look like Dirk?"

She shrugged, turning onto her belly. He reached out and smoothed his palm over the swell of her rump.

"The more control you have over it the more wolf-like you'll be. Most people are so afraid of it that they let go of any kind of power they might have over it. They don't know how to safely let it out because they're resisting it. It fights against the human half and can't completely emerge. That's when it becomes something like Dirk. I'm hoping you'll be able to shed your skin like I can, but I don't know how difficult that might be for you."

He turned to face her, his gaze sharp.

"Show me how you do it."

Agatha was no longer afraid to show him everything about her Birthright nature. She had been hesitant early in their relationship to reveal her other form because it was disturbing to witness the actual change, but he needed her tutoring now. She rose up on hands and knees. Without preamble, she allowed her skin to split and slough off. It fell onto the quilt in a pile of bloody strips. In the guise of a grey and white wolf, she stood above him. She shook out her flattened pelt to fluff it, her tail whipping loudly.

Nick stared wordlessly. It was quick and surprisingly less gory than he had expected. The skin scraps were wet with blood on one side, but it hadn't been a violent or particularly bloody event. He reached out to brush her fur with his hands. It had a pleasantly coarse texture, thicker and heavier than a dog's. He ran his fingers along her underside, finding eight prominent nipples. She growled softly when he tweaked one. He let go and lay back with a contented smirk.

A cloud of fur filled the air as she changed back. It floated down to the bed and onto the floor in thick clumps. She frowned at the debris, kneeling in the middle of her old skin and fur.

"Well, I've made quite the mess," she muttered. "I don't suppose it's fair to ask Mrs. MacLeach to clean it up. I'd best get the broom."

CHAPTER THIRTY-ONE

"There is no life without freedom"
Paradeus, werewolf revolutionary

Nick struggled daily to maintain his usual calm demeanor. It was becoming more difficult as the full moon neared, but he felt that he mastered it sufficiently to avoid the concrete room at Buren's. If he became too wild the first time, he would accept the offer in the future.

The day before the moon reached its bloated zenith, Agatha took him out into the bush. It was safer to be as far away from human habitation as possible. It was a warm night and Nick was feeling the feverish preview of what awaited him. They camped by a small creek but did not light a fire. They did not want to draw attention to their presence should anyone be traveling in the area. If any escaped convicts happened to cross their path it would go badly for the former prisoners.

Agatha was asleep against him when the moon's influence reached its peak at dawn.

From a dead sleep, Nick let out a scream, suddenly feeling the gnawing presence of the wolf inside him. It pawed against his skin with fury, trying to push its way out. It was growing within his body and it was demanding to be set free.

Agatha leaped to her feet. She watched helplessly as he contorted in agony, straining to keep the wolf at bay. She could see his skin stretching on his arms and bulging under his jaw as the wolf pressed outward against the fragile barrier of his flesh.

His screams resounded off the hillsides.

"Don't fight it," she told him furiously. "This is what you are, Nick. Let the wolf out."

He looked up at her with terror stricken eyes a moment before his skin peeled away to expose the dark fur of the wolf beneath. It struggled, clawing and tearing at his flesh and clothes. He shrieked with pure agony as it burst free from the last vestiges of his human body. His scream became the howling cry of a newly born werewolf.

He hunched over the torn shreds of his human remains, breathing heavily.

While he hadn't achieved Agatha's wolf shape, he was more wolf-like than Dirk. He could stand on his reshaped hind legs like a man, but it was more comfortable on all fours. His front paws were longer than that of a wolf with flexible digits for toes. Thickly hooked claws tipped those digits, matching those on his long back feet. His ribcage was rounded like a wolf's and he had a shorter neck than Dirk's. Although his face retained no human characteristics, his eyes were still blue. His head was awkwardly heavy, being fully that of a wolf. His fur was charcoal grey down his back, blending into a silvery white on his chest and belly. Sitting back on his haunches, he realised bemusedly that he had a weighty appendage protruding from the top of his flanks in the form of a furry tail. He gave it a preemptory wag to test his ability to use it. It worked.

"How do you feel?" she asked with a beaming smile.

He found he couldn't speak but his tail thundered on the ground in response.

It was exhilarating. There was nothing holding him back from giving in to his basic impulses. He could feel the pounding of the universe's heart all around him. It was like being enveloped in a giant womb of wilderness.

"Are you ready to hunt?" she asked with a gleam in her eye.

The tail pounded again. His system was revving like an airship's engine. He had to unleash it or he would explode.

Agatha joyously flung off her skin and joined him. They nuzzled each other with unabashed ecstasy, learning new ways to communicate with body language. With an inviting yip she bounded forward. She glanced back over her shoulder to see the awkwardness in his movements as he adjusted to coordinating four legs instead of two. He took a few unsteady steps towards her, deliberately placing his feet to keep his balance. After several steps he began to realise it was not as complicated as he thought. He began to gain confidence.

He suddenly bolted past her in a burst of speed, disappearing into the night shrouded bushes. She lunged after him in excitement.

Nick stumbled more than once as he negotiated the terrain on his new legs. The ground came up hard to meet him and he tumbled head over tail. He didn't let it slow him down. He was back on his feet in a flash, racing after Agatha like a hound on a fox.

She was fleet of foot, sailing over the landscape with enviable ease. This was her comfort zone. The earth flew by under her paws.

They reached an open rise and slowed to enjoy the view. He stood beside her in the glow of the sunrise, ears arched forward.

The valley stretched out below them, bathed in nascent light. Trees glittered as the wind caught their leaves and they shivered in the pale light. The valley seemed to go on forever, meeting the sky's edge and flowing beyond the horizon.

They caught the scent of prey at the same time as the breeze brought it up the slope. It was familiar to Nick. He had smelled kangaroo before, but not like this. It was so much thicker, coalescing on his palate more like a flavour than an odor. The mob was resting quietly near a stand of gum trees but he knew what they were capable of. He'd seen what one had done to Agatha so he was hesitant to offer pursuit.

Agatha had no such reservations. She had a score to settle with the beasts. She lunged down the hill at a brisk clip. She had already selected the one she wanted.

Nick galloped in an ungainly fashion downhill, having problems with the angle of the land and his hind end gaining on his front end. Gravity was not something to be trifled with. He went down again, rolling to the bottom of the slope in an undignified heap. He hopped up, shook off and chased after Agatha.

She had already reached the mob, sending them fleeing towards the trees. She ignored all but the one she had her sights set on; a small male. She didn't know if Nick would be able to keep up, but she could see out of the corner of her eye that he was only a few strides off. He was holding his own fairly well for his first time out.

He followed her lead as she spurred herself on to cut the small male from the mob. He saw that she had a particular scrubber in her scope and was pacing it with deliberate care. It tried to rejoin the mob, bounding to the right in one massive leap. He headed it off. It turned again and he was able to match its move. It was amazing.

Agatha drove the kangaroo into a stand of trees, her teeth gnashing at its flank. It chuffed in panic, finding no way to escape. They needed to bring it down before it could stop and make a stand. If it faced them directly there was a chance it could use its hind claws to injure one or both of them. Nick was not sure enough yet on his canine legs to be able to avoid a direct strike.

Nick saw her jaws snapping at the scrubber's powerfully leaping hindquarters. The wolf instinctively responded. He wasn't aware of making the move, but he found himself suddenly on the scrubber's back with all his claws sunk into its blue-grey hide. The creature bleated pathetically, trying to dislodge him. He clung to the animal's lurching back, closing his jaws on the nape of its neck. He heard and felt the crack of its vertebrae as they shattered in his mouth. The kangaroo's forward momentum stopped at once and he rode it to the ground in a plume of dirt, leaves and rocks. His jaws were locked on its neck, drinking in the blood that flowed from the wound.

Agatha was incredibly proud that he had made his first kill. She approached with a happy bounce in her step only to be met by bared teeth and flattened ears. He lowered himself in a pseudo submissive posture, still flashing his teeth. He was guarding his kill.

She was tempted to let him keep it and enjoy the spoils of their effort, but he needed to learn that they were a team and there was sharing involved. It was a lesson for all young werewolves. They had to learn the hierarchy of the pack quickly.

Hackles up, she took a warning step toward him. He snapped at her, lowering himself further to the ground. He wasn't defying her exactly, but he wasn't rolling over either. He had tasted blood and it gave the wolf a boost of courage to push its limits. He could feel its power growing, taking control of his actions.

He pushed back. He forced himself to think of what made him human. Keeping his mind focused on memories of his life as a man he was able to bring it under control. It acquiesced to his demands. His snarling ceased. That was the answer to keeping it in check. He had discovered the means to subdue it. He had been a man first. The wolf could not force him to forget that.

He turned over, displaying his belly.

Agatha could not allow his insolence to go unpunished, though she knew it was not his fault. The wolf had made an attempt to take over. He had successfully restrained it, but he had given it a moment to challenge her and that was not acceptable.

She gently gripped his throat in her teeth and growled. He understood his mistake.

Releasing him, she stood over the warm carcass. He came up beside her, rubbing his muzzle against her cheek for forgiveness. She returned the gesture of affection then took a ripping bite out of the kangaroo's flesh.

Nick was overwhelmed by the scent of blood. Despite his success a moment ago at putting the wolf in its place, he let it come forth to claim its reward. He tore into the scrubber's belly with claws and teeth, dragging organs out onto the grass to devour them with bestial satisfaction. The flavours in his mouth were more intoxicating than wine. He pulled and tugged to get all the viscera free of the abdominal cavity. Agatha reached in to assist him in getting to the juiciest parts. Together they gorged on the kangaroo's organs and meat until the sun fully appeared and they could swallow no more.

Sated, they lay on the crimson smeared grass. She rested her head on his ribs and dozed off.

Nick remained awake, drinking in the sights and sounds around him. He had never noticed how the trees moved in such a flexible dance as the wind came through their limber branches. The bright glow of the sun was radiant beyond anything he had seen in his life. He could hear birds chattering a mile away. He could hear their wings beating as they took to the sky. The world was so much more intense and beautiful than he had realised. He didn't regret his decision to become a Sauvage, but he was saddened that he couldn't have experienced this as a human.

As the afternoon wore on, the full moon's hold over him began to wane. As Agatha watched, patches of dark grey fur began to fall away leaving pink skin exposed. It took nearly an hour for the transformation back to his human shape to be complete. The wolf was reluctant to go back into hiding. Nick groaned in pain, but it was not the same depth of pain as his initial change to wolfshape. She waited patiently for him to finish before shedding her own fur and joining him naked in the grass.

His blue eyes searched the sky, convincing himself that the morning's escapade had not been a dream. He turned his head and found himself gazing at the eviscerated carcass of the kangaroo a few feet away. Raising his hands, he stared at the dark red stains on his skin. It was real.

"How do you feel?" she asked timidly, fearing his response.

He sat up, swirling his tongue around inside his mouth. He spat a translucent red stream of saliva onto the ground.

"I did that," he said, nodding towards the dead kangaroo.

"You certainly did," she answered with a mother's pride. "I hadn't thought you'd take to it so naturally. You still need to work on keeping the wolf under control, but you did very well for your first time. Did you…enjoy it?"

He considered the question. To say no would be a lie. To say yes would be to admit that he liked the animal side of himself.

"It was…" he struggled for the right words. He met her expectant gaze. "Unbelievable."

She laughed and flung herself on top of him. Their bloodied, slippery bodies collided with a wet smack.

The moon's effects hadn't entirely worn off. There was enough of the wolf's power to give rise to a new hunger. Nick grabbed her around the waist with both hands, pinning her hips in place. She sat upright, breasts bouncing. He ran his hands along her ribs as she wriggled energetically in his grasp. His fingers painted her skin with blood. She was slick in his grip, sliding along the length of his body. He felt his penis swelling in anticipation, throbbing with an aching need. He maneuvered her into position to spear himself inside her inviting depths. She contracted her vaginal muscles, squeezing him firmly. With a slow, deliberate motion she began to rise up then come back down quickly. She used this rhythm until he was ready to scream with the pulsing force building in his loins. He clenched his hands on her hips and shoved one final time inside her, bringing forth their mutual climax.

Agatha sank down on top of him, drawing patterns in the blood on his chest. She licked around one nipple, savouring the combined saltiness of the blood and his sweat. She raised her mouth to his and forced her tongue past his lips. He met its inquisitiveness with his own tongue, dueling playfully.

"We can do this every full moon, if you want," she said, leaning back. "We'll need to for awhile until you have complete control. It takes practice."

He reached up and fondled her enticing breasts. He never grew tired of touching her.

"I'd like that," he sighed. "But we can't leave Gilgai. We have to make sure no one sees us. The Elders have ruled that you can't leave the property and if they find out what I am…" He shook his head. "I don't know if we can stay here."

Agatha got to her feet, golden eyes burning down on him.

"What do you mean?"

Nick sat up, feeling vulnerable in his naked state. He'd brought extra clothing, but it was back at their campsite. That was miles away. Then he realised he had no reason to be ashamed or anxious. He was in his element now. His natural state was ideal for this situation.

"I won't make this another reservation where you're a prisoner. You came to Australia for freedom and so help me, you'll have it. I'll sell Gilgai and we'll find a place where we can both live in peace."

She was horrified that he would think it was necessary to leave this place for her sake.

"No," she said, angry tears stinging her eyes. "This is your home, our home. I don't care if I can't leave it, I don't want to leave it. The Rez was a prison. This is paradise. Please don't make me leave."

It struck him then that she was frightened by the idea of deserting Gilgai. She had established a home for herself and her children. Abandoning that was like losing her identity, her security. She had left one familiar life by coming to Australia, now he was talking about robbing her of the life she had built in Falmormath. She would rather live out her future within the confines of the station than be torn away from what she had come to love about it.

"You're alright with being confined to Gilgai?" he asked unsurely. "You don't feel trapped?"

"No." A tear trickled down her cheek. "I don't need to go anywhere. I don't like the people in town and they don't like me. I don't have any friends besides Buren and Bloem. They can visit any time they like. I have everything I want and need right here. I have you and our children."

Nick clambered to his feet, glancing down at the red streaks over his body. He looked at her, seeing the blood that caked her skin as well. They had slaughtered an animal and bathed in its blood, had sex while covered in it. Its flesh filled his stomach. They had staked a claim to their territory. He knew they could not leave it.

"You're right," he agreed. He stepped forward and took her in his arms. There were rusty chunks of dried blood in her hair that scratched his cheek. "We have our home right here. We aren't going anywhere."

CHAPTER THIRTY-TWO

"Honesty should be followed wherever it leads."
John Nigel, philosopher

Life resumed a somewhat normal pace at Gilgai. Nick threw himself into his new wine making venture with complete abandon. He continued to convert the station into a vineyard and the buildings into production facilities. He was in the paddocks during the long summer days, leaving Agatha home with the babies who were developing into interactive individuals. His evenings were spent with his family, relaxing and playing with Luna while attempting to make peace with Logan. He still had not said anything to the station hands about being Sauvage.

Bloem began to emerge from the shadow of her grief. An unexpected visit from her daughter, Beshka, seemed to provide the cure.

Beshka was a slightly shorter version of her mother. She was the youngest of the van Amersvoot children and lived in Sydney while attending university. She had come home briefly for her brother's funeral before returning to the city for final exams. Now, finished with the semester, she had decided to return home for her mother's sake. She was staying at Willowbrook with her father while Bloem remained at Gilgai. She understood that her mother needed time to recover.

On a lazy evening, after Nick's third full moon, the two families gathered for a relaxing meal under the sky in the garden. Beshka would be returning to Sydney in a few days. There was a jovial atmosphere among the diners, with plenty of laughter echoing through the orchard and into the yard.

Beshka held Logan, bouncing the heavy baby on her thigh. He had a fist stuffed in his mouth that barely muffled his delighted squeals. It was difficult for Nick to watch, but he knew that he had to be patient. The time would come when Logan would welcome his touch again.

Agatha knew Beshka from her time in Eliza's bridal boot camp. She had encountered the pair in a passionate kiss which led to the disclosure of the fact that the young elf was sexually involved with Eliza. Homosexuality among Birthrights was practically nonexistent. Their animal drive to reproduce was not something that could be altered or explained. They instinctively sought out mates of the opposite gender. Beshka and Eliza's affair was something Agatha couldn't easily comprehend, other than to rationalize that two people could love one another in an untraditional manner. She thought she understood it better now being with Nick. They were of different races and, with her non-human grasp of Victorian society's standards, she equated it with the unconventional relationship between the women.

As she watched Beshka playing with Logan, she commented, "It's too bad you and Eliza can't have children."

Beshka had not thought it necessary to instruct Agatha against mentioning her relationship with Eliza. She had assumed it was an unspoken understanding that it be kept private. Her face went white with horror at Agatha's innocent remark.

"What about you and Eliza?" Buren demanded, putting his wine glass down so hard the stem snapped. French Bordeaux went flowing across the table in a dark red tide.

"It's not what you're thinking," Beshka answered with an accusing look at Agatha.

Before Nick could prevent it, Agatha said to her, "What's wrong? You told me you loved Eliza."

"This isn't the time or place to talk about it," Nick told her sternly. He wished he could make her understand without going into a long, involved conversation. Her confused eyes met his. "I'll explain it to you later, alone."

"How long have you and Eliza been together?" inquired Bloem with brows arched over her questioning eyes.

Bloem had a renewed radiance. Her appetite had returned and her skin was filling out. She spent most of her time in the garden and orchards, reconnecting with the essence of the natural world. It was with the beneficial aid of the elements that she was able to heal. She was recovering slowly but steadily. The pain of Lars' death would never truly be gone, but it was becoming tolerable. She had come to accept as well that Dirk's fate was sealed. Two of her children were lost to her, but she had Beshka to keep her going.

Buren was relieved to see her blossoming once more. She had taken Lars' death harder than he could have expected. He had anticipated a dark time of grief, but he had not predicted the intensity of her depression. She had all but given up living. He had thought he was losing her until Beshka returned from Sydney to find her mother falling apart. Having their daughter home had brought Bloem out of her self-imposed bereavement. She had made the turn back to wellness.

He had heard nothing from Holt. He wasn't sure if that was bad sign or a blessing. He had considered contacting him, but decided he didn't want to know. As long as Dirk never returned it didn't matter if he was alive or dead. Now he had to contend with his daughter's sexual proclivity. Gods, would it never end?

"Since I moved in with her at the beginning of school," said Beshka somewhat defensively. "And yes, I do love her. We love each other very much."

"Aren't there any young men you like?" Buren ground out. He wasn't precisely against his daughter's choice, but it ended any hope for grandchildren like a door slamming shut.

"A few," Beshka replied with a derogatory sniff. "Eliza could teach them a thing or two."

Buren's expression might have been comical under other circumstances. He looked ready to burst a blood vessel. That sort of talk was not acceptable at the dinner table or anywhere else.

"I think we've discussed this enough," said Bloem, always the voice of reason. She laid a hand on her husband's tense arm. "If you're happy then we're happy for you. It would have been considerate if you had told us privately at some point before now, but that is neither here nor there. We shall have to invite Eliza out to Willowbrook to get to know her better. I assume she will be part of your life for some time. It would be nice to meet her formally as your lover and to welcome her into our family."

Buren shuddered at Bloem's generous words, but said nothing. He silently mopped up the spreading wine stain with the napkin Nick offered. He wanted his daughter to get married someday, to have a family of her own. He couldn't very well demand it of her, although he was certain there were fathers who would. With a mental shrug, he decided that if he had been able to accept and continue loving his son as a Sauvage, the least he could do was open his arms to his daughter's female lover. At least this was a secret he wouldn't regret keeping.

After that, the mood brightened.

Agatha was seated next to Bloem, who lovingly cradled Luna in her embrace. Agatha was still confounded by the direction of the conversation, but all seemed to have gone well. Bloem's strength was not back to normal and even the slight weight of the sleeping baby tired her. She placed Luna in her mother's arms. As her fingers brushed Agatha's abdomen she sensed the spark of new life. She smiled, knowing her services would be in demand again.

"It seems there will be another addition to the Buchanan family," she announced. She placed her hand on Agatha's belly, measuring the strength of the life energy that dwelled within. "About mid October, I should think."

"A Birthright baby," Agatha said, looking up at Nick with cheerful eyes.

"It can't be a Birthright. Nick's human," said Beshka, who had not been included in Nick's secret. She didn't know that he had taken the

Bite and no one had thought it necessary to reveal it to her. She was close to her uncle, Holt, and they feared she would tell him. When everyone around her froze with apprehension, she realised what Agatha meant. "By Gods, Nick, are you a Sauvage?"

He nodded, watching her reaction with cool blue eyes.

"Papa, you knew about this?" she asked, turning her horrified gaze to Buren. Her secret paled in comparison to this.

Buren stared at his plate for a moment before answering. It was going to be difficult to make her understand. He met his daughter's accusatory glare.

"We thought it would be best if you didn't know," he told her straightforwardly. "You cannot tell Holt."

It was a shock to her that not only was Nick, the man she knew as her uncle, now a Sauvage, but her father had been aware of it. He had hidden Dirk's condition and that had led to Dirk killing Lars and three other men. What was going to happen to Nick?

"How could you? Look what happened to Dirk," she demanded. She immediately regretted her words. "I'm sorry, Papa. I didn't mean that."

"I know how you feel," Buren replied, keeping his emotions in check. "This was not a decision I made lightly, nor was my decision to protect Dirk made without much deliberation. I weighed the options and chose to do what I felt was right. I don't expect you to agree. He's your brother, as was Lars." His voice caught. "Nick is not like Dirk. Dirk was tainted by the Birthright that gave him the Bite. Whoever she was she suffered from depravity and cruelty that your brother has inherited. He's not in his right mind. Nick has all his faculties about him, as you can plainly see for yourself. You haven't had any reason to suspect he was a Sauvage, have you? You've been here all this time and you never saw anything different about him."

Beshka couldn't refute his statement. There had been nothing in Nick's attitude to alert her to his condition. He was more easily provoked than she remembered, but she had been away for years and could easily have forgotten the finer points of his personality in that time. Details tended to fade as time passed.

"But, still, Papa," she pleaded. "Shouldn't he ask for an exemption?"

Bloem answered with more venom than anyone had heard from her before.

"They will not give him a second chance after the debacle with Dirk. All Sauvage will be under suspicion. We could shout Nick's praises from the hillsides and they wouldn't hear it. They would make an example of him."

Agatha's heart almost spilled out of her chest at the thought of what that meant. Nick clutched her hand in a gesture of comfort. Their eyes met and silent words of encouragement passed between them.

Beshka watched their voiceless exchange and knew that Nick was a different person than her brother. He was stronger man than Dirk had ever been. If her parents believed he had overcome his infection then she could not betray that confidence.

"I will say nothing to Uncle Holt, unless it needs to be said," she told the gathering. She turned beseeching eyes to Nick. "Please don't make me do that."

"If it reaches that point, your father will take care of it. The Guardianship will never need to know," he promised her solemnly. "I wouldn't put you in that position."

She nodded, reassured for the moment. It would always be in the back of her mind.

Beshka returned to Sydney a few days later. Her knowledge of Nick's condition gnawed at her night and day. She finally broke down and told Eliza what she knew. Beshka refused to keep anything from Eliza. As they lay in bed one night she brought up what she had learned about Nick.

"I've been meaning to say something for awhile now about something I found out when I went home," she said. She reclined against a hillside of pillows. "Agatha gave Nick the Bite a few months ago. Apparently, he was badly injured and it was the only way to save his life."

Eliza propped herself up on an elbow, gazing down on Beshka's chagrinned face.

"Copernicus? Sauvage?" She wagged her head, unable to comprehend such a thing. Agatha must have been desperate. "What's he like now?"

"Honestly," Beshka mused, "I couldn't tell the difference. They had to tell me."

Eliza hummed to herself, deep in thought. At one time the news would have come as a terrible shock and a potential blow to her business. She had more werewolf clientele now. Her concerns were closer to home. She knew that if Agatha had been pressed into giving the Bite to her husband, it had been done between consenting adults and did not deserve the judgment of others. Like her relationship with Beshka, it was no one's business what they did together.

"I also told my parents about us."

That got Eliza's attention. She stared into Beshka's worried eyes.

"I can't imagine they were pleased. I don't know what they would think the worst part of it," she muttered gruffly. "The idea that we're both women, that I'm human or that I'm significantly older than their little girl."

"You sound like you're some kind of predator," Beshka admonished. "They were fine with it, after my father picked himself up off the floor. They were hoping for grandchildren. I was their last chance for that."

"I don't see any reason why you can't still give them grandchildren," grunted Eliza, sliding her arm around Beshka's waist and pulling her close. "We'll just have to find you a man for a night. I put up with it for years. All things considered, there are worse hardships than sleeping with a man."

Beshka kissed her and let her hands roam over Eliza's ample breasts. They were warm and soft in her palms.

"I wouldn't feel right being with someone else, man or woman," she said. "And I don't want children anyway."

"Good," Eliza muttered, slipping her fingers between Beshka's legs. "Because I wasn't going to let anyone else have you. I just needed to hear you say it."

The heavy fragrance of moist soil and tropical blossoms filled the air inside the glass walled atrium at Eliza's house. Moisture formed runnels of water on the clear panes. It was where Eliza received her more informal guests, especially if they were fae. The fae had a deep connection to the earth and felt more at ease in the humid setting around the plants and various water features. It was a sanctuary in the midst of mankind's urban sprawl.

She was dressed in a sleeveless Grecian style gown of cream silk with gold cording. It was ideal for spending time the atrium entertaining Holt Threadwell.

He wore a crisp white shirt with a dark brown leather vest and houndstooth trousers. The damp heat didn't faze him. He reclined easily on a cushioned hardwood bench, sipping on lemon barley water.

His duties to the Guardianship left him little time to work on his favor to Buren. It was a personal matter. He had been making discreet inquiries for months, but had received precious little information on the state of the crime and those involved. He fervently hoped to avoid alerting his family of the incident. Any rumors would fly on fairy's wings to Threadwell ears. They were a force to be reckoned with and would not hesitate to pull strings to clear their name. Bloem did not need that on top of everything else.

"What a pleasant surprise to see you here," said Eliza, pouring herself a glass of chilled refreshment. They had already discussed the newest acquisitions to her conservatory. Now it was time to talk business. "I used to see you at my parties all the time. Now you're too busy with Guardianship business to have a social life. Which leads me to believe this is not a casual visit."

Holt inclined his head. She had a shrewd head for business.

"It is not," he agreed. "I've been hearing about an influx of werewolves into Australia over the last year. I was wondering what you might know about that."

She had suspected that this would be his concern. As the primary marriage broker in New South Wales it was no surprise that he would expect her to know more than the average citizen on the street. She had her fingers in too many pies to count. Her local and international network of agents was as extensive and convoluted as a rabbit warren.

"I'm flattered," she said. She took a long slow drink to draw out his anticipation. He was a powerful man in the elf world, but she had prominent allies among all the major races. She could afford to make him sweat. "I have heard about a large number of werewolf immigrants of late. Why does that bring you to my doorstep?"

Holt set his glass down on the mosaic topped table between them. His gaze was direct.

"I'm investigating a report of an attack on a human by a Sauvage. I believe you know both individuals. They are former clients of yours." Eliza's brows rose in query. "The Sauvage is Dirk van Amersvoot and the victim was Copernicus Buchanan."

Eliza's face paled and her hand trembled because she already knew that Nick was Sauvage.

"Copernicus Buchanan? Was he killed?" she asked, disguising her anxiety with a façade of concern.

"Fortunately, he was not. He survived his injuries. What do you know about the two of them?"

Breathing easier, Eliza took another long drink to settle her nerves.

"Copernicus Buchanan is a hard working, decent man. A second generation grazier, not a British import. He was a widower and he came to me for another wife."

"Did you find him one?" Holt asked, studying her face for deception.

"Yes." Her expression betrayed nothing. "A lovely young American woman named Agatha Whistleton."

Holt's eyes narrowed briefly. That was a telling bit of news.

"What part of the American Territories is she from?" he inquired suspiciously.

"I don't know what difference that makes. You're asking about Copernicus Buchanan and Dirk van Amersvoot," she reminded him sharply.

"And now I'm asking a question about Agatha Whistleton," the elf replied with equal irascibility.

"You presume correctly. She's from Colorado." Eliza saw no point in continuing to skirt the issue. "And yes, she's a werewolf. A Birthright."

Holt's nostrils flared.

"Before your blood gets hot, elf, let me remind you that there are no laws against werewolves immigrating to Australia as yet. The Victorian government has not yet made a ruling on their status and your own High Council can't seem to be bothered to decide their fate. They may not be welcome, but they have every right to come here like any human, elf or fae."

"You allowed a werewolf to marry a human?" he bit out.

"They're a good match, if I do say so myself. Agatha comes from venerable stock. I always do research on my brides and I was impressed to discover that she can trace her bloodline back to Paradeus himself. I don't think she realizes how important that is. She's rather humble like her husband."

"Does she understand the potential danger if she gives her husband the Bite?"

Eliza scoffed at his pathetic mother hen attitude. Elves could be so melodramatic when it suited them.

"What happens between husband and wife is no one's business. I realize elves have a corporal law regarding Sauvage, but it's not really up to you to pass judgment on every werewolf in the world. The Paradeus Uprising was three hundred years ago. You elves certainly hold a grudge. If she does give her husband the Bite that's their business. I will stand by that. I strongly encourage you do the same."

Her threat hung in the dank jungle-like air.

"Tell me about Dirk van Amersvoot," Holt said, taking her words under advisement.

Eliza swirled her lemon barley water, listening to the ice cubes clink on the glass.

"He wants Agatha. He's contacted me several times to get information about her," she said with a deep frown. "I don't know what he's about, but he's not well."

Holt's head tipped slightly to the side.

"In what way?" he asked casually.

She picked up on his attempt to sound relaxed, but he was definitely on alert.

"I think his Birthright was unstable. He's just not able to comprehend why Agatha chose a human over him. It's eating him up inside and I don't think he knows how to get over it. Perhaps I shouldn't be surprised he attacked Nick. It's a sign of his illness. Not everyone can handle the infection."

"Very few can," Holt muttered darkly.

Eliza squared him in her forceful gaze. She was a stormcloud about to unleash its ferocity.

"Because they don't receive proper education or treatment," she said to him in a tone like thunder. "Rather than treat them like criminals, we should be taking the time to get them the help they need. A positive attitude towards them can make all the difference. They had a place in society once. Birthrights were human companions for thousands of years. They served us faithfully until we used them to generate war machines. Don't forget that the Sauvage were human first. Brave and devoted men stepped up to take the Bite to serve their masters. When Paradeus made a stand, humans and elves took offense. And why? The Sauvage wanted independence, so they fought for it. We created the problem by turning their infection to our advantage and our answer was to banish and execute them. One struggle over equal rights and freedom turned the world against them. How many wars have been fought by humans, elves and fae over the millennia for far less noble ideals? And yet not one elf or human or fae is killed on site for being what they are. Why are werewolves of lower value than any other race?"

Holt found his tongue too heavy to respond because she was right in every way. She was a convincing, passionate believer in empathy for all creatures. She certainly wouldn't be a successful business woman in her chosen occupation if she didn't practice what she preached.

"It's not to say that all werewolves are decent people," she continued. "We see it among all the races. There must be regulations regarding the Bite and penalties for those that pass the infection recklessly. That's what I believe happened to Dirk van Amersvoot. He didn't take the Bite willingly. It was forced on him and he has never been taught how to control it. If his Birthright gave him the Bite out of anger, or for any negative reason, then he'll never be able to get past that. It makes him dangerous."

"He's killed four men, including his younger brother," Holt pointed out. "I'm sure his sister has told you. She does stay here while attending school."

"Lars was a gentle soul," she whispered to herself. She was well aware of the killings for she had comforted Beshka through her grief. Her gaze rose to meet Holt's. "I had a delightful girl selected for him, too."

"Dirk is a wild animal, Mrs. Forth-Wright," said Holt. "Out of respect for my sister, I am trying to resolve this issue quietly. Any help you can give me would be appreciated."

"I have had several American werewolves come to me of late, looking for places to live in peace. I've helped them connect with one another. I felt it was only right since they were new here and had no resources. They are all Birthrights," she added to allay his concerns. "Not a Sauvage among them."

Holt accepted her judgment. He picked up his glass and sipped at the now tepid liquid.

She would be his best accomplice to track down Dirk. She had the means to make further inquiries without drawing undo attention to his cause. He just needed to sweeten the deal.

"I hope I can count on your assistance in locating Dirk van Amersvoot as quickly as possible. In exchange I can bring you several influential gentlemen in need of wives."

She smiled and tipped her glass toward him in a toast of acceptance. There was nothing to be gained by turning away his business.

CHAPTER THIRTY-THREE

"Alpha is as Alpha does."
werewolf proverb

By August Agatha was displaying a prominent belly. Her body was familiar with the routine and it was giving the baby plenty of room to grow. With two months to go, Bloem had some concerns that the baby might be quite large by its due date so she kept a close eye on its growth. She had returned to Willowbrook in May but visited frequently.

From an early point in her pregnancy Agatha could feel the baby's wild spirit. Its wolf was already making itself known, especially at night. She wasn't sleeping well, which worried Nick. He did all he could to make her comfortable, but no amount of feather pillows or warm quilts could help her nocturnal restlessness. Like its brother and sister, the baby was most active when the sun went down. It felt like a tumbleweed rolling around in her belly. It was worse during the weeks when the moon was approaching its peak. During those nights she got no sleep. On the full moons she still went out with Nick to keep him from hurting himself or causing trouble on a neighboring station. Other nights she tossed and turned, kicking and whining. She woke herself up at times and kept Nick awake. She offered to sleep in the spare room, but he decided that if he needed sleep that badly he wasn't much of a man. His ego wasn't really a detriment considering the vines were dormant in winter so much of his time was spent undertaking less taxing endeavors.

Mornings were a time of restoration for Agatha. She took long hot baths to rejuvenate her tired body. The baby seemed to find it a peaceful time, too, finally coming to a rest. Bloem recommended an infusion of lavender oil in the bath water to help calm them both. Agatha preferred rose oil, but she acquiesced to the midwife's prescription.

After one particularly violent night of sleeplessness she soaked in the deep tub, eyes closed and dozing lightly. Her chin rested on her chest. The water was a warm cocoon around her body.

She heard the hall door open, but didn't stir. Mrs. MacLeach usually came to check on her once or twice to make sure she hadn't drowned. The rustle of clothing didn't rouse her either. She did wake when the water rose and she felt Nick's body sliding against hers. He lowered himself into the large tub behind her, framing her with his arms and legs. She reclined into the comfortable shape of his thighs and upper body. Her head fell back against his shoulder. He entwined his fingers with hers on top of her swollen abdomen to feel the motion of their baby as it rolled lazily in her womb. They stayed like that, not speaking, until the water went cold.

※

That afternoon Nick was sequestered in his office going over plans to add another plot of vines in the east paddock. He gnawed on the stem of a pencil as he poured over figures jotted messily on notes scattered across his desk. He had been studiously organized prior to the Bite, but he now found his concentration wandered occasionally. He worked hard to keep himself on track with the winery because he wanted it to succeed beyond anyone's expectations. He had a few noses to rub in it.

He didn't allow the sound of a steam wagon rattling into the yard to distract him. He used his fingers to count as he drew out equations for how to accomplish the new planting. His focus was already strained and he concentrated with a tremendous effort. The full moon had recently passed, which contributed to his short attention span.

Agatha was putting the twins down for a nap when she heard the vehicle arrive in the yard. It took her a few minutes to make her way into the salon to look out at who it was. She hadn't thought Bloem would be coming over that day.

The wagon belonged to Tim Rushgrove, a long standing friend of Nick's. Despite the warnings of the Elders, Tim continued to make trips out to Gilgai to learn from Nick. He was considering converting his property into vineyards. On this day, he was playing taxi to someone needing a ride to the station from town.

Agatha peered out the front window to see the wagon already departing. That was curious.

A knock on the door drew her attention. She waddled over with a sense of trepidation. No one just came out to Gilgai.

The familiar young man standing before her caused her knees to buckle. Adam Steelcuff caught her before she collapsed. She gazed up into his face with utter disbelief, wide eyes searching his face for confirmation that what she was seeing wasn't a hallucination brought on by lack of sleep.

"I thought you were dead," she breathed when she had enough air in her lungs to speak.

He grinned with that charming lift of his lips that melted women's hearts. Hers had once been a victim of that disarming smile.

"Not yet," he said. He half carried her towards the sofa. "Let's get you sitting down before you fall down."

She couldn't help herself. Her hands caressed his smooth face, ruffled his light brown hair. She couldn't believe that he was alive and right in front of her. It couldn't be real. She had to touch him to make sure she wasn't imaging him.

"They said the Regulators killed everyone," she whispered, giving in to the joyous tears that sprang from her eyes. "That was over a year ago."

"They found out we were planning to stage an attack so they preempted us. Most of the Rez was wiped out, but we managed to escape with about a dozen others."

"We?" she echoed, not daring to hope.

"Me and Lance. He's here in Australia, too. In Sydney. We've been in touch with a woman named Eliza Forth-Wright. She knew where you were. I had to see you. I had to know you were alright. That woman said you were, but I needed to see for myself. I can see you're doing very well."

She nodded, her smile returning.

"I am." She sat back, hands in her lap. "But you. Where have you been all this time? How did you even get out of America?"

Nick's ears pricked at the sound of two voices. He lifted his head and listened. He recognized Agatha's, but the other voice was male and foreign. American. He left his sketches and notes where they lay. He came out of his office, the back of his neck itching with hackles wanting to rise.

Agatha turned to see Nick's dark expression as he approached. His wolf had identified an interloper and was none too pleased. He was obviously not in control at the moment. Though he could usually keep the wolf subdued they were far from best friends.

"Nick," she said, struggling to get off the sofa. Adam helped her, putting his arm around her waist, which didn't make his first impression on Nick any better. "Wait."

He was already on top of Adam, teeth showing through taught lips.

"Who the hell are you?" he demanded, his face tight with ill-concealed animosity.

Adam immediately, wisely, backed away. He lowered his head in deference to Nick's authority.

"My name is Adam Steelcuff, sir," he answered, eyes on the floor. Any eye contact would be construed as a challenge and for Agatha's sake he wanted to avoid that. "I'm from the same reservation as Agatha. We grew up together. She's like a sister to me."

Nick's eyes narrowed and he sniffed at Adam's throat. It was not a behavior Agatha had seen before and she realised that he was definitely under the wolf's hold. Adam, as the trespasser onto Nick's territory, rolled his head to the side and submissively bared his throat.

"Nick, stop," Agatha commanded.

His hardened glare turned towards her.

"By Gods, he's not here to fight with you," she snapped. She growled low in her throat. "But I will if you don't back down."

Nick read the intent in her features. He took a step away, shaking his head to clear it. What had come over him? The wolf was displaying its natural mannerisms and he had allowed it to come to the surface. He battled it down, but it was not willing to hide.

"I'm sorry," he said. His face was hot with humiliation. "I don't usually let wolf get its way like that."

Adam hesitantly looked up. The danger had passed for now. He still didn't like the stiffness in Nick's shoulders, but he couldn't blame the man for protecting what was his. The way he'd referred to his wolf told Adam that he was a Sauvage, which was what he had suspected right away.

"I understand," he replied, keeping his eyes away from Nick's to demonstrate that he understood Nick was the alpha of the situation. "I didn't come here to cause a problem."

"You haven't," Agatha assured him with a harsh look at Nick. "You're welcome here."

Nick wasn't as accommodating, but he kept that to himself. Instead, he relinquished the decision making to Agatha. She supposedly knew the man well and was a better judge of his purposes. He didn't like having virile young competition for her attention. At least the young man seemed to acknowledge that Agatha was Nick's mate and was submissive. It was best for all involved if it stayed that way.

"I'll have Mrs. MacLeach make up the extra room," he offered with curl in his lip. "Our home is open to you."

"No, I don't want to intrude-"

"You aren't," Agatha answered quickly. There was so much they had to discuss, seemingly a lifetime to catch up on. "You can stay as long as you like."

Nick's brows arched stiffly. She was being too inviting, but her unbound happiness tempered his urge to scruff the pup and toss him out into the dirt. His wolf was so irritated that he was allowing Adam to remain at Gilgai that it was bringing out his worst side. He was surprised by his own reaction toward someone from Agatha's mysterious past. He had hoped that someday she would have closure, but when faced with the reality of her past he didn't want to accept it. He needed to take his aggression down a notch to maybe learn more about his wife's history. There was nothing to fear from Adam Steelcuff. Nick knew Agatha was devoted to their marriage. She would not be tempted by this newcomer. Still, he was ready to take action if Adam tried anything.

After a dinner of raw wallaby and goanna, Agatha and Adam strolled in the garden. Nick had grudgingly given her time alone with her old friend to speak in private. He couldn't monitor her every moment of the day. He had to trust her.

"We went to Mexico first," Adam said, gazing up at the ink stained sky as they walked arm in arm among the wintering plants. There were no blooms to be seen. "It's fairly safe there. Lance stayed in Mexico City, but I went down to Peru for a while. There are several large packs there. One of the most powerful packs is made up of mystics. They live in a stone city on the most remote mountain peak. It's stunning. They were willing to let me stay because of my medical background, but I wanted to find you. I had to see you again. I went back to Mexico to find Lance and we came here. There aren't many werewolves in Australia yet, so it wasn't too difficult to find you. That woman in Sydney, Mrs. Forth-Wright, said she found you a husband and you moved out to the bush, whatever that is."

"It's what they call the wilderness here," she explained. She leaned her head on his shoulder as she had done as girl. For her it was an innocent gesture, reconnecting with her childhood companion. "I haven't met many others since I've been here other than the female Birthrights that came with me from America. There is one Sauvage that scares me, but he's been reported to the Guardianship because he attacked Nick."

Adam paused under the bare branches of an orange tree and she turned to face him. His hand went to her stomach in a gesture that was far too familiar for their current situation. It crossed the line from friendship to intimacy. She tensed visibly and he withdrew. He reached up and broke off a few small twigs.

"I never expected you to marry a Sauvage," he said, peering at her from beneath the long forelock that fell over his brow. His hazel eyes were as charming and mischievous as she remembered.

She leaned against another tree, watching him with a dreamy gaze. He interpreted that glazed expression as girlish fondness for him, but she was actually thinking about Nick.

"He wasn't a Sauvage when I married him."

Adam's head snapped back. His face was a mask of incredulity.

"What? Then how did he-You? You gave him the Bite?"

She nodded, bracing for his reaction. It had to be one of the most shocking revelations he could never have seen coming. It was something she had felt so strongly against that he had to find it nearly impossible to accept.

To the look of thunderous disapproval that clouded Adam's face she said, "He asked me for it."

"I don't care what he asked for. That was something you said you would never do. You told me you would never give the Bite because of what happened to Paradeus. You didn't want to repeat that mistake."

"I saved his life with it," she told him. Tears lingered in her golden eyes. "I would have lost him."

Adam took three long strides to reach her. He gripped her arms and gave her a shake.

"You swore to me."

She tore herself away and retreated to the relative safety of a large red cedar. She pressed her face against the cool bark.

"He's my husband," she said with deliberate enunciation. "His world has been turned upside down since he married me. There isn't anything he wouldn't do for me. There isn't anything I wouldn't do for him."

"Evidently that includes breaking a promise you made to yourself," Adam replied with disappointment clear in his voice. His expression was dour. "How could you do that?"

"Even someone opposed to killing would do it to if it meant defending their life or their loved ones," she pointed out. "We do what we have to in order to survive."

Adam exhaled long and loud. He paced an angry path between her and the edge of the garden.

"Do you know why we were put on reservations to begin with?" he asked, slanting a glance in her direction.

Her features darkened.

"So the humans could have all the land to themselves."

He wagged his head. There was much their generation had not been told about their history in the UAT. He had only learned the truth since fleeing America.

"About a hundred years ago the UAT broke ties with Britain. The Victorian government wouldn't let their profitable new acquisition go without a fight." He paused, lips taught across his front teeth in a soundless snarl. "The UAT used Sauvage to win their independence."

Agatha couldn't have been more shocked or appalled. To learn that her own country had once created Sauvage for their self-seeking benefit made bile sear a trail up her throat. She spat the bitter taste onto the ground.

"They used us then turned against us," he went on, watching her reaction with satisfaction. "We made America what it is and we get nothing for it. Now you know why they've isolated us on those Gods forsaken reservations and refuse to allow us to live as we are. They're afraid of us. You know they want us dead. They want to make sure nothing like that happens again. We never knew that when we were on the Rez. They kept that from us. It's why they killed the generations before us, so they couldn't pass down that knowledge. They drilled into our heads that it was illegal to give the Bite without telling us what they had done. We just knew what happened when Paradeus stood for our freedom so we made sure we kept the infection from spreading. Do you see now why I just can't believe you would have done that? You can't love anyone that much."

She smiled in way that seemed to light the darkness around them.

"I do. I didn't think I could ever trust a human, much less love one," she said, reliving her initial hesitation at being with Nick. "He's shown me that it was the Regulators who were evil. Whatever happened back on the Rez isn't my problem, Adam. Nick has given up the life he knew to be with me. He's brought me happiness and given me freedom."

Adam stepped closer to her. He searched her face for falsehood. As far as he could tell she was speaking the truth or at least it was what she had convinced herself to believe.

"That's not what I heard from the man who brought me out here. He said you can't leave this property or you risk being killed by the townspeople. How is that better than what you left behind? You've just found new walls to keep you in."

The sting of his words cut deep. Nick had said essentially the same thing. Were they right? Had she traded in one reservation for another? There was a significant difference between Blackpaw and Gilgai. She had remained at Blackpaw because she had no other choice. She stayed at Gilgai because she had a choice. She had weighed the value of her options and chose to stay out of love and a commitment to her future.

"There are no walls around my heart," she said definitively. "It doesn't matter where I live, as long as I'm with my family."

Adam shook his head. She was in denial.

"Do you honestly believe that?" he asked. He picked up the gold ring that lay on her chest and twisted it in his fingers. "Do you think this place is any better than Blackpaw?"

Her shoulders went back defensively and her gaze turned stony. She slapped his hand and the ring dropped onto her breasts. She did not appreciate his insinuation. After two years apart, he had no claim to her life. Any potential romantic feelings they might have shared while on the Rez had died there. She was grateful that he was alive, but he was a lone werewolf coming onto her territory and challenging her judgment. She wasn't as threatened as Nick by his presence, though she resented his assumptions.

"If you stayed here for any length of time you'd see for yourself," she said. "It's better than anything you've ever known."

"Maybe I should stay for awhile," he agreed, slyly inserting himself back into her life. "Do you think Nick will mind?"

"Of course," she replied with a sigh. "He sees you as competition. Can you blame him?"

Adam smiled, shaking his head. He understood where Nick was coming from. He would have to watch his step. One false move and the next full moon could be his last.

CHAPTER THIRTY-FOUR

"Man is often at the mercy of his own devices."
Nathaniel Elliott, scholar

From the top gallery, Dirk looked out on the courtyard of Dumfries Castle. He studied the rag tag men that gathered there. He had been overseeing the recruitment of Sauvage soldiers for months and was satisfied with the progression of his army. The human population of Australia was comprised of Aborigines, escaped convicts, squatters predominantly descended from the criminals sentenced to the Victorian penal colony or direct British imports. There were plenty of disgruntled citizens living in less than ideal conditions that were easily manipulated into joining a military campaign against the current regime of the Victorian government. He had commanders working to gather platoons of soldiers in other parts of the country as well. Of course the recruits didn't know they would become Sauvage.

Anatoly Goreyevskiy had upheld his end of the bargain by bringing in droves of Birthrights from Russia to support the effort. Like their ancestors, they were lured by the promise of riches and power.

Against Dirk's order Anatoly made a plea to the Victorian government and the elf High Council leaders to attempt a peaceful resolution. Dirk had known there would be no chance of their agreeing to the formation of an Alpha Council to compete with their authority. Disgruntled, Anatoly had set about collecting soldiers. They were stationed outside Perth in another isolated compound, building an army in the west.

BIRTHRIGHT

Dirk wasn't concerned that word was spreading about the gathering of werewolves and the creation of thousands of Sauvage across the continent. The humans meant nothing to him. Their defenses were pathetic. By the time their local government was aware of the true danger, it would be too late for Britain to respond with any military force. As easy as it was to pass the infection there was no way to contain the problem. If they were smart, the Victorian government would cut all ties to the new country, leaving it open to domination by Dirk and his new regime. He had no intentions of creating more Sauvage than necessary to accomplish his goal. He wanted to open the continent to Birthrights from all over the world. He only needed the Sauvage to take the country by force then he would be able to establish an Alpha Council to govern the remaining werewolves, and anyone else who chose to make Australia their home. Once the war was over, he would make sure the soldiers he'd created were dealt with appropriately. He had no intention of allowing thousands of Sauvage to run rampant and cause mayhem every full moon. For now they were cattle.

To make the newborn Sauvage into the terrifying beasts of legend they were locked in dark holding cells immediately after taking the Bite and left alone with the wolf inside them. It took most men only a few days to break under the strain of fending off the wild animal trapped inside their skin. Stronger souls lasted until the first full moon before losing what had ever been human about them. The few who could tolerate their new internal guest were made into officers under the command of Birthright commanders. The bulk of the Sauvage were then housed in barracks where infighting was rampant. On the full moon all soldiers, even officers, were securely locked down, left to endure the pain and rage of their change.

Dirk was in constant contact with his commanders via the dingoes. Those little orange dogs could pass messages in no time. For their fair share of the continent in exchange for their part in Dirk's war, Wollaweroo was willing to join the effort. The dingoes were Dirk's spies and messengers. They could infiltrate the more remote communities to keep tabs on human activity. They also kept him apprised of Agatha's condition and Adam's as yet unsuccessful attempt to bring her into the fold. He would only give the American Birthright so much time before taking stronger action. He already knew that Nick was Sauvage. Wollaweroo had personally delivered that message after Nick's accident.

As he leaned on the stone rail, brooding over Agatha's second pregnancy, he was joined by another American Birthright, Lance Highmoon.

Lance had quickly risen to a position of power within Dirk's ranks through his ruthless acquisition of humans to turn into Sauvage. He gave no mercy to humans and cared little about elves or fae. The elves were another enemy altogether. The fae would be considered collateral damage if they interfered.

A few fae species were willing to sign up to fight against a common foe. Dragons in particular had felt centuries of persecution at the hands of humans and elves. There were few left in the world, but those few were prepared to join the battle. Lance had met two of them in Mexico shortly after fleeing the Rez. They had readily agreed to round up their kin and relocate to Australia. A dozen dragons had descended upon the continent. They lived in the caverns close to the castle, biding their time.

"What have you heard about Agatha?" Dirk asked without turning to acknowledge Lance.

Lance was taller than Dirk, an impressive feat. Thick black hair fell over his shoulders like a cape. He was narrow of frame but wired with lean muscle. He wore a tanned leather tunic over cotton trousers. It had been the uniform of the males on the Rez and he wore it to denote his pride in escaping America. As was most Birthright's custom, his feet were bare.

"She isn't coming."

Dirk slammed his fist on the stone. He had promised the Birthrights that he had Paradeus' descendant on his side. If she didn't come around soon he would lose credibility and vital support. She was crucial to his success. Some of the Birthrights regarded him as a loose cannon. They wanted to reach a mutual agreement with the humans and elves without spilling blood. Their reasons for supporting his rebellion were varied. There were those who merely sought equality. Others were fed up with their three hundred year exile and desired a werewolf dominated society as did Dirk. They all wanted freedom. To realize the full potential of his vision he required Agatha at his side. Birthright and Sauvage alike would respond to her as an Alpha Queen.

He had to have her.

"Tell Adam he has no more time," he said, teeth bared. "Either she comes of her own accord or against her will. I don't care. Bring her here."

Lance grinned. He was looking forward to bringing Agatha down from her bucolic pedestal. She had refused him as a mate in Colorado. This would be ideal revenge.

Social circles in all major cities around the country were buzzing with rumors of a new werewolf uprising. It was history repeating itself. All over the continent concerned citizens boarded ships and departed for safer shores.

The Victorian government called an emergency session to discuss the issue. It was their opinion that they should remove the governor and valuable parliament members from the line of fire until the full measure of the threat was identified. They had received intelligence that there were dragons on Australian soil, which caused further concern. Reports of unusually large dingo packs moving into populated areas were widely dismissed. The native dogs were of no consequence. Dragons and Sauvage took precedent over the cowardly canines when it came to fire power and brute strength. Dingoes were merely a nuisance.

The elves convened the High Council and called several concerned parties to the table. It was their understanding that the

Sauvage leading the rebellion had been responsible for a host of other problems.

Buren was summoned to Sydney. Agatha's presence was also requested, but her pregnancy was too advanced to allow her to travel safely. Bloem defied the Council and refused to permit Agatha to attend. Nick reluctantly took her place, leaving Agatha at Gilgai with Bloem and Adam. Whatever was happening was his business as well. It involved Dirk and in some way had to lead back to Agatha. He was terrified to come face to face with the High Council. If they figured out he was Sauvage they could order his execution. It was a chance he had to take.

The High Council building was a brick edifice on the edge of Hyde Park. The façade was laced with ivy vines like the stitching on a quilt. It was surrounded by natural gardens tended by nymphs. It was a popular destination for human males to wander past in hopes of glimpsing one of their nubile, naked bodies.

The interior was lushly appointed in varying types of marble with dark wood accents. Huge ceramic containers housed a veritable forest throughout rooms and halls. Brightly coloured fairies darted like butterflies along corridors, delivering messages on paper-thin wings. There was a great deal of activity inside the building as elves and their fae allies organized efforts to gather information on the state of the werewolf army. All manner of creature flooded the halls and crowded into offices.

The fae were divided into hundreds of species, all of which maintained their own form of governing body. It was virtually impossible to get them to come together, even under the threat of war. They had not been involved in the Paradeus Uprising and they wanted nothing to do with the fighting now. Only the fae directly impacted by the situation sought aid from the High Council.

Nick had never been around so many non-humans in his life. He was eternally grateful that Buren was with him. Etiquette had never been his forte. He was a man of few words and none of those seemed to fit the circumstances. He followed Buren's lead and hoped he didn't offend anyone too badly. He wore his finest suit, which seemed more like second hand rags compared to Buren's formal robes and crown of eucalyptus leaves.

The clatter of hooves on the marble floor approached as they waited in an antechamber off the main hall. A slender faun slipped into the room through a tall door. His short curved horns were polished to a shine as were his small split hooves. His torso was unexpectedly hairless above his white and brown spotted goat legs. He wore a wreath of wheat sheaves on his head which denoted his lower rank.

"Come with me, please."

Nick took a deep breath, glancing to Buren. The elf did not make any polite conversation with the faun so neither did Nick. They followed their guide down a long private hall to another room where they were left to wait.

This room was larger with more comfortable furniture. Its windows overlooked the park.

"What now?" Nick asked, completely out of his element.

Buren patted him on the back in encouragement. He sympathized with Nick's unease. He had only been in the High Council building twice before and each time he had felt near sick to his stomach with nerves.

"We wait some more."

Nick had to release some of the anxious energy building within him so he started making slow laps around the room. His wolf was quiet. It was eerily timid at the moment, afraid to make its presence known.

As he passed close to Buren, he whispered, "Won't they know what I am?"

"How do you think werewolves have survived this long? They blend in extremely well. I won't let anything happen to you," Buren promised.

"I wish I had that confidence," grumbled Nick. "No offense, but I'm not sure your word carries any weight."

Before Buren could respond, the door through which they had entered opened. Both men turned, not knowing what to expect.

Holt Threadwell and Eliza Forth-Wright were led into the room by a different faun. He had fully curled horns and dark legs with the same wheat crown adorning his brow as his fellow fae. He escorted them inside then left.

The four stared at each other for a moment. Eliza, the consummate hostess, made the first move. She walked up to Nick and gave him a light embrace.

"How is Agatha?" she asked.

Nick couldn't believe her calm attitude in the face of their predicament. He floundered for a response.

"She's well. The baby's due in a few weeks so she couldn't come," he said, looking dumbly to Buren.

"Another baby?" Eliza brightened. "Congratulations. How are the twins? A boy and girl, I understand."

Nick nodded, brow furrowed in consternation. It seemed an odd time and place for small talk, catching up on old times.

"They're good. A year old now."

She smiled, nodding cheerfully at the news. Her gaze travelled to Buren.

"How is Bloem? This must be very difficult for her."

"Yes, it is," was all Buren would say on the subject. His glare was pinned on Holt.

Holt stood by the fireplace mantel, gaze turned away from the eyes boring into the side of his head. He could feel Buren's resentment like a hot match on his skin.

"I did what I could to keep this from getting out of hand," he said, bringing his face around to meet Buren's frigid blue glower.

Buren turned and marched to the far side of the room. He needed space between himself and his brother-in-law. He believed that Holt truly had done all he could to prevent this disaster. It came down to the fact that he, himself, hadn't followed the law and his inaction had put the country in the peril it was in now. He hated thinking in terms of "if this" or "if that", but if he had done the right thing in the first place Lars would be alive and Australia wouldn't be on the brink of a war with werewolves. He had put Bloem's emotional attachment to her illegitimate son before the law. He had as good as handed the country to Dirk.

"Holt came to me for help obtaining information on Dirk's whereabouts and in the course of my inquiries I learned that there was a dramatic increase in the numbers of Birthrights coming into Australia from all over the world," said Eliza.

Holt took over, "That led to the discovery of camps where the Birthrights are creating Sauvage by the thousands. They're churning out soldiers as fast as they can. Our intelligence reports that in the past few months they've created over ten thousand Sauvage. And that's a conservative estimate. Those are only the ones we know about."

Nick sank into a dark green chair. His head was spinning.

"What are the elves going to do about it?" he asked, running his hand across his face.

Holt pursed his lips. He wandered to the window and gazed through the sheer curtains at the people strolling through the park.

"That's what we're going to find out."

"Why do they want to talk to us?" Nick demanded. "I'm sorry, Buren, but I can see why they would want to question you, but what do the rest of us have to do with this?"

"Buren came to me about Dirk," Holt answered with remorse. "He did the right thing. I was obligated to take my knowledge to the Council, but I couldn't. It would have exposed our family's dirty little secret and I wanted very much to keep that under lock and key."

Nick looked up, brow cocked.

"What secret?"

"Bloem's affair with a human that produced a *helf*, a half-elf. Dirk," answered Buren.

"I didn't realize that was a secret," Nick said lamely. "I knew."

Buren smiled at his charming human innocence. There were

many reasons he liked Nick and that was one of them.

"You're as close to family as anyone can get. Bloem and I have never kept anything from you," he said. "But among the elf community, her affair would have been damaging to her family's reputation. I went to Holt because of his influence in certain circles. I hoped he would be able to locate Dirk and put him down without creating a scandal."

"When the Council learned that I had been aware of Dirk's condition and that I hadn't turned in an official report, I was removed from my post pending an investigation," Holt said. "Now that this has grown into a second potential Paradeus Uprising I have to answer for my ethical lapse."

"And you?" Nick asked of Eliza.

"I brought Agatha to Australia, as well as other werewolves," she sighed. She took a seat on the settee opposite Nick. Her vibrant red hair was coiled atop her head like a turban. "They are holding me accountable for all of this as well."

"Shit," Nick muttered. He shook his head in wonder. "What do they think Agatha has to do with any of this? Dirk attacked her, too. She isn't responsible for this disaster."

"The Council has concerns about where her allegiance lies," Holt told him. "She may be married to a human, but she is a werewolf. More than that, she *is* the direct descendant of Paradeus. Her influence among the werewolf population would be monumental. She could unite them in this war."

Stunned into silence, Nick slumped in his seat. His tortured gaze sought Buren. At that moment his concern for his own safety could have fit into a thimble. He had to protect Agatha at all costs.

"What are they going to do to her?" he asked with a tremor in his voice.

"For the moment, nothing," assured Holt. "We have to assure them that Agatha isn't a threat in any way. She isn't responsible for creating any Sauvage and isn't part of Dirk's planned conquest of Australia."

Immediately Nick and Buren looked at each other. The glance did not go unnoticed by Holt.

"Is there something I need to know?" he queried.

"No," Nick said, staring at his hands in his lap. He turned them over, recalling the texture of Agatha's fingers twined with his as they had lain in the bathtub feeling the movement of the baby inside her. How had their world suddenly fallen apart?

Buren had made one terrible judgment in error by keeping Dirk's secret. He could not in good faith make the same mistake twice.

"Nick is a Sauvage. Agatha gave him the Bite to save his life."

Nick's astonishment at being betrayed was nothing compared to Holt's genuine horror at the realization that their situation had just gone from bad to worse with one statement.

"How could you tell them?" Nick exploded. "Are you trying to get me killed?"

"They aren't going to do anything," Buren said rationally with a stern glare at Holt.

Eliza seized upon the opportunity. She came to Nick's defense, positioning herself at his side. She put her hand on his shoulder.

"This is what I was telling you," she said to Holt. "It should not be a crime if a husband or wife gives the Bite to their spouse. How can it be wrong for two people who love each other to share that kind of connection? Doesn't it bring them closer?"

Holt was painfully conflicted. His inner turmoil would have to wait as they were summoned to the Council chamber by a somber female elf. The four individuals came together and followed her in silence.

CHAPTER THIRTY-FIVE

"Beware the wolf asleep among the sheep."
fae proverb

From inside the twins' room Agatha heard thunder. She glanced at the window, but the day was clear. Her heart doubled its pace with foreboding. It was not the weather acting up.

Logan stood in his crib, gripping the rail for balance. Luna lay on her back at his feet. She had not begun to stand yet. She was still small, half her brother's size. Her development was taking significantly longer. Both had their father's pale blue eyes. Logan's hair was darker, like Nick's. Luna had the same tawny strands as her mother.

Raising her head as she heard another thunderclap and the breaking of glass, Agatha felt a cold finger travel up her spine.

"Mrs. MacLeach?" she called out. "Bloem?"

There was no response. The house was silent.

Fearing another attack by Dirk she left the twins in their room and pulled the hall table in front of the door to block it. It wouldn't stop anyone, but it would slow them down.

She debated changing to wolfshape. She would definitely be more agile without this belly in her way. The downside was that she wouldn't be able to communicate. She decided if she needed to change she could do it quickly enough.

"There you are," said Adam, coming through the back door.

He filled the hall in front of her like a barricade. Someone was standing behind him. Her wolf went on alert, scratching to get out.

"What's going on?" she asked, stepping back.

BIRTHRIGHT

The other figure made itself known. Lance Highmoon stepped out from behind Adam, head lowered in a challenging posture. He was another ghost from her past.

"Lance?" she breathed, pressing her back to the wall.

Any joy she might have experience at seeing him again shriveled like a withered flower. He was not there for a social call. The expression on his face was menacing. Before Agatha could step out of her skin to defend herself, he made a quick jump at her and shoved a foul smelling cloth against her nose and mouth. In the few seconds she had before blacking out, she raked her claws across his cheek. Then darkness overcame her and she went limp in Lance's arms.

"Be careful," Adam warned.

His affection for Agatha was still as strong as it had ever been. He knew that Nick had put up with his presence on the station for the past month out of consideration for his wife's well being, but there had been no mistaking that Nick was willing to shred him to pulp if given the chance. Only the lull between full moons had offered Adam protection. Now he was taking Agatha by force and his only means of staying alive was to remain at Dumfries Castle where they were taking her. Once Nick learned that she had been abducted he would be out for blood. Adam knew that Nick would not be able to penetrate the thick defenses of Dirk's fortress by himself, which would keep Adam alive.

"What about the twins?" Lance asked. His lip curled. "We should clean up her bloodline for Dirk. I wouldn't want another male's cubs around."

Adam cut him a sharp look. He stood in Lance's way. Out of respect for Agatha, he could not allow her children to be slaughtered, even if it was the way of their kind. He was only participating in this scheme to make sure she wasn't harmed.

"Dirk didn't say anything about what do with them. He only wants her," he pointed out. "If he wants them dead he can do it himself."

Lance agreed. They had what they had come for. As a message to Nick, he yanked the wedding band from her neck and threw it on the floor.

They carried Agatha's heavy body out to the yard where an immense red dragon waited. It wore a passenger basket attached to a harness that fitted its lean body to perfection. The basket would hang suspended beneath the beast's belly as it flew, much like the design of a hot air balloon. It was large enough to hold four bodies, which was only for the comfort of the travelers. Dragons could carry an impossibly heavy load.

The dragon's reptilian head came down from its twenty foot elevation, turning towards them on a long flexible neck. Its eyes were dark with orange veins like magma showing through cracks in the surface of a lava field. Its yellow pupils widened before contracting into thin vertical lines. A thin stream of smoke rose from its nostril slits.

"That's her?" Torric asked in a seething telepathic voice. "Hardly impressive."

"That's not your concern," snapped Lance, loading Agatha into the basket. He climbed in after Adam. "Just take us back to Dumfries."

The dragon reared up, great wings pounding the air, shattering windows in the house. It rose into the morning sky as the station hands rode in from the paddocks on lathered horses. They had seen the dragon coming and returned to the homestead as fast as their horses could carry them. Not a man among them had seen a dragon with his own eyes, but they recognized the massive lizard-like creature for what it was. There could be no mistaking it for anything else once it opened fire on the barns and rows of vines with a blue flash of its sulfuric breath. The stench of rotten eggs filled the air.

Ed flew off his horse as it skidded to a stop by the front gate.

"Agatha?" he bellowed, hurtling the fence in one leap. His boots crunched loudly on broken glass as he reached the open door. "Agatha?! Bloem? Mrs. MacLeach?"

The other men were manning the fire pump, trying desperately to staunch the flames. Most stations had separate wells dug near the homestead buildings as a precaution against fire. Those wells had specialized hand pumps, in some cases steam or gas powered, to provide high water pressure. The men wrestled with the heavy canvas hose, dragging it to the barn. The fire would not be quelled easily.

Ben Farnsworth was on Ed's heels, spreading out to search the house. He spied Agatha's wedding ring on the floor and picked it up. His chest shrank inwards until his heart was pounding directly against his ribs. He shoved the hall table away from the bedroom door. He opened it to find Logan still standing at the side of the crib with tears dribbling down his plump face. The baby didn't make a sound as Ben scooped him up. He gathered Luna in his other arm.

"Are they alright?" asked Ed, peering in the doorway.

"Yeah, yeah, it looks like it. Where the hell is everyone?" Ben replied. "What happened?"

Ed shook his head and bolted out the back door. He sprinted to the kitchen where he found Mrs. MacLeach and Bloem bound and gagged, but alive and unharmed.

"Those mangy werewolves took the Missus," wailed the housekeeper the instant her gag was removed.

Ed cut through the rope binding the women's wrists and ankles with his utility knife. He slipped it back into its sheath on his belt.

"You have to save Agatha," Bloem urged, allowing Ed to help her to feet. "I don't know where they've taken her but I'm sure it's to Dirk. I know my son is behind this."

Ed nodded.

"We have to make sure you and the babies are alright first," he said reasonably.

"No," Bloem insisted, clutching the front of his shirt. "You have to find Agatha. Get word to Nick in Sydney right away. He has to know what's happened. Notify the High Council and the Victorian government. Dirk's made his first move."

Nick stood between Eliza and Buren with Holt on the other side of the hugtandalf as they faced the authority of the High Council.

The room had a high domed ceiling with a grand mural depicting the pantheon of their revered ancestors. Those severe face were almost more intimidating that the faces of the living elves around them. The elves were seated on risers in a circular fashion like the Roman senate. There were more than thirty grave expressions staring down on them. It was called the High Council for several reasons. They were the highest ranking members of their race in Australia. The room was designed for them to sit above the level of mere mortals. The more colloquial reason was that they held their arrogant heads so high that they needed a domed roof to keep them from hitting the ceiling.

"We know that a war is brewing," pronounced the Grand Council, Rhionna Greenhill. She was seated directly in front of the four suspects. "Our understanding is that each of you has been in some way responsible for allowing Dirk van Amersvoot to reach the point of forming a significant army of Sauvage." Her moss green eyes settled on Holt, who refused to show his discomfort. "I am saddened to see you here, Guardian Threadwell. While I appreciate your desire to protect family honor, this had wider reaching implications that you should have considered."

He inclined his head in agreement.

"Had I any idea that Dirk was capable of achieving such a feat as this, I would most assuredly have taken the appropriate steps," he said with humility. "It was not something I could have imagined."

"Indeed, it was not something anyone could have imagined," agreed the stately female elf. Rhionna looked to Buren. "You, as well, put family first which is a noble sentiment. Your devotion to your wife is commendable. Raising a helf bastard is not a task many men would take on. I commend your sense of responsibility."

Her condescending comment forced Buren to bite his tongue to prevent a scathing remark from leaving his mouth. His mustache twitched. This was absolutely not the place to fire back in anger. He nodded stiffly instead.

"And yet when it became clear that Dirk was no longer able to control his wolf you did nothing to ensure the safety of those around you. In your refusal to take action, you allowed him to kill four people, including your other son, Lars. Am I correct?"

Buren nodded again, tasting the blood in his mouth from grinding his teeth into his tongue.

"I am sorry for the loss of your son Lars," said Rhionna. "No parent should lose a child, no matter the circumstances."

Buren said nothing. His nostrils flared as he breathed heavily with resentment.

"We also understand that a Birthright female was attacked and raped?"

"My wife," said Nick bluntly. He did not have the same sense of respect for the High Council as Buren and Holt. They were not his government. His wolf grew bolder. "Her name is Agatha Buchanan."

Eyebrows were raised all around the room at his outburst, mild though it was. They expected no less from a human. He was, strictly speaking, out of his element among the Council. With the current status of the Victorian government, he had no protection against the elves' legal decision in this matter.

"Yes, Agatha," said Rhionna. Her slender hands were folded together on the ledge in front of her. She glanced at a file that rested on the flat surface. "Formerly Agatha Whistleton of the Blackpaw Reservation in Colorado. She is the sole descendant of the Sauvage, Paradeus. Are you aware of that?"

"I am," he replied.

"Do you understand that as such she would be a powerful tool in this war?" asked the Grand Council.

"I am now," he grudgingly admitted. "We didn't even know about this war until recently. We want no part of it. All we want to do is raise our children in a healthy environment. We don't want to be involved. Can't you leave us alone?"

Buren and Eliza placed their hands on his back in mutual support.

"Unfortunately, Mr. Buchanan, the situation is such that you are involved," answered Rhionna with a sympathetic tilt of her head. "In fact, you may be in over your head. Did you think we weren't aware that you are a Sauvage?"

Panic struck Nick like a hammer blow. Only Buren's strong hold on him kept him from dropping to his knees. Eliza stepped in front of him to address the speaker. Her back was up and she wasn't going to allow the elves to run roughshod over her friends.

"With the greatest respect, Madam Grand Council," she said in a tone that could have cut glass. "It was his wife that gave him the Bite, not out of selfishness or in anger, but out of a loving necessity to save his life. They have young children. Would it not have been a crueler fate to rob them of their father?"

"Why did you make no effort to secure an exemption, Mr. Buchanan?" Rhionna inquired with a direct look at Nick.

"Because of what I knew about how your system works," he replied, meeting her formidable gaze head on. The wolf no longer needed to hide. "If I had applied and been denied, I would have had a death card hanging over my head. With Dirk's murders so fresh in the Council's minds, I felt it more than likely I would have been rejected for an exemption. For my family's sake I couldn't take that chance."

Rhionna leaned back with a satisfied nod. She closed the file and pushed it aside.

"You might have been right about that at the time," she admitted. "We do have a corporal law that allows the dispatching of Sauvage. It was something we took extremely seriously in the first century after the Paradeus Uprising. Over time our concerns with the Sauvage have become less significant. We no longer automatically cut them down when we come across them. The more severe the debilitation of the individual the more quickly we take action, however, in most cases we merely keep an eye on them from a distance and monitor their behavior. If we deem their condition to be well managed, we allow them the same freedoms as any other fae creature. It is only when they are not in control of their wolf that we step in. Are you in control of your wolf, Mr. Buchanan?"

BIRTHRIGHT

"Agatha helps keep me on course, so yes, I am."

"Good. Your exemption papers will be filed. Now, about your wife. You claim she knows nothing about Dirk and his army?"

"Hell, no," Nick snapped. He did need to keep the wolf from getting its way for the time being. It wanted to let out a more aggressive response to all the questioning. "Agatha doesn't know anything about it. She knows nothing about her history. She was taken away from her parents when she was born and was raised by human missionaries that tried to make her into something she wasn't. She knows that she's related to Paradeus, but she has no clue what means."

The Grand Council consulted the file once more. Her face was somber. She looked into Nick's eyes with a sharpness that made him flinch.

"Her birth name was Aconitia Winterbourne, the same name as Paradeus' Birthright."

A rumbling murmur went through the High Council as they digested that information.

Nick was not impressed. She was Agatha Buchanan and always would be. She was his wife.

"What difference does that make?" he growled. "She's never known that name."

"It may not make any difference to her, but it will to every other werewolf," declared the Grand Council. "If, as you believe, she does not understand the importance of her position in the greater pack, then she will learn as this war unfolds."

"You don't feel we can prevent it?" asked Holt, addressing her directly.

"I don't see how," Rhionna answered.

"What if Agatha stood up against Dirk?" suggested Eliza. "What if she publicly opposed him? Would you support her?"

The Council members exchanged looks. It was a proposition they had not considered.

"That is something we will need to discuss privately," said Rhionna. "And we shall when this session has ended. Right now we are determining the role each of you has played in this situation. I am inclined to be most lenient with you, Mr. Buchanan. You were brought into this through the dealings of Mrs. Forth-Wright. And while she should have done more to educate you about your decision to marry a Birthright, she could not in truth have prevented you from marrying Agatha. The heart decides for itself in these matters and no amount of wisdom can alter its course. It is our decision that you receive an exemption. You are free to go."

The female elf that had brought them to the Council chamber stepped forward to lead Nick out. He looked back at Eliza, who was apparently never out of confidence. She smiled at him with that bold insouciance of hers. He turned and followed the elf.

CHAPTER THIRTY-SIX

"Trust not the man with nothing to lose."
vagabond adage

Cold stone walls surrounded Agatha when she woke. The hard stone floor had made her stiff from lying on it. She didn't know how long she had lain in the dark. After three failed attempts to get to her feet because of the awkward distribution of pregnant weight she removed her clothes and split her skin to use four steady feet to regain her balance. The baby remained human inside her, which left her wolf belly uncomfortably distended. It would not be able to change its shape until after it was born. She stood amid her own bloody remains and took stock of her situation.

Her nose twitched, pulling in the overwhelming stench of vomit, feces and urine from beyond her cell. The rancid odor of terror counted among the vile smells that assailed her scent organ. She could hear whimpered pleas and violent screams vibrating through the stone walls on every side of her. The pain and torment of Sauvage newborns closed in on her like water closing over her head. She couldn't avoid breathing it in and drowning under its pressure.

Inside her cell there was no straw for bedding. There was a grate in the floor to be used for bodily functions. There was no window, not even a slit for air ventilation. It was suffocatingly dark.

She padded to the rusted metal door, sniffing at the flap located close to the floor. A thin strip of light from under the door broached the eternal night of her prison. It gave her visibility that was four feet wide and two inches deep. She raised her snout to check for a latch.

The door was completely flat, no hardware of any kind except for the bottom flap.

She would have to wait until someone came to let her out. She remained in wolfshape because it was warmer with a fur coat in the icebox of a cell. It would also be more comfortable to curl up on the stone floor. She picked a corner at the back of the cell and folded her legs under her. She nuzzled her uncomfortably swollen abdomen, realizing that she hadn't felt the baby move since she'd awakened. With a trembling sigh, she rested her nose against her stomach and waited.

At Eliza's house that evening, Nick was reunited with his fellow conspirators, if that was what the elves had decided they were. They took dinner in the formal dining room, which was by far more formal than any back home. Eliza liked to keep her house up to the highest standards so the men were dressed in proper dining attire with black jackets and stiff white shirts. She wore an amethyst gown with a deep purple and black brocade corset that strained to keep in her considerable girth. Beshka joined them, her slim figure caressed by dark blue satin. She remained a silent figure at the table, avoiding her father's gaze whenever it came her way.

Although the Victorian government tried to maintain the façade of a moral modern society, the balance had been upset decades ago with the decline of the penal colonies. The country was no more than a wilderness outpost and dumping ground for criminals. Cities were bastions of culture where people of all races could pretend they were isolated from the uglier side of reality. Sydney's nickname of Lesser London reflected the country's desire to rise above its reputation as mere Victorian chattel. The immature country desperately sought its own identity apart from Britain, though it refused to relinquish the customs of Victorian society.

"What happened after I left?" Nick was dying to know how the events had shaken out. "I'm hoping none of you has a death card over you."

BIRTHRIGHT

There was light laughter from the others. They were more relaxed than they had been all day.

"I've been removed from service to the Guardianship," Holt revealed, cutting into his poached trout with elegant silverware. "It won't be easy to find another position in the government, but I'm sure I'll find something. I'm not financially in any danger. It's only my reputation."

Reputation was everything to an elf. For him to be so flippant was evidence of how deep the wound went.

"They suggested I stick to arranging human marriages in future," chuckled Eliza. "I'll do as I damn well please. I don't answer to elves. No offense, gentlemen."

Holt and Buren weren't in the least bothered by her sentiment. They stood behind it one hundred percent. She was human, after all. She was only required to mind the laws of her Victorian government.

Putting down his wine glass, Buren said, "I suppose I got off easy, all things considered. They granted me a full pardon for not following the corporal law, or reporting Dirk sooner. I think they felt a father's protection of his child took precedence. The Grand Council is a wise woman. She wields great power in the elf world."

"And it doesn't hurt that Herself is related to you by marriage," Holt pointed out.

Nick was the only one not eating. The raw calf's liver sat untouched on his plate. It had been warmed to body temperature for his dining pleasure, but he had no appetite.

They would not know if or when the High Council would make its decision to support Agatha's opposition to Dirk's army. He could only pray that their strategy would be enough to keep war from breaking out. The Council's decision could take days. Elves were not ones to rush into anything.

"At least the Victorian government is being proactive," said Eliza, tucking into her trout with gusto.

Nick only peripherally caught her comment. He turned his distracted gaze toward her.

"I'm sorry, what?"

"Your human military is preparing to defend its rights to this continent," answered Holt. He dabbed at his mouth with a crisp white napkin. "They aren't going to just roll over, no pun intended. They're massing ships, both air and sea, to support a land campaign. They've sent for more forces, but I don't know that Britain is that attached to this big rock to take on another Uprising. They may just let him have it."

"If they could make up their minds sooner rather than later it would be a great help," sighed Nick. He poked at the liver with a knife, pushing it around his plate like a finicky child. It was one of his favourite dishes now that he was Sauvage, but tonight he couldn't bring himself to eat it. "It could save us all a headache."

The others agreed wholeheartedly.

A servant came into the dining room and offered an envelope to Nick. He glanced at Eliza, who shrugged. With a tight feeling in his chest he opened the mysterious missive. All colour drained from his face as his eyes scanned the message. The letter drifted to the floor as his hands began to shake. A gold ring fell out of the envelope and rolled across the carpet.

"This can't be happening," he gasped.

He planted his elbows on the table and clutched his head in his hands. He trembled violently. His stomach was repeatedly turning itself inside out. If he had eaten anything he would have vomited. He pressed his tongue against the back of his throat to stop the bile that rose up.

Buren snatched up the letter, reading aloud, "*Agatha has been abducted* stop *Children are safe* stop *Return as soon as possible* stop *Edison Finnerty.*"

"He's got her," Nick moaned, giving in to racking sobs. "He's taken Agatha."

"He won't hurt her," Buren told him. "She's the secret to his success."

Nick looked out from between his palms, tears spilling across his cheeks. They fell, mingling with the blood that pooled in the shallow recess of his plate. He wanted to believe Dirk wouldn't do anything to harm Agatha, but he had no delusions about what Dirk was capable of. If Agatha resisted him there was no telling what that lunatic would do to her or their baby.

Eliza knelt beside Nick and wrapped her arms around him to quell his tremors. He twisted in his seat and clutched her tightly. She was the only thing keeping him from succumbing to the rage of his wolf. She looked to Holt.

"How do we stop him now?"

"I have an idea," the elf replied. "It's a tremendous risk and there are no guarantees that we can pull it off, but it's the only thing I can think of."

"What are you thinking?" Buren demanded. He stood behind Nick's chair, his hands on his best friend's slumped shoulders.

"Nick has to convince Dirk that he wants to join the Sauvage army."

"Are you insane?" Eliza shrilled. She released Nick and loomed up like a fully hooded cobra. "Agatha's life is already in danger, you'd put Nick in harm's way as well? Dirk would never fall for it."

Holt shrugged.

"I didn't say it was great plan, but it's all we've got. Any attempt to use force will be met with more force. He's got the humans outnumbered. He doesn't have to wait until the next full moon, either. If he's been using the traditional method for 'training' then his soldiers are under their wolf's power at all times. It's a brutal tactic, but effective. They'll be strongest under the full moon, but he doesn't need it," the elf sighed. "He can attack whenever he wants."

"How would I convince him I was willing to join?" Nick asked. He forced his weaker emotions into a box deep within himself and locked it. The tears that glimmered on his lashes were the only sign that he had ever given in to them. His eyes took on a hard glint. "I can't very well walk up to his front door and announce that I'm there for the party."

"I'll have to get an audience with Herself, the Grand Council," Holt replied, glancing to Buren who nodded against his better judgment. Holt's gaze shifted to Nick. "We'll need official support if we're to make you a double agent. If the High Council declares you a Sauvage and puts death card over your head then Dirk will hear about it. He'll know you don't have many doors open to you. He might just open his. He'll have Agatha's life in his hands as a means to keep you in line, so he knows you won't do anything rash. It'll be up to you to prove you have what he wants in a soldier."

Nick's resolve was unflinching. He would do whatever it took to get Agatha back safely. If that meant forfeiting his own life then he would do it without hesitation.

"Have Bloem bring Logan and Luna here," he told Buren. "Falmormath is too wide open to protect it from a Sauvage assault. I'd rather they were here in the city."

"I'll send a message right now, and I'll contact Rhionna for a meeting tonight. She won't be pleased, but I think she'll come around once we state our case."

Agatha lost track of time inside her tomb. There was no natural light by which to judge day and night. She shifted from wolf to human to reach her arm out through the door flap in an attempt to reach a latch or lever, but her hands were stepped on by thick soled boots and she learned to keep her hands to herself. She didn't dare stick her muzzle out. Adam brought her meals, which consisted of the same raw meat and water, but he said nothing to her. There was no routine feeding schedule so their arrival offered no hint if it was morning or evening.

At least the baby had become active again. It was her only company. She didn't know when it was due anymore. It could still be four weeks away, or it might only be days. She was losing touch with reality.

In moments when frustration and anger took over she would

claw the walls just to lash out at something tangible. She would howl and scratch with fury, raking furrows in the stone. She didn't know how often she was doing it until she transformed into human form and realised the tips of her fingers were wet and raw where the skin had been rubbed away. Her fingernails had split, becoming jagged shards. She slapped her hands against the door in futility, screaming with aggravation.

At times she felt there was something moving under her skin and she scratched at her arms to make it stop. In those moments she didn't recognize her own wolf. She pulled at her hair as the wolf lashed back, tearing a hole in her scalp from which blood dripped down her neck and shoulder.

She was going crazy and she knew it during her more coherent periods. This was the brutal, inhumane training method used for the new Sauvage to break them. It was working.

CHAPTER THIRTY-SEVEN

"Madness dwells in the hearts and souls of men."
fae proverb

Choking on his nerves, Nick approached the Birthright casually loitering near the fish pond in Hyde Park. Flowers were beginning to bloom around the water's edge, hinting at spring's arrival. He was within view of the High Council building and he knew that several pairs of eyes were following his every move. He glanced over his shoulder at the building behind him, steeling himself for what he was about to do. The weight of Agatha's wedding band on a chain around his neck kept him grounded.

Through the Guardianship this Birthright had been identified as a recruiter for Dirk and had been under surveillance for two weeks, determining his routine and the means by which he made contact with potential recruits. He was a young Russian Birthright brought in by Anatoly Goreyevskiy. The decision had been made for Nick to establish contact via this method, rather than going straight to Dumfries Castle where Dirk was holed up. He would appear more cautious and desperate by going through clandestine channels. He was supposedly a wanted man. It was vital to maintain that ruse under any circumstance.

During those two weeks Nick had been going out of his mind with worry. The single good thing that had happened in those two weeks was that Logan had begun to accept him again. It seemed that the child realised that without his mother Nick was better than nothing. He didn't relax when Nick held him, but he did not scream or

BIRTHRIGHT

resist. He seemed resigned to Nick's touch.

Swallowing a deep breath, Nick walked up to the other werewolf and tapped him on the shoulder.

Oleg Skelekov turned to see the older gentleman standing close to him. He sensed the man's wolf and nodded obligingly. Domesticated Sauvage were rare.

"I understand you're waiting for some friends to join you," said Nick, leaning in and speaking softly. He kept his hands in his pockets.

Oleg looked him up and down. Ideally they wanted younger, fresher meat, but an established Sauvage could be an asset as an officer. This man was clearly in control of his wolf. He would set a good example.

"Yes, you're the first to arrive," he replied. "We'll be meeting tomorrow morning at the Bulli Airyard. Do you know it?"

"I'll find it," Nick assured him.

"Be there at dawn. We won't wait."

Nick nodded in understanding. As he walked away, towards the High Council building, he took his hands out of his pockets as a positive signal to those who watched. He had been recruited into Dirk's army. He was now on his own to get to Agatha.

❧❖❧

Nick arrived at the airyard almost an hour prior to the appointed time. He had not been able to sleep so there was no sense wasting effort. The sun was still beneath the horizon and he could see his breath. He wore canvas trousers, a heavy cotton work shirt and his most comfortably worn in work boots as he approached dock thirteen.

Blue lamps lined the half dozen landing strips further out from where the ships were moored. He stared in fascination as an airship was being towed in by a team of oxen. Regulations prohibited use of fuel powered engines in the airyard for safety purposes. The dirigible's landing gear crunched over gravel as it was guided into its docking hangar. Ground crew came forward to tie down its large hydrogen laden body. Nick watched the men work. He was impressed by their speed and skill as they made short work of securing the land lines to steel cleats.

The crew of the airship on which he would travel was already in action, preparing the craft for flight. The massive envelope was filled taught with hydrogen, hovering above the long passenger cabin.

"You're here early," announced Oleg, coming up behind Nick. He clapped him on the shoulder. "I commend such enthusiasm."

"There's nothing to gain by being idle," said Nick, who abhorred laziness.

Oleg laughed heartily.

"The humans say 'idle hands are the work of the Devil,'" he remarked with a grin.

"'Idle hands are the Devil's playground,'" Nick corrected without thinking. He met Oleg's arched brow with a negligent shrug. "I can't forget everything about being human, can I?"

Oleg cawed with laughter. He liked Nick's unassuming demeanor.

"Ah, here comes our commander," he said, pointing to a figure striding towards them from the hangar.

When the short, thickset Birthright reached them he gave Nick a shrewd once over.

"So, you are one of our newest recruits?" It was a question and a statement. His accent was straight from London. "I am Commander Collin Stafford-Hines. You may call me Senior Stafford-Hines. You are Copernicus Buchanan, the Sauvage being hunted by the Guardianship."

Nick was taken aback that the man recognized him, but he didn't let it show. He hoped it didn't show. He hadn't expected to be identified so easily. Apparently the elves had been more than thorough with his cover.

Nick inclined his head, but kept silent.

Stafford-Hines smirked, but it was without humor. His deep set eyes were calculating.

"Your name is familiar to us. Our esteemed Alpha Leader is

eager to meet you again. He is understandably curious about your motives."

"I have nowhere else to go," Nick said with an appropriate amount of bitterness. "My land and my children have been seized by my own government, which has now turned its back on me. The elves in their infinite kindness have placed a death card over my head because my wife gave me the Bite. If that isn't reason enough to sign up for your little rebellion, I don't know what is."

"Your wife gave you the Bite?" Oleg echoed in surprise.

"She thought I was being unfaithful, so that was her way of punishing me." Nick found lying easier than he'd thought.

Oleg and the commander exchanged looks.

"Yet you are in control of your wolf," observed Stafford-Hines.

"More often than not." Nick grinned. "I guess it likes me."

"It must like you, indeed," guffawed Oleg. "There certainly aren't many Sauvage like you."

Stafford-Hines went off to check on the state of the airship's readiness. Oleg lit a cigarette and offered one to Nick, who declined.

"I'm afraid my only bad habit is an affinity for the grape," he commented wistfully.

"Wine?" Oleg scoffed. "Ah, wine is weak. You should drink vodka."

While they debated the merits of wine versus vodka other recruits began to trickle in and the airyard came to life around them with cargo ships heading out one after another.

There was mandatory overnight grounding for inspection at all major airyards. Every thousand air miles the ships were carefully checked for leaks, rust, faulty equipment and any other hazard that could lead to a potential crash. It was a necessary safety precaution.

Nick was the only one among the dozen or so men who was already a Sauvage. They were captivated by him, hounding him with questions about the process of receiving the Bite. He hesitated to offer them his perspective. His experience had been a good enough one. They were going to be tortured and turned into monsters. It made his gorge rise to talk to these healthy human men, knowing what awaited them at Dumfries Castle. He finally halted their incessant chatter by declaring he was too tired to keep talking. He took a seat at the back of the cabin and settled in for the flight.

<hr />

She wasn't sure what day it was when the door finally opened. Agatha sat at the back of her cell, scared and cold, hugging her stomach, rocking back and forth. She used a mound of her shed fur as a nest. Dried curls of her old skins were scattered around the floor.

There was a deep echo of metal on metal that reverberated through the stone walls. Her head came up as the door opened. Startlingly bright light flooded the room, momentarily blinding her. Dirk van Amersvoot stood in the opening, casting a shadow that reached across the floor to her feet. She tucked her feet up, away from the dark shape.

"Good morning, Agatha," he said.

She squinted up at him, eyes refusing to focus clearly. She turned her head slightly to stop the light from piercing directly into her pupils.

"Is it morning?" she asked. "What day is it?"

"You've been here about two weeks," he said, stepping into the cell.

She calculated in her head that the baby was due in another two weeks. She still had a chance to get out before it arrived, if she could figure out to do that.

Lance Highmoon lounged in the doorway, leaning against the steel frame. He was there to make sure she didn't try anything stupid.

"I hope you don't think me cruel for keeping you like this," said Dirk, kneeling in front of her. "I'm afraid it was a necessary evil to keep you from hurting yourself. Or anyone else."

"Like you?" she hissed. She blinked constantly against the painful glare of light that burned into her eyes. "Why would I hurt you? Because you killed my family?"

"I haven't hurt your family," he replied. "Yet. Whether I do or not is up to you."

Her face turned upwards, hope blooming like a flower in the desert, fragile and short lived. She saw the mocking gleam in his eyes and knew he was lying. She bared her teeth in a show of defiance.

He slapped her once, hard. Blood seeped from her lip.

"Don't challenge me," he warned her. He adopted a pious tone. "We need to present a united front for our soldiers' morale."

"I don't love you, Dirk," she said, licking the blood from her split lip. "Why can't you just accept that?"

"This has nothing to do with love," he replied, rising. He looked down on her with false pity. "I've never loved you. I only wanted you for your bloodline."

She blinked up at him uncomprehendingly.

"What does that have to do with any of this?" she whined, hating herself for showing weakness.

"You really don't know, do you?" he sneered. He snorted in disdain at her naïveté. "You're the only living descendant of Paradeus. Your parents named you after his Birthright, Aconitia Winterbourne. Every werewolf will look to you as their Alpha Queen, whether you accept it or not."

"I'm not-I can't-" she stammered, shaking her head. She pulled herself into a fetal position and pressed her arms close to her belly as though she could keep her baby from hearing his words. "I don't want that."

He laughed in a cold, emotionless manner.

"Whether you're my mate or my trophy, you will stand beside me as I take this continent," he promised.

He walked to the door and Lance moved aside. Without a backward glance, he shut the door and sentenced her to a pit of darkness.

"How long do you think it will take?" inquired Lance as they made their way along the stark stone corridor.

"It will only take one thing to convince her," said Dirk. "I'm just keeping her locked up until that mutt is born. She'll do anything to protect it. After she's done what I want her to, it's dead. It's of no use to me. I need to plant my seed to create a true Alpha pack. I can't have Buchanan's mutts hanging around. That includes the two you took care of."

Lance paused as they reached the exterior door and prepared to enter the courtyard. He wasn't about to let Dirk know that they hadn't done anything to Agatha's twins. He would find a time to rectify the situation.

"Speaking of Buchanan, I hear he's coming in on the next airship from Sydney."

Dirk's smile was inhuman.

"So he is coming," he said, nodding with approval. "I want a proper welcome prepared. I'll be in my quarters when he arrives. I expect to be notified at once." As Lance walked away, Dirk said, "Don't lay a hand on him. I want to know what he's about."

Lance nodded and continued on his way.

※

The airship came in on time.

Nick stared out at the behemoth fortress built on a mountain top with steep, thickly wooded slopes on all sides. It was imposing and appeared impenetrable to the casual observer. Dirk had expanded it to include barracks, holding and training cells and a landing pad for airships, all contained within the towering stone walls. It sprawled across the entire surface of the mountain's flat terrain. The valleys spreading out below had been cleared of forestation and turned into internment camps for the Sauvage, complete with tall wire perimeter fences and pens for holding the unstable new soldiers. It became clear how Dirk had managed to amass such a large army so quickly. The Sauvage in the camps below were almost all Aborigines. He was rounding them up like the Regulators had done to the werewolves in America.

The local limestone caves had begun attracting naturalists' attention in the last decade, but with dragons currently in situ there were

BIRTHRIGHT

no longer visitors to the stunning, cathedral-like caverns. The karst landscape was the domain of the fire-breathing lizards.

Nick felt his heart creeping into his throat as the airship descended into the north courtyard nearest the soldiers' barracks. He swallowed firmly to return it to where it belonged in his chest. His gaze scanned the compound for any sign of Agatha. He didn't expect to find her like Juliet, on a balcony waving a handkerchief at him, but he had hoped to see her somewhere in one of the fortress' open areas. It was disheartening that she was nowhere to be seen.

"Alright, mutts, out you go," bellowed Stafford-Hines. He gave the last man to clamber out of the airship a stiff kick in the ass before jumping down himself. "Form up!"

Nick stood shoulder to shoulder at attention with the other new recruits in a straight line across the yard. His eyes continued to rove around the area.

"Eyes front!" roared Stafford-Hines, positioned directly in front of Nick.

"Yes, Sir!" Nick barked. He did as he was told.

Stafford-Hines looked into Nick's intense blue eyes. They stared unblinkingly at one another for a painful amount of time until the commander was satisfied. He turned and moved down the line. Nick blinked, breathing heavily in annoyance. His wolf wanted to take a piece out of Stafford-Hines so badly that it ached. He again mentally thanked Agatha's influence for the control he had over it. He couldn't imagine what would have happened if he was a Sauvage like these poor sods were going to become. It would have gotten ugly in a hurry.

Lance stood on the second floor gallery, watching the exchange between Buchanan and the commander. The man knew when to listen. Lance took his time descending the steps the led to the courtyard. He didn't take his eyes off Buchanan.

Nick caught a glimpse of a tall black-haired Birthright striding across the courtyard, but he didn't shift his gaze to see the man clearly. The man did that for him. Lance stepped into Nick's line of sight and walked straight at him.

"Commander Highmoon," greeted Stafford-Hines, strolling back along the row of new soldiers. "What brings you to review my newest batch of mutts?"

He couldn't miss the fact that Lance was staring at Nick with undisguised hatred, but he chose to ignore it. They weren't supposed to get personally involved with their soldiers. Whatever was going on between Highmoon and Buchanan wasn't his business.

"I'll be taking this one to the Alpha Leader," Lance replied.

He grasped Nick's arm and pulled him violently forward. Nick would have fallen if he'd still been human. With the wolf's reflexes he kept his feet and matched the tall werewolf's strides without any difficulty as they marched towards an archway that led to another courtyard. He said nothing to the American Birthright who was at ease without conversation.

As they mounted a circular stone staircase in one corner of the open yard, Nick caught sight of a familiar face out of the corner of his eye. He turned his head to follow Adam Steelcuff as the traitor disappeared through a large metal door on the far side of the courtyard.

A moment later Nick's nose tingled as Agatha's scent drifted on the clear air. It came from the same place where Adam had gone. He could detect the unhealthy condition she was in. The wolf was chafing against his skin in its desire to go to her. He had to find the right time. He could not act out impulsively.

Soon enough he found himself dragged in front of a massive wooden door with iron findings. Two large guards stood on either side, armed with static spears. The tips of those weapons could pierce flesh and send an electrical charge powerful enough to stop the heart. Harnessing electricity was still a young science and only for those who could afford it. It was no surprise that Dirk was using every weapon at his disposal. Lance nodded and one guard opened the door. Lance shoved Nick through and backed away.

Nick heard the door slam shut behind him like a death knell.

"Well, well," said a gratingly familiar voice from his right. He

BIRTHRIGHT

turned quickly and was face to face with Dirk van Amersvoot. "Uncle Nick. What brings you here?"

Adam hurried down the corridor to Agatha's cell. He had been bringing her twice daily meals since she'd arrived and he knew that she was deteriorating. That was what Dirk wanted, but Adam was not convinced it was the right way to handle her. Like a rock with an unseen fissure, she appeared strong, but she could be shattered if struck the right way.

He carried a tray with a freshly killed rabbit and a bowl of water. It was a treat today. If Dirk learned that he had altered the routine he would have Adam lashed, or worse, thrown in his own cell.

He lifted the door flap and slid the tray across the floor. It barely passed into the cell before she was on it, tearing at the rabbit's flesh with rabid energy. He could see her muzzle as she tore into the animal's small brown carcass with crushing teeth. There was other blood on her lower lip and he could smell that it was hers.

Had she injured herself? He didn't know if he wished that was the case or if it was easier to think that Dirk had probably struck her. One possibility meant she was one step closer to the brink of insanity. The other meant Dirk's concern for her was at an end. Either answer was a bullet through his heart.

"Agatha?" he whispered, kneeling to speak through the narrow opening. "I'm sorry. I want you to know that."

Her throaty growl made him back away. He caught a metallic gold flash from her eyes as he closed the flap. By Gods, what had he done to her?

CHAPTER THIRTY-EIGHT

"The past cannot be changed. It is a lesson learned."
John Nigel, philosopher

A cool draft filled the sitting room in the castle's tower. The windows were open to allow fresh air to flow freely. Heavy brown velvet curtains barely moved in the breeze. The room was decorated with thick, dark furniture. Tapestries depicting violent hunting scenes hung on the walls. A depressing atmosphere filled the air.

Dirk sat in a high backed, throne-like chair with arms that were carved into lion heads. His legs were crossed in a sign of authority. He was dressed like a military leader: tall black boots, khaki trousers, matching long- sleeved shirt with a double row of brass buttons up the front. His expression was deceptively laconic as he regarded his guest.

Nick's wolf desperately yearned to get loose and sink its teeth into the smug face across from him. It was straining his self-control to its limits. He clenched his fists at his sides.

"I hear things didn't go so well with the elves," Dirk mused, flicking lint off his thigh.

"So you know there's a death card over my head," Nick replied. "I'm not happy to be here, but I can be an asset to your efforts. You can use my wolf to your advantage."

"To my advantage?" Dirk scoffed. "How will you be an asset? I've attacked you, raped and abducted your wife, killed your children and now you come to me with this delusion of becoming my ally? I never took you for a fool, Nick."

BIRTHRIGHT

"Desperation will make a man do things against his nature. This is the only place I have left to go," he said. His eyes were hard as ice. "I've lost everything. You have Agatha. You've won and I might as well be on the winning team in this war. That's the best I can get."

Dirk smiled conceitedly. He met Nick's unrelenting stare.

"Yes, I do have Agatha, or should I say Aconitia?"

A muscle flicked in Nick's jaw. His eyes narrowed for a fraction of a second and the wolf came to the surface.

"Her name is Agatha," he ground out, wrestling the wolf back. "I would prefer if you called her that."

"I'm calling her by her true name, the one her Birthright parents gave her. They gave their lives to bring her into this world. Don't you think their dying efforts should be honored?"

Nick let a long breath out through flared nostrils, but he nodded.

"The truth is I can use you," said Dirk with a bemused grin.

Nick waited apprehensively.

"As much as I'd like to kill you outright, I can use you as example of what happens to anyone who tries to challenge me," Dirk informed him.

It felt as if cold water had suddenly been poured down Nick's back. He had walked willingly into the wolf's den. What had he really expected from Dirk? A welcoming party with streamers? He had hoped that his life would be spared, but it would seem that Dirk had other plans.

"What do you have in mind?" he asked with far more bravado than he felt.

Dirk's head came up slightly.

He'd known Nick his entire life. Nick had carried him home when he'd broken his arm trying to ride a ram on a dare from Lars. It had been Nick who had allowed him to tie a rope to a tree overhanging a deep pond on Gilgai, so he and Lars could spend hot summers keeping cool away from their parents' prying eyes. Even as a grown man Nick had joined them in that boyhood thrill, flinging himself with reckless abandon from the rope to splash down like a cannonball. When his father had come down on him for sneaking out to join friends for a drinking party in the hills, Nick had stepped up and pled his case, getting him off with a warning rather than a bruised backside. Nick had been there through all the major events in his life, never once judging him for being a helf bastard. He owed Nick more consideration, but that part of his life was dead and rotting in the concrete cell his father had built. The insecurity and arrogance brought forth by Natassia's influence would not allow him to give Nick any leniency. Nick was a threat to everything he had built and would have to be dealt with.

"I'm not sure yet, but I'm sure I'll think of something….original."

Dirk called to his guards and the muscular brutes came in immediately, like well trained hounds. He instructed them to take Nick back to Commander Stafford-Hines in the barracks. He knew the senior officer wouldn't let Nick get away with anything. Maybe Nick would prove himself useful as a soldier after all.

That night Nick lay awake on his bunk in his sleeping trousers, listening to the distant screams of the newborn Sauvage as they suffered. After basic military training was completed, the men he had arrived with would all be taken to a part of the castle where Birthrights waited to give them the Bite. There were whispers in the dark room as the men murmured about the cries and howls in the night. They had been told that those were prisoners being tortured. They did not realize that, soon enough, they would be the ones fighting against a wild animal forced unwillingly into their bodies, and the unholy shrieks would be theirs.

His thoughts turned to his primary objective. Somewhere inside the walls Agatha was trapped and he didn't how bad her condition was, he just knew that she was not in a good state. Was the stress too much for her? Had she already given birth? If so, was their baby alive? Had Dirk taken it away from her and killed it? Too many visions of horror filled his head. He pushed his fists into his eyes to stop them.

He wouldn't know anything until morning. Turning onto his side,

BIRTHRIGHT

he envisioned Agatha's lean body naked beside him. He could see her lively sparkling gold eyes gazing back at him until tears blurred her face. He reached out to touch her, but she disappeared. He quietly cried himself to sleep, his wolf whimpering within.

***

He was awakened before dawn by a hand pressing firmly against his mouth. His eyes shot open to see Adam Steelcuff next to his bunk. It was Adam's palm that silenced him.

"Don't make a sound," Adam warned in a breathy hiss. "Come with me."

Nick used all his Sauvage stealth to move silently. He changed into his work trousers before following Adam past the rows of snoring recruits. He pulled on his shirt as they slipped out into the corridor. Adam led him through several halls until Nick was completely lost. He had no idea what Adam wanted with him or why Adam was acting so strangely. He tugged on his boots as they worked their way through the maze of corridors.

They were just sneaking down a stairwell to the courtyard where Nick had first arrived, at last something he recognized, when a group of officers appeared through an arched doorway. They took one look at Adam and Nick and stopped in their tracks. The courtyard was well lit by tall lampposts around the perimeter so they got a full look at the suspicious pair.

"I hope you'll forgive me someday," said Adam softly, landing a hard blow into Nick's ribcage.

Nick groaned, falling back.

"What's going on?" demanded Rutger Schaefer, stepping forward. He was of equal rank to Adam. "Senior Steelcuff?"

"A little extra training," Adam replied. "This one doesn't know how to show respect to an alpha."

Nick's wolf was done being kept down. He lunged forward, catching Adam in the stomach with his shoulder and taking his back into the wall at full speed. The air went out of Adam's lungs in a loud huff.

"Seems like you're the one getting schooled, American," laughed Rutger.

Adam could barely breathe, but he whispered in Nick's ear, "Take it easy. I'm on your side."

Nick withdrew with a suspicious glower, only to have Adam's fist connect with his jaw. It made his teeth rattle in their sockets.

Without the full moon he was weaker than a Birthright, but not by much. The moon was waxing in the sky and it would be only a few more days until it peaked. His wolf felt stronger than ever before despite the lack of the moon's influence.

The two men squared off with a growing audience. Adam got in another blow to Nick's jaw and Nick spat blood.

Nick had every reason to go for Adam's throat, but he didn't understand why Adam was giving him the chance. If what Adam had said rang true, then this was a ruse of some sort. A painful ruse, to be sure. The look in Adam's eyes told him that Adam wasn't interested in hurting him. He was putting on a show because they had been caught. If he wanted a show then Nick's wolf would oblige.

Adam saw the wolf rising in Nick's clear blue eyes and realised that he had to put an end to the demonstration before things got out of hand. If they let this go on one of them was going to get hurt. There would be no avoiding it.

"Enough, mutt," he declared.

With the strongest effort of his life, Nick forced his wolf to back down. It resisted valiantly and he swung once more at Adam, but didn't land the blow. Resentfully accepting his authority, the wolf receded. Nick stood with head lowered in submission, his cheek already starting to swell.

The officers and guards applauded as Adam led Nick away.

"I should kill you," Nick growled at him.

They passed beneath the archway leading to a smaller courtyard. Nick tested the air for signs of Agatha's presence.

"I'm not the one you should waste your energy on," Adam told him. "I'm the reason your children are still alive."

BIRTHRIGHT

"Why does Dirk think they're dead?"

Adam halted in the shadows and Nick did likewise. Their eyes locked in a silent struggle for dominance.

"You're still learning what it means to be a werewolf," Adam sighed. "Male werewolves don't keep other males' cubs around. They only want their own bloodline to continue."

Nick staggered back, whispering, "What about this baby?"

"He'll kill it after it's born."

"She hasn't had it yet?" Nick said in relief. "I can still get her out of here before she does."

Adam nodded. He placed his hand on Nick's arm.

"I didn't mean to hurt you just now, or hurt Agatha ever," he said earnestly. "I believed in Dirk's vision of a united country for our kind and I knew that Agatha would be able to bring that vision to life. He sent me to try to convince her to join him. He thought someone from the Rez would stand a better chance of bringing her into the new pack order. I was supposed to kill her husband and children, but when I met you I realised how much she loved you and what you've given her. I couldn't take that away from her."

"But you did."

Adam looked away, embarrassed. For a moment he couldn't meet Nick's eyes.

"If I had thought for one minute that Dirk planned to 'train' her, I would have taken him on myself. He's crazy. Lance is completely enamoured of him and his grandiose plan to take over this Gods' forsaken continent. Between the two of them Agatha doesn't stand a chance." He looked directly into Nick's intimidating glare. "I've been keeping an eye on her and she's going downhill. The moon madness is already setting in."

Nick wasn't familiar with that diagnosis. It sounded frightening.

"What the hell is moon madness?"

"It's when the wolf and human can't tell each apart anymore. They begin to attack each other. She'll end up tearing herself apart, physically and mentally," Adam explained. His voice softened in reaction to Nick's mortified gaze. "Very few survive and those that do are left scarred, inside and out."

"You're telling me that she's going to start hurting herself if we don't get her out of there? What about the baby?"

"She'll do more than just hurt herself. It's the worst thing you can imagine. I've seen werewolves rip off their own limbs and claw out their eyes. The Regulators liked to use it to make examples of anyone who challenged them. I don't know what she might do to the baby."

Nick suddenly remembered Dirk's words. Was the same punishment in store for him? It didn't matter what happened to him. His only concern was Agatha and the baby she still carried. He blocked out any thoughts of what injuries she could inflict upon herself. He couldn't allow that to interrupt his focus.

"How do we get her out of here?"

"The moon will be full in three days," Adam replied. He glanced out at the graying light in the courtyard. The sun was rising. "Dirk's planning to move on the cities. His army will be at full strength then. His commanders are waiting outside Perth, Melbourne, Sydney and Brisbane for orders to move in. But first he wants to parade Agatha around to whip his troops into a frenzy. He plans to show her off to the troops massing outside Sydney. He's taking her there tomorrow."

"She can't go anywhere in her condition," Nick protested. "It's too dangerous."

Adam leveled a look at him that told him he'd stated the obvious.

"I think I can get him to take you along then we'll have to make something up as we go. There will be some point when his guard is down. We'll have to take it when we can."

Nick wasn't content to just wait as Agatha tore herself up.

"I have to see her."

"There's no time right now. You have to get back to your barracks. Stafford-Hines will make my beating look like a tickle if you're not there at first call."

Nick glanced into the empty courtyard and bolted across the broad square towards the door where he had picked up Agatha's scent the day before. Adam shot after him, dragging him into the shadowy recesses before the guards saw him.

"Are you out of your mind?" he snarled in Nick's face.

"I have to see her."

"By Gods, you are in love with that woman," Adam mumbled. "Only a fool in love would do what you just did. Wait here."

Adam quickly formed a scheme. He had always been one to think on his feet. He grabbed Nick by the nape and made his way to the thick wood door that led to the training cells. He addressed the two guards, telling them that he was bringing in a new "trainee". They opened the door.

Once inside the dank corridor, Adam headed straight for Agatha's cell. He had learned to tune out the sounds of misery long ago, but Nick flinched at every scream that filled the hall.

"She's right there. You have thirty seconds."

Nick dropped to his knees and lifted the door flap.

"Agatha?" he called into the darkness.

He was met by a snapping, snarling muzzle that shot out of the opening. It was joined by a partially human arm, covered in grey fur. Black claws scrabbled on the stone surface, reaching for him. Nick threw himself back, crab-crawling across the floor until his back slammed into the opposite wall.

"Holy shit!"

"You've seen her. Time to go," announced Adam, hauling him to his feet.

"No, wait, I have to talk to her-"

Adam pushed him against the wall.

"She isn't in any mood to talk, in case you hadn't noticed," he said, using his forearm to pin Nick by the throat. "You need to keep your wits about you right now or you're going to be the death of her. Now let's get you back to your barracks before Stafford-Hines turns this place upside down looking for you."

Adam lied to the guards, telling them he had brought the wrong "trainee". He said something about a mix-up in paperwork and dragged Nick out into the brightening courtyard.

Because Nick was fully dressed when he returned to his barracks and the other men were just climbing out of bed, they assumed he was trying to make points by showing them up. They commented on his puffy, bruised cheek but he didn't respond. He was standing at attention when Stafford-Hines came in. His fellow soldiers were still getting dressed.

"I like a man with initiative," Stafford-Hines said with an appraising nod. He gripped Nick's chin in his fist and turned his head to get a better look at the bruise. "It would seem that your wolf had a little fun at your expense last night."

"You should see the other guy," Nick replied coldly.

"Hm." The commander walked away to continue his inspection of the troops.

Nick felt a knot in his belly that would not unwind. His time was running out to save Agatha.

CHAPTER THIRTY-NINE

"New life breeds new hope."
Edward V. Schuster, philosopher

Dirk leaned over a map of the continent spread out on a large table, studying the positions of his troops and those of the humans. The elves were still non-committal at this point. That had been their initial stance three hundred years ago. Maybe this time they were going to keep their elitist noses out of it.

"I want another dragon deployed in Perth," he said, moving a red puck to the southwest corner of the map. "It would be too easy for the Victorian colonies in India to send more ships to that port. I want every ship burnt to its keel in the harbors and anything in the sky brought down."

Lance nodded. He turned to a young Birthright runner and repeated the order. The werewolf sprinted away to relay it to the dragon's representative.

Dirk regarded the line of his troops as it formed a crescent moon shape around the landlocked portion of Sydney. There were also pucks representing the human resistance blocking his ranks from the city's center. They were pitifully outnumbered by Sauvage. Even with superior weaponry the humans were no match for what he was going to unleash.

"You know they'll be ready," said Lance, gazing at the map.

"Ready to die for our noble cause," Dirk replied with a grin. "Get the commanders to rally their men. Prepare Aconitia for transport. We're going to Sydney."

Adam entered the room, bringing the news that he had feared. When he had just brought Agatha her meal he had smelled blood and something new, unfamiliar. She didn't come forward to attack her food. She hung to the back of the room, whining. He realised with a sinking feeling that what he smelled was amniotic fluid. Her water had broken sometime in the last few hours. Her labour starting was a blessing and a curse. It meant that Dirk couldn't take her with him to Sydney. Even he wouldn't risk that. She would be of no use to him now until after the baby was born.

"I'm sorry, but she won't be able to join you just yet," Adam informed him. "I've just come from the training cells. She's in labour."

Dirk snatched a tall silver candelabra from the map table and hurled it across the room.

"I swear she must have planned this," he snarled. "Fine. We'll go ahead without her. She can join me after she's pushed out Buchanan's mutt." He looked to Lance. "I can trust you'll take care of it?"

With a calculating glance at Adam, Lance answered, "Just like the other two."

"We didn't touch the other two," Adam retorted, seizing a potential opportunity. He turned to Dirk. "They're in Sydney with your family."

"What?" Dirk roared. Another silver candelabra went flying. "Why the hell didn't you kill them when you grabbed Aconitia?"

Adam managed to appear contrite as he answered, "You only ordered us to get her. You didn't tell us to do anything about the twins."

He took the damaging blow from Dirk's fist with stoic resilience, although he nearly went down.

"I know you aren't that stupid," Dirk snapped. "Find out where they are in the city. I don't want a dragon torching the wrong house by mistake. Once I've burned most of Sydney to the ground I'll take care of them myself."

Adam swore that a better opportunity could not have presented itself. With Dirk away from the compound it would leave only untrained Sauvage and a few officers behind at Dumfries. It would be a simple matter to deal with Stafford-Hines's raw recruits and the remaining guards. He had a surprise in store for them. He would have to make sure Nick was left behind as well. That was crucial for Agatha's sake. Dirk would be too preoccupied with battle lines to be worried about Nick. That left Lance to deal with.

By early afternoon, airships were rising into the skies, joining the iridescent crimson bodies of six dragons as they burst from the limestone caverns like a stream of erupting magma. The lead dragon, Torric, carried the passenger basket with Dirk and his two closest commanders.

Adam watched from the parapet as they shrank away in the distance, heading towards the unfortunate citizens of Sydney. The people there were not his concern. He had only one person on his mind. Agatha.

He scurried to the stairwell and was met by Lance coming up.

"I was going to make sure Buchanan's other mutts were dealt with so Dirk didn't have to find out how incompetent we were," Lance said harshly.

"What difference does it make now? He'd rather get his own hands dirty anyway," Adam said reasonably. His eyes tracked movement behind Lance. "And you get to wring this mutt's neck yourself. That should make you happy."

Lance grunted angrily and took a step back. He collided with Nick. He hadn't heard Nick's stealthy approach. Nick's arm looped around the Birthright's neck and he pulled tight. His wolf was giving him strength and he wasn't going to make it go away any time soon.

Adam stood and smiled at the astonished expression on Lance's face.

"I think you should reconsider who's incompetent," he said to Lance. "You let a Sauvage get the drop on you. I'm shocked."

Lance pushed against Nick, forcing him backward. Nick's hip struck the stone rail and he winced. He glanced down at the hundred foot drop to the forest below.

"I'm still stronger for three more days," said Lance, pivoting in Nick's hold. He cracked his forehead against Nick's brow and Nick staggered away, briefly disoriented. "I don't even need to change shape to prove it."

Adam moved closer, but Nick waved him off.

"Get to Agatha," Nick said, ears ringing from the skull blow. "That's all that matters. I've got this."

Adam didn't need it repeated. He lunged down the stairwell, leaving Nick to it.

Lance smirked, taking slow steps towards where Nick crouched. He wasn't intimidated by the bared teeth that invited him to fight.

"I'm going to enjoy tearing your throat out," Lance said with shining eyes. "It's so much more satisfying to take down a Sauvage. You shouldn't even be allowed to exist."

He loomed above Nick, glaring into the older werewolf's turbulent gaze. A silver sheen flashed across Nick's pale irises. Lance hesitated. He recognized the sign of an emerging wolf. It was impossible for Nick to change now. The moon was nearly full, but its power wouldn't be complete for three days.

Nick welcomed the wolf.

"You know who my Birthright is, don't you?" he growled, tasting blood as the roof of his mouth began to split. "You keep thinking she's the only living descendant of Paradeus. Everyone's forgotten that makes me one, too."

He gave over to the wolf and before the shards of his skin hit the stone he was in the air, aiming for Lance's unprotected neck. Lance stumbled back, calling to his wolf. It wasn't quick enough to fend off Nick's teeth as they plunged deeply into his flesh. Lance clawed at him, unable to bring his wolf forth. It cowered submissively to the rage and power of Nick's dominance. Lance had never been an alpha. His pack position had always been a beta, secondary to the pack leaders. When faced with stronger alpha, his wolf showed its belly. It was his human side that did not know when to surrender.

BIRTHRIGHT

Nick brought him down, bringing his teeth together through bone, ligament and muscle. His fangs cut easily through the tissues, severing the carotid artery. A large splash of blood spread across the stone.

Lance stopped resisting.

With a final shake, Nick released his hold on the Birthright. He looked up at the brilliant blue sky in wonder. How had he been able to change before the full moon? Had he been right that the infection passed from Agatha included some of Paradeus' rumored ability to change at will?

Agatha.

He focused himself on changing back to his human shape. The wolf was reticent to retreat, but it understood his urgency and gave in. Feather-like clumps of dark fur blew away on the breeze, drifting down to the treetops far below. He collected his discarded clothing, pulling on his ragged trousers. His shirt was torn, but still buttoned, and he slipped it over his head. He didn't need boots. His bare feet pounded on the stone as he rushed to reach Agatha.

———

In the black abyss of her prison, Agatha leaned against the wall as another sharp pain gripped her abdomen. There was pressure building low in her pelvis and she knew the baby would be born soon.

The guards didn't challenge Adam as he approached them on quick marching feet. He had known they wouldn't. He had authority to be in the training cells and they were far down in the order of the greater pack. They allowed him to pass without question.

Adam could hear one shrill cry rise above the riot of screams in the corridor. He had to work quickly. He went to the main mechanism that operated the locks on the cell doors. Without thinking twice he pulled it back and a series of clanks reached his ears as the doors opened simultaneously down the length of the corridor. He used the first door as a shield, hiding behind the steel the barrier as he pressed against the wall. The cell's mutated occupant emerged on four thin legs. It was joined by other misshapen Sauvage from the cell on the other side of the hall. They lingered in the corridor, unsure about their freedom.

Adam pressed himself in as tightly as he could then called out, "Guards! I need help!"

The two Birthrights came barreling into the corridor, static spears at the ready. Thirty psychotic Sauvage in every conceivable state of transition met them, charging at their captors. The "trainees" made short work of the guards before following their noses outside.

After the last one left, Adam extricated himself from his hiding place and made his way to Agatha's cell. He pulled the door open to find her with her head down, leaning against the wall on her forearms. There was a large stain on the skirt of her dress. She arched her back, whining loudly as a contraction gripped her. Adam went to her, helping her to lie down on a bed of her own wolf fur with her legs spread apart. Her face was red with the exertion of pushing. He pulled her dress up and tucked it under her breasts.

"You're doing fine, Agatha," he said. "You're doing just fine."

He knelt between her knees, evaluating her condition. Adam could see that she was on the verge of delivering. The skin of her perineum was swollen as the baby's head pressed outward on its journey towards daylight.

He had been trained as a doctor's assistant on the Rez because of the lack of medical care the werewolves received from the Regulators. The more sympathetic missionaries had felt it prudent to teach basic first aid to some of the more intelligent, submissive Birthrights. Though it was illegal to breed on the Rez, werewolves were amazingly fertile and forbidden births were common.

"Keeping pushing, Agatha. Push," he encouraged her. "You can do it."

She groaned, gasping for breath between contractions. She bore down with formidable muscles, bringing the baby closer to Adam's waiting hands.

BIRTHRIGHT

※❖※

Wiping Lance's blood from his face with his sleeve as he ran, Nick was able to reach the east tower where the female Birthrights were housed without crossing paths of any of the Sauvage. Dirk had been an equal opportunity recruiter. While the Sauvage were all male, he had brought in male and female Birthrights to give the Bite. Most of the castle's occupants had departed for Sydney with Dirk, but there were enough left behind for the uncontrolled Sauvage to massacre.

The courtyard below him was a gruesome battlefield of slaughter. The human recruits with whom he had arrived were on the galleries shooting down on several cornered Sauvage. Birthrights and Sauvage were engaged in a dance of death on the floor of the courtyard. There were dead and dying werewolves and humans scattered about like autumn leaves. The carnage extended to the halls and rooms throughout the castle. It seemed nowhere was safe.

Running along the gallery to reach Agatha, he passed Stafford-Hines. The commander changed to wolfshape in front of him and leaped onto the stone rail overlooking the courtyard. His clothes fell to the floor. He paid no attention as Nick raced by. The Birthright was caught up in the action below him. Most of the newborn Sauvage were from his last platoon that had been undergoing the brutal training process. He threw himself down onto the back of a Sauvage and tore into the creature's skull.

Nick narrowly avoided being grabbed by a Sauvage as he squeezed through the door to the training cells. Its claws tore his sleeve but he slammed the door on its paw, leaving a mass of bloody pulp on the floor where the severed fingers landed.

"Agatha?" Nick's voice rang out on the stone walls.

"Nick!" Adam shouted. "Hurry! In here!"

Nick skidded into the cell as Agatha howled, straining to force the baby out. He dropped to his knees on the sharp pieces of her dried skins. He didn't feel them clawing into his skin like fingernails. He was only aware of Agatha's struggle to give birth to their child.

There were now screams coming from beyond the training cells as the out of control Sauvage hunted down anyone left in the castle. After several minutes they heard fewer gunshots and less yelling.

Nick could see a pale round shape protruding from between Agatha's widespread thighs. He took her hand, letting her squeeze tightly through the pain. The compressed features of his newest child became visible as the head fully emerged.

Adam guided the bald head with gentle fingers as it slid into his hands, followed by the slippery body in a splash of retained fluid. The baby was covered in a patchy coating of waxy vernix, making it look unnaturally grayish and wrinkled. There was no mistaking the gender.

Nick was too emotional to speak as his son was laid on Agatha's bare stomach. The baby wailed, its eyes screwed shut and gums showing in the wide open mouth. Its arms and legs floundered like a fish stranded on a beach. With sharp teeth, Adam bit through the rubbery blue umbilical cord.

"Here, wrap him in this," he said, wiping blood from his mouth. "We need to keep him warm."

Nick used Adam's vest to bundle the baby, swaddling it as tightly as he could before placing it on its mother's chest. Agatha looked down at her son then at Nick. Reality came crashing in and tears rippled down her cheeks. The moon madness disappeared with the antidote of his presence at her side.

"You're here," she gasped, touching Nick's face. "You're really here."

"I'm not leaving you again," he told her, pulling her and their son into his arms. His tears saturated her lank hair. The baby wriggled between them, still crying. "I'm never leaving you again."

Adam stepped out of the cell to give them a few minutes alone. He also needed to think of a way out for all of them. It wasn't going to be easy with agitated Sauvage running rampant in the fortress. They would attack anything that moved. Dirk had sealed all potential except routes, leaving only the main gate for access in or out,

BIRTHRIGHT

making the castle a veritable cage. Adam knew where the former exits were located. He could think of only one that was fortunately close at hand.

"We have to get moving," Adam announced, leaning through the doorway.

"She can't go anywhere," Nick objected. "She's just given birth. She needs to rest."

Agatha pushed the baby at him and slowly climbed to her feet. The hem of her soiled dress dropped down around her ankles. Rusty fluid trickled down her legs. She swayed like a sailor on shore leave. She put one hand on the wall for balance. With a final effort of her internal muscles the placenta landed on the floor between her feet with a wet slap.

"I can make it. Get me out of this place."

Adam looped his arm around her waist and led her through the door into the corridor.

"Why are you helping us now?" Agatha asked, stopping briefly to lean against the stone wall. "Where are my children?"

"They're at Eliza's," Nick answered, adjusting the baby in his arms. "They're fine."

"Are you sure?" she insisted, her pitiful gaze finding his. "You've seen them?"

"I've seen them, they're alright," he promised. He kissed her tenderly then rested his brow against hers in their familiar gesture of affection. "Buren and Bloem are taking care of them. No one is going to let them be hurt. They're safe."

"For now," Adam interjected. "Dirk intends to go after them after Sydney falls. He knows where they are."

Nick's heart sank. He closed his eyes to still the wolf's angry response.

Agatha turned her furious glare to Adam standing beside her.

"You brought me here. You betrayed me," she growled. "In all the years I've known you I never thought you were capable of this."

"And I never thought you would give the Bite. You betrayed my

- 317 -

trust," he said, equally angry. "I didn't intend for this to happen to you. I didn't know how far Dirk would go."

"Let's just get out of here," Nick suggested. He kissed Agatha again to reassure himself that was she was really there and not a figment of his imagination. "We can debate ethics later."

Adam took them to the far end of the corridor and down another narrow hall to find a door that had been boarded up. It looked to have been like that for years. He began to pull the planks away.

"Dirk had this sealed up to keep anyone from getting in," he explained. "I don't know who he thought that would be, but he wasn't taking any chances."

With the boards removed Adam pried the door open. It dragged on the floor, scoring grooves in the stone surface.

They looked out at the dense foliage of the forest. It was going to be a long hazardous trek.

Nick tucked the hem of his shirt into his trousers and put the baby inside it like a sling to carry it more easily. He kept one arm around it for support, keeping his other hand free to fend off any kind of violence they might encounter.

It was well into evening when they were met by a wide patrol that was combing the area for pockets of human resistance. Local towns had mounted a counter offensive, but were subdued with little hassle. Isolated stations still offered a chance to scrap which the werewolves relished.

The commanding officer was an English Birthright by the name of Ridgeley Carter. He was of average height and slender build, with black hair and a neatly trimmed mustache. The insignia on his uniform sleeve denoted his rank as a major.

While his men surrounded the weary travelers, he cut Agatha from their small group. Nick and Adam tensed, but Agatha was not concerned. She was not going to be intimidated by a lower ranking werewolf. She glanced at Nick to make sure the baby was securely

BIRTHRIGHT

protected before confronting the werewolf in charge.

Ridgeley inhaled her potent alpha scent, instantly aware that she was of an ancient bloodline. His green eyes narrowed and he took a step back. This was the female Dirk van Amersvoot had been bragging about. What was she doing wandering about in the bush? He recognized the authority of Adam's uniform, but Nick's clothes were torn and bloodied as were Agatha's. He looked to Adam first for an explanation.

"There's been an accident at the castle," Adam told him. "Newborns were released prematurely and they're loose inside the walls."

Ridgeley shuddered to imagine the bloodshed occurring at Dumfries.

"Who are these two?" he asked, eyeing the soiled and tattered couple who stood close to each other. He saw the bulge of Nick's shirt move. "What do you have? Give it to me."

While Nick and Adam watched with growing trepidation, Agatha raised her head. Her glare pierced Ridgeley's suddenly uneasy gaze like a dagger. There was no exhaustion apparent in her worn out body. A glow of strength exuded from every inch of her. A primary law of nature was to never come between a mother and her child. Ridgeley had crossed that line.

"Do you know who I am?" she asked, advancing on the other Birthright.

Ridgeley nodded, averting his eyes to show his respect for her dominance. He offered no challenge. He waved off his men. They were properly conditioned to obey. They retreated, weapons lowered.

"You're Aconitia Winterbourne," he said with a degree of awe, eyes still turned away. "The only living descendant of Paradeus. What are you doing here? Why aren't you with your mate in Sydney?"

The baby uttered a hungry wail and Nick rubbed its back through the fabric of his shirt to soothe it. It wriggled against his bare skin and he could feel its soft moist gums seeking food and comfort. He didn't have anything to offer and it would have to wait for Agatha's stand-off to play out before she could provide it with nourishment. He slipped his index finger inside his shirt and let the baby's mouth close on it. That would have to suffice.

Forgetting his place, Ridgeley's gaze went from Nick to Agatha. The truth suddenly registered. His eyes widened.

"You aren't Dirk's mate," he surmised correctly. "He's been lying to us."

Adam spoke up, "We need to reach Sydney to stop him."

"It's too rough to travel these canyons at night," said Ridgeley. "We'll take you to our campsite and get you transport in the morning. By the look of all of you, rest is what you need most."

Agatha addressed Ridgeley with the natural air of an alpha leader. Her voice and glare were not to be opposed. She assumed the mantle of leadership with a grace and ease that surprised even her. She had not wanted any of this, but it was now her place to step up and handle it.

"Send word to your commanders that their troops are to cease hostilities until I decide what further action is to be taken."

Nick looked at her with startled eyes. She had stepped flawlessly into a position of power and it suited her. He was impressed and a little nervous that she seemed so confident in the role. It occurred to him that he had never seen her behave as a real alpha. An alpha needed a pack to command to fully realize their potential. She had one now. One that spanned a continent and beyond.

"That could take days," Ridgeley stated. He lowered his head submissively. "I'll get the order out when we reach to camp."

Under the near full moon Nick and Agatha had a brief respite from the enforced turmoil that had entered their lives. They were able to spend some time alone together while Adam and the troops kept watch for wandering Sauvage. They took time to wash in the lake near the campsite and refresh their bodies as well as their spirits.

While he waded naked into the cool waters, she stretched out on the grassy bank and nursed the baby. Nick didn't mind the chill of the water as long as he could wash away what remained of Lance's blood on his skin. He sank under the surface, peering up at the sky through the undulating window of water. The stars appeared within his reach, floating on the clear surface above him. At last he came up for air, shaking off diamond droplets.

Agatha watched him walk towards her. Silver moonlight glistened on his skin. Seeing him in his natural state, glowing under the light of the moon, she realized that giving him the Bite had been the best thing for all of them.

Her gaze was caught by a glint of gold on his chest. As he drew near, she realised it was her wedding ring strung on a chain around his neck. Her heart caught in her throat.

"You have my ring," she said in a tremulous voice.

He knelt in front of her, slipping the chain over his head and draping it over hers. The gold band rested on her breast next to the baby's cheek. His gaze was on the peaceful face of their newest son as the infant curled against her bare skin. He had fallen asleep with his mouth still around her nipple. His lashes were long and dark, sweeping plump cheeks. She could see Nick's features in his face already.

Nick reclined on a blanket spread out on the grass beside her, waiting until he was dry before dressing. He was amazed at how uninhibited he had become since taking the Bite. He would never have been comfortable lying naked out in the open before now. Agatha's influence had stripped away that layer of self-consciousness. He found that he enjoyed the more relaxed lifestyle. It was the most liberated he had ever felt. It was as though Birgitta had never been part of his life.

"I'll take him," he said. "You should wash up. The water feels good."

Agatha let him take the baby, who didn't seem to notice the exchange.

"We decided on Gavin for a name, didn't we?" she said as she stepped into the bracing water. She shivered for a moment as her body adjusted to the change in temperature. "It was Grace for a girl and Gavin for a boy."

Nick's blue eyes searched the sleeping face in his arms. The baby was hard asleep.

"Is that who you are?" he asked, kissing the soft brow. "Gavin Buchanan?"

The infant gave no indication one way or the other if he had an opinion about his name. Nick pulled the blanket around them to keep Gavin warm against him. He turned his gaze to view Agatha as she splashed her way further out. He caught a glimpse of her pale backside as she dove into deeper water. When she broke the surface he noticed how her full breasts resembled the swollen moon in the sky. She was a creature of moonlight and forest, a truly wild thing.

"You had Lance's blood on you," she said, scrubbing away the crusted evidence of Gavin's birth from her thighs with a handful of sand from the bottom of the lake. "What happened?"

"I killed him."

It was that simple. Nick felt no remorse. He had protected his family as any alpha male would. He did not have any regrets about defending what was his.

Agatha had suspected that was the case, but she wanted to hear him say it. He was finally growing into his wolf, not the other way around.

Once satisfied that she was as clean as she was going to get, she joined him on the bank. She nestled against him with Gavin wedged between their bodies. They fell asleep as a family under a sheltering blanket of stars.

CHAPTER FORTY

"A man can be forced to take desperate action against the nature of his heart."
Thrace Summit, elf elder

Bloem closed the curtains to block out the terrifying view of the city in flames. An orange glow stained the midnight sky above the rooftops. The assault on Sydney had been going on for days.

She huddled on the bed in an upstairs room, cradling Luna to calm the baby's frightened cries. Mrs. MacLeach held Logan and walked with slow strides back and forth across the room. He was crying louder than his sister. Both children were inconsolable with the sounds of fighting going on in the city. Beshka sat in a chair in the corner, knees drawn up to her chest. She had a quilt pulled around her, but it was of no comfort.

Eliza was downstairs with Buren and Holt, armed with a Wetherell twelve chambered pistol in one hand and a brandy in her other. She wore tan canvas trousers, work boots and a dark blue shirt that had belonged to her late husband. Her hair was braided into a single rope that hung over her left shoulder. Even a moon mad Sauvage would be foolish to take her on.

The men were similarly armed. They had moved large pieces of furniture in front of the downstairs windows to slow any intruders, and used the upright piano to blockade the front door. The red felt surface of the billiard table had been turned into an armory. Eliza's late husband had been an avid collector of modern weaponry. There were even flash bombs and shrapnel grenades. They would be able to make a formidable stand.

Ships were burning in Sydney Cove, Cockle Bay and Woolloomooloo Bay. The bridge to North Sydney had collapsed in cinders into the hungry waters below, effectively isolating that part of the city. There would be no further military aid to any area north of the bay. Everything on the water was in flames as dragons continued their patrols above the city. They had already brought down the entire Victorian air corps. The hydrogen laden airship bodies had been floating bombs, waiting for the dragons to light the fuse. Massive explosions had rocked the city in the preceding days. Smoldering debris had rained down to set the city ablaze. The bells of fire engines racing from one side of the city to the other could be heard day and night. Their resources were stretched thin, yet they valiantly attempted to provide rescue and medical attention to those in need. Looting and pillaging were rampant as desperate citizens struggled to find supplies and food.

The Sauvage forces were pushing the human military back towards the decimated city. Packs of werewolves had broken through the lines and were making their way through the streets, wreaking havoc on the terrified residents. They gave no mercy.

It was worse in Melbourne, Perth and Brisbane. The cities were collapsing under the onslaught of Dirk's armies. The Victorian government was unable to defend them. Perth's population was less than ten thousand people, and approximately ten percent of those were elf or fae. Australia was not equipped for a major war on its own soil. It had been intended as a resource colony. The Victorian government had been prepared to protect itself from an outside invader, but not to engage a massive force from within its own borders.

Not even remote regions were spared from the invasion. Millions of angry dingoes poured into small towns and overran stations across the continent. Orange waves of the small dogs flowed over hills and into valleys as the no longer timid canines revealed their strength. The days of treating them as vermin were over. They trapped humans in their homes, killed them if they caught them out in the open, tore through their food stores and laid waste to sheep and cattle. They

BIRTHRIGHT

were taking back their lands.

As they had three hundred years before, the elves kept to themselves during the first days of the battle. They had evacuated as many of their own as they could before the main battle, and gathered a large number of those left behind within the walls of the High Council building as a precautionary measure. They knew that the werewolves were targeting the human populace, but they were prepared to take action if the tide of war turned on them. The High Council determined that as long as elves were not specifically being singled out they would not intervene. They could pick up the pieces when the smoke settled.

Inside Eliza's house the mood was dim, but no one was giving up hope. They waited and listened for a break in the fighting. Eliza had stopped importing brides several weeks ago. She had not wanted to bring innocent women into a potentially hostile environment. That left the house empty except for herself, Holt, the van Amersvoots, Mrs. MacLeach and the Buchanan twins. Eliza had let her servants go be with their families while the conflict raged.

There was a cold cellar packed with enough fresh meat to last for weeks. There were fruit trees in the conservatory that produced all year round. An extensive pantry was filled with dry goods and canned products. They had enough fire power to keep a herd of charging elephants at bay. They just had to wait it out.

Buren sat by the carved marble fireplace in the game room, a glass of scotch untouched on the table beside him. The gun rested next to it, both within arms' reach. He listened to the twins crying with tears in his eyes.

"Don't beat yourself up over this," said Eliza. She touched his shoulder with a strong hand. "You didn't know what Dirk could accomplish. No one did."

Holt looked over. He reclined on a high backed sofa by the window, keeping a watch through a small opening in the curtain. He kept his hand on his pistol as it rested in his lap.

"The High Council absolved you of all guilt related to Dirk and his actions," he added. "And the Victorian government can't touch you because you aren't human. You should be thinking about Beshka and Bloem, not Dirk."

"I am thinking about Beshka and Bloem," Buren replied in a tone harsher than he intended. He couldn't bring himself to apologise. "I'm thinking that Dirk is going to march in and destroy them as well as this entire city. And I can't stop him."

Eliza hoisted her pearl-handled Wetherell proudly. It was a large weapon, advertised as *"All the firepower you'll ever need"*.

"I can."

Holt chuckled darkly at her unbridled optimism.

"We'll do what we must to keep everyone safe," he said. "There may not be anything we can do to save the city, but we can save everyone in this house."

Eliza nodded. She had no intentions of giving an inch to the werewolves.

Nick, Agatha and Adam reached the outskirts of the city as the sun cleared the horizon. The main force of Dirk's army had already moved on towards Sydney's center, leaving an open wound in its wake. Their caravan of military wagons had been passing scores of refugees on the road during their journey from Dumfries. All they found as they neared Sydney proper were homesteads destroyed by the fighting and stragglers trying to gather what they could. The ground was scorched and pitted from artillery fire and dragon flame. The bodies of soldiers, werewolves and civilians could be seen scattered around the countryside. Hungry goannas were already gorging themselves on the carrion. Magpies formed clouds in the sky as they awaited their turn at the dinner table. Blackened timbers were all that remained of entire towns and homesteads.

They rumbled past a derelict general store where people were looting to survive. Children with ash stained faces watched them drive by.

BIRTHRIGHT

They were traveling in a convoy of steam wagons carrying support troops toward Sydney. Ridgeley had given his command over to Agatha. His officers accepted her authority without hesitation. The lower level troops gave her their allegiance as well, responding to her as their Alpha Queen as Dirk had predicted. They showed Nick the same deference, offering total submission, which made him uncomfortable.

Agatha stared out in disgust at what damage Dirk had wrought on the country. No one deserved to live as a scavenger. It was a dark reminder of the reservations. Dirk had never lived on one, but she recognized the survival instinct that drove decent people to behave like animals. If he had come from the same background as she and Adam, he might have taken a different route to reach his goal. She doubted it, but it might have altered the course of things.

Her son was asleep in his father's arms on the bench seat next to her. She reached down and touched the hairless scalp. Her children would not know this world as their own. They would know only freedom and peace if she had to give her life to make it happen.

Nick met her determined glare. He stroked her cheek, his thumb brushing her lips.

At dawn on October third, Dirk prepared for his final push to overtake Sydney. The full moon was expected to peak before noon and he wanted to take full advantage of it. Melbourne, Brisbane and Perth were already in his grasp. Canberra and Adelaide had surrendered with little resistance. Other cities were finding it wise to simply give in and save their citizens from the horrors of a Sauvage invasion.

Only Sydney continued to resist because the Victorian government had its largest military base stationed there. Even with their airships and navy destroyed they had ground troops and artillery at their disposal. They would not quit until there was no fight left in them, but even they understood that when the moon went full no amount of cannon fire would stop several thousand werewolves from crashing through their defenses. They were bracing for the slaughter.

Just before noon, at ten fifty eight, the moon completed its cycle and was a perfect white orb in the cloudless sky above the city. With his own wolf pressuring him to be let out, Dirk gave the order to attack.

Legions of Sauvage overtook Sydney. Massive packs of wolf-like creatures ran through the streets, taking down any human they encountered. They were ruthless in clearing the city of resistance. They fell when shot, but more took their place in a seemingly endless parade of violence. They smashed into buildings, dragging the occupants into the street to rip them apart. Men, women, children; it made no difference. The Sauvage were driven to keep killing. Nothing sated their bloodlust. They acted out of blind rage and a pathological desire to destroy.

Torric drew in his sixty foot wingspan as he lowered the passenger basket onto the roof of a stone faced house in the Peddlington suburb. Most of the area had been left intact as requested by Dirk. The leafy tree lined hills of the district were predominantly untouched by the ravages of the battle that was taking place all around it. It stood as an oasis amid a desert of devastation. The moon would soon lose its hold on the Sauvage, but until then they continued to storm through the streets.

The dragon wrapped his articulated hind toes around the stone ledge of the roof and settled his impressive figure there like a giant red gargoyle. Fragments of limestone crumbled under his weight and crashed to the ground. Grey wisps of smoke rose from his nostril slits. He folded his wings behind him as he waited for Dirk's orders.

The occupants felt the structure tremble. The cracking of rafters resonated throughout the halls as the dragon positioned itself on the roof. The entire building groaned under its weight.

"What is that?" Eliza whispered, eyes wide.

BIRTHRIGHT

"A dragon," replied Holt. He had seen it approaching from his vantage point at the front window. He glanced at the stockpile of weapons on the billiard table. "We don't have anything that will take one down."

Dirk stepped out of the passenger basket onto the flat roof. Despite the powerful pull of the full moon on his wolf, he refused to allow it to come out. He had learned, in his years in the holding cell that his father had built to contain him during the full moon, how to suppress it for a short period when the moon first peaked. He allowed it to become fully enraged, about to explode through his skin, before he unleashed it.

He cocked his head, meeting the dragon's orange veined black eyes. The molten yellow pupils regarded him emotionlessly.

"Break it down."

The dragon rose into the air, making the house rattle with the buffeting wind from its wings. Windows shattered. Furniture toppled over. Anything not nailed down was sent crashing to the floor.

Beshka screamed as plaster rained down from the bedroom ceiling. She covered her head with her arms. Her mother shielded her with her body. Mrs. MacLeach leaned over the cradle to protect the wailing twins.

Buren and Holt pounded up the stairs in tandem, guns in hand. The ceiling in the hall was spider webbed with fractures. Holt flung open the bedroom door.

"Downstairs, now!" he yelled.

The women gathered up Logan and Luna, clutching them close as they ran down the main staircase. Beshka hesitated, looking at her father. Holt pushed her forward and she bolted after her mother like a spooked rabbit. He paused on the stairs, looking back at Buren who remained on the second floor.

"What are you doing?" he demanded, leaning heavily on the balustrade as he stared up at the hugtandalf.

Eliza was already sweeping all the weapons she could into her arms to take them down into the cold cellar. Bloem, despite holding

Luna, and in direct conflict with her nurturing elf nature, grabbed a rifle. She was not going to let anyone take the babies unless it was from her cold dead hands.

"I won't hide from my son," said Buren. "If it's a fight he wants, I won't disappoint him."

Holt admired his courage. He turned and followed Beshka to the cellar, gathering weapons as he went.

As Agatha entered the decimated city, she absorbed the enormity of what Dirk's arrogance had done. Nick sat in silent horror next to her. His eyes were huge as he took in the devastation. His body was numb. His arms unconsciously tightened around the baby.

The assault had stopped per her orders, but there were still pockets of activity. The dragons had come to roost on rooftops around the city. Their bright red-gold bodies could be seen like beacons in the distance. The Sauvage had slowed their reign of terror, but there were still some that needed to be brought under control by their Birthright officers. Bringing them to heel required a heavy hand.

Troops recognized their own vehicles as the convoy made its way toward the abandoned Victorian Government House. They began to fall in line behind the line of steam wagons, following out of curiosity. Once Agatha's potent alpha scent reached their noses, they surged ahead to spread word of their Queen's arrival.

Dirk realised the fighting was winding down. He had given no command to cease fire and it infuriated him. Once he had dispatched Buchanan's twins he would address the issue.

Torric touched down in the street. The forceful draft from his wings bowled over trees and broke windows in neighboring houses. He gave one lash of his horny, spiked tail and the front door to Eliza's home splintered into kindling. The piano blocking the entrance groaned deeply as it was crushed by a second blow.

Dirk leaped down to the street, landing in a crouch at the dragon's clawed feet. He straightened and walked confidently into the house. He stepped over the broken wood and glass, remembering the last time he had been there. He could recall every detail from that night, including the sight of Agatha departing with Nick as his wife.

The wolf howled beneath his skin, pushing against the fragile bars of its cage. He raked claws across the wall, tearing great furrows in the imported, hand painted wallpaper. Eliza would be livid. He could smell the fear and defiance of the house's occupants. It sent his wolf into a frenzy. The flesh swelled along his arms as it struggled to get free. Crimson fissures appeared across his body as his skin reached the breaking point. He clenched his fists, forcing the wolf to obey. It would not wait much longer.

Buren came down the wide staircase to the broad landing above the foyer. He had the gun in his hand, resting at his side. It weighed like an anchor in his grip.

"Dirk."

The Sauvage raised his head, nostrils flaring. Metallic sparks flashed in his eyes.

"Father," he said with a mocking grin. "Well, you're not really my father, are you?"

Buren stared at Dirk with grief carved deeply into his face. His eyes were the frigid blue of an arctic ocean. Even their icy depths couldn't cool the fire in Dirk's contaminated soul.

"I've always been your father," he replied. His voice cracked under the strain of his emotions. "And you've always been my son."

Dirk's shoulders rose as the wolf strained, writhing inside. Blood dribbled from his lips. He spat a red streak onto the glossy marble floor.

"You locked me away during the full moon, when I had every right to let my wolf out!" he roared. "Look what you did to me!"

Fiery needles pierced Buren's heart at the sound of Dirk's words.

"If I had known that what I was doing was wrong, I would have done it all differently," he said in a voice barely audible. His body was rigid with angry tension, making speech difficult. "But I didn't know. I thought I was saving you from the infection."

"Well, you didn't," Dirk growled, losing the struggle to keep his wolf at bay. His face began to tear into strips. One long thread of skin fell away, revealing a section of dark fur. "You made me what I am."

"And I'm sorry," said Buren as a tear crept from the corner of his eye.

He had never seen his son change into his other shape. It was nauseating to watch as flesh tore away from Dirk's body, falling with wet slaps onto the marble. The thing that emerged was tall and lean with a coating of thick black hair. It didn't look like a wolf or a man, but some gruesome blend of the two species melted together.

Buren raised his pistol, aiming at the raging blue eyes.

Dirk made a long leap toward him. His mouth was wide open, saliva stringing from his sharp teeth. His breath reached Buren first, hot and reeking of madness.

Buren pulled the trigger once.

A cloud of brain and blood filled the air as the bullet blew through Dirk's head. His body continued forward, landing on the steps at Buren's feet with a solid, heavy thud. With the gun clenched in his trembling hand, Buren stood and stared at what had been his son. The killing jaws were agape in a silent cry of rage. A limp wet tongue was draped over savage teeth. The silver gleam had vanished from the crazed eyes.

Holt burst through the cellar door ahead of Bloem and Eliza. They stopped in their tracks when they saw the dead Sauvage sprawled on the dark wood stairs below Buren. Beshka and Mrs. MacLeach remained in the cellar with the twins, waiting until it was safe to emerge.

"I'm sorry," was all Holt could choke out.

Bloem looked at the inhuman corpse, seeing nothing of her son in its grotesque appearance. She mounted the stairs to reach Buren, careful to step around the carcass. Her green eyes met Buren's distraught gaze with an expression of forgiveness. He fell into her arms, sobbing on her shoulder. The gun clattered to the floor.

"I only wanted to help him," he moaned, clutching her tightly.

"You did help him," she said, stroking his short hair. "You set him free."

"But he was our son," he replied gruffly, furious with himself. "I killed our son."

Bloem tilted her head back to peer into her husband's agonized eyes. She smoothed her fingers over his stubble roughened cheek.

"Our son died years ago," she told him with a ragged sigh. "I was the one who couldn't let him go. You only did what I asked, what any father would. You forget that the heart has a mind of its own and it isn't always that wise."

It took several minutes before everyone realised there was an eerie quiet outside. There were no more bloodcurdling howls from the attacking Sauvage and the artillery firing had suspended. No one knew what to make of it.

The house was rocked again as Torric shoved his long head and neck through the gaping hole where the front door had been. Tin tiles clattered to the floor as the dragon's recurved horns scraped the ceiling. The volcanic eyes surveyed the scene in one sweeping glance. His gaze settled on Holt.

"Does this mean the elves will be getting involved now?" he asked. His voice reached into every head.

"No," Holt answered firmly. "This was a family matter."

CHAPTER FORTY-ONE

"Even at the cost of her pride, woman is always by her husband's side."
Excerpt from the Victorian pamphlet, "A Woman's Place"

The further the convoy got into the city the more they found the roads littered with abandoned carriages, broken furniture, bricks and beams from exploded buildings and the scavenged remains of bodies. Enemy blockades forced them to change direction several times, but they met with no resistance. The Victorian military had pulled back to the waterfront, where it waited with what little force it had left. Eventually the werewolf convoy realised that all roads leading to the Government House were completely blocked by debris. The wagons came to a rattling stop with a thousand meters to go to reach their destination.

It had been Dirk's intention to introduce Agatha as his mate, once victory was in his grasp. His goal had been to use the human's own palace of power to demonstrate his conquest of their race and their country, as well as his conquest of Agatha.

Ridgeley had been trying all morning to ascertain Dirk's whereabouts, so they could safely reach their destination without confronting him directly. If they could get Agatha there first, they could address the army and expose Dirk's manipulation of werewolves across the globe. He had used Agatha as a pawn to gain their trust and support, tricking them into joining him in Australia to fight a war they would otherwise never have agreed to take part in. None of the officers they met seemed to know where Dirk could be found. He had told no one his plans.

Word had spread that Aconitia Winterbourne was in Sydney. Every werewolf in the city was gathering in the Royal Botanic Gardens, their numbers spilling over into The Domain as well. They spread out through streets, alleys and on rooftops to await the arrival of their Alpha King and Queen. Dirk had been promising to introduce her to their troops once they took Sydney. They were ready. They howled in anticipation.

Nick rallied against the pull of the moon, repressing the wolf when it was at its most determined to emerge. It was obvious to all around him that he was strong enough to keep it inside against the tide of the full moon, which was considered impossible for a Sauvage. Agatha held him as he shuddered with the effort to resist its advance. The wolf was merely responding to instinct in its drive to come forth. Although he considered the wolf no longer his adversary, he needed to keep his wits about him and that was more easily accomplished in his human form.

Before she met her audience, Agatha had a more pressing matter to attend. She had to find her children and assure herself they were alive and well. Judging by the ruination of the city, she was losing hope. It had been years since she had set foot in Sydney and the last time she had been there she had just come off the boat from America and had no perception of distance or direction. She was completely lost once again.

"Where is Eliza's house?" she demanded, sticking her head out the open window.

She sucked in a deep breath through flared nostrils. Under normal circumstances she could have picked up their scent, but the acrid stench that filled the air hurt her nasal passages and she couldn't smell anything but death.

"That way," said Nick. He remembered it well. He would never forget where he had first fallen in love with Agatha. It was as instinctive as a salmon swimming upstream. "It's not too far, but I don't think it's safe to go out on foot. Not with the baby."

Adam and Ridgeley took charge of the troops in the convoy.

They barked orders and the soldiers fell into ranks around Nick and Agatha. They formed a wall that was nearly impenetrable. Agatha carried Gavin close to her breast and Nick had one arm around her shoulders to keep her against him.

She wore a pair of mens' trousers that had been altered to accommodate her shorter legs. A belt kept the trousers cinched snugly around her waist. A long sleeved white shirt with hung long and loose on her frame. The sleeves were rolled up to her elbows. Nick was dressed in a soldier's uniform that replaced his tattered clothes. They could almost have passed for members of the military.

As a single unit they made their way through the nearly uninhabited streets. They could see ghostly faces peer out of smoke smudged windows as they passed. Two harpies were fighting over a corpse, but they took to the air with a fluttering of black wings at the werewolves' approach.

They reached Sittella Lane without incident, though the howling and chanting from the waiting werewolves carried clearly on the still air. The crowd was getting restless.

Torric heard the padding of bare feet on the cobblestones and withdrew his head from the house. His horns caught on a support beam and he pulled twice before it snapped and part of the second floor collapsed into the foyer, narrowly missing the people inside. He shook dust and clutter from his scales before turning his body to face the approaching werewolf troops.

Ridgeley called a halt. The soldiers arranged themselves as a shield in front of Agatha and Nick.

Torric recognized the female. He had seen her the day she had been abducted from the vineyard in Falmormath. She was the one Dirk had wanted more than anything in the world. Torric also recognized Adam as one of the two that had been there that day to take her by force. The dragon saw that the female now carried a babe in arms and was in the close company of a man who was old enough to be her father. Did that make her child Dirk's?

"*You are Aconitia Winterbourne, yes?*"

BIRTHRIGHT

The voice pierced directly into their heads, but it was clearly directed at Agatha.

The magnificent and terrifying creature stood in Eliza's front yard, blocking access to the house.

Nick tried to hold her back, but Agatha walked fearlessly toward the dragon. He knew nothing of dragons, except that they were all but extinct. This one was absolutely immense. It could blast them all with one breath and turn them to ash. What the hell was she thinking? He snatched Gavin from her arms and passed the infant to Adam before following at Agatha's side. She barely seemed to notice.

"I am Agatha Buchanan," she told the dragon, stopping a respectable distance away. "I am the descendant of Aconitia Winterbourne and Paradeus. Will you give me your name, fire breather?"

The dragon lowered his head in a gracious bow. Flattery was a good option when dealing with dragons. Their vanity was legendary.

"I am Torric," he said with feigned modesty. "You are the mate of Dirk van Amersvoot?"

"I was his prisoner," she answered, not the least alarmed by the close proximity of the giant lizard. "I was never his mate."

While occasionally unpredictable and dangerous, dragons did possess tremendously advanced social skills and were a highly cultured species. They were dignified and honorable for the most part. At one time in history they had lived in palaces formed of mountain peaks and hosted grand events attended by fae and elf alike. Poaching and trophy hunting by humans had eventually reduced their numbers to the twelve that survived now. It was rumored that a few smaller species of dragon still existed in remote mountain ranges, but no evidence had been found to prove or refute that claim.

"Then it pleases me to inform you that he is dead."

While it was something she and Nick had both dreamt of hearing, it still came as a shock.

"Are you sure?" Nick asked and immediately regretted opening his mouth as the wedge shaped head swung toward him and those magma laced eyes focused on him. His belly clenched with fear.

Torric understood the need for proof of an enemy's demise. He inclined his long neck and head toward the house.

"I invite you to behold with your own eyes."

Nick just wanted to get out of the line of fire if the dragon decided to become unfriendly. Taking a risk that he would ordinarily never consider, he took Gavin from Adam and skirted close to the crimson dragon to reach the rubble of the front entrance. Holding the baby tightly in his left arm, he used his right hand to help scramble over the pile of timbers and brick to get inside the house.

The first thing he saw was the familiar shape of a Sauvage on the stairs. It was the same ugly creature that had attacked him in the bush. He would never get the images of that moment out of his head. He felt slightly nauseous.

"Copernicus!"

Eliza charged towards him, lowering her gun. She reset the firing mechanism for safety so it wouldn't accidentally discharge before shoving the barrel into the waist of her trousers. She smothered him in her overbearing embrace, but he couldn't find a reason to complain. Stepping back, her eyes dropped to the baby he held. She feared he might fall over in his shock at seeing Dirk like he was; the back of his skull blown out and his brain splattered on the floor. She took Gavin from Nick just in case his legs did give out. She carried the baby to the billiard room where the other women were gathered.

"By Gods, are you alright? Where's Agatha?" Holt asked, putting a steadying hand on Nick's back. He steered him towards Eliza's office, the place where he had first laid eyes on Agatha. "Come in here and sit down."

"She's out there with the dragon and I think…" Nick doubled over. "I think I might be sick."

Holt retrieved a waste basket and placed it between Nick's feet to catch anything that might come out.

The only thing that was coming out was his wolf. His guard was down and the moon was full. It was not trying to assert dominance.

BIRTHRIGHT

It was reacting to the natural draw of the moon's influence.

Holt stepped back, watching flowers of blood blossom on the back of Nick's shirt as his skin split under the fabric. The elf had not witnessed a werewolf's change before. It was a fascinating process of transformation that happened quickly.

Most of Nick's sloughed skin was retained in his clothes, but he tore out of them with teeth and claws until he stood on the floor as a long limbed, nearly human wolf. With his ability to change at will he had achieved the level of a Birthright. There was no doubt of Paradeus' blood connection.

Buren entered the room, his face a somber mask. He stopped when he saw Nick. Dirk could never have accomplished that successful of a transformation.

"Agatha's with the twins," he told his friend. "They're alright."

Nick nodded. He needed to change back as soon as possible. He was tired, but there was no time to rest. They still had to get to the Victorian Government House to address the baying mob and convince them that Agatha was their Alpha Queen. He would not allow himself to consider the consequences if they failed.

In the billiard room, Agatha was reunited with Logan and Luna. She held them in her lap while Logan greeted her with loud cries of, "Mum! Mum!" and grabbed at her with eager hands. He stood in her lap, his little arms clinging to her neck. Luna was still not able to stand, so she snuggled against Agatha's stomach, making happy noises as she pressed her face into the comfort of her mother's warm scent. Unable to contain her joy, Agatha gave in to the tears that threatened to sweep her away in a flood of relief. She hugged her children so tight they squealed in protest, but didn't resist.

Mrs. MacLeach stood by, cradling the most recent member of the Buchanan family. Beshka slipped her arm around the urisk's shoulder, her own tears falling without care. Bloem was some distance away, isolated by her grief. She was not yet prepared to allow happiness to return to its rightful place in her heart. She was glad that Agatha and her children were safe and sound, but there was emptiness in her soul that would not be occupied by anything but sorrow.

In Eliza's office, Holt addressed the wolf version of Nick.

"She has to speak to them now," he said. "If we wait any longer, they'll think she doesn't exist and without Dirk at the helm they'll go rogue. If you think they were dangerous when they were under orders, you don't want to think about what they will do when turned loose. The officers won't be able to control them. They'll turn on each other. Those that don't will start to migrate into the bush and you could lose any hope of containing them. They will take over this country in the worst possible way."

Understanding that it was inevitable, Nick began to shake. A cloud of shedding fur surrounded him until he was human, crouching naked on the carpet. He raised his head and looked at Buren.

"I'm sorry about Dirk."

Buren nodded stiffly.

"I'll find you some clothes," he said. He turned and left the room.

Eliza passed him coming in and took a seat by the fireplace. Nick moved into another chair, suddenly feeling awkward with his blatant nudity. It made no difference that she preferred women. She did not need to see him naked.

"How do we convince thousands of werewolves that she is who we say she is?" he asked, hands in his lap to cover himself.

"They'll know," answered Holt. "It's ingrained in their genes to recognize an alpha of any kind. And believe me, she is the greatest alpha this world has seen in three hundred years. There's no mistaking it. Surely you know that."

"She's my wife," Nick replied without humility. "Of course I think she's the greatest alpha. It's getting those mutts to acknowledge it that concerns me."

Holt shook his head at Nick's foolish worries.

"They will. Trust me."

BIRTHRIGHT

"What do we do about Dirk?" Nick asked.

Holt smirked.

"Leave that to me."

Adam and Ridgeley waited outside with the soldiers and the dragon for word from Agatha.

She came out of the house wearing a full length dark brown bustle skirt. The white blouse had a high collar and small elk horn buttons, imported from America. An underbust vest corset in the orange, yellow and green of the Buchanan tartan tucked in her newly narrowed waist while giving her full breasts more room than an overbust style corset. It would have been cruel and painful to confine them in their current nursing condition. Eliza had been holding onto the outfit as a gift for Boxing Day, but felt it was more fitting for Agatha's coronation.

The werewolves lowered their heads reverently as she approached them.

"You will be my escort to the Victorian Government House," she said. To Torric, she said, "I need you to do something, if you would."

CHAPTER FORTY-TWO

"A woman's potential is rarely overestimated."
Excerpt from the banned publication, "The Voice of a Woman"

With the children tucked up at Eliza's house guarded by Beshka, Bloem and Mrs. MacLeach, the royal procession started out along Sittella Lane.

Nick wore the outfit that would have been his Boxing Day gift from Eliza. He had not donned a kilt in years, but it felt as comfortable as his wolf skin as he strode confidently beside his wife. Her hand rested on his raised arm. His white shirt matched hers in a more masculine style with a Mandarin collar. His look was completed by a brown leather vest and a sporran made of spotted quoll.

They walked with steady, determined progress towards their destiny.

The sun was leaning against the horizon when they reached the furthest edge of The Domain. As her scent reached them the werewolves turned to find its source. The crowd opened to allow them clear passage through the tightly packed assemblage. There was confusion at first when they noticed that Dirk was not the one at her side, but they quickly detected the connection between Agatha and Nick.

Birthrights were first to display their fealty to their Alpha King and Queen by taking the knee as they passed. Soon, row upon row of Sauvage went into a submissive posture, lowering themselves to their knees with heads bowed. It was like a wave reaching across the vastness of the park.

BIRTHRIGHT

Nick did his best to remain calm while thousands of Sauvage soldiers showed him their undying respect. His wide blue eyes swept the crowd, finding not one that would meet his gaze. There would be no challenge from what, he realised with shock, were his subjects. These people were granting him their unquestioning loyalty to his position as their one and only alpha male. It was almost too much to take in.

Agatha moved through the ocean of kneeling werewolves with a confidence that surprised her. She had been born on a reservation in southwestern Colorado, been raised by human missionaries, had moved to another country and married a human sheep farmer. In the wake of such humble origins she was now the most important werewolf in the world. Werewolves around the globe were looking to her with hope for their future. There was no explanation for how the Fates worked.

The Victorian Government House had been abandoned by the humans. It stood as an empty reminder of their hold over her kind. Its crenellated roofline and turrets mimicked castles in Britain and Europe.

Ridgeley led his team inside to clear the area, making absolutely certain that no humans remained that might pose a threat. Once it was determined to be safe, Agatha and Nick were allowed in. They were led up to a door that opened onto a stone balcony facing the park and the prostrating field of werewolves that filled it as far as the eye could see.

A red spark appeared in the sky above and swiftly became a wildfire as Torric descended towards the building. He landed on the roof of the portico, cracking the limestone mortar. He carried Dirk's body in his jaws. A stunned silence settled over the crowd. He dropped it onto the stone drive and exhaled a stream of blue fire that set it ablaze.

While the flames burned themselves out, Agatha addressed the assembly. When she spoke, not even the wind took a breath.

"You have come to know me by the name Aconitia Winterbourne," she declared, using the throat muscles that allowed wolves to howl at great volume over long distances. She wanted to be heard by every ear. Her tawny hair fluttered wildly around her head. "My name is Agatha Buchanan. My mate…" she paused, looking up at Nick. She laced her fingers in his. "My husband is Copernicus Buchanan. Dirk Van Amersvoot started this war out of revenge against the humans. While I share his vision of our place in the world as equals among humans, elves and fae, I have never advocated the use of violence to achieve it. We are not animals. We are werewolves. Our bloodline is ancient and venerable. We can trace our ancestors back to the First Forest, from which all creatures emerged in the Time of Mist. We are werewolves!"

A ululating howl erupted, thunderous and deafening, from every corner of the park.

Nick felt a sense of pride that transcended mortal emotions. It was as though the universe was agreeing with every word she said.

"There will be no more fighting," she announced. Her golden eyes scanned the crowd as it fell quiet. "We have brought great ruin upon this country and we will be the ones to repair it. Dirk had a dream of making Australia a place where we ruled above all other races and species, but we are no better than they. We will not show our belly to anyone, but we will not take what we want by force. It is my goal to establish a true Alpha Council that will govern in conjunction with the High Council and a new human government. Humans will be welcome here. We know better than any what it means to be victimized. We must learn from our past and present mistakes to prevent this tragedy from happening again."

Another roar of approval filled the air with its volume and ferocity. The cheering continued well after Agatha turned and went inside. Nick was on her heels to catch her as she collapsed just as she passed through the door, out of the view of her adoring public.

<hr />

Nick studied her placid features as she slept.

He lay under the sheets beside Agatha in a large four post bed in what had been the former Victorian president's private chambers. Lace curtains formed a delicate barrier around them, shutting out the world. Moonlight traced an intricate pattern on her features as it passed through the lace.

She had given so much of herself lately that she had simply run out of energy. Her body was drained from giving birth. Her heart was overwhelmed by too many emotions to name. She had done more than any normal person could.

Her eyes flickered briefly before opening. She peered up at him with a weak smile, leaning into the palm of his hand as he caressed her cheek.

"It's over now, isn't it?" he asked. "We can go home."

"Only the war is over," she answered. Her voice was soft and tired.

"What does that mean?"

She took a deep breath to build enough strength to answer. She felt like an empty grain sack, limp and useless.

"It means we have to remain here to help rebuild," she said. "We have to put together a strong Alpha Council. Otherwise there will have been no point to any of this."

Nick flopped onto his back, folded arms propping up his head. He glared at the lace canopy overhead.

He hadn't signed up for a war or to take the throne as an Alpha King. Some part of him was still the man who had grown up in the country on a sheep station, who only wanted to hone his craft making wine and raise his own family. He resented being thrust into a position of responsibility that was beyond his simple wants and desires. Another voice spoke in his head. Agatha had not been a willing participant in this turn of events, either. She had been forced into this as well. She had more to lose than anyone.

"You're angry," she guessed, picking up on his tension.

"I'm tired," he sighed. "I'm tired of everything. I don't think I can take anymore."

She turned to face him, letting her hand rest on his bare chest. He brought one hand down and gripped hers.

"It won't be forever. Once the Alpha Council is set up and running smoothly we can go back to Gilgai."

"I don't think I'll ever leave the station again," he muttered. "This isn't the world I knew."

"This is our children's world now. Everything we do from this day forward is for them. We have to give them the best possible future we can."

He agreed with a nod. A subject that had been nagging at him since her speech reared its head.

"What about the Sauvage? The elves will be calling for their destruction."

"I can't in good conscience order the execution of thousands of Sauvage and yet spare my husband," she replied with difficulty. "I have to stand up for them through this restoration process. This wasn't the way they were expecting things to go. I know many of them will have to be put down. They're just too far gone. I'm going to push for retraining and education for the rest. We're going to have to rebuild everything anyway, we can start by building facilities to hold them and teach them to work with their wolves, not against them." She paused. She was drifting towards sleep. "I won't just abandon them. I know it's going to be an uphill battle, but we have to find the way to do this right."

Nick hated to say it, but he had to.

"I can't stay in Sydney."

She pulled away, suddenly awake, using what little strength she had left. She stared at him with a deeply hurt glare. After all they had endured, he was willing to leave her alone when she desperately needed his support? She didn't even have the energy reserves to form tears.

"I don't understand," she whispered. Her lips trembled as she spoke.

Realising how she perceived his intentions, he hurried to reassure her. He gathered her into his arms, nuzzling her hair.

"I'm not leaving you," he said, kicking himself for alarming her in her vulnerable state. "I need to get the station back on track and ready for you to come home. I'll be right here while you need me. Then I need to get back and set things right. I don't want you and the children coming home to a wreck."

She exhaled in relief and wilted in his embrace. He cradled her against him until sleep overcame his senses as well.

CHAPTER FORTY-THREE

"A noble head will rise to bear the weight of the crown."
Roman Emperor Causius, 1089-1102

Agatha was awakened by a thousand thoughts churning in her mind. There was too much to be done in the wake of Dirk's defeat for her to think clearly. She had to make decisions quickly, but she didn't want to make bad choices just because it was urgent to correct the state of things. She could easily make the situation worse if she chose unwisely. She required a strong pack to work with her and assist her through the turmoil. It was only through the power of the pack that made an alpha successful.

Nick grunted in his sleep and turned over. His hand instinctively went out to feel for her, but she had slipped out of bed long ago. His eyes opened to find her in her nightdress, staring out the tall windows. Sunlight bathed her with an otherworldly glow.

"You need more rest, come back to bed," he mumbled, pressing his face into the pillow.

The past weeks' events seemed unreal, like a complicated and unending dream. He found it almost impossible to believe that he was now some kind of werewolf monarch. He was a simple man with no such aspirations. Until two years ago he had been content to raise sheep and keep his family's name going by remarrying and having a few sons. Now the future of werewolves in Australia lay on his shoulders. It rattled his mind to think back and realize everything had occurred since that New Year's Eve marriage ball at Eliza's when he had first laid eyes on Agatha.

"I need to start fixing what Dirk broke," she replied in a tone sharper than she intended.

Nick flung his legs over the side of the bed and sat for a moment, gathering his bearings. The bed sheets were the softest cotton he'd ever felt. Beneath the sheets was a down filled mattress that had cradled his body during the night and he was loathe to part from its company. He couldn't remember his last sound night's sleep.

The room around him was exquisitely appointed. It had been the Victorian governor's suite before the man had wisely fled the continent with his contemporaries in the face of the Sauvage onslaught. It was tempting to remain in such luxury, but he only wanted to wrap up his part in the Restoration, as Agatha called it, so he could return to their true home in Falmormath.

"What's first on the agenda?" he asked, wiping a hand across his face.

"I need to establish a new governmental authority," she said decisively.

"Can't the elves run things?"

He pushed himself to his feet and staggered to the water closet just off the bedroom. He had never thought that indoor plumbing would be such a blessing, but he was grateful he could relieve himself without trekking through the bush to reach the dunny. With his newfound influence as Alpha King, maybe he would be able to have plumbing run to the station.

"Do you want our fate decided by the elves?" she replied.

As he stood urinating into the porcelain bowl, he thought about his experience with the High Council and answered honestly, "No, not really."

Agatha felt the pressure building in her breasts and turned away from the window. She had seen the blackened, charred mark on the stone drive where Dirk's body had lain after Torric had set it ablaze. It had thankfully been removed. The Sauvage were noticeably absent from the park and she found it disturbing. She had to find out what had transpired overnight, but right then she needed to feed Gavin. An emergency meeting with the people she trusted would have to wait.

The baby was sound asleep in a child's doll bed that had belonged to the governor's daughter. She was surprised he had slept through the entire night. As newborns, Logan and Luna would have been screaming to be fed by now, but Gavin was much more relaxed. Bloem and Buren had kept the twins in their room ostensibly to give Nick and Agatha a modicum of peace and quiet. Nick and Agatha knew that the presence of the toddlers brought Buren and Bloem light in the shadow of their grief and gave them renewed optimism.

Nick came out of the water closet to find Agatha curled up on the bed with their newest son in her arms. The sight brought a proud smile to his face. He poured cold water from a ceramic pitcher on the dressing table into its matching basin and set about giving himself a sponge bath. In the mirror he could watch Agatha nursing and he was again mystified by the direction his life had taken. It was going to take some considerable getting used to.

Agatha found Gavin to be a pleasantly mellow baby. Logan and Luna had been avid feeders, suckling aggressively. Gavin was more lackadaisical about it. He let the nipple slip from his mouth several times as he continued to gum at the air like a fish. She had to redirect him to her breast to make him focus on the task at hand. He possessed a completely different personality than his brother and sister.

A knock on the door startled them. Nick grabbed a pair of trousers that had been laid over the back of a chair. Mrs. MacLeach had made sure they had everything they needed before she had retired the previous night. Tugging them up his legs he made his way to the door.

"Who is it?" he asked.

"Adam Steelcuff, your Majesty."

Nick glanced questioningly over his shoulder at Agatha.

"Well, let him in," she said somewhat brusquely. She was too tired to keep her tongue completely civil.

"You aren't covered," he pointed out, more out of his own

discomfort at her being seen by others as she was with their son at her naked breast.

She rolled her eyes and pulled the top sheet over herself, concealing Gavin as well. Nudity meant nothing to a werewolf. Satisfied, Nick opened the door.

Adam entered the room with Ridgeley, Buren and Holt behind him. They stayed close to the door out of courtesy. The relationship between the men and their sovereigns was new territory and in need of clear boundaries.

"We're sorry to intrude, your Majesties," said Adam, head lowered submissively.

Nick didn't care for the words or the tone in the beta werewolf's voice, but he realised that his world had changed literally overnight. He did not want to be put above his friends, but he could not alter the fact that he was now royalty and no longer a common man. There was no avoiding the conflict between his rise to prominence and his desire to remain ordinary. He wasn't familiar with the protocol to be followed within the greater pack or how it translated into his private life. It was going to be a delicate balance until the wrinkles were ironed out. Against his will, he would be treated differently from this day forth.

"Please, can we not be so formal in private?" he asked. "I can't handle that right now."

Buren grinned.

"You are the Alpha King now," he said. "Even elves have to show you respect."

Holt also smirked, but his expression was less jovial.

Agatha looked on from her impromptu throne at the head of the bed. As she shifted Gavin to her other breast the sheet fell away to expose her upper body. For Adam and Ridgeley it was a moment of tremendous honor to witness their queen as she nursed their prince and possible future king. Their awe was evident and they quickly took a knee in deference to the sacred bond between mother and child. As Alpha Queen she was also the spiritual mother to all werewolves, representing their connection to the earth.

Holt looked away. It was not appropriate for a woman to bare her breasts in the presence of strangers, even when feeding an infant. Elves were far more priggish about their bodies.

Buren felt a myriad of emotions at the sight of Agatha with her son. It brought to light the pain of losing Dirk and Lars, but also reminded him of the most basic link between any mother and child. She was entitled to display her affectionate and nurturing side. The Gods knew that in the past few weeks she had suffered deeply and she would be expected to display a strong veneer to the public. An intimate moment such as this was to be cherished.

Nick marched to the side of the bed and pulled the sheet over Gavin's head, shielding Agatha's breasts. She understood his possessiveness and embarrassment. It made no difference to her, but he was still struggling to shed his human tendencies.

Adam and Ridgeley rose, keeping their gazes averted. They could no less demonstrate their place in the greater pack than they could make the sky change colour. Nick and Agatha were their alpha leaders in every sense of the word.

"I didn't ask for this," Nick sighed. He picked up the shirt that also hung over the back of the chair and dragged it on. "I don't want this."

Although she knew he felt that way, it still twisted Agatha's heart to hear the words.

"Then you need to form an Alpha Council quickly," said Holt, relieved that Agatha was covered.

Adam cocked his head in a decidedly dog-like manner.

"There hasn't been an Alpha Council in over a thousand years," he said.

"What's the Alpha Council?" asked Nick, seated so he could pull on socks and boots.

Agatha adjusted Gavin again as his mouth released the nipple. His lips smacked empty air until she realigned them with her breast. He latched on and set about working milk into his belly. He took only few swallows before falling asleep, flopping back in her arms with his mouth open. If this was any indication of his personality she realised he was going to be a gentle, sensitive man like his father.

"The Alpha Council is something like the elves' High Council," she explained. "When werewolves came out of the First Forest with the other races they realised they needed a ruling body. There was an Alpha King and Queen, but they relied on the Alpha Council for maintaining law and order. The Alpha King and Queen are mostly figureheads. It's the responsibility of the Alpha Council to actually run the show."

Nick's exaggerated sigh of relief came as no surprise to anyone.

"I thought that would make you feel better," she said to him before going on. "It's up to us to establish that Alpha Council and make sure we have the right people on it. It's no simple matter to remove someone from the Council once they've taken a position. We need to get it right from the start."

"I vote for Adam and Ridgeley," Nick said quickly, lacing his boots.

"It would be an honor, your Majesty," said Ridgeley, head still lowered.

Nick's face tightened, but he forced himself to ignore the resentment that lurked inside him. At least the wolf seemed pleased with its promotion. He supposed it was more aware of its innate authority because of Agatha's alpha influence. She had placed it inside him and it was part of her dominant nature. He would have to learn to rely on its senses and instincts during his reign.

"Of course Adam and Ridgeley will sit on the Council, if the two of you accept our appointment," said Agatha. Gavin twitched in her arms and she carefully extricated him from beneath the sheet. She managed to keep herself concealed as she did so. Nick took him from her. "If either of you don't want to take on that responsibility, we understand. Adam, I ask that you stand as Alpha Prime, the head of the Council."

"I accept your charge, your Majesty," Adam replied humbly.

"As do I," echoed Ridgeley.

Buren walked to the window and peered out on a gathering of werewolves in the front yard. The Birthrights milled about unsurely, hoping to get a glimpse of their king and queen. There were no Sauvage in sight.

"I think your subjects are feeling lost," he observed. "You need to make some decisions right now."

"Adam, Ridgeley, I need to you to oversee the rounding up of Sauvage. I know it's going to be a huge undertaking and probably the most difficult task anyone will have to handle," said Agatha. "Will you do it?"

They nodded. Their loyalty to her had no limit.

Getting thousands of Sauvage under control would be a monumental challenge with no guarantee of success. They had to move swiftly to prevent too many strays from leaving the city and working their way into the bush. Then they needed somewhere to put them once they were captured and a means to get them there. It was going to involve some ingenuity and luck to have any hope of restoring order among the Sauvage and to keep further mayhem to a minimum. In their favor, the commanders of Dirk's army had remained at their posts and were already engaged in damage control.

"Now that the moon's fading they are somewhat more manageable," replied Adam. He shared a look with Ridgeley. "The commanders have been following Dirk's orders. He wanted them destroyed once he captured Sydney. He didn't want them wreaking any more havoc than necessary to achieve his goal. It was always his plan to wipe them out when he didn't need them anymore. With Dirk dead, there's no reason to keep them alive. It's going to take months to clear them all out, maybe years. We may never get them all."

She didn't desire to kill every last Sauvage if it wasn't necessary. She knew that there would be a significant number that could not be managed or rehabilitated. They would have to be euthanized to protect the larger population. In her head she knew it had to be done. In her heart she wished it could be different. These Sauvage had been men forced to become monsters. They had been given no choice. Whoever they had once been would likely remain a mystery. They were now violent creatures that had to be dealt with in a detached and clinical manner.

"Corral them as best you and do what you can to salvage the ones that aren't too far gone," she said with a catch in her voice. She choked on her emotions. "I want to save those that we can."

"What do you intend to do with them?" Adam inquired. His gaze was haunted by the memory of werewolf history. "You aren't planning to keep them are you?"

"They can't all be lost causes," she replied sadly. "We have an obligation as Birthrights to work with those that can be helped. We have to catch them first. To protect the greater population I'll talk to Torric and have the dragons burn any that they find beyond the cities. Even that may not be enough to keep people safe."

"What do you mean *burn them*?" Nick demanded. Gavin squeaked as Nick's grip tightened. "Burn them alive?"

She turned hollow eyes up to meet his horrified expression. She refused to allow tears to fall for the Sauvage who would soon die, but inside she was a wreck.

"If it comes to that. We need to prove to the citizens of this country that we're going to make amends," she answered. She tried to keep her voice level, but it trembled slightly. "We don't have the luxury of treating the Sauvage with compassion. We need to destroy them as quickly as possible to get life back to normal. These people have already suffered enough. We have to rebuild and reestablish law and order. I don't know if the elves will give us any help, or what the humans will do now. We can only control our own people and demonstrate our strength. We need to get the Alpha Council going and start making the right decisions. What we do here and now will be our legacy. All werewolves will be judged by our actions from this day forward. I will not let my people down."

There was a soft, hesitant knock on the door and Beshka's voice reached them.

"I'm sorry to bother you, but the Grand Council is requesting an audience."

"Tell her we'll let her know when we're ready to talk," Nick snapped. He patted Gavin's back until the baby brought up a bubble of air. The warm weight of the infant against his shoulder kept him grounded. It soothed his wolf, as well. "Agatha still needs to rest."

"Herself won't be please to be kept waiting," muttered Holt. "Right now the elves are your best allies. You should hear what she has to say."

Agatha yawned, covering her mouth with the back of her hand. Trying to solve the world's problems was taxing, but it wasn't something that would keep.

"Is she here?" she sighed.

"She's in the drawing room downstairs," said Beshka.

"Keep her entertained. I'll be down shortly." Agatha caught Buren's studious gaze. "I wish this had all gone differently."

He agreed without saying a word.

She looked to Adam, who cautiously raised his eyes to meet hers. When neither she nor Nick made any attempt to correct or chastise him, he boldly lifted his head.

Even with the shift in power she was still the girl he had grown up with on the Rez. He pictured her when she was maybe four or five years old, well before they were branded, running through the white poles of the aspens with her wheaten hair streaming behind her. He remembered her before her innocence had been shattered. He had never been able to pick up those pieces for her. Perhaps now he could repair some of that damage by standing at her side as her friend, protector and confidant.

"I never want to see your head lowered to me again when we're in private," she told him. "You're my friend. Any differences or disagreements between us are resolved. I need your help and advice right now. We both do. This is a new world for all of us."

Adam smiled. His eyes glinted with that peculiar metallic sheen that indicated the wolf was near the surface. He and his wolf owed her their lives. It was hers for the asking.

"I'm glad you still consider me your friend," he said with an outpouring of gratitude. "I will always be here for you both. My life is yours."

"May I suggest one decision you should make sooner rather than later," offered Holt. "There will be humans who want you dead for what's happened. Their government may have thrown them to the wolves, but the humans that inhabit this country are not as willing to give it up. They fought valiantly and should still be considered your enemies. You need protection until they realize you're on their side."

Nick reeled with the awareness that Holt was right. There were people who would actively seek to kill any werewolf involved in the war. They had not resolved any of the friction between werewolves and humans yet. If anything, the chasm was wider than ever.

"I'll be at your side," Buren assured him. "They'll have to get through me first."

"You may be a target as well," said Holt with a look at Buren. "Dirk was your son."

Buren's cold blue gaze sliced through the other elf's haughty demeanor.

"And I am the one who brought him down. I want that known," he said through clenched teeth.

"So we need bodyguards now?" Nick inquired, returning Gavin to his cradle. He straightened up and faced the small crowd of men who would serve him faithfully. "When is this going to end?"

"It's not going to end," said Agatha from the bed behind him. Her voice was small and soft. "Unless you want to go into hiding, this is how our lives are going to be from now on. I'm sorry all of this was forced on you. If I could change it, I would."

Nick crossed to her and sat on the edge of the mattress. He took her hands in his and looked into her shimmering gold eyes.

"When I married you, I had no idea what to expect," he admitted. He stroked her hair. "If I had seen this coming, I might have run the other way. No one could have predicted this. Honestly, I don't think anything would have stopped me from marrying you. Eliza tried and she sure as hell couldn't stop me. As crazy as all this is, I'll do whatever it I have to. I told you once that you're my wife and partner in all things. Nothing's changed that. Let's hear what Herself has to tell us."

CHAPTER FORTY-FOUR

"A woman's appearance should reflect her thoughts, understated and well organized."
Excerpt from the periodical, "Ladies of a Victorian Age"

The drawing room had an ornately painted high ceiling and pale blue carpet. The furnishings were French antiques. Generic oil paintings of European gardens hung on the white walls. It was a cold and impersonal space.

The Grand Council Rhionna Greenhill was perched on the edge of a cream divan as she waited with growing impatience. She was the highest ranking elf in Australia and the newly appointed Alpha King and Queen were keeping her on ice until they deigned to put in an appearance. It was blatantly rude, but what could one expect of werewolves? She had thought, based on her interrogation of Copernicus Buchanan and his consequent infiltration the Sauvage army, that there might be some promise of civility and honor among the new order. So far she was not impressed.

Mrs. MacLeach hovered nearby to attend to their elite guest. She was far down the cultural ladder from a high elf such as Herself. The urisk knew her place and remained there.

The first people to enter the drawing room were Buren and Eliza. They were both armed with gun belts and they visually swept the room to assure the safety of their charges. Eliza had taken up the reins as Agatha's personal guardian without a word needing to be said on the matter.

Ridgeley and Adam had gone to meet with the commanders in

Sydney to strategize the optimal method by which to collect, sort and designate the Sauvage for their fate. They needed a system in place for the process to proceed. Their king and queen had also assigned them to determine the most suitable candidates for the Alpha Council. They would be busy.

Holt aided Beshka in wading through mounds of correspondence that kept flooding in from all regions of the continent and from more distant shores. The telegrapher was transcribing faster than he ever had as the telegraph key clattered non-stop. Messengers continued to arrive with dispatches from every corner of the globe. Much of the communication from within Australia's borders was for reparation of property destruction, loss of land and assets. There were also open threats. Those were handed off to Birthright soldiers who were charged with tracking down the offender if possible and assessing the legitimacy of the potential threat. If it was deemed to be sincere they would handle it as they saw fit. The outside world demanded to know what the werewolves' plans were at this point. There was fear that the fires of rebellion would spread to other countries.

Bloem stayed up in the governor's suite with Gavin, who slept through everything, and the twins, who were into everything.

Nick and Agatha entered the drawing room without ceremony.

The Grand Council got to her feet to greet them. Her formal attire consisted of a long sheath dress in muted earth tone patterns beneath her Council robes. Her hair was swept away from her face, held in place by delicate silver and onyx hairpins. The style exposed her tall thin ears.

Agatha didn't have many clothing options at the moment. Her wardrobe was back at Gilgai. Mrs. MacLeach had commandeered the clothing left behind by the governor's wife. It was either entirely too frilly and inappropriate or it was frumpy and ill fitting. She had chosen a sleeveless blue gown that matched Nick's eyes and adjusted a dark brown corset to fit her waist as best she could. It was not ideal for her first contact with the elf Grand Council, but she made it work.

Rhionna's initial impression of the Alpha Queen went far beyond her fashion sense. It was that Agatha Buchanan was a woman who would not be intimidated. There were lines of exhaustion in the werewolf's beautiful face, but her eyes reflected the strength and fierce will that had brought her to Australia in the first place. The Grand Council was inspired to hope for a positive outcome.

"Your Majesties," she said, inclining her head respectfully.

Agatha's eyes raked over the elf. Her wolf was reacting to the other female's dominance. It wanted to challenge the Grand Council, but she kept in check. The elf was not her enemy at the moment. She knew that could change in an instant depending on their conversation.

"Madame Grand Council," Agatha responded with a nod.

Buren and Holt had given her a briefing on how to speak to the prominent elf. Agatha might have made a fool of herself without their quick coaching.

"I understand you've recently given birth to a son. May I offer congratulations," said Rhionna.

Nick circled the elf, not realizing his animal behavior had kicked in. As with Agatha's wolf, he felt the silent challenge the elf presented. He stood behind her, ready to pounce if she made a wrong move. He listened with two sets of ears. His human side heard the words while his wolf was in tune with their intent.

"Thank you." Agatha gestured to the sofa. The women sat facing each other. "Shall we speak frankly? I know it's considered impolite to get directly to the heart of the matter, but I don't think we have time to waste. Wouldn't you agree?"

As Mrs. MacLeach bustled forward with fresh coffee for Agatha, Rhionna answered, "I agree completely. There is much to discuss."

Nick took a seat in a low backed chair close to Agatha. He rested his elbows on his knees and leaned forward. His gaze was focused on the elf's inscrutable features. He had been in her presence only once before, but he believed she was an intelligent woman who acted rationally. He wanted to trust her.

"We are currently in the process of eliminating the Sauvage,"

Agatha said, taking the cup of coffee the housekeeper presented to her. Rhionna's teacup rested untouched on the table beside them. "It will be a long and difficult endeavor, but we are committed to eradicating the Sauvage that cannot be retrained or otherwise salvaged."

Rhionna's surprise showed for an instant.

"You believe any of these Sauvage can be saved?"

"I don't see why not. They aren't all mindless beasts. I've seen many that could be taught to accept their wolves. My husband is an excellent example of proper conditioning," said Agatha, adding quickly, "for a Sauvage."

The ghost of a smile appeared on the elf's lips. Her gaze briefly flickered in Nick's direction before returning to Agatha.

"And you think you can accomplish such a feat?" Rhionna shook her head. "We are willing to provide you with assistance to form a new government and establish ties with other countries if you wish. In other words, the High Council is offering to invest in your future."

Nick didn't mean to sound ungrateful, but he had to ask, "Why would you do that? You sided with the humans during the Paradeus Uprising."

Rhionna acknowledged that it would be rough going at first to make them understand. There were centuries of prejudice and misinformation to lay to rest.

"At that time there was no clear authority to provide competent rule in the event of Paradeus' success. He was barely more than a Roman foot soldier. Yes, he had control over his wolf to the point of near Birthright status, but he was no leader. If he had succeeded there would have been chaos. We stepped in to prevent that. We have always supported freedom and independence for Birthrights."

Agatha's lip curled. She didn't appreciate the elf's condescending attitude.

"Why haven't elves ever done anything about it?"

Rhionna addressed her with the tone of a mother politely correcting a child.

"We aren't werewolves," she said. To mollify the anger she saw rising in Agatha's face, she went on. "It has never been our practice to invite ourselves into another race's conflict. If we are approached we will take all things into consideration. We usually provide aid."

Agatha's temper flared. Buren cleared his throat to stem her outburst, but she was in charge and her alpha side wouldn't be silenced.

"You've let us think we were the scum of the earth for three hundred years," she snarled. The porcelain cup shattered in her hand. Coffee and blood spilled onto her lap. "When all we had to do was ask for help?"

Rhionna understood her rage, but Agatha was directing it at the wrong race.

"Who would have asked?" the elf inquired. "There was no Alpha Council, nor a king or queen in control of any segment of werewolf society. You were fractured after the Paradeus Uprising. So I say again, who would have asked us for help?"

Agatha was stopped in her tracks by the elf's logic. Her wolf instantly backed down in the face of reason. Rhionna's common sense observation had never occurred to her as it probably would not occur to any werewolf. They had given up, allowing themselves to be scattered and mistreated.

"Then I humbly ask for the elves' help through this Restoration," she said with total humility. She was beginning to feel the sting in the palm of her hand. "We're in dire need of your knowledge and experience. We don't know what we're doing."

Nick nodded, coming forward to see to her injury. It wasn't deep, but it was still bleeding. He took a cloth napkin from the table and knelt beside Agatha. He began dressing the wound.

"You're already making progress," said Buren. He stood by the door with thick arms crossed and feet apart. He was a man anyone would want to avoid antagonizing. "You know what you need to do. You just need help getting there."

Eliza stood on the other side of the door with slightly less rigid posture. Her bright red hair was in a heavy plait down her back. She wore men's trousers and a flannel shirt. With the addition of the studded gun belt around her ample hips she could have passed for an American outlaw.

"He's right, Agatha," she remarked. "Don't sell yourself short. I saw that spark in you the first time I laid eyes on you. Do you honestly think I would have let you go with Copernicus if I didn't think you were capable of holding your own?"

Nick pulled a face at her audacity to claim credit for their marriage.

"You let her go with me because I doubled your fee," he said gruffly. "And I wasn't taking no for an answer."

Eliza smirked, conceding.

While Nick continued binding Agatha's hand, her mind closed around a particular thought. She turned curious eyes to his focused expression.

"How much did you have to pay?" she asked.

Nick didn't feel it prudent to discuss her purchase price. They had not once spoken of it in their few years together and it didn't bear mentioning now.

"I don't think that's relevant."

"Two thousand dollars, if you must know," announced Eliza. She saw no reason to keep it a secret. It was her business after all.

It was a staggering amount.

"Where did you get that kind of money?" Agatha demanded, her mind leading her along a path that no one else seemed to be following. "The station barely breaks even, even when you had sheep. That money could go a long way now."

Since Nick was reluctant to speak about finances, Buren answered.

"You remember the rubies you wore on the night of your wedding celebration at Willowbrook?" She nodded, gaze alternating between him and Nick. "Those came from mines on Buchanan land to the north."

"You own jewel mines?" Eliza echoed, stunned. "And you live like a pauper in the bush?"

"Those mines haven't seen use since my father died," Nick replied sharply. His voice was laced with heartache. "They're closed."

When he offered no further explanation, Buren filled in the blank.

"Nick's father died in a mine collapse in '39. We were never able to recover his body. The mines shut down after that."

"My God," Eliza gasped. "I'm so sorry."

It didn't matter that the accident was more than thirty years in the past. It was as though he was getting the terrible news all over again. Hard emotions came careening through Nick like a tidal wave.

He had been nineteen at the time, too young to lose his mentor, father and friend. His pain had been exacerbated by not being able to say a final farewell and see his father laid to rest in the family cemetery. His father's tomb was a cave in a hillside. He hadn't been to the mines since the day the rescuers had declared an end to the search for survivors.

As a young man he had not been able to reconcile his grief. Now it was fresh in his thoughts once again, but he could manage it. It also brought to the forefront of his mind the fact that he had stepped up and taken control of the station when he had been lost and unprepared. At that time he had been forced make the hard decisions that kept the place functioning. He was back in those same shoes. He had done it once, becoming one of the most prominent and successful men in Falmormath. He was older, wiser, more sure of himself today. He had married Agatha with the idea that she would be able to take root and thrive in difficult conditions. Those conditions couldn't be any more difficult than right now. If they didn't stand together, they would lose everything and take every werewolf in Australia down with them.

"You've never told me how your parents died," Agatha whispered.

His face was close to hers and she pressed her cheek to his. He gently pushed his face back against hers in an affectionate wolf-like gesture.

"I didn't want you to think about how you lost your parents."

Rhionna seemed to have been forgotten. She understood Agatha's line of inquiry. She was not questioning her monetary value, but rather was searching for a means to finance the Restoration.

"Do you still have access to those mines?" the elf asked, ignoring their joint glares.

Nick tightened the knot on the temporary wrapping around Agatha's hand. He slid in next her on the sofa. He peered over her shoulder at the Grand Council with brows sunk low over stormy eyes.

"Why?"

"If you could fund the Restoration yourselves as Alpha King and Queen then you will silence many who would oppose you," she replied logically. "It would make you that much more powerful in the eyes of your enemies to have your own financial backing. They'll know that you can manage this country without foreign aid. You won't need to go outside Australia's borders to seek support. It will help you to stand alone as an independent nation for werewolves. Isn't that what this infernal war was about?"

Agatha turned her head to look at her husband. If Nick refused to open the mines she would back his decision without hesitation.

Nick struggled with his old emotions as they battled with his adult reasoning. He had to put the past where it belonged if he was to focus on the future.

"If I reopen the mines, who's going to work them? The conditions are brutal. We used convicts that had been sentenced to hard labor and they had a rough go of it. We lost at least one or two a month."

"You have an unending supply of slave labor," said Eliza. She nodded toward the window. "Put those filthy Sauvage to work in the mines. They're stronger and more durable than any human convicts. If they die it's no real loss." After the words were out she remembered that Nick was a Sauvage. She muttered, "Apologies, Copernicus. I didn't mean-"

"You're absolutely right," he said. He shared her sentiment towards the violent and mutated Sauvage. He was not like them so he did not think of himself as Sauvage. To his way of thinking, he was a werewolf like Agatha. "They are a potential resource."

Rhionna spoke again. She was a shrewd politician as well as a benevolent nature spirit.

"How will you control them? It's one thing to force them down a mine shaft, but what will you do when they come back out?"

"You're talking about pure slave labor," Buren protested. He couldn't bring himself to share the same feelings towards the Sauvage as the others even with what had happened to Dirk. "Working them to death."

"No," said Agatha. She was beginning to tire and her hand ached. She leaned back into Nick's solid chest. His arm came around her waist and she felt his strength bolster hers. "They will not be mistreated. They will be handled appropriately, which may seem harsh, but in no way will they be abused. You have my word on that. I also want any Birthright responsible for creating Sauvage arrested and put to work in the mines as punishment."

"I'm sure many have fled the country," said Rhionna.

Agatha's eyes burned with amber flames.

"I want them found. I don't care where they've gone," she declared. "I want them brought back with their tails between their legs. They created the Sauvage and they will pay for it. They can break their backs in the mines alongside their offspring."

She suddenly took a shuddering breath and closed her eyes. Nick pressed his nose behind her ear. She sighed, opening her eyes a sliver to prove that she hadn't fainted as he feared.

"I think we're done here for now," Nick announced. He held her tightly. "Agatha needs to rest. Madam Grand Council, we will gratefully accept any help the elves offer. If you would like to return this evening for dinner, we would be honored."

Rhionna could see the weariness clouding Agatha's face. There was a great deal more to discuss, but she recognized it was time to end this session of negotiations.

"I shall do that," she accepted before taking her leave. "In the meantime, I will speak with a few key Council members about your plans."

As she walked along the exterior arcade to reach her carriage, Rhionna reflected on her opinion of the Alpha King and Queen. She had feared they would be weak, as had other werewolves throughout history, or they would be too eager to prove their dominance and become tyrants. To her surprise and chagrin they had proven to be normal people with their own fears and foibles. They merely needed a firm hand to keep them on track but, all things considered, they were off to a good start.

CHAPTER FORTY-FIVE

"The balance of power is as fragile as the balance of nature."
elf proverb

With the Sauvage control efforts underway across the continent, it was time to cement their decisions for the Alpha Council members who would continue to oversee the Restoration. Adam and Ridgeley gave their lieges a list of names, providing background information and an explanation for every werewolf they put forward. It was not a particularly long list, but it took time to contact the individuals, especially as several of them were not currently residing in Australia. There was no defined number of members that could sit on the Alpha Council, but there needed to be balance. Too few and they faced the danger of the Council collapsing under the weight of pressure and expectation. Too many and they risked too many voices and not enough decisions. Historically, the magic number was seven. The only hard and fast rule was that it be comprised solely of Birthrights. Agatha also insisted that none of them had been party to creating the Sauvage army. If they had served under Dirk, but not actually been responsible for giving the Bite, she would take that under advisement. Had Anatoly Goreyevskiy not committed suicide upon learning of Dirk's demise, he might have been a candidate, despite his involvement with Dirk. He had served werewolves well in his years in Moscow before his downfall in Perth and he had made an attempt to prevent the bloodshed. His loss was another werewolf's gain.

Nick was hunched over the writing desk in the sitting room of the Alpha suite, renamed in their honor, head in his hands. His frustration was running at an all time high as they went over the list again in their deliberations. They had whittled the field down to ten and were debating minutiae to make the last selections.

"Remind me again why you want Shen-Li Huang and not Arnold Kopelson?"

The other person in the room was feeling the stress just as oppressively as Nick. Agatha was seated on the long sofa with Gavin. Because he was so young she would not be parted from him for more than a few hours at a time. Logan and Luna were content to be with their extended family in another part of the building.

They only had one chance to get it right. Removing someone from the Alpha Council meant a physical challenge and fight between the Council member and the one demanding their replacement. It was a vicious system set in place by their nature as animals. Some things required resolution through tooth and claw.

"I know governing Australia is our primary objective, but we need to think in broader terms," she said tiredly. "Shen-Li Huang represents Australia's connection with Polynesia and Asia. She would make a fierce advocate against the use of werewolf organs as medicinal cures. I like her stance on promoting cultural systems. I think she would be an excellent addition to the Council. Kopelson has a history of siding with humans to save his neck. I'm not sure why they included him on the list."

"Because he has ties to the shadow fae realm," Nick replied, reading through the dossier for what seemed the hundredth time. His eyes were beginning to cross. "So maybe we should include him and leave out Aldo Storan or Kjurtaergen Nommerfeld."

"Aldo and Kjurt are both strong alphas," she countered, kissing Gavin's round cheek. The baby let go with a long string of drool that fell onto her blouse. She mopped it up with the towel that rested on her shoulder. "But they're both in Europe."

"Alright." Nick pushed their files aside for the moment. He was reaching his breaking point. If they didn't come to a consensus soon he would throw darts at the files to have it done with. "That leaves us three in Australia. Ben Stroud, Dyra Cooper-Renwell and Egan McCoy. Egan's American by birth. I'd think you would have chosen him already."

"Lance was American." She cradled Gavin in her arms and gently began rocking him to sleep. "Don't think I'm going to appoint someone just because they're from America."

"I didn't mean it like that," he said, turning in his seat to look at her. Seeing Gavin snuggled against her chest he felt a surge of pride and love. He had to protect his children and his country. His children would always come first. "I was thinking that he would be more inclined to sympathise with the plight of werewolves in the UAT and work to loosen the Regulatory government's stranglehold on them. I know you want that to happen at some point."

She nodded, placing her lips on her son's bald head, breathing in his clean, innocent scent. She looked over at Nick with heartfelt affection and commiseration. He was ready to quit and she was fed up as well.

"Maybe we can have nine on the Council," she said with a shrug. "It would give us a deeper perspective on the issues."

He took a long breath and overlapped the files on the desk in front of him.

"That means we need to decide who's *not* going to be on the Council," he announced. "My vote is Arnold Kopelson. I don't think we need his connections to the shadow fae to establish strong ties with that faction. They aren't well organized anyway. We need to keep our focus on solid foundations."

"I agree. He'll be held out as an alternate should someone else decline the offer."

Nick pushed his chair back and let his head roll forward. He rubbed his nape to soften the tense muscles. Agatha set the sleeping baby on the sofa and padded towards Nick on quiet, bare feet. He felt her gentle fingers take over as she massaged his neck and shoulders with expert manipulation.

She kissed his ear, working her mouth down the side of his jaw. He let out a contented sigh.

"You need something to help you relax," she murmured.

Her hands came around the front of him and unbuttoned the flap of his trousers. As she had surmised, he was ready for action. His penis rose up to meet her gentle caress. His head fell back and he closed his eyes to savor the warm, squeezing action her hand performed. He thought back to their first days together, when he had been aroused by the mere sight of her. His attraction to her and his desire for her had not diminished, but with regular attention to his needs he had reached a point where his body was able to hold back until the time was right. He was glad the time was right now. He had been denied her touch for weeks.

As she was quickening her strokes there was a knock on the door.

"Go the hell away!" shouted Nick, just about to reach his release. He put his hand over hers and kept her at it until a glistening tide of semen spilled out of him. He groaned loudly.

"Is everything alright?" asked Beshka through the door.

They could hear Eliza's deep, knowing chuckle.

"I think everything's fine," she laughed. "Sorry to bother you. Let's go. They need some time alone."

"Oh. Oh!"

Their footsteps receded.

Agatha pressed her face into Nick's shoulder to smother her laughter.

"I'll go see what they want," she said, leaving him with a kiss on the side of his head.

Nick wasn't as amused. His moment of bliss had been interrupted. His entire life had been interrupted by this war and his ascension to the werewolf throne. He couldn't wait for the day to come that he could get any part of his former life back. The station needed him. There was a complete rebuilding to do after Torric burnt the vines and barns. Edison and the boys were working overtime to restore order, but he was needed there as well.

BIRTHRIGHT

※

"It's those damned dingoes," grunted Eliza from her position by the door of the drawing room.

Agatha stood by the grand fireplace, staring into the empty hearth. In the room with her were Nick, Eliza, Buren, Bloem, Holt and a few other Birthrights that she deemed worthy of being part of her inner circle. Her children were in Mrs. MacLeach's excellent care. She trusted her friends explicitly, but she knew that she needed to include more of her own race in the picture if she was to present a united werewolf government to the world. This collection of her advisors and guards had assembled in record time to deal with the latest crisis.

Apparently the indigenous canines were wreaking havoc on outlying stations and towns. In their rage at being denied their due, they were going after humans with a vengeance.

She had not realised the dingoes had become a problem. She was just learning that Dirk had promised them a large chunk of the country in exchange for their communication skills as spies. She was not inclined to give the little orange bastards anything, but if there had been an agreement reached she would need the specifics to make an informed decision. The dingoes had been in Australia first. It was the werewolves who had started a turf war, after the humans had laid claim to dingo lands. She supposed that was splitting hairs. It was also of importance to make certain the native humans kept their identity and lands. Though they were human, they had been mistreated by their own race over time and again more recently by Dirk. Agatha could afford them some sympathy.

"Do they have some sort of governing body?" she asked. "Is there a liaison or representative we can meet with?"

No one in the room knew for certain. The dingoes were elusive.

"With respect, your Majesty," said Declan Burke. He was a rugged, broad shouldered Birthright from Melbourne. He had been a staff sergeant at Dumfries, but had refused to create Sauvage. His allegiance to his Alpha King and Queen was unshakable. He had already accepted a position on the Alpha Council. "I believe the dingoes have more of a collective conscious, but no particular ruling body. If memory serves, Dirk kept in close contact with one named Wollaweroo. Perhaps that one has some sort of influence over the rest."

"How do we find this Wollaweroo?" Buren asked. He was unimpressed with the idea of giving dingoes any benefits. As a grazier, he supported wiping them out. "What are you going to offer him?"

"I want to know what Dirk promised them first." Agatha's golden eyes swept the faces around her. Her wolf was spoiling for a fight. "If it's reasonable, I'll honor it. If not, the dingoes will feel my teeth in their flanks as I chase them out of my territory."

There was agreement from all present.

"The elves are keeping order until the Alpha Council is confirmed," she said, moving away from the fireplace. She paced the length of the room, hands clasped behind her back. Her left hand was still bandaged, but it would be healed in another day or two. "I will see to the dingoes personally. Track down this Wollaweroo and make sure he knows we're coming. I'd rather see his tail than his face, but I'll meet him head on if that's what he wants."

Nick came to her side. His concern was evident. Apparently he was more worried about her than she seemed to be. If he didn't keep an eye on her she would push herself too far.

"Are you sure that's wise? You only had Gavin a few weeks ago. You aren't in any shape to fight."

"I don't think we'll hear back from our little orange friends right away," she assured him, resting her hand on his chest. "In the meantime, I want the areas where they are causing the most problems to be protected. I want them shut down."

"Most of our resources are tied up with the Sauvage effort," said Declan apologetically. "I don't see how we can spare any bodies to deal with the dingoes."

Agatha glanced at Holt. He shook his head.

"Don't bother asking the elves. They don't care if humans are under attack from dingoes."

"The dragons?"

"They're involved in the Sauvage purge, remember?" said Nick.

Agatha despised feeling out of control. It was her duty and responsibility to make sure the country was put back together with as little conflict as possible. This was an enormous conflict.

"May I make a suggestion?"

All heads turned in Eliza's direction. Several expectant gazes focused on her face. She was never shy to be the center of attention.

"I do have contacts among the fae, shadow and light. More light than shadow, mind you, but I could pull a few strings to get you some help."

Agatha nearly sagged with relief. She should have considered Eliza's tangled web of associations. Her reputation crossed racial borders from Australia to Zaire. Who didn't the woman know?

"I'll make some queries and see what I can bring to the table. We'll stop those sons of bitches in their tracks. That I can promise you."

Nick wrapped his arms around Agatha and tucked her in close. He nuzzled her loose tawny hair.

"The sooner the better, I guess," he muttered.

The entire room agreed.

CHAPTER FORTY-SIX

*"A house is built one stick a time.
A home is built one heart at a time.
A nation is built one step at a time."*
Evelyn Wild-Winter, author, "Family Foundations"

While they waited for word from their other chosen Council members, and about the dingoes, Nick and Agatha made their presence known in Sydney. They actively pitched in with the physical activity of removing debris and offering aid to those who had lost their homes and businesses. They were thickly surrounded by bodyguards, but most of the citizens seemed genuinely grateful to see them. Agatha wanted the people of Sydney and Australia to know that she and Nick were there for them. They toured the hardest hit sections of the city, though Nick put his foot down on Agatha entering any areas where the dead were being housed awaiting disposal. In her post birth condition he didn't feel she needed to view or come in contact with the decaying remains.

To have the Alpha King and Queen on the front lines in the Restoration effort boosted their credibility. They received offers of aid from several countries. The strongest support came from Russia, where werewolves had kept a prominent profile in the centuries following the Paradeus Uprising. Even in death, Anatoly Goreyevskiy's name carried weight among the wealthy and powerful in the land of tundra and ice. All assistance was humbly and graciously accepted. There remained a stony silence from Britain. The Victorian government washed its hands of the messy affair and formally disowned its former colony. It attached a name to the events that had transpired, the Dirk Rebellion. The name stuck.

Although Dirk had successfully brought werewolves out of the shadows and back to prominence among the major races, it was too soon to grant him heroic status. His ruthless tactics were far too fresh in the minds of the victims to consider him anything other than a beast and a traitor. It would take time, if ever, for him to earn the same distinction as Paradeus. Most of that honor was applied to Agatha.

During the days immediately following the battle, Agatha dedicated her time primarily to the children orphaned by the hostilities. She made it clear that there was no preference or prejudice. She organized several orphanages to get the lost children off the streets and into structured environments where they would be fed, sheltered and given the love and attention they deserved while relatives were tracked down. She brought her own children with her to visit, against the advice of her informal ministry. It was important to her that her children be seen by the younger generation and that the people of Sydney realise she was a mother, too. It would be her children leading them when they were adults and there was no point in keeping Logan, Luna and Gavin sequestered from the public. Nick was appreciative of her endeavors because it kept her mostly indoors and out of harm's way. There were still solitary Sauvage roaming loose and the streets were not safe.

Improvement could be measured day by day. Airships arrived at all hours in every part the country, bringing supplies and brute force to add to the Sauvage control project.

Former training grounds were transformed into internment camps while the Sauvage were reclassified and divided into those that could be salvaged and those to be euthanized. To Agatha's deepest regret, more than half the Sauvage required termination. Dirk's attempts to manufacture mindless monsters had paid off. More than five thousand Sauvage were destroyed on the orders of Adam and Ridgeley. The rest were still being catalogued for rehabilitation. It was probable that more would be put down before the entire process was complete.

Because at some point outside aid would dry up, Nick sent word to Gilgai to begin work on clearing the entrance to the primary sapphire mine. He offered jobs to anyone in the Shire who was willing to take on the daunting task. There were those who had been part of the rescue party the day the shaft had collapsed, trapping and killing his father and four other men. Others in Falmormath had heard the stories. They were reluctant to disturb the dead, but their esteem for Nick's reputation and family history won out. Falmormath wouldn't exist if not for Barker Buchanan's determination to carve a life for his family out of the remote and unforgiving bush. They owed him some sweat and sore muscles.

"I have to go out there and take care of this myself," Nick said as they undressed for bed after a long day spent helping to rebuild a school. Even his bones ached from lifting and moving heavy objects all day.

"Are you sure?" she queried, taking Gavin from his doll's bed cradle. She settled herself on the bed and prepared to nurse him. "I don't know if I like the idea of you that far away. Bad things seem to happen when we're apart."

Nick crawled across the mattress and lay down, using her thighs for a pillow. He could closely watch her breastfeeding and it brought a smile to his face. Gavin's mouth moved with slow, deliberate actions. He still let go of the nipple from time to time and had to be reintroduced to it. During one such episode, Nick snuck his finger into the infant's smacking mouth and received a squawk of disapproval.

"Then eat what you're supposed to, little one," Agatha chided her son.

He seemed to learn his lesson. His mouth closed tightly on her nipple and he didn't relinquish it until she forced him to so she could switch him to her other breast. His attention span soon waned and he resumed his lazy feeding style.

Nick gently stroked the hairless head as Gavin pretended to nurse.

"I don't want to be away from you either," he said, delighting in the simplest moments in her company. "I don't see how it can be helped. It could be a year to get the mines up and running. We have to build some kind of work camp for the Sauvage and living quarters for the people who'll be involved in controlling them. It's going to have to be a small town of its own out there, away from Falmormath. I don't want to leave anything to chance. I need to be there to make sure it's done right."

She met his encouraging gaze. Her smile was tinged with worry.

"You'll take Buren with you," she insisted.

"I couldn't get rid of him if I tried," he replied, grinning. "He's probably sleeping outside the door right now."

They shared a moment's respite from the stress in their lives as they succumbed to a bout of uncontrollable laughter at the picture of the tough and hard-edged elf lying on the floor in the hall beyond their door. It felt good to laugh. There had been little enough to find humor in of late. Nick worked his way up to the head of the bed alongside her. He rested his forehead against hers and they allowed themselves time to relax while watching their son fall asleep in her arms.

A military convoy accompanied Nick and Buren to Falmormath as a precautionary measure.

Gilgai looked much the same as when he had left, with the obvious exception of the paddocks and barns. Nick had not witnessed the destruction before now. As they drove closer to the homestead in the back of a sleek four-door steam wagon, Nick seethed at the sight that greeted him. The burnt barns had been razed and the foundations for new structures were well underway. He found the blackened hillsides the most disturbing. The paddocks were a waste until another season passed. All the time and energy that had been put into planting the grapevines had been undone by one fiery exhale of a dragon. He could see that the station hands had not been idle in his absence and it tempered his anger.

The troops pulled into the yard to find his men in the process of raising a newly constructed wall for the largest barn. Hopping out of the vehicle before it stopped, Nick joined them in hoisting it into place. Buren was at his side as the men secured it. It was a balm to his spirit to be back at work on the station. This was where he belonged, not in Sydney in the Alpha House. The potent smells of the station welcomed him home.

The men were overjoyed to have him back, but their greetings were gruff and awkward. They were at a loss about how to address him now that he was royalty, even more so because he was a werewolf. A Sauvage at that. The soldiers put them off, too. Nick gave his guards clear instruction that they were expected to stay out of his way. Once the station hands realised that he was the same man they had always known, and he encouraged them to think of him that way, there was much back slapping and crude mutterings about the condition of the country. Nick was still their Boss, no more, no less. These were men with simple lives and basic needs. Sydney might as well have been on another planet to their way of thinking. Apart from the dragon's damage, their world had seen little change with the war.

Nick was alarmed to hear their discussion over dinner that evening in the bunkhouse. He wanted to reconnect with his friends, so he made himself as approachable as possible. He had spent years in their company, eating and carousing with them. Dining in the main house seemed ridiculous and counterproductive to regaining a normal way of life.

It seemed that dingoes were invading the Shire. The men had been shooting them daily, but they kept coming. The outer stations were being the hardest hit by the invading predators. Sheep were being slaughtered in droves.

Buren shared Nick's unease. Hearing about the dingo situation and being in the middle of it made them realize the potential for an incident was high. Maybe they could send a message to this Wollaweroo through the mangy creatures here in the Shire.

BIRTHRIGHT

Work on the mines commenced the following day. Not only had Nick returned with a company of soldiers for protection, they were also willing to put their backs into the undertaking. The crew was a mixed bag of races, including a few humans, but they were dedicated to the resurrection of their country and they set aside any former bigotry. Shoulder to shoulder they sweated as equals alongside the men of Falmormath.

In addition to manpower, they had brought machinery that would make the chore of moving the tons of rubble easier. The steam powered rock crusher rattled and shook while it hammered at the largest stones guarding the entrance to what was being called Barker's Mine. Once the boulders were broken into smaller fragments, they were loaded onto a conveyor belt that took them to a secondary crushing device. Under the steel hammers inside the machine they were pulverized into fist sized bits and dumped into waiting carts. Centaurs pulled the carts nearly a mile to a stretch of river where the contents were deposited. They were creating a dam that would provide water to the mine's working population. It was a scheme designed to make the most of the natural resources.

On the fourth day of excavation, the men uncovered the remains of the victims from the 1839 mine collapse. There was profound silence as the mummified bodies were brought out to be identified through their personal items and clothing.

Nick instantly recognized one of the five shrunken bodies as it came out into daylight. He didn't need to judge by the clothes or the shaggy red-brown hair and thick beard to know the desiccated features belonged to his father.

He had wondered for over thirty years how he would react if he was ever able to extract his father's mortal remains from the earth's clutches. Staring at the dried out husk made him realize that he had put too much emphasis on his father's death and not enough on his father's life. The thing before him may have once housed Barker Buchanan's spirit, but it was not the man he had known as his father. It was time to properly bury the past.

They held a simple funeral for all the men who had tragically lost their lives on that day, giving them all a final farewell as they were interred in the Buchanan family cemetery. There was no need for more than that. Temporary wooden headstones would be replaced with official marble markers once the stone carver in Falmormath finished them.

After the men solemnly trailed out of the cemetery's gate, muttering long overdue condolences as they passed, Nick stood alone at the foot of his father's grave. His mother's plot was right beside it. Wildflowers grew with abandon in the soil that covered her body. At last they were reunited. He allowed long withheld tears to creep down his face.

Nick stood on the hill overlooking the bustling activity around the mouth of the Barker Mine. He was pleased with the progress they were making. A slouch hat shielded his face from the sun. His tan short-sleeved shirt and canvas trousers were smeared with dirt, sweat and a little blood. It was symbolic of the dedication and hard work that was occurring across Australia.

From the corner of his eye he spied furtive moment among the ferns and tree trunks. He turned to see an orange shape disappear into the shadows. With a glance at Buren a few feet away, he gave chase. Buren was on his heels as he made his way into the trees.

They trailed the solitary dingo for a few hundred yards until they came out into a clearing and found a gathering of the beasts waiting for them. Buren drew his Riggins, keeping it low and steady. Nick's wolf surged forward, but he forced it back. He wanted to communicate with them if he could.

"I don't suppose any of you are Wollaweroo?" he asked, keeping

BIRTHRIGHT

his eyes moving from face to face as the small dogs surrounded them.

A familiar tall white dingo stepped forward. Its fur began to shed in large sections, exposing the shape of a slender young Aborigine woman. She rose up, mindless of her nudity in the presence of the two men. Her smooth skin was the colour of honey. She had long black hair and her eyes were dark and hypnotic. She was a strikingly beautiful woman.

Nick looked to Buren, who was just as shocked.

"I am Wollaweroo," she told them. Her voice was the wind that rustled through the trees. "I am the one you have been seeking."

Nick was floored. She was a native Australian Birthright. He hadn't thought to consider that there would be any. He felt an idiot for not realizing that werewolves were all over the world, of course there would be some in his own backyard. As members of the same genetic family, they shared a far reaching ancestor.

"Are all of you Birthrights?" Nick asked, hoping not to sound completely ignorant.

She smiled intriguingly, but it had a wicked undertone.

"After Paradeus failed and our people were scattered to the four winds, our forbearers came here. They had no need for their human skins, so they lived as wolves among the indigenous population. For generations, they took mates among the dingoes and produced scores of Kindred. I'm one of the only Birthrights left that's native to Australia."

Nick couldn't wait to tell Agatha about this revelation. There were werewolves already living in Australia. It certainly would come as a surprise.

"I've been watching you for some time. You're the new Alpha King, but are you an honorable man?" Wollaweroo demanded, showing none of the respect he was due as her lord and master. "You and your mate have picked up the pieces Dirk van Amersvoot left behind. I want some of those pieces. I was promised that my people would get most of the Northern Territories and the far lands to the west. We did our part to hand you this country on a plate. We only expect what's ours."

"I'll take that under advisement," Nick replied. He wasn't going to make any decisions without Agatha and the Alpha Council to back him up. "In the meantime, you need to back off. If we hear any more accounts of dingoes attacking stations or towns we'll take action."

Wollaweroo's dark, alluring lips worked their way to a mocking smirk.

"Of course you will," she said, baring small white teeth. "You're the Alpha King. I'd expect nothing less than a show of force. Your fae friends are already doing a good job on your behalf."

Behind him, Buren squared off against some of the bolder dingoes that had come forward.

"I'm not refusing your demands," Nick assured her. "I just can't make that decision right here and now. It's become a more complicated political issue. You'll need to meet with the Alpha Council to make-"

She jumped forward, nearly catching him off guard. His wolf reacted more quickly than his human half and he was able to grasp her outstretched hands before her claws reached his face. He twisted her arms behind her back. Her small breasts pushed into his chest as she writhed in his hold. She was surprised that as a Sauvage, without the moon's influence, he was able to overpower her. What she had heard about was true. She had needed to prove it to herself.

Buren fired into the dirt at the paws of the first dingo to make a move to come to her aid. The dingoes held back momentarily. They were prepared to attack if their leader called on them.

"I'm not going to debate this with you," Nick said into her snarling face. "I can drag you back to Sydney as my prisoner or you can wait to hear from me. It's your choice."

Wollaweroo relaxed in his grip. She found his strength and forcefulness arousing. Her eyes offered him promises of pleasure. Nick shoved her away. He was a legitimate alpha and he had a mate. She knew from her own observations that his bond with his mate was indestructible. She consoled herself that it never hurt to try.

BIRTHRIGHT

"I have no need for your city or your Alpha Council," she snapped, head turned aside. His rejection still stung although she accepted it. "We've survived for centuries without one."

"So you'd rather slink off into the bush and live like refugees than accept the future that's coming," Nick taunted. His wolf wanted to sink its teeth into her throat for her impudent attempt at seduction. He found that his alpha side came out naturally when challenged. "You may not like it, but you will not undermine our efforts to restore this country. We don't want to start a fight with you. We'd like you on our side. I'll call off the fae if you call off your people."

The Birthright slunk backwards towards her pack. They closed around her like a russet cloak.

"We want no part of your world," she sneered, lips pulled away from her teeth in a derisive smile. "You can find me through my people when you make up your mind."

Her umber-hued skin fell away and the white dingo reappeared. She led her pack into the trees.

Buren spared a glance at Nick, who was shaking with nerves and anger.

"I think that went well," he remarked drily, holstering his gun.

Nick closed his eyes, collecting his breath. He had not expected to confront the infamous Wollaweroo on his own property and his wolf was whining to go after her and bring her down. With tremendous effort, he held it back. It was like holding onto an unbroken horse with a piece of string.

He didn't want an incident between werewolf factions. They needed to be united to bring valuable harmony to the country. What would it take to make the dingoes their allies rather than adversaries? It might be in everyone's best interest to just give the dingoes their chunk of the continent. He had to contact Agatha to put things right.

※

Agatha's initial reaction to the incident between Nick and the dingo leader was explosive rage. How dare that dingo bitch threaten their efforts to rebuild what was their nation as well? After she finished her tantrum, in which several pieces of antique furniture lost their lives, she settled into a state of simmering resentment, which eventually faded into discontent. She desperately wanted Australia to be whole. It would only hamper their efforts if Wollaweroo opposed them. As she had once pointed out to Nick about the sheep being the ones eating the grass meant for the kangaroo, she realised the dingoes were the indigenous species. She could afford to be generous and grant them the lands they wanted. It was the right decision for all concerned.

The partially assembled Alpha Council signed off on the measure to bestow much of the central and western portions of the country to the dingoes. Clear lines were marked and Wollaweroo was warned that any deviation from those boundaries would result in severe retribution. The dingo leader did not respond immediately, but dingo attacks stopped in areas along the wrong side of the border. It felt as though a moderate truce had been reached.

At last, the restructuring efforts were solidified and the country breathed a collective sigh of relief.

CHAPTER FORTY-SEVEN

"A man must often choose between his own fate and that of a higher power."
John Nigel, philosopher

It was well into summer when Agatha was finally able to return to the home she had built with Nick in Falmormath Shire. The air was warm as she rode in a new kind of steam wagon driven by Adam Steelcuff. Its rounded brass fenders gleamed in the sunlight. It had comfortable leather seats and made far less noise than the utility trucks used on the station. The canvas top was down and her tawny hair twirled in the breeze as they drove through familiar valleys. They wore goggles that were small and sleek to protect their eyes from the wind and sun. She breathed in the scent of home, letting the delicious flavors roll across her palate.

In the backseat Gavin was swaddled in a bassinette that was securely strapped down. It would be his first trip to the home where he would grow up. Nick had made several trips back to Sydney to keep tabs on the advancements she was making. He often brought Logan and Luna with him on his visits. They had felt it best that as young as he was, Gavin should remain with her, but the older two were just too much for her to handle with her other responsibilities. It was during one of those trips to Alpha House that she conceived again. Because of their age difference, she wanted to bear children close together as possible so that they would have a good lifetime to be with their father. He was thirty years her senior and wouldn't be around as long as she would. It was something that never left her mind.

The physical rebuilding of the devastated country brought new jobs and a boost to the economy. Immigrants of all races poured in with dreams of their own to live in an open society. In cities from coast to coast the sounds of construction became as common as birds singing. Smaller towns popped up where there had been nothing, although the border was enforced and there was no building allowed on the dingoes' territory. Unfortunately, with progress came the growing pains suffered by all new kingdoms. It would take time to bandage the wounds of the nation.

War was, indeed, a strange animal.

As the steam wagon bounced over the dirt track towards the homestead, Agatha put her hand out, gesturing for Adam to stop. The wagon pulled onto the grassy edge. She blinked in disbelief at what she saw in front of them. There was a new main gate with guards blocking the road, but that was not what caught her attention.

Gone was the stone wall with its metal worked lettering. In its place was a new wooden sign. In hand painted script it read:

Paradeus Vineyards, est. 1875

She took several gasping breaths, reading and rereading the bold, gold-outlined black words. She stepped down and approached the sign. Her trembling fingers traced the lettering several times.

"Looks good, doesn't it?" Adam asked with a knowing smirk. He leaned on the driving wheel and watched her with an amused gaze.

She gave him a narrow eyed glare.

"You knew about this?" she demanded as she climbed back into her seat.

He chuckled, putting the wagon in gear and driving forward.

In her absence, the property had been transformed from a plain frontier homestead into a majestic manor with formally landscaped grounds befitting their status. The house was a two-storied, stone-fronted gothic revival with wrought iron scroll work on the balconies. The barns, previously burnt to the ground by Torric, had been replaced with proper buildings for making and storing wine. The place bore no resemblance to the humble home she had left nearly a year ago. She drank in the splendor with shimmering gold eyes.

They were met by a large crowd of family, friends and station hands. More than fifty people filled the yard as they pulled in. Security was tight, but the guards remained in the background. They were always present in the shadows.

Nick was in front of the mob, holding Luna on his hip. He lifted her hand to wave at her mother. Her motor skills were considerably delayed and the simple action was beyond her capability to comprehend, but she was fond of smiling, which she did from dawn to dusk. Her protracted development meant that she was the darling of everyone around her. Everyone went out of their way to work with her and spend time in her simple and uncomplicated company. She was more of the Alpha Queen on the station than her mother as every soul unabashedly doted on her.

Logan stood next to Mrs. MacLeach, hiding in her skirt. He kept his distance from his father. In his young mind he was still not able to understand the fear and anger he felt towards Nick's wolf. Nick bent over backwards in his efforts to appease the child's emotional confusion, but Logan was out of his reach. There was a rift that Nick could not seem to overcome despite his best efforts.

Edison Finnerty unloaded the trunks and bags from the back of the wagon while Agatha was mobbed by a bevy of well wishers. He was happy to have her back. The Boss made a right bastard of himself when he was missing her.

Agatha walked towards Nick with a beguiling smile. It hid the weariness that had built up within her over the past months. It felt as though her very bones were tired, but as was her nature, she kept it to herself.

"I like what you've done with the place," she said, leaning up to receive his kiss, "but why did you change the name?"

He hoisted Luna up higher on his hip as she squirmed, wanting to get to her mother. She could only bounce in place and utter urgent noises. To stem her forthcoming outburst he handed her to Agatha.

Luna promptly fell into a contented state with her head on Agatha's chest. Logan's uncertainty was overcome by jealousy when he saw his sister in their mother's arms. He suddenly rushed forward and clamped his arms around her legs, crying, "Mum, Mum, Mum!" She reached down and ruffled his dark hair.

"I thought it was appropriate," Nick answered unrepentantly. "Do you mind?"

"Mind? Why would I mind? We've restored Paradeus to his rightful place as a heroic figure in our culture's history. His name stands for our people. I think it's absolutely appropriate."

"If you're finished mobbing your wife, the rest of us would like to enjoy her company," said Buren as he came up behind Nick. He clapped a hand on Nick's shoulder. "We haven't seen her in some time either."

Amid laughter and high spirits the party went inside.

***

It was hours past midnight when the welcome home festivities wound down and the host and hostess were able to get time alone.

They shared the duty of putting the children to bed, though Logan fought Nick with a fierce resistance that surprised Agatha.

"He still won't let you touch him?" she sighed, taking over the task of undressing the struggling toddler.

Logan relaxed at once, but his eyes stayed distrustfully on Nick standing behind her.

"He fights me tooth and nail any time I have to handle him," said Nick bitterly. He tried not to take it personally, but it carved him up inside and his wolf occasionally lashed out. "You'd think he was the Sauvage."

"I know it doesn't make it better to tell you he can't help it," she offered, laying Logan down in the crib. He and Luna still slept together. There was no quiet in the house if they were parted. "It's just something that's going to take time."

Nick's disheartened gaze rested on his son. Logan's eyes were closed, for which he was grateful. It gutted him when Logan looked at him with fear and apprehension. He understood now some of what Buren had suffered.

Something that had been on his mind for weeks came back to him and he finally felt ready to talk to her about it. It was a delicate topic and he wasn't sure he would handle it correctly so he simply plunged in.

"What if Logan was like me?"

Agatha's face twisted in a bemused frown. She didn't pick up on his meaning.

"He is like you," she said with a light laugh. "Stubborn as anything."

Nick shook his head. He took a moment to consider his words before deciding there was no gentle was to say it. He just blurted out, "Can you give him the Bite?"

Agatha went reeling backwards as if struck by a physical blow. The surprise in Nick's eyes at her reaction told her that he had no idea that what he was suggesting would kill their son.

"I know you don't mean that," she said slowly.

"Why not?" he retaliated, stunned by her burning glare. "He's my son. I can help him."

She took a menacing step towards him, blocking him from the crib as though he was a threat. Her eyes glinted angrily with a familiar sheen as the wolf brushed the surface.

"Have you forgotten what you went through?" she said furiously. Her face was a tense mask. "He's still a baby, he wouldn't survive the infection."

Nick's wolf reared up in response to her maternal protectiveness. They met head to head.

"As young as he is, maybe he would adapt to it," he countered. Desperate tears filled his eyes. He couldn't stand losing his son because Logan would never know the benefits of having whole wolf inside him. "Maybe he would be more like a Birthright and grow up with it like you did. He wouldn't know any different."

Agatha slumped to the floor with a heart wrenching moan,

clutching her head in her fists. Why was he asking her to destroy their family? When would he understand that the Bite was not meant to be used recklessly? She had given him the Bite because he had been on the verge of death when he asked. She would not have done it otherwise, no matter how deep her love for him. There would never be another time when she would give the Bite to anyone, even if meant losing someone she loved. Dirk's instability and his use of Sauvage as weapons had hardened her to the reality of what the Bite could do. She could not allow it to continue.

"I'm so sorry," he sobbed, falling to his knees beside her. "I was wrong to ask. Maybe when he's older we could think about-"

"No. Not ever."

He sat back on his haunches, watching her face twist with pain. He realised too late that what he was suggesting was a grievous mistake. He was asking her to do something unforgivable. Giving him the Bite had gone against everything she believed and he was begging her to do it a second time to assuage his personal guilt over not being able to connect with his son. She would know better than anyone what would happen to Logan. She had probably seen firsthand the results of the infection in children. He would rather have Logan at arm's length than not at all.

His tears slowed as his resolve firmed. If she was telling him that it could not be done then he would have to live with the onus of having a Kindred child that would likely never accept him. He loved Logan unconditionally. He could keep the pain inside. Logan would never know how much it hurt him. That was his obligation as a father.

Logan and Luna had slept through their heated exchange. Gavin was snoring lightly in his own crib next to theirs. He was definitely his father's son.

Agatha felt an urge that had been denied for too long. Their turbulent emotions called to her wolf. It needed to get out. She crawled submissively to Nick, whispering, "Let's hunt."

They left the homestead without being seen.

BIRTHRIGHT

~~~❖~~~

Using a blanket of damp grass, Nick laid Agatha down in the moonlight. The sheer excitement of the kill aroused them into a state of agitated pleasure. He took his time to savor every inch of her blood and sweat slicked body with his mouth. He licked the salty juices from her skin with long strokes of his tongue, moving up from her ankle to her thigh, across her belly and down her other leg. She writhed on the grass, clutching at the earth in her joy. He reared up over her, using his hips to push her thighs apart. With a deep groan, he sank inside her, slowly filling her with his thickness. Her warm flesh closed around him and he let out a loud roar of exhilaration. She moved under him, creating a brisk friction that sent tremors through their veins. Their bodies rose and fell in a dance as old as time itself. He tried to hold out and make it last, but he could feel the rise of his desire and it would not be held back. He exploded into her, head thrown back and a victorious howl bursting from his throat. She bit into his shoulder as she felt fire fill her belly. Her hips shuddered against his, slowly coming to a rest.

They fell apart, gasping for air.

The world around them was quiet, only the rustling of leaves in the trees above them could be heard over their racing hearts.

"Do you think that werewolves will ever become equals with humans?" he asked.

She rolled onto her side and reached out to draw her fingers along the length of his arm. His hand smoothed circles across the surface of her slightly distended stomach. He was thrilled to have another baby on the way. He would never have guessed how fertile werewolves were. It was little wonder there were so many orphans living on reservations in America. He intended to correct that situation if it was at all possible.

"I'm not going to hold my breath," she answered honestly. "I think we're making progress. Only time will tell if we accomplished what Dirk set out to do. That's our responsibility now. Both of us. I know Paradeus is your dream, but you can't just hide here."

"I know," he agreed.

He sighed and intertwined his fingers with hers. They lay on the wet grass, silent with their own thoughts.

They heard the sound of movement among the underbrush and assumed defensive positions side by side. He grabbed his trousers and pulled them up his lean legs. His first reaction was still a human one. Agatha released her wolf. Their eyes scanned the ferns and grass for signs of danger. The same smell reached their noses, but only Nick could put a name to it.

"What are you doing on our land, Wollaweroo?" he demanded. "You're on the wrong side of the boundary."

The sensual human shape of Wollaweroo emerged from the darkness. She had not bothered to cover herself. Moonlight bathed her with its milky white glow. There was a part of her that still wanted Nick, but one look at Agatha crouching next to him put a momentary damper on her desire.

"I've come to accept your conditions," she told them. Her head was raised in an arrogant tilt. "You've honored Dirk's promise."

"And then some," muttered Nick. "We've given you control over those lands, but we are the ultimate authority in Australia. You understand that?"

The dingo leader inclined her beautiful head. She met Agatha's jealous, suspicious eyes. Two alpha females in the company of a handsome, dominant male were likely to fight, but Wollaweroo was wise enough to concede to Agatha's prevailing authority. Her gaze went to the gold ring shining on its chain around Agatha's neck. She smiled at the snarling Alpha Queen.

"You best appreciate what you have in this one," she said, grinning wickedly. "Men like this come along once in a blue moon."

Agatha nodded, teeth showing in a savage grin of understanding.

"You may not see me again," Wollaweroo said to them. Her dark gaze slanted towards Agatha. "My people will stay where they belong. If you need us, we'll be there. This country belongs to all werewolves now." She vanished into the dark depths of the trees until only her voice remained. "I wish you well, your Majesties."

※

The struggle to unite Australia under werewolf rule continues for Nick and Agatha in the as yet untitled second book of the Shepherd's Moon Saga...

They started off slowly, trotting side by side. He was larger than Agatha and his shape was not fully wolf like hers. He had an anthropomorphic appearance, more like a wolf that could stand upright. His fur was a blend of dark ash grey with a pale belly. She was a lighter grey mottled with darker hues.

Shoulder to shoulder, they padded up the hillside through heavy brush. Both were aware that feral Sauvage could be anywhere so they did not stray from the other's side.

Nick lowered his nose to sweep the ground for scents. His head worked side to side until a faint smell trickled into his snout. He picked up the pace. Agatha matched his quicker stride, though she felt sluggish and out of sorts. She detected the kangaroo's scent as well. They weren't planning to make a kill, or even give proper chase, but the blue-grey beasts still made for entertaining sport.

The small mob was ahead of them in the trees, grazing in a relaxed fashion. They milled about, ears twisting and turning to pick up on movement around them. The wind changed, blowing the scent of the werewolves towards them. One head reared up and was quickly joined by the rest. They scoured their surroundings with cautious eyes.

Nick lowered himself to the dirt, hiding in a clump of ferns. Agatha sank down beside him.

She was beginning to feel an ache in her belly that she hadn't experienced before. She shifted her position to see if that would help. It faded to a dull throb like a bruised muscle.

As they watched, the scrubbers began to display their anxiety, sensing the presence of hidden predators. The large animals began to shuffle uneasily, uncertain if they should flee. They were confused and it was making them agitated.

Excitement clouding his better judgment, Nick sprang forward.

Out of the trees on the far side of the mob came a dark giant shape. The rogue Sauvage lunged at the closest scrubber, hooking its claws into the kangaroo's hide. A scream burst from the kangaroo's throat as it pulled away. Its flesh tore, leaving a ragged wound in its side. A long flap of skin hung loose down the animal's ribcage, slapping wetly against exposed muscle as it bounded into the trees.

The other terrified animals sprang into flight, leaping away from the marauding beast.

Nick skidded to a stop, claws splayed in the dirt. He hadn't picked up on the Sauvage's scent because he had been intent on the kangaroo. There hadn't been any Sauvage reported in the Shire so he was completely taken aback. He was caught in the open and that meant Agatha was at risk, as well.

The Sauvage spotted him. It briefly debated between pursuing the scrubbers and attacking the Birthright in its path. The challenge of an alpha werewolf was more enticing. It lifted its wedge shaped head, dark brown eyes trained on its prize.

Nick rose up to meet the other werewolf's charge. Any fear he might have felt when he was human was overpowered by the wild nature of his wolf. It took over, giving him the strength to match his opponent's lunge.

They collided with mouths open, each seeking to get a hold on the other's throat. Claws raked through fur and flesh, scattering feathers of coarse hair on the wind. Thickly muscled hind legs were braced to provide balance and to prevent being pushed backwards. Their growls rang out like thunder.

Agatha cowered in the ferns, feeling the increase of discomfort in her abdomen. Fear made her muscles constrict and that put pressure on the fragile sac that held baby securely inside her. She whined, wanting to join Nick in defending himself, but she couldn't make

BIRTHRIGHT

herself move. Her body was betraying her.

Another Sauvage broke from the thick shrubbery behind her. Her reaction was swift once she was in direct jeopardy. She spun about, teeth flashing. Dirt and debris went skittering as she came around to face the taller werewolf. Her wolf would defend her under any circumstances no matter the toll. Put in a position of self-defense, she was forced to ignore her body's warning signals.

She could hear the clashing of the werewolves over her shoulder. Nick was winning against his rival. The other Sauvage's snarls were loud and rasping. She had not doubted that Nick would be the victor in that fight. He was protecting his mate and unborn child. No creature on earth, with the obvious exception of a dragon, could beat him with that motivation.

The Sauvage that loomed over her was hesitant. It watched her for a moment, breathing in her scent. It recognized her elevated alpha status and slowly began to circle her. She wasn't sure if it was trying to remember how to behave in the face of a supreme alpha or if it was searching for a weak spot to attack. It bared long fangs, hissing defiantly.

Agatha prepared to meet its advance. Her belly was tight, hurting. She knew what it meant, but she couldn't allow that to break her focus. If she lost concentration for even a split second she could be severely injured or killed.

As the Sauvage lunged at her Nick came shooting over her head like an arrow. He slammed into the other Sauvage with his full weight, knocking it back into the trees. Tree trunks shattered like they were made of glass as the werewolves crashed through them. The pair of Sauvage went tumbling into the brush and Agatha lost sight of them for a moment.

CPSIA information can be obtained at www.ICGtesting.com
Printed in the USA
BVOW010207280812

299003BV00001B/56/P